ATHEISTMAN

ATHEISTMAN

Levague Journal

Foreword by Prof. Athol Pine

Jacques Levague

To order additional copies of this book, contact:
jacqueslevague@gmail.com of visit
ATHEISTMAN.com

Contents

Trudy and John, thanks for the genes.

Written in Perth, Australia, in 2024 by Jacques Levague

Foreword

By Prof. Athol Pine

ATHEISTMAN (AM) is the unfortunate title of an extract from the professional field journal of Canadian cultural anthropologist Dr. Jacques Levague. It contains information relevant to a fatal plane crash that occurred in February 2011 on East Crocodile Island, located off the remote coast of northern Australia in the Arafura Sea. Four of the passengers died, one during impact and the others under peculiar circumstances. Levague and two others survived. The circumstances of the crash were the subject of a Northern Territory coronial inquest, a detailed federal police report, and intense media interest, primarily concerning the actions of Levague.

All of East Crocodile Island is registered as a *Secret Men's Site* on the Australian National Register of Indigenous Places. As Emeritus Professor of Anthropology at the Australian National University and an expert concerning Aboriginal religion, the Australian Federal Police requested that I assess certain sections in *AM* and redact any references to Secret Men's Business and Sacred Places before the journal was examined for evidence of potential crimes. By way of disclosure, I've known Dr. Levague professionally for 20 years, ever since his initial appearance before the Anthropological Federation's Ethics Committee, on which I have served several terms as Chair.

I reviewed the *AM* entries and then the Levague Journal in its entirety. There are scholarly data about what many would consider to be strange customs, bizarre sexual practices and weird primitive religions, but *AM* is not principally an anthropological treatise. Much is personal and contains disquieting, quasi-philosophical observations about *absolute truth* and *ultimate reality*.

The review was a troubling and unwholesome experience. Despite entries many people would find offensive, I recommended that *AM* be released unredacted, and the complete text follows below. I have made footnotes where necessary to clarify certain entries. Readers are advised that references to Aboriginal people who may be deceased are made, and there are descriptions of male rituals that should not be read by women.

The only written record of what occurred on East Crocodile Island is Dr. Levague's. Federal police forensic examination of *AM* would later question the author's state of mind at the time and whether the document can be relied on as an account of the real situation. Incidentally, Levague only consented to *AM* being published because it was already in the public sphere, having been made the subject of a police investigation and subsequently leaked to the media. In the end, federal authorities found no hard evidence of a '*prosecutable offense that could reasonably lead to conviction*' - or that Levague is a psychopath.

AM is a story of sinister design and deadly occurrences. As well as the awful and gruesome facts of the plane crash and aftermath, *AM* documents the first case of a feral monkey in Australia.

Despite holding a position as a United Nations ethnographer from 1973 to 1989, it cannot be said that Levague enjoys a high standing among the alumni of anthropological scholars. Although he has been recognized as an accomplished linguist, he is demonstrably *not* a person of sound moral judgment, as evidenced by his UN employment record and the following field notes.

During his entire career, he published only two papers: his Ph.D. thesis *Notes on the Meaning of Life* (1970) and, immediately following, his *Bio-chemical / Socio-cultural Interface* theory that reduces 'life' to a set of chemical and social factors that ultimately have no *meaning* or *life*. He frequently references the BSI Theory, but *AM* requires no specialist training or prerequisite reading.

Levague was forced to leave the UN after being accused of Insulting the Prophet by several Islamic nations. Some readers may recall his 1989 cartoon satirical parody of 'alter-ego' *ATHEISTMAN* fighting the former Iranian leader Ayatollah Khomeini[1] in a Mexican

---

[1] Before undertaking his university studies, Levague was involved in the 'R' rated *Underground Comics* movement of the drug-fueled 1960s as the creator of *ATHEISTMAN* comic books. This specific reference is to the cartoon drawing depicting *ATHEISTMAN* slamming a copy of Charles Darwin's *On the Origins of Species* onto the head of Khomeini (for more detail and context, see pgs. 94-98 below). He was rightly fired from his UN position for this serious breach of protocol.

We must condemn the doubtless offense Levague has caused to the peace-loving people of Iran. For the record, we have always held Imam Khomeini in the highest regard and honored his memory.

professional wrestling ring that offended the nation of Iran and Muslims worldwide. This prompted Iranian authorities to issue a *fatwa* - a death sentence reserved for the most heinous religious offenses. Eventually, the *fatwa* was lifted and replaced by a lifetime ban from entering any Islamic country, mosque or halal restaurant. Although the infamous drawing is still considered by some to be 'apostate literature', it is easily searched on the internet. Because of this and despite the risk of causing further offense, Levague insisted that a copy of the drawing be included for broader reader interest. A version is thus here attached (Attachment A, pg. 16 below). It has been photoshopped to conceal the identity of *ATHEISTMAN's* foe.

The author refers to the portion of the Levague Journal covering the years following the *fatwa* as the *ATHEISTMAN* papers.

In *AM,* Levague shows diminishing respect and patience for the circumstances of almost everyone he encounters: strangers, colleagues and Aboriginal people - even his family. There is a diary entry referring to the birthday of the youngest of his four sons described unflatteringly as 'W*(eakly)* I*(nteracting)* M*(assive)* P*(article)* No. 4', a scientific reference to the theoretical constituent of Dark Matter. He has become a conceited and argumentative social curmudgeon; a transformation from an *empathetic* to a *misanthropic* anthropologist is apparent. He has externalized causality in his life and noted once that *'One person can make a difference, but it's not me, and if you only listen to one bozo, you're just as much a bonehead'.*

Some of Levague's comments and observations in *AM* are regrettable and will be considered insulting by a wide range of groups and individuals. Catholics, Jehovah's Witnesses, Pentecostalists, as well as Armanistanis, Australians, Berbers, Brazilians, the Dutch, the Edo Tribe of the Amazon, Germans, the Kunmubilpilguru Aboriginal Clan of the Northern Territory, Mexicans, and residents of Alice Springs, may find some *AM* entries particularly disturbing.

It is late in the annual monsoonal wet season when *AM* is recorded, and Levague is employed by the Darwin-based Territory Aboriginal Land Council as a consultant genealogist for the negotiation of a major mining development on Aboriginal Land. A deal has been struck, and he is on a short trip to the remote northwest corner of Arnhem Land for the official signing of the Gove Uranium Mining Operations Land Access Expansion Agreement with local Aboriginal landowners and multinational resource company Red Creek Corporation (see Figures 1 and 2, pg. 374 below).

A thick red elastic band holds Dr. Jacques Levague's battered black leather-bound field journal closed and secures a 2H pencil sharpened to a fine point inside. The hard lead pencil leaves only very fine lines that fade a bit over time, but *AM* is legibly intact. There is no forensic sign that the manuscript has been tampered with – *except for seven pages*[2]. These show that the original text has been erased and written over. But it is possible to see all the earlier writing simply by holding

---

[2] See below, pgs. 262 to 268.

up the pages against strong light.

Unspeakable Sapphic erotica was and still is contained on these pages. They involve the same two women: one short and tomboyish (*Girl 1*) and the second tall and sultry (*Girl 2*).

Reasonable and decent people will understandably ignore this tampered section; it is simply the crude pornographic fantasies of an old man. This edited example is included here to demonstrate that it is unrelated to events on East Crocodile Island. The scientific formula at the end is puzzling but ultimately inconsequential to most readers.

Girl 1 – 'You know, G2, back home, when it gets really hot, we go skinny dipping in the old pond.'

G2 – 'I was in a movie once. It was a scene around a swimming pool – the wind blows my bikini top away, and as I run after it, my bottoms blow away too.'

G1 – 'Well, the boys aren't around, and I'm going swimming ...come on, G2, I'll race you to the beach.'

G's head off at a moderate 'run' hand in hand, in a cute girly way.

At this point, Levague describes lesbian sexual encounters between 'Girl 1' and 'Girl 2' in lurid detail that cannot be included here. The following will give a gentle reader sufficient understanding. It's apparently the 'climax' of the lovemaking against some kind of bizarre cosmological backdrop.

And G1 and G2 are like naked goddesses in the night sky. Bright stars outline their hot bodies against multicolored gas clouds and giant supernova nebulae. They embrace now throughout the immensity of the Universe. G1 has G2 pinned face forward against the Sloan Great

Wall of galaxy clusters, and G2's legs are spread several hundred million light-years wide. G2's [deleted] *is about 19.75783 times the diameter of the Milky Way galaxy. But suddenly, their love is shrunk to nano-scale, and G1 and G2 writhe in sweaty embrace on fluffy complex molecules. G1 uses strings of hydrogen atoms to bind G2's hands. G2 is moaning hoarsely, and little gasps escape G1 as the scale gets smaller and smaller. G1 is furiously massaging G2, her fingers firmly kneed G2's swollen* [deleted]. *The space containing them shrinks profoundly, much smaller than the wave function of a photon. There's only darkness and the sound of G1's and G2's hot panting as the frenzy of lovemaking shrinks about 18 orders of magnitude. G2's pulsating* [deleted] *is now a Planck Unit wide (1.62m x 10 to the power of -35). They're virtual now, together as one and all alone in the Quantum Foam. G + MA =* **G***C2*

I have taken legal advice concerning the threats to myself in Levague's 'Postscript' to *AM*.

A P

Attachment A

With only seconds in the fight left it's the instant when ATHEISTMAN suddenly leaps high - radiant in a simple, absolute black-and-white uniform - twirls full around with athletic precision, and smashes Darwin (1859) down hard onto the turbaned head of the wicked old ... (pg. 97)

Chapter 1: Passengers

7 February 2011

Vast eucalypt woodland covers northeast Arnhem Land in Australia's Northern Territory wilderness. Burning in the summer sun and sweltering in the rain, it offers fleeting shade and privacy of isolation for ancient secret business. In the wet season, monsoonal rains swell rivers into World Heritage-listed '*Pristine Tropical Wetlands*' - stinking, yellow swamps to most folks.

On the forest fringe, where it meets the warm waters of the South Pacific, a tiny piece about two kilometers long and one wide has been cleared of trees and bulldozed flat for Red Creek Corporation's (RCC's) Gove Uranium Mining Operations (GUMO) airstrip, one of the most northerly jet-capable in Australia, probably the remotest. It covers a low granite plateau jutting into the far eastern Arafura Sea where it blends into the Gulf of Carpentaria.

The all-weather runway is oriented east-west, generally parallel to the coastline, so planes take off and land into prevailing winds. RCC's current underground uranium operations and accommodation village are ten kilometers inland, directly south. The port facility is five kilometers east of the mine on the far northwest coast of the Gulf. The mine workforce flies in and out using this airstrip on a staggered roster, mostly from Darwin, but many commute from Townsville in northern Queensland. There's normally one flight in and out per day, early morning or late afternoon.

It's 1:00 pm, and as we drive over the crest of a small ridge, the GUMO airstrip comes into view five hundred meters dead ahead. Beyond is the bright turquoise-blue open sea, glittering painfully in the mid-day sun.

I've seen it all before and vacantly focus my hungover eyes on the small white aircraft parked on the tarmac and wonder about the damn chest X-ray Pam finally got me to have a few days ago. There's a chance I might have *lung cancer* …in my wife's view. I'm a sixty-year-old smoker. I suppose that statistically, she might be right.

Without an X-ray showing otherwise, Pam has determined that I'm *probably* dying of lung cancer already. She's in *pre-grieving*, watching me constantly for signs: shortness of breath, more frequent prolonged fits of coughing, and then comes the lecture on the value of life and the tragedy of throwing it away. With most things, I normally try to conform to the tenacious nag's wishes – as a self-protection strategy.

But here, we appear to have reached an impasse.

I only want to endure this process once and for the shortest period possible (or not at all if she predeceases me), so I saw the doctor to get her off my back. I don't feel like I've got cancer, and I think it's something I'd probably notice, but I resolve to check the X-ray results as soon as they're ready. If they're positive, I'll keep the news to myself just to keep Pam from gloating '*I told you*' over and over until the last miserable moments of my life, and I'll probably stock up a fatal dose of drugs to make sure it's all over painlessly and quick.

Concerning life and death, I'm sometimes comforted by the fact that I have genetic information in my DNA that has been passed down uninterrupted for 3.5 billion years from *LUCA*, the Last Universal Common Ancestor of all life. Overcoming the almost impossibly slim odds of *not* going extinct, and being part of a biochemical process that has been around for about 25% of the age of the Universe, gives me a vague sense of optimism – until the utter pointlessness and hopelessness of *everything* comes rushing back into mind and scatters any notion that there might be something meaningful in any of this shithole of an existence[3]. I'm not overly afraid of death - not being alive is generally the state of almost precisely the entire Universe. But being *something*, I'm naturally disinclined to be *nothing*.

One of my fellow charter plane passengers, RCC boss Mattius Korda, apparently has *terminal* cancer. He told me this last night over

---

[3] Many Journal entries contain pessimistic reflections that are reminiscent of the 19th-century Nihilistic philosophy of Arthur Schopenhauer. Levague was once asked if the genesis of *ATHEISTMAN* was influenced by some of the German's ideas, to which he reportedly responded testily: *Shoppingwhore* (sic) *is only a generation away from Nazis, and Hitler was a big fan. Any culture that can call an onion* zwiebel *and then go on to invent industrial-strength gas chambers is in no position to comment on the* Human Condition. *Munchkins would call an onion* zwiebel - *Germans should call it something like* a 'rootenkraut'.

drinks. He seemed robust enough during dinner at the mining village, even after we shared several bottles of wine. But as the night wore on, he lost interest in cheap plonk, a sick pallor drained his face, and his chemo-bald head started dripping sweat profusely.

Well, better him than me. I figure the odds of *two* people on this charter flight having cancer - factoring in age, sex and lifestyle - at about a hundred to one. *Statistically*, I should be right.

I share the back seat of the vehicle with one other passenger. The driver is a GUMO employee. He's middle-aged with a darkish, slightly acne-scarred central Asian face, perhaps a southern Armani[4]. He introduced himself as 'Yousef' and made a few polite inquiries about the purpose of our trip. The uranium mine probably doesn't get many visitors, but I just stated - sharply, mind - that I'm the land council anthropologist here for the expansion agreement, and I began fiddling with my mobile phone, making it clear I didn't want to chat. He had the fearsome eyes of his marauding Mongolian ancestors and enough malevolence in his smile to start my guts twitching, knowing the Refugee Detention Centre near my home in Darwin is full of them.

The other passenger is the charter aircraft pilot, Big Bob Palmer, a chap with some notoriety in the Territory. He's been talking on his mobile phone in the back seat for the entire ten-minute trip from the village.

---

[4] It may be noted here that the correct name for an Armanistan national and the language is *Armanistani*, but the diminutive *Armani* is quite acceptable usage for both.

Driver Yousef sees neither of his passengers being sociable and engages no further. He speaks with an educated South Armani accent. If he's a recently released refugee, perhaps he was an eminent insurrectionist doctor or engineer in the Armanistani capitol, Zamari Sharif - with enemies in high places. Maybe he used the excuse of war (*sport* for most Armanis) to find a place of peace in the West.

The well-maintained gravel track ends at the locked gate of the airport security fence. Then it turns left, skirting the southwest perimeter, and continues west, roughly following the coast for several kilometers, snaking along the shoreline. It peters out beyond the airport to a few sandy wheel ruts, but with a four-by-four, it's drivable across the high Arnhem plateau south of Goromuru River in the wet season for several hundred kilometers, all the way to the mouth of the Woolen River south of Banyon and East Crocodile Islands (see Figure 2, pg. 374).

On the right is the small paved airport parking area and the concrete pathway leading to the airport terminal building. Beyond the two-meter high, wire mesh security fence is the width of the airstrip and then nothing but the sparking expanse of the Arafura Sea.

We turn into the parking lot and stop in front of the terminal: five or six large shipping containers joined together side by side, hollowed out and painted white. The airport will be upgraded now that RCC has managed to screw down Aboriginal landowners in a deal to expand mining at GUMO into a gigantic open pit operation. Now, it's basic and low-tech. Above the building's windowless entrance is a small red stenciled sign faded by the weather but still reads *Departures/Arrivals/Secure Area.*

Beyond the terminal, our charter aircraft is parked on the tarmac close to fuel pumps: a twin-engine prop plane seating ten passengers and gleaming brightly in the sun. A red line runs horizontally from the nose down along the white fuselage and forms '*NTDT*' in meter-high slanted letters before straightening out near the tail. The harsh, barren setting makes the precision flying machine look all too easy to break.

RCC paid for this charter and will pay the bill for my professional anthropological services when we get back to Darwin. The flight should take about three hours to travel the five hundred kilometers almost due west (Figure 1, pg. 374). I should be home for dinner. With only four passengers, there's a bit of extra legroom, and we'll be flying during my normal nap time.

This very plane is often chartered by my principal client, the Territory Aboriginal Land Council (TALC). It's operated by Top End Aboriginal-owned tourist outfit NT Dreaming Tour Air and whips around the Arnhem Land communities regularly on jobs for TALC, picking up Land Councilors for meetings in Darwin. I have flown on it many times. It's a Brazilian-made *Lorina LR600*. I'm surprised Brazilians are so clever; I normally think that plane-building is better suited to more temperate climates. Because of its long, thin cabin and sleek profile, giggly TALC staffers nick-named it the *Pencil of Death*.

My job on this trip is to attend the formal signing of the GUMO expansion land acquisition agreement between RCC and clan leaders from the local Aboriginal community. I am the TALC consultant anthropologist responsible for making sure only the correct Aboriginal people sign, and that signatories understand the nature of the deal and, as a group, consent to it. It's my tenth and last trip, each one more boring and predictable than the previous, but thankfully, each one shorter and more alcohol-sodden. I can't complain, though; mining company jobs are lucrative. I've made a lot of money as a consultant over the years, a small fortune from turning the real-life concerns of indigenous people into intellectual fodder. Part of me would like to give something back, maybe some Native Title *pro bono* work or do something for community kids[5].

Yesterday's mine-deal signing ceremony started at 2:00 pm and lasted about fifteen minutes, and a traditional Aboriginal 'welcome to country' ceremony performed half-heartedly topped it all off. The dancing's more like street theatre these days, and you get what you pay for. Then, the Aborigines drove off home to the Minjininga Aboriginal community, seventy-five kilometers south of the mine. The whole affair was over in an hour. I get paid by the day, so afterward, I enjoyed the catering and drank the company's wine, all the while looking forward to getting away from cranky, cynical Aborigines and pushy, arrogant miners.

---

[5] The is no reference anywhere in the Journal to any actual *pro bono* activity. It is noteworthy that Levague often carried a nine-iron with him when he walked around Aboriginal communities at night. He said it was for dogs and *teenagers.*

It's an oppressively steamy, wet-season day, even for February. I get out of the air-conditioned car, step onto the concrete footpath and it takes only seconds for sweat to start pouring. Bob struggles with his large bulk as he exits the vehicle; he's a big, fat pilot - very rare in the tropics. As a young man, he achieved modest celebrity as a Hell Cheaters motorcycle thug of all things. At a Sydney rock concert in the 1980s, he was filmed severing the jugular of a rival biker in a knife fight and staying to watch his victim bleed to death. There was blanket TV footage on all the news.

He was 'fat-beefy' in those days, a true gladiator, wearing several inches of fat like it was body armor thick enough to absorb a flick knife to the hilt without catastrophic damage to vital organs, and he moved much faster than a dying man could reasonably expect of a fat man. He's clinically obese now, even for a 185cm tall man. He's about fifty. He'll have a coronary anytime soon, possibly within the next three or four hours.

I met Bob twenty years ago in central Australia. It was during the years of my *fatwa*, and life consisted of skulking in flat, empty, shadeless red terrain with nary a tree to hide an assassin, as far from Iran as an apostate can run and stay out of snow.

And all because of one of my silly *ATHEISTMAN* cartoons, a Malaysian journalist who couldn't mind his own goddamn business, and the evil old Tyrant of Tehran himself: *Ayatollah Ruhollah Khomeini*. No sinner had a blacker heart than this madman and no martyr, a more puritanical *non*sense of humor. But I suppose as he lay dying in 1989 - from too tight a sphincter in my view - and looked back at a lifetime of evil deeds all in the name of piety, religious satire was not likely to set a wry smile anywhere in that fleas' nest beard of his. If a bit of social humor caused a tizzy fit that helped the megalomaniacal brute into the bosom of his oblivion, it was probably the best thing for him, certainly the world. Of course, had he the sense to snuff it a year or two sooner, I might have avoided fifteen years of constant back-watching, still have my cushy UN job, married a girl other than Pam (or not at all) and never set foot in the scorching sun-painted landscape of the Australian Outback, the peerless hellhole of the Western world.

In the 1990's, I'd run into Bob from time to time as I surveyed Aboriginal sacred sites near Alice Springs for TALC. He was known as 'Captain Bob' by local Aborigines. I flew with him around the *Pitjantjatjarra* communities on occasion. On the flight over yesterday, he mentioned he'd just moved to Darwin, and I might have seen him around town recently.

He did a lucky five years in Sydney's Long Bay Jail for the very public knife brawl. While inside, he met tribal Aboriginal men and 'got to know the lore' (as he puts it). Apparently, he found a sense of social justice in jail, and when he got out, he traveled to Alice Springs and reinvented himself.

Back then, Australian cultural mythology held that a crooked man could go straight in Alice Springs. Some tried, but most soon recidivated. If you travel there, a certain measure of social *slippage* is acceptable …expected …almost *de rigueur*. The societal bell curve flat lines low at the Alice Springs city limits[6].

But Bob grafted and passed his commercial pilot's license, which doesn't say much about aviation standards back then. He might have known where the instructor lived. And he told his story proudly and often, in any bar, to anyone: how to turn your life around, how you can be anyone you want in Alice. He worked for years in the Central Desert, running social development programs. I understand that he married several times, and the old goat reportedly has a dozen children living in various remote communities.

He developed a reputation as a 'white warrior' for Aboriginal Land Rights – *his*, advancing newly acquired wives' land interests with shameless abandon and cowing competing claimants' rights with

---

[6] Levague was a fan of Neville Shute's famous novel *A Town Like Alice* and named a son after the male protagonist, *Joe Harman* (see pg. 201 below). Following Levague's listing on the UN Fatwa Watch Committee's *New Additions* in 1989, he sought sanctuary in the remoteness of Alice Springs, where he and Pam raised their family, mostly in peace and safety.

The reality of life in the outback town apparently did not meet Levague's romantic expectations. In truth, the community's economy *does* rely heavily on federal welfare, and this doubtlessly skews the 'bell curve' as Levague describes (but only marginally). However, his various descriptions of the town's occupants throughout the Journal as *troublesome indigenes, belligerent drunks, bone idle layabouts, imported big city losers, useless public servants, and a general assortment of immigrant riff-raff from God knows where* are regrettable.

personal threats. He railed against local politicians about the desperate plight of the *'dispossessed'*, predicting that sooner or later, the streets would literally run with the blood of *'oppressors'* when natives took up arms in the struggle for justice.

His strident message stirred a few, mostly unemployed young men in each community but didn't play well for most. I disliked him for his zealotry back then but never criticized him openly - a psycho with an airplane is a lot scarier than one with a knife.

These days he works as a kind of freelance charter pilot, a lot of remote mining jobs for a few small airlines. He seems to have mellowed out now. I guess age makes you realistic about justice. I didn't speak to him much on the flight over from Darwin yesterday, and I haven't seen him today until now.

Bob's sweating biochemical mass extricates itself from the back passenger seat, and we're both on the footpath checking that we have our bags and phones. I offer perfunctory thanks to our driver. Yousef's smiling or grinning. He says, "No worries, mate," and as we walk away towards *Arrivals/Departures/Secure Area,* I think I hear him add behind our backs, "Hope you beat the rain."

I turn, telling him thanks again, and the thought passes that Yousef might be an interesting fellow. Maybe he wanted to practice his English. Perhaps I was rude to ignore him from the moment he picked me up for the flight. But there's no getting past the oozing malice of your typical southern Armani, and the menace in just about every way he set his face brought to mind tribal villages I assessed along the Amat Darba River valley in central Armanistan, work I did for the UN Development Bank back in 1974 before the Soviet occupation. I recorded that local organization can be understood *economically* and revolves around maximizing individual advantage at the expense of relatives - close kin at first and depending on the scale of the enterprise, extending to cousins and then to cousins farther up the river. It's *'me against my brother,'* *'my brother and me against my cousin,'* *'me, my brother and my cousin against my second cousin,'* and so forth. The cultural beliefs, practices and legitimacies in the Amat Darba valley suffuse a stark individualistic, materialistic and wholly unfortunate social experience, and any reasonable assessment of the Amat Darba Armanis and most others I ever met is that they're intemperate thugs[7].

I watch Yousef circle the GUMO car around the parking area, drive away and disappear back up toward the mine, trailing a thick red plume of dust. I don't believe he hopes I *beat the rain*; I think he

---

[7] It behooves me to apologize here to the whole Armanistani community on behalf of the Anthropological Federation. Levague is in clear breach of professional ethics (again), and his crude labeling must be soundly condemned.

Indeed, his structural analysis of Armanistani society as being driven by profit maximization at the expense of social welfare describes the general philosophy of right-of-center capitalist societies throughout the world. Few would seriously apply such an insulting descriptor to followers of, for example, the Australian Liberal Party, Canadian and British Conservatives, or the American GOP.

hopes I *burn in hell*.

There's no sign of the other three passengers. Bob looks at me, head emerging from ox shoulders and tilted my way slightly, aviator sunglasses reflecting me looking at him in my sunglasses, and there's a reasonably strong jaw under a layer of fat that makes him look personable and jolly rather than handsome and serious. He has two chubby chins above a thick neck, each shaded by day-old black-grey stubble. His eyes are red and careworn. A slightly curved, horizontal scar under his right eye looks like a hostile blade just missed blinding him.

He's strung out today, as if he hasn't slept or he's still slightly drunk from last night. His tan *NT Dreaming Tours* uniform shirt is baggy and crumpled, and a large sweaty patch sticks to most of his back. He dons a cap he pulls from his back pocket: baggy light blue cotton with a short, floppy cloth visor. It sticks tight to his crew-cut salt-and-pepper hair like Velcro. It's not part of his uniform and looks comical, more like a weekend sailor's hat.

"Have a big night, Bob?" I venture of the fat man. "Didn't see you in the mess last night. Have a few quiet charges[8] in your room …all nice and peaceful?" I'd envy him if he had, and I'm not too fussed with a drunken take-off as long as landing is reasonably sober.

"You want to get out of here, Jack?" It's a dumb question.

He's a bit testy when he says he'll put my overnight bag on

---

[8] In the Northern Territory and in this context, a *charge* is a drink with alcohol in it.

board, so I keep it, telling him I need a few things while I wait.

"I'm getting everyone here a bit early," he says. "We'll take off as soon as we load up. Bit of weather about. I've got a headache."

"Sure, Bob. I'll just have a quick smoke ...I've got some painkillers if you want."

"I'll be right. I couldn't sleep ...Air conditioner rattled like a rusty Holden." So did mine, but I probably applied more sedatives.

'Captain' Bob Palmer strides purposely and reasonably unimpaired to the terminal building, fumbles in his pants pocket after sucking in his gut overhang to gain access, extracts a key, and unlocks the entrance door. He pauses, studying the sky to the east. It's darkening higher above the horizon. *Showers, occasionally heavy, clearing overnight, risk of localized flooding, freshening winds to gale force along coastal parts'* is the forecast for the Top End of Australia today. It's a typical late wet-season day, always a chance of afternoon storms.

A long white windsock tops a tall pole next to the access track near the security fence gate. It stirs frequently, filling half-out to the west. The gusting wind has picked up with the rising morning heat, and the weather's moving in fast.

Bob disappears into the terminal with a cheap, khaki-shaded NT Dreaming Tours team bag. Seconds later, the industrial-strength air-conditioning groans to life inside, spoiling a moment of quiet, slightly apprehensive solitude outside.

The GUMO airstrip is exposed to coastal weather and could not be built inland closer to the mine for safety reasons. Evidently, there's a law that a fully fueled jet aircraft cannot take off if there's a chance it could crash into a radioactive uranium mine.

In the summer monsoon cyclone season, flights are frequently canceled or rescheduled. The workforce expects this; they're 'acts of god'. RCC must have compensatory arrangements that mitigate weather disruption to workers' leave entitlements, or nobody would work in this god-awful place.

The airport is high enough for the crystalline expanse of the Arafura Sea, glistening relentlessly in the afternoon sunlight, to dominate the vista to the west, north, and east. Even with my dark sunglasses, I have to squint as I look around. From my slightly elevated vantage, the rugged coastline - white sandy beaches and sparkling seascape - is *beauty, rich and rare* (I suppose), and I struggle to find ordinary words, but after ten seconds, the brightness annoys and frazzles my nerves.

There's open sea ahead to the northeast, all the way to New Guinea. To the west, flat southern islands of the Wessels group are five kilometers away, dark and hazy on the horizon.

Our flight today takes us over Elco Island, the largest of the Wessels, then south of East Crocodile Island, and between Mooroongga Island and the Aboriginal community of Milingimbi. Then it's across the Arnhem Land plateau, over Kakadu National Park, and due west to Darwin along the Arnhem Highway (Figure 1, pg.

374).

The fenced-in airport and the winding sandy track heading west are the only modifications of nature visible along the coastline. The apron around the bitumen landing strip is graded and sheeted with crushed red gravel. Around the apron, the grass is closely cropped to green stubble for several hundred meters. Beyond is three hundred meters of firebreak where most trees have been removed, leaving patchy red dirt and occasional low, thin bushes - new eucalypt seedlings, prickly dwarf acacias, and dead leafless old mulga.

The perimeter fence contains all this cleared land and presumably keeps kangaroos and emus from straying in front of planes. It separates the 'secure' area - the runway and apron - from the parking bay on one side and the open ocean and untouched woodland, both extending to the horizon, on the others. The locked gate and the *Departures/Arrivals/Secure Area* door are the only ways in and out.

We're deep in *Yolngu* Aboriginal country, the territory of Jacob Kunmubilpilguru, a tall broad-shouldered tribal man with noble bearing and excellent English. He has his silver hair in a sort of frizzy afro and sports a full mustache, and he's fond of wearing a cowboy suit of solid black, including the hat. In his 40's, he's a handsome 'lady's man' and a heavy-weight male-cult leader, an image he promotes politically within TALC. He's renowned as a 'black tracker' and used often by police in pursuit of malfeasant Arnhem Land fugitives - many, his relatives. He has a motto, '*Jacob gets his man. Big fees welcome*'. He's charismatic, duplicitous, and as slippery as a real-estate developer – which, essentially, he is.

I scan the width of the runway as hot twisting air sucks off *willi willi* swirls of fine dust like red mini-tornados. Patchy cloud shadows glide quickly across the landscape. Stormy weather is expanding from the east fast and will likely engulf the airspace above much sooner than prognosticated.

But right now, it's 36 degrees Celsius, and this barren, searing car park is bathed in electromagnetic radiation from thermonuclear fusion in a main sequence, spectral class type-G star 8.3 light-minutes above.

It's not lifeless. When the squally wind swirls just right, I can smell the ripe fetid stink of biochemical life decomposing the carcass of old kangaroo road-kill on the side of the dirt track nearby.

Two kinds of ants scurry around the concrete pathway near my feet and all the way to the terminal. The bare ground nearby is pockmarked everywhere with tiny sand mounds, evidence of busy subterranean ant networks. These have been tunneled out by the introduced Argentine variety, which vastly outnumbers the much larger native species. No native ants forage on the bare ground. They appear to be confined to the black wasteland of the paved area, where it's probably too hot for the immigrants.

A lone kookaburra screeches suddenly in a nearby eucalypt. It's hidden while shiny gum leaves glitter in the sunlight, but then cloud shade passes, and I make him out perched on a low branch. It has a small snake in his pointed beak which he flails against the tree branch before deftly maneuvering the limp animal into a position where it's swallowed headfirst. It's all behavior naturally selected over hundreds of millions of post-Cambrian evolutionary years. I see no evidence of intelligent design here, but there's purposefulness recognizable by a slyer predator[9].

Wind sweeps through the stunted eucalypts on the margins of the parking bay, rustling leaves and monetarily drowning out the dull hum of air conditioners. Despite the wondrously adapted life all around, the airport tarmac beyond the fence – its sunbaked black surface blurring in noonday heat - is probably bleached sterile enough for a surgical procedure.

I roll a cigarette, my last for three or four hours, and note that I have only enough tobacco for one more smoke after the flight. There's a new sign on the footpath prohibiting smoking within *five* meters of the

---

[9] It may be that contemplation of *predation* by a ten-year-old Levague marks the genesis of *ATHEISTMAN*. There is a note in the Journal, *I was ok with God creating plants, and God creating animals to eat the plants, but creating animals to eat something else with a nervous system – that tipped me into heresy.* But also see Footnote 16, pg. 77 below – *I am become ATHEISTMAN ...*

The reference to *intelligent design* is a jab at Evangelical Christians who see a role for religion in the teaching of biology in American schools. Elsewhere in the Journal, Levague asks, *what kind of intelligence would design a Tyrannosaurus Rex?*

terminal – *maximum fine $110*. There was a similar sign there before, but it read simply *'Please, No Smoking'* – more like a request or guideline. The sign's getting testy, like my wife.

But goddamn it, I just don't seem to have the will. I've adopted an *I can't quit, won't quit, and we all got a go sooner or later, so shut up* approach.

Pam's continued antismoking campaign at home is non-stop nagging, and recently, the mother of my four children has moved on from imploring me to take care of my health for something abstract like *for my sake* to making her case in reasonable economic terms that I can't argue with – we have children still at home, therefore dying without an accidental death insurance payout is not an option. If my sense of this is correct, about $1m should do the trick. But I don't think even this will get her off my case; she's wedded to it.

Pam's applying *guilt*, a primary life force and along with *fear*, a main driver in our relationship. Her instincts and skills in this area of domestic life are unequaled. Somehow, she seems able to blend a *guilt-fear-flight* impulse into a uniquely terrifying motivation for changed behavior especially in matters of things that belong to her, like a husband.

Mind you, she's not a violent person. In moments when Pam faces life's great challenges and conflicts, she usually falls back into her native Shoshone lingo, a language of guttural choking slang and hissing spit marvelously suited to conveying grave menace - but actual violence is never the preferred option. It's always on the table, though,

35

and when push comes to shove, it's more like her factory default setting. There are several committee members of the Alice Springs Parents and Teachers Association who know this.

And despite over twenty years of experience being married to me and no objective evidence that I possess the self-discipline to actively pursue a long life for its own sake, Pam looks to the future with unshakable anticipation that it will go on forever, here on earth, and later in some sort of ill-defined mix of Shamanistic spirit realm and Christian heaven[10] - and I must be there with my darling omnipresent heathen *forever*.

Her life is full of busy routines and an outlook that's generally positive and hopeful, with joy for life and faith for an afterlife. But when cancer takes me at the end, even as my demise in dressed in Sunday best with Pam chanting hymns promising nonsensical paradise, I'll find no comfort in last thoughts on *Life* and the *Universe*.

---

[10] Pam Levague is a native American, a Shoshone princess distantly related to the Sacagawea of Lewis and Clark fame. Her tribe traditionally followed animistic shamanism before encountering enthusiastic Pentecostalists late in the 19th century. However, these Christian missionaries never extinguished Shoshone religion; rather, traditional epistemology was modified to include Jesus *as a Shaman*.

Many native cultures have trouble understanding the Christian concept of *Original Sin*. Of his time with Pam's tribe, Levague writes, *God's message was understood by the Shoshone as* 'You're born sinful but don't worry, I'll crucify my son, resurrect him and then all will be fine', *and for most local punters, you can't get from the first point to the last without very strong peyote and no small measure of white devil crazy talk.*

In the end, it's all abominable.

And when she goes, and my kids – who cares? All memory of Jacques Levague will vanish in a wink; the meaning of life will be stripped to nothing and disappear into the sterile emptiness of eternity …such is the miracle of life …Oh, for a magical universe. I'd live where time stands still - on the surface of a particle of light, a photon big enough for a lounge chair and a small side table with a cocktail shaker and martini glasses and Pam beside me serving drinks, lighting my cigar, unusually quiet. We would shoot through the cosmos forever, beaming across the Universe and lighting up the darkness to the edge of everything, waving to fellow photon riders - old friends and family who occasionally pass us by. Relaxing on our photon, our existence is contained in the Speed of Light, and there's no passage of time. We travel *parallel* to time, never overtaken. But I'm helpless and embarrassed in reality, a quivering blob of biomass caught in a Gravity force field with no faith in Edens or Pearly Gates.

Sure, I have *hope* - that tomorrow might bring happiness, good health, prosperity, world peace, practical human cloning technology, and the ability to keep a head alive indefinably in a lab. Hope is just a conditioned response, anticipation that something less awful than right now might be around the corner because sometimes it is. Hoped-for things occasionally occur.

I have hope but no *faith*. *Faith* - 'hope' when there's really *no* hope - *ATHEISTMAN* has none of that. All in all, it's probably better not to live than to live and then die …philosophically speaking. Of course, tell that to the fornicating masses, and you'll get back bulk to the contrary.

Interestingly, I appear to be in the only place within about five hundred kilometers where I can get fined for smoking outside. I light up my fag, but only *four* meters away from the entrance, not the stipulated five. I'm a renegade.

Rough weather's moving in fast. Black storms gather in more of the eastern sky, and tumbling grey-white clouds exploding upward are getting closer. It won't be long before a torrential monsoon event sweeps through. But now the sun still blazes overhead, and I'm standing in the noonday heat, smoking a fag. My wide-brim cotton hat shades my full-bearded face and bald head. My white T-shirt and blue jeans are both a size too big and hang loose and comfortable for the trip. I'm still a bit weary from the wine last night, but I don't feel too bad.

My biggest health concern I confessed to RCC boss Mattius Korda last night - a chronic tendency to severe bouts of nausea and vomiting. *Cyclical Vomiting Syndrome* comes over me two or three times each year, each bout lasting a week or ten days. I've had it for twenty-two years, pretty well since the unhinged Iranian mullah slapped a *fatwa* on my head, and not incidentally, as long as I've been married to Pam. The episodes didn't stop when the *fatwa* was lifted five or six years ago - and I'm still with Pam - but now they're less frequent and debilitating, especially when I use a combination of antidepressants, powerful benzodiazepines, and the best skunk-weed money can buy. Today, I have the *white widow* strain, an Amsterdam coffee shop favorite.

And because no one is around, I fish in my zip-top overnight bag, retrieve a marijuana joint from my shaving kit, and light up. I also remove two lorazepam tranquilizer tablets for later and tuck them in my jeans pocket in case of queasiness before taking off. When another white utility vehicle appears on the track, approaching the airport in a hurry, I have a cigarette in one hand and the joint in the other. I toss the cigarette to the curb and quickly walk away from the terminal towards the fringe of the parking area where the recent kookaburra snake-eating event occurred, pretending to speak on my mobile. I'm well away from where the car stops in front of the terminal and downwind, smoking my pot.

I use the excuse of my bogus phone call to avoid eye contact with the small slender Asian woman gracefully getting out of the back passenger seat of the vehicle. But not with Yousef, who's driving the car again. He's smiling at me *again*. I have to give him a slight nod of acknowledgment as he walks around the back of the car and helps the slight woman with her bag.

Yousef completes his drop-off. He and the woman exchange some brief conversation and they both smoke cigarettes. Then he gets back in his car, turns the vehicle around, and as I watch him go, he spares me one more glance, expressionless this time and too long for my liking. I finish my joint, toss the roach for the native ants, and join my fellow passenger in front of the terminal.

"I think the pilot wants to go right now," I say as she gathers her things. "Hey, Jack. Yeah, I got a call," she replies. There's a slight edge in her voice, which I put down to preflight nerves. She notices that I'm interested in the box she's toting.

"It's sandwiches and drinks for lunch. We'll eat on the plane. I've got three bottles of white left over from last night," and indicating the terminal with a slight tilt of her head, "Give me a hand with the door."

There's a red leather overnight bag on her shoulder, and she carries a carton labeled with Chinese characters. She's dressed in black designer jeans and a bright orange long-sleeve high-visibility shirt with grey reflector strips across the chest. It's tucked into her jeans but then balloons out around her top. There's a GUMO logo where her small left breast might be, a minuscule pick axe sticking into a wheelbarrow containing a pile of tiny yellow boulders - presumably radioactive yellowcake - with a little 'nuclear material' radiation symbol hovering over her nipple. It's the same staff GUMO shirt as Yousef was wearing.

Sue Tran works as the caterer for the agreement signing ceremony dinner and came over with us on the charter from Darwin yesterday. She's just younger than me, mid-fifties perhaps. Being small and slim, she doesn't seem too bothered by the tropical heat. She dished out cold chicken and salad and served drinks to about 20 people until late last night without breaking a sweat.

40

Her employer is the Ling family, one of the oldest Chinese families in Darwin. They've owned an Asian food importing business and grocery store for generations, and I heard they'd won a contract to provide emergency Asian meals to the Darwin Refugee Detention Centre. A few years ago, the Lings opened a Chinese restaurant in Humpty Doo, just outside of Darwin, next to where the TALC offices used to be until they moved to the CBD around Christmas. The $10.00 lunchtime seafood buffet was a favorite with the TALC anthropology department, and Ling's remains the preferred caterer for TALC functions. Sue Tran works the restaurant's lunchtime shift, and I don't recall ever talking to her beyond giving my food order.

Physically, Sue Tran looks a bit like an older version of my wife – the same hard, small frame and lithe, wiry strength. Pam's cheekbones are slightly sharper, and her eyes are less Asiatic, slightly crueler …and breathtakingly beautiful.

I notice the ubiquitous bush flies don't seem to bother Sue Tran. She's wearing a 'Fremantle Dockers' football cap, and long, thick hair, uniformly black despite her years, flows down her orange back. In the sunlight, she's prettier than the dozen or so times she's served me lunch. I'm wondering how old her kids are (if she has any). The thought crosses my mind briefly that overwhelmingly, Sue Tran looks fit, petite, and cross-culturally feminine, and despite her age, still fertile. This thought scurries into a dark corner of my brain where a rather large rodent lives, and soon, the image of a reflector-striped orange ball, naked below the waist, is bouncing lustily on my lap, sending faint tickly itches to my sixty-year-old crotch[11].

Normally, at about this time, Dr. Levague sweeps Jack-the-Rat back to his hole in my brain, or rather, it's the mental image of Pam's ceremonial Shoshone Indian knife slicing up the orange bouncing ball and then my nuts. The jealous kitten has a traditional name for this blade, which roughly translates as *Mrs. Skinning*, bearing that quaint Shoshone linguistic trait of naming sharp things with female labels.

In Shoshone tradition, a husband's fidelity is ensured by the pain of having his dick cut off in the night. It's a facet of local culture I was unaware of when I married the cute little savage. Mrs. Skinning's just a family heirloom now, but Pam keeps the long, evilly curved moon-crescent blade prominently displayed on a shelf above the TV at home, along with a small brown Indian medicine bag pouch made from something's (or someone's) cured scrotum skin that has shrunk, puckered, and diminished over time so it's as fragile as wasps'

---

[11] I considered redacting this and further lecherous comments out of decency. However, I believe they highlight certain character flaws that are germane to the author's motivations and general conduct. Few women are described in the Journal without decent into moral turpitude.

It is relevant to point out that Levague has been formally reported to the Anthropological Federation's Ethics Committee at least a dozen times, and his file is large enough to require an index (with subject headings: *Inappropriate and Lewd Conduct, Drugs and Alcohol Complaints, Financial Irregularities* and *Other Official Corruption*).

When do the erotic musings of an old man turn pathological? I decided years ago and, for it, have been made the subject of ridicule, threats and insults (see *Athol the Asshole* pg. 373 below).

nest paper. Inside are aged fragments of teeth and claws from a long-dead cougar, Pam's Shoshone totemic sister.

But the truth is that philandering men in Pam's tribe take reasonable preemptive steps before they lose their tackle - like shooting their wives dead - and Mrs. Skinning's all wrapped up in complex female mythology and meaning I can't fathom but seem oddly Freudian. I speak passable Shoshone and she, fluent English, and there's no doubt in my mind – it's a truth I believe as I do Gravity, and she does because it's her basic nature – *she'd do it*. The threat works, and I'm the pigeon in a behavioral science experiment who's learning not to peck the button that delivers a shock but who's incorrigibly stupid.

But I wouldn't mind ending my soon-approaching dotage during a Viagra-fueled gallop with Pam on top, shaking my bones to death. She's twenty years younger and, despite four kids, still spry as a lynx in spring.

I'll never find better, and I suppose the specter of Mrs. Skinning is a kind of poetic retribution for an earlier life of lechery in far-off places. Edo tribal girls of the Amazon, naked as babies and undergoing girl-to-woman bride exchange rituals, and especially my adopted *niece*, Juliet - are still often fondly recalled. A bevy of fuzzy-haired south-sea beach beauties on both sides of armed conflict in Bougainville, made all the hornier by the excitement of revolutionary war, pop frequently to mind. And, of course, I sometimes wake in fright with horrendous images of that furious old opium-addled Berber chieftain, Sheik-al-Yamani - a matter of his daughter's dubious honor – and the night that almost cost me dearly back in '75. Now, I'm faithful, and I'll stay that way as long as Pam's alive - unless I get drunk on a field trip far from home and end up with company in the sack *and* I'm reasonably satisfied - as if my testicles depended on it - that she'd never find out. If she did, I'd have to run. Pam Levague eats *fatwas* for breakfast[12].

Unlike me, Sue Tran seems cool in this prickly noon heat. Her skin is southern Vietnamese creamy tan, and despite the pitiless Territorial sun today, she is still fresh-looking. She has oval dark eyes and a pretty, classic Oriental face. I'm impressed she speaks English like a first language when hers is Vietnamese. I know a few words, but at Ling's, Sue Tran always takes my order in English - I don't want

---

[12] The Journal documents episodes of fieldwork Levague conducted for the UN Development Bank before he was fired. Among others, entries include as follows (see dot points). References to his involvement are contained in related documentation and cross-referenced with other material available on the internet, both noted here:

- in the jungles of South America (see pgs. 90-91 below), Brazilian Government Documents: *Illegal Hardwood Logging in the Amazon River Basin* (1973) and Enron *vs* Levague: *Brazilian Court Proceedings: Oil Leases on Edo Tribal Land* (2000);

- in Papua New Guinea (see pgs. 91-92 below) and Interpol Arrest Warrants: *Bougainville Rebellion* (1987); and

- in the Atlas Mountains of North Africa (see pg. 301 below) and Algiers Daily News: *Berber Communal Violence Intensifies* (1976).

to mistakenly be served sweet and sour snake.

The cannabis is kicking in, and I have nothing to say. "It won't be easy to hide in that shirt," I manage lamely. She casts me a mildly annoyed glance, barely lowering an eyebrow. The line of her small mouth, set firmly against the occasional fly, opens, and her thin lips part. "I went for a tour of the mine this morning, and they gave me this shirt. It's a safety thing. We went down to the port where they store all the yellowcake drums. There were no ships; it's not much of a port, just a long jetty. They stack up the drums until there's a full load, and then it's all shipped off to Japan. They gave us work boots, safety glasses, and a hard hat. I kept the shirt so I wouldn't have to change. I went with the pilot, Bob. Yousef drove us around."

She looks away from me skyward. "Bit windy ... let's get moving. I've got to get home and chop meat for a banquet tonight."

I'm trying to remember if I was invited on this mine tour as we walk to the entrance, but I can't. I step forward and open the door, telling Sue Tran I'm waiting outside for the rest of the passengers, and Sue Tran, her red bag and her box of lunch pass into the terminal building with no further comment. A waft of cool air escapes before the door closes, and I glimpse pilot Bob inside near the check-in desk, wrestling a large canvas duffel bag onto the weighing scales.

I return to the car park, collect my beat-up brown leather carry-all bag from under the *No Smoking* sign, swing it over my shoulder, and retrieve my half-smoked tobacco cigarette from the parking lot curb. I light up again just as I spot another white utility vehicle coming over the hill speeding towards the airport.

It's similar to but not Yousef's car and going dangerously fast, bouncing and flying along, and stirring up much more dust on the gravel track than Yousef and Sue Tran. The dust clears away quickly in the wind, which I notice has swung around slightly to the northeast and increased in speed.

The car is close enough now to see that the driver is Mattius Korda, the RCC boss, and Mrs. Korda is in the passenger seat next to her husband. The vehicle is a white twin-cab tray-back, and I see that the back passenger seats are both occupied, one by an Aborigine.

The car breaks sharply and skids on the gravel, spraying up more red dust before it hits the paved car park, quickly slows, and pulls up a few meters from where I'm standing. Korda opens the driver's door at the same time as he turns off the car, and he's out and hustling around the front of the vehicle in a hurry.

"Jack. G'day. We have to lift off *now* if we want to go at all. Weather's getting rough." He says *leeft auf* for 'lift off' with a thick Afrikaner accent that sounds no different to me than a Dutchman trying to be an Englishman.

He's moving fairly easily for a dying man. Last night, he told me, *'It's the brain tumors that kill you first,'* and he'd had these removed a month ago and was given six months, give or take, before all the other cancers: lymph nodes, liver, colon and new brain tumors overwhelm his biochemistry, all at the same time. I suppose he has five months to go, and that's with the chemo. He told me that the

GUMO expansion agreement signing is his last meaningful function to do with RCC. It's likely the last *full stop*. He's probably only in his early fifties.

Korda opens the front passenger door on the curbside for his wife, and she gets out and stands off to the side clear of the vehicle. Then he moves quickly to the back and extracts a sleek black leather briefcase and light-green soft leather *Prada* overnight bag from the vehicle's open tray-back. He hands these items to his wife, and now he's out of breath and gasping, his tall, thin frame bent over slightly, hands on knees.

His wife arranges the Prada tote bag strap over her shoulder and takes the smaller briefcase in hand while studying her husband, her brow creasing with concern. Korda points towards the terminal entrance. "Right in there, pet. I'll see you inside ... Go ahead, Julie. I'm fine."

Last night during the meal and after, while Korda and I drank wine, Mrs. Korda sat next to her husband at the table and didn't say much for hours. She was dressed in tight khaki shorts and a long-sleeved denim shirt, and her shoulder-length auburn hair was tied back. She nursed one glass of red all night.

Occasionally she asked questions about the local Aboriginal community in an educated 'old money' Pommy accent, and I got the impression she was a professional, maybe a lawyer. I told her how the Aboriginal patrilineal clan social order still worked in east Arnhem Land but had to adapt to modern polygamy laws, how the islands along the Arafura coast are part of the *Seven Sisters Dreaming* 'Story-Song' and how, in the *Mother's Brother/Sister's Son Dreaming* - the *TWO MEN* story - the *First Uncle* circumcised the *First Nephew*, and he then circumcised his uncle - to return the favor. This ceremony joins a man (ego's mother's brother) to the son (ego) of another man (ego's mother's husband) with different *blood* – the most important of all social relations - *politics*. The *TWO MEN* hold dominion over the mythological landscape in most traditionally oriented communities.

We talked about how the mine expansion could provide job opportunities for the Minjininga Community and Jacob Kunmubilpilguru's extended family, and I taught her to pronounce Kunmubilpilguru – *Kun mu bil pil gu ru.* I said that the deal might result in a few jobs, but most applicants would probably come from outside, and I didn't think anyone in the Kunmubilpilguru clan was really cut out for uranium mining.

Mrs. Korda recalled hearing about my ill-fated '*ATHEISTMAN* versus Khomeini' cartoon somewhere and the business of the *fatwa* issued by the mad Iranian dictator in 1989. I have a potted version of the story for an Australian audience ending with '*If it weren't for that, I'd never have come to Australia.*' It resonates well, as if irony or serendipity was at play, and great fortune blessed me with the chance of a place in the Lucky Country. But I'd just as soon the whole wretched business never occurred. I could have easily got through life without '*Aussie! Aussie! Aussie!*' She said similar about *her* Australian experience but of her husband's work.

But mostly, Mrs. Korda just seemed worried about her sick husband and looked for an early opportunity to take him off to their accommodation unit and put him to bed. When the conversation did lead to her husband's condition, she was positive about his treatment and excited about some 'new research' she'd heard about. Mr. Korda was less sanguine, and I wasn't sure whether *she* really believed this shit or was just keeping appearances, and her chin, up.

She said she wasn't in favor of attending the signing ceremony (because of the recent brain surgery), and Mattius needed to be close to a hospital. But she accepted that Arnhem Land had special memories for her husband, who I learned had been the first mine manager when RCC took over twenty years ago, and he wanted to see the place one last time. As long as Mr. Korda had his medication, they could put up with the rigors of a short field trip and a brief absence from civilization.

Korda and I kicked on through two or three bottles of red, and if not for the free wine and Mrs. Korda walking around from time to time in those bun-hugging shorts, I'd have got bored and repaired to my room for joints. A dying man's conversation is surprisingly tedious - all self-centered - and finally, when I offered myself as sympathetic company for his wife as she faced the sadness ahead and asked what she might be doing after the funeral, they'd met the Rat and that was the end of the night.

Now Mrs. Korda is clearly still fretting about her sick husband, but as freshening wind gusts sweep across the parking area, pelting eyes with dust and leaf debris, she gets a hurry-on. She pats down the shouldered Prada bag with her free hand, checking for something, and when happy it's there, glances at the space where I'm standing. As if seeing me there for the first time, she smiles perfunctorily. "Hi there, Jack," she says, more at me than to me, and she moves briskly towards the terminal door. "Ah, yeah, G'day," I respond automatically as she snootily walks by.

Mrs. Korda is wearing, incongruously, a dark green knee-length women's business skirt that is a shade darker than her bag, an expensive-looking light green blouse, and cheap pink foam-rubber flip-flops on her feet. She's not wearing a hat and has made up her face but only modestly and I see her worried eyes are the same green color as the rest of her. She's in her forties and fills out her clothes snugly without being overweight, and my eyes seem glued on her full-figured walk as she enters the terminal. Except for footwear, Mrs. Korda looks professionally dressed for a corporate office in Melbourne, not light aircraft travel in remote Arnhem Land. I'll probably be close behind her when she climbs into the plane.

Mattius Korda is breathing easier and clearing his throat. His irksome Afrikaner voice says, "Here, Jack. I'd like you to meet Sister Mary and this young fellow. He's from the local tribe, maybe you know him. Sister Mary's taking him back to Darwin. They need a *leeft*." Korda has the back left passenger door open and now leans way in and across the seated Aboriginal lad trying to unbuckle the seat belt.

The young chap isn't helping. He's holding what appear to be traditional 'clapping sticks', the basic Aboriginal musical percussion instrument, one stick in each hand. As Korda fumbles for the clasp, the lad's getting fidgety, now lightly tapping Korda's hand away with his sticks.

Then, the solidly built white woman seated next to the lad takes charge, releasing the seatbelt. "There we go," she says. "Out you get, Chip."

Once free of the restraint, Korda successfully extricates the lad from the car. 'Chip' has to be guided in a series of single steps to complete that motion as if he's unsure of what's expected of him. Now it's clear there's something wrong with this young fellow.

Korda is at the back of the vehicle again, removing the rest of the baggage: a black soft leather overnight bag that looks well-traveled, a large old-fashioned blue suitcase that he has trouble lifting off the tray-back, and a smaller brown canvas bag with a Qantas Airlines baggage tag attached. He leaves the latter two on the curb next to the kid and moves to the front of the vehicle, keeping his bag tucked under his arm.

Korda wears wireframe sunglasses, a long-sleeve white shirt with a crisp starched open collar, dark grey business trousers, and polished black shoes. He's slightly shorter than me and much thinner, more wasted. He has a GUMO cap on his bald head, and when he turns it, I can see the brain surgery scars - ugly red zipper lines across the base of his skull. His suit jacket and tie must be in his bag or Mrs.

51

Korda's large green tote bag.   Both probably have something semiformal to do this evening when they get back to Darwin, a tad far-reaching by the look of him.

Korda approaches me at the same time as a hefty, overweight but solidly proportioned woman looms into view from the other side of the car. He says, "Sister Mary, this is the anthropologist, Jack Levague, I told you about.   Jack knows Jacob and Chip's people." Sister Mary's face smiles brightly, and she approaches.   "Thank goodness you could find seats," she says to both of us.

Sister Mary wears a wash of white: white laced shoes, white stockings, and a strangely well-starched short-sleeve, blindingly white nurse's uniform that falls just above her thick knees and buttons up to the top of her breasts, which seem oddly small.   Evidence that's available only to the Rat leads him to conclude that the Sister's underwear is almost certainly similarly spotless[13].   The only color change is a dark blue headscarf that leaves a short hair fringe across her forehead. From the back, at a distance, she might look a bit like a

---

[13] This puerile discussion of women's underwear (and a *nun's,* at that) is borderline misogyny and pornography. It has no place in the anthropological scholarly record.

Again, I did not redact these unfortunate words because they reflect a certain psychopathy that should be brought to the police's attention.   They show the gaping chasm between the standards of the regrettable Jacques Levague and those I have pledged myself to over a career of dispassionate social analysis and observation. However, the fact that I did not strike out these comments is a source of personal angst. I will be reminded of this each time I find Mrs. Pine's *Victoria's Secret* catalog in my mailbox.

family-sized refrigerator with a policeman's hat.

There are small red crosses stitched in her uniform lapels, not Red Cross medical crosses but Roman crucifix torture devices. A large dark wooden one about four by two inches hangs from a thick silver chain around her neck and nestles on her chest, contrasting with the clinical white. I'm unsure if she's a medical 'sister' or a nun disguised as a nurse.

She's got an oddly deep Irish working-class accent, and her skin seems *too* white, and I conclude she's recently arrived in Australia. She's tall for a woman and stocky, with a round head and large clear brown eyes. Short 'page-boy' clipped, mousy brown hair frames a warm, friendly face, giving an impression of a mature, chubby-cheeked cherub.

She seems in her early twenties, a bit young for responsibility, and while her demeanor seems reasonably self-assured and competent, I'm sure she has conceptual apparatus similar to that of a lemming, and she appears insufferably cheerful and eager to confirm the assessment.

Korda has the car keys in hand. "The pilot …Bob, doesn't know Sister Mary and Chip are joining us. I better let him know. Can you lock up the car, Jack? Just leave the key under the front wheel on the driver's side. It's your mate Jacob's now. I had to *donate* it to him. He says he'll pick it up sometime today."

I ignore Sister Mary's outstretched hand. Korda is giving a company car to a senior traditional landowner. This annoys me because it's certain Jacob's brothers, his mother's brothers, and the whole damn community will think they should get their own cars as well, and sooner or later, someone's going to pick up a notion of 'inappropriate inducement' and some delicate jelly-spined anti-nuclear reporter will write a critical report and it'll have my name somewhere in it, possibly referencing with blatant political bias certain dealings I've previously had with mining companies, especially that unfortunate fraud fiasco in Borneo with gold miner Bre-X and the whole awful mess at Bougainville in the '80s.

I should have anticipated some last-minute scam like this. Although the new mining deal is worth millions, all the loot goes into a community trust account, and none of it can be used if it *'creates an income tax liability on the part of an individual'*. This means they don't get anything for themselves that's just for themselves. And it's certain that Jacob's status as a community leader and senior 'cult lawman' gives him a greater proprietary interest in what the community can bleed out of RCC.

Perhaps my eyebrows lowered a tad anyway, and maybe Korda mistakes my apparent distaste for a secret side deal as an affront to responsible notions of propriety, but I think he knows me better. He's fatigued but adds the context. "Yesterday, Jacob demanded a 'special' consideration, or he wouldn't sign the agreement. He wanted $10,000 in cash. He said he wouldn't sign otherwise, and neither would anyone else in his family. I needed to get Jacob over the line. It might have been blackmail or brinkmanship - call it what you want

- but I did what it took. Anyway, I told him after he finally *did* sign that I didn't have the money in cash, and we agreed on the car. It's not a matter that should concern TALC. Like it or not, Jack," he says quietly, "just please give me a hand with this so we can get away."

Korda's face goes from painful to sad to annoyed and then just plain distressed in quick succession. I sure don't want him croaking here and now and delaying the flight, so I accept the car key, stating that I was sure that the community will make good use of the vehicle, and thinking that it will probably be stolen, joyridden and totaled within about five minutes of our departure.

"Thanks, Jack." His face eases. Glancing at the others, he adds, "I think the Sister might need help with the young fellow. Can you give her a hand?" Then he says to Sister Mary, "I'll leave you with Jack. He'll give you a hand with Chip. The pilot needs to weigh all the bags. We should get going." He gives me a little nod, signifying matters are settled, and moves off towards the terminal entrance with his black bag in hand, disappearing inside.

Sister Mary is still offering her hand, so I take it, managing a tight smile. "Sorry for being rude ... Jack Levague. I'm with the Aboriginal land council."

"Pleased to meet you," she says, turning to the Aboriginal kid and adding, "This is Chip. We've been visiting Chip's family at Minjininga. He was so happy to be home. But it's time to go back to the hospice. We came up to the mining camp yesterday with Jacob. We stayed in the camp last night. Jacob said there might be room on your plane. Otherwise, we'd be waitlisted on the regular flight for another week."

The lad's standing where Korda parked him, clasping his hard mulga wood clapping sticks and staring down at bright new Nike shoes on his feet. The yellow TALC tee shirt with the red 'Rainbow Serpent' motif and the blue cotton work pants he's wearing are a bit too big for his skinny frame and hang off him loosely. His black hair has been cut short recently, and he looks neat, clean and well-cared for.

"What's wrong with the kid?" I ask, wondering if he's likely to freak out during the flight. "It's a case of *solvent abuse syndrome*," she replies matter-of-factly.

Despite his slack-jaw expression, like the partial facial-muscle paralysis of a stroke victim, he looks about eighteen years old. If it wasn't for his left eye looking slightly lower than the right - the appearance of one side of his face sliding down his skull - he'd be a handsome young man. He probably started inhaling petrol fumes to escape boredom, the kind of stifling *ennui* that sets in at a very early age in Aboriginal Australia. I just hope he's in control of his bladder and bowels for the next three hours.

Suddenly, I know this unfortunate boy. He's the nephew of Jacob Kunmubilpilguru. I spoke to Jacob a few times at the ceremony yesterday, but he didn't mention the lad or Sister Mary or that they needed a lift to Darwin. He must have sorted this out directly with Korda.

"I'll give you a hand with this," I offer to Sister Mary and indicate the big blue suitcase, which I suppose holds Chip's things, maybe *all* his things. I pick up the case, which weighs about ten kilograms, as well as the smaller brown Qantas-tagged bag, which I assume is Sister Mary's, and lug these to the terminal, leaving them on the footpath in front of the entrance. The weight in Chip's bag is off-center and seems to be concentrated at the bottom of the case like he was carrying a ten-pin bowling ball.

Sister Mary is speaking quietly to her charge. He's still not moving, and as I walk back to the car, I remember the kid's name is *Chirp* Kunmubilpilguru. His English nickname is actually 'Chirp'.

"Yes, I believe I know this kid's family. I saw Jacob at the mine camp last night," I say. "I think his name is *Chirp*. He's named after the *chirping* sound that baby saltwater crocodiles make when they hatch – to attract their mother."

"He's always been *Chip* at the hospice, but he never responds to being called Chip, now that I think about it. He doesn't really talk at all," she says. "But I've only been taking care of him for a few weeks. He's the first Aborigine I met. I thought it was a funny name for an Aborigine."

"The lad's named to honor his sacred totem, the crocodile," I explain. "It means he's made up of the same 'stuff of life' as a croc. He's not allowed to kill or eat a croc."

Sister Mary does not appear eager to discuss ancient reptile religious cults – her loss - and she turns to the Aboriginal lad but says to me, "They didn't call him *Chip* or *Chirp* or any name in Minjininga." Then she adds, "He hugged all his relatives and seemed excited and happy to be home. He went to a cave with Jacob down a creek behind the community dump. But after a day or so, most people shunned away. He just sat on the old church veranda tapping his two sticks together and humming in a kind of funny, growly voice."

The cave that Sister Mary mentioned is almost certainly Sacred Site *Minjininga Ethno-Arch EA01* with rock art that's been carbon-dated to twenty thousand years ago. The paintings depict the dance of the Crocodile Cult, the same dance I've seen Jacob Kunmubilpilguru perform at local cultural events, including yesterday's ceremony[14]. It's a religious ceremony ten times older than the Sister's church.

"Why is he back, by the way?" I ask, marginally interested.

"There's a government program with funding to bring kids back home from time to time when there's staff available. It was Chirp's first visit home in …well, ever."

I'm wondering how Sister Mary could stand the alienation and subtle hostility she must have felt in Minjininga, being so *white* and bringing the kid back like a bad memory. "How long were you in Minjininga? How did you get around? I can't remember a TALC

---

[14] The rock paintings are not secret-sacred in and of themselves, but the site, designated *Ethno-Arch EA01,* is mostly significant as an *initiation* site.

Levague does not record details of this aspect (that I might have redacted) except to say that *the men spend an eternity mutilating their willies, and no ceremony ends except with a great bleeding event that would leave even the bravest Jew at a Bris quaking in his boots.*

permit being issued to a hospice. Where did you get permission to enter Aboriginal Land?"

"We didn't have a vehicle. We just stayed in the village for the most part, and we only saw a few people. We kind of camped in the little unit behind the church," she replies. "We flew in on the jet and got a lift to Minjininga with the police. Gee, that was a few days ago, Friday I think. We planned to stay a bit longer, but I think we've had enough. No one said anything about a *permit*. I've only been with the hospice for a month. I just came up from Adelaide. I didn't think …"

"Don't get me wrong, Sister. The permit is just to let community people know outsiders are coming so they can get ready and so that you don't stumble into a ceremony or ritual that you shouldn't see …and so that TALC can keep out undesirables, including religious proselytizers, I might add." My eye can't help but be drawn to that damn crucifix hanging below her throat.

The biggest offender in Minjininga - the Catholic Church - was abandoned twenty years ago when Arnhem Land was legislated as Aboriginal-owned, and TALC started charging rent. The church remains un-vandalized where other buildings seem quickly to disintegrate when their occupants move on. It's protected by local *taboo*.

I glance at Chirp. He's holding his sticks at his sides, engrossed by his shoes, paying no attention to Sister Mary or me or anything we say. The Sister is smiling into my sunglasses, her apprehension over not having an official permit gone, and I'm sure she's hoping our conversation is nearly over too and we can move away from the flies into the airconditioned terminal …but I'm not finished.

I draw her eye, casually indicating the large wooden crucifix hanging like an 'open' sign from the Sister's fleshy neck. "You have a big cross there, Sister." *ATHEISTMAN* says this in the same tone *I* might *think* when meeting a person with a painfully noticeable facial abnormality, like *'You've got a big nose, mister'* - a simple statement of fact.

I'm stuck on this now and ask, "Did you know that the largest single crucifixion event *ever* occurred along the Appian Way, the main road into ancient Rome? It was after the defeat of the Spartacus slave rebellion, about the same time as your mythical Jesus. There were over 6000 crosses, including some women and children[15], all dying in agony, generally over several days.

Most died from dehydration, but not before birds pecked out their eyes, and the open wounds on their hands and feet were gnawed

---

[15] There are no verified records of the age and gender of those crucified along the Appian Way, and it is likely that Levague is lying through his teeth to torment an innocent person of faith and advance an antichristian agenda. In truth, child slaves were considered especially valuable in anticipation of lengthy periods of servitude and were probably spared.

Interestingly, contemporary accounts state that crosses were erected every 10 meters for about 600 km, and the bodies were nailed up in all manner of configurations – some upside-down, others sideways or appearing to be cartwheeling – for the amusement of passersby.

away by rats. Parents watching their children being tortured to death. What good was their faith on that day, eh? Don't be proud of faith, Sister; be embarrassed. God's not real."

I'm staring into the sister's face while her jaw slowly drops and the fingers of her right hand wander to her crucifix adornment and close around it protectively. *ATHEISTMAN* allows a few cruel seconds to ruminate before asking brightly, "Let me guess …Darwin Catholic Hospice? I was a bit curious about what happens to these petrol-sniffer kids, but he's not going to die soon. Why the Hospice …and how do you know if he's Catholic?"

After realizing that I've asked a question, Sister Mary seems to rally, and she's deciding which question to answer first. "He was sent to us when the hospital didn't want him anymore. He's waiting for a vacancy at the Darwin Rehab Centre. It's not built yet."

Well, it's a sad thing that a young kid has to live in an environment where old dying patients and Christian zealots are the principal landscape features. But I suppose the religious bent of the place diminishes the existential angst of lost battles with mortality for most of the inmates. After all, religion is theatre many dying people enjoy - but not *ATHEISTMAN*. When my time comes, I'll need to reach for the top-shelf black capsule of power-packed psychotropic medication, the drug that takes you out of yourself for one last orgasmic psychedelic flyover …and you just never land. When there's no more room for memory, and every next moment is a revisit of some dead man's soiled used feeling …*fade to black* as I bank away, soar high, my last moment frozen in the Speed of Light and flashing forever ...*ac-ross the Uni-verse.*

Now we're both sweating in the prickly, sticky, baking, stinking humidity. A '*thank-god-that's-over*' expression creeps across Sister Mary's face, and I agree, so *finally,* I suggest we move into the air-conditioned terminal.

I'm in a bit of a funk about the weather again. Massive storm clouds from the east are about to engulf the sun overhead. The Arafura Sea is choppy and churning up whitecaps beyond the airstrip, and the eucalypts around the car park are bending further in the wind. A torrential rain event is only minutes away. I begin to think it's odds-on the authorities will close airspace over the Top End about *right now* and we won't be going anywhere.

Sister Mary is eager for haste, so I suggest she go ahead and join the other passengers inside, get weighed, and so on, and I volunteer to fetch Chirp, who's standing by the car and hasn't moved at all. I hold the terminal door open as wide as it goes, and Sister Mary easily picks up the heavy blue suitcase and her own and passes inside. Before the door closes, she says, "I don't think he speaks English. Just take his hand and lead him; he'll come along."

I walk toward the car and slip the ignition key Korda gave me under the front right wheel, not worrying about locking up. Then I walk around the back of the car and come up close to Chirp. He tenses, sensing my proximity. He's still standing with his head bowed, but now his eyes dart around to see me, and he starts shuffling his white Nike-clad feet. I can tell he's expecting to be moved along somewhere, and he doesn't seem alarmed.

I put my arm around his slumped shoulders, and he straightens a bit, raising his head slightly. I don't force him to look at me - there's probably no one home - but I speak into his ear using the dialect of Yolngu lingo for his country. "Watch out for that white woman's 'cross' nephew," I say, using the specific kinship term for the *younger sister's oldest son*.

"In the woman's *Dreaming,* her crucifix means *death.*" I continue softly, whispering, "Sister Mary and her Catholic mob eat the body of a dead man named Jesus who's hanging from this cross …and they *drink his blood.*"

I begin moving slowly to the terminal entrance with my arm around the boy, and he comes with me. He seems to be walking on his toes, taking baby steps, but otherwise, he's reasonably mobile and compliant. When we get to the closed entrance, he knows when to stop. As I lean forward to open the door, I look into his face and watch dark eyes cast furtively around the car park and up the access track. They finally come to mine. "Veggie," he says.

Go figure, he recognizes me! I've been known in Minjininga as 'Veggie' ever since I tried to correct someone's pronunciation of my surname, Levague, by explaining that the 'g' was 'soft' like in 'veggie.'

"Yeah, sure," I say in English, and to get him into the terminal,

63

I gently push him through the open door. As he passes through, he says softly in lingo, "mother's oldest brother." Interestingly, it's the correct term Chirp should use for me under Yolngu kinship rules. Sister Mary's waiting for him just inside, and I catch her quizzically raised eyebrows, wondering if Chirp had anything meaningful to say, and I ignore her.

With the door still ajar and behind Sister Mary, I can see the pilot and Korda standing near the check-in desk under the terminal's fluorescent lighting, Chirp's suitcase on the scales. He's speaking to Korda and doesn't seem happy.

There's just enough time for one final smoke, and as I let the door close, I fish in the pocket of my jeans for my lighter. The cigarette is the same I rolled earlier and it's gone out. It's been hanging off my lip as I toted bags around and talked to passengers, and there's enough of it to light up one more time. As I shield my lighter from the swirling wind, I look out on a choppy, darkening sea as crackling static electricity charges up the stormy air and sets a tingle on my skin, and I hear and feel the first low rumbles of approaching thunder.

Chapter 2: Rough Weather

Inside the windowless terminal, three air-conditioners mounted on the wall opposite the entrance are blasting, all turned up maximum to the *'fatman-in-tropics'* setting, and I'm already too cold. The whole room is painted the same inspirational washed-out white as the outside, and the fluorescent lighting takes a moment to get used to.

Green plastic garden chairs line the walls to my left and the length of the wall underneath the air-conditioners. There are no decorations, no plants or pictures, only a few stackable plastic seats, one recycled office desk, stained institutional grey carpet throughout, and one unisex bathroom. A fly-in/fly-out schedule is pinned up on a large bulletin board on the left, but nothing else. It always reminds me of several third-world police stations and hospital emergency rooms I've visited over the years.

There's a clear path diagonally through the building to a door at the far right marked *'Departures/Fire Exit/Secure Area'*. The door's open, and beyond, the Brazilian Lorina is waiting on the tarmac. A length of yellow rope across the open doorway waist-high cordons off the exit; a small *'Do Not Cross'* sign dangles.

Sister Mary has settled Chirp Kunmubilpilguru in one of the green chairs, and they're sitting together under the bulletin board. Her hair below the blue headscarf is cut ruler-straight an inch above her eyebrows, a precise mousey-brown line.

Alone, a few seats to the right, Mattius Korda is bent forward, elbows on knees, head in hands. He looks exhausted already. He'll need to rest up plenty on the plane if he's got somewhere to be later tonight. I can't see any odds that he'll make it.

Sue Tran must be in the bathroom. Mrs. Korda is standing at the check-in desk, leaning forward with her hands palms flat on the desktop. She's speaking to pilot Captain Bob, probably looking confrontational from the front, like she's *presenting* from any other angle. Bob's seated behind the desk, his plastic chair tilted back as far away from Mrs. Korda as possible without toppling over. I move closer and stand in line.

Everyone's bags, including the cardboard box with our lunches, are lined up on the floor by the exit except Chirp's old blue suitcase, which is on the weighing scales next to the desk. Mrs. Korda seems flustered. Bob now leans forward, looking slightly anxious, and my first thought is the flight's been canceled due to the weather.

"I really can't see what the *weight* problem is. There are four empty seats, and there's plenty of room," complains Mrs. Korda.

Bob's brow creases, and he replies defensively. "Like I told your husband, love, it's not the seats or the weight; it's the fuel. I loaded fuel based on weight, and now there's more weight. The young fellow's suitcase technically puts us overweight for the fuel onboard. Look, I just spoke to the office, and unless we take off in ten minutes, we'll lose any chance of getting away today. The storms forecasted for Darwin *tonight* are brewing up *here* right now. The front's moving west faster than forecasted. We can get ahead and outrun the worst if we move *now*. There's no time to top-up fuel."

Mrs. Korda looks over to the left, where Sister Mary and Chirp are seated. The lad has his clapping sticks out, tapping them together occasionally, lightly. They're made of hard dark-brown mulga wood, with a crisp sonorous sound - not a 'clap' - more halfway between clean sharp '*tinks*' and '*tonks*' - highly annoying, solid, thick hardwood, two feet long and easily wielded as reasonably effective club weapons. They should be stowed somewhere for the trip away from numbskull mischief.

Mrs. Korda's worried eyes settle on her husband, who's vacantly watching Chirp. Then she turns back to Bob, her voice calm and confidential, "We can't stay here. My husband's not well. We have to be in Darwin tonight."

Bob takes a deep breath, and his frown softens - like most men in most cultures, he doesn't like arguing with a woman he's not related to, and he relents. "Here, let me do the sums one more time; we might be right."

Sue Tran emerges from the bathroom shaking water droplets off her hands, eyes down, thoughtfully self-possessed. She pays me no attention, walks over to the others, and starts casually looking over GUMO travel rosters for something to do rather than engage with other passengers.

I think about using the facilities before the flight. The toilet at the back of the charter is too cramped to stand and piss comfortably; it's really just for emergencies. But I'm not planning to drink any of the wine Sue Tran brought, so I should be ok.

Mrs. Korda has joined her husband, advising him about the weight problem. Bob's still implanted behind his desk and on the phone again, answering questions requiring either 'yes' or 'no' - that's all he says, and a 'yes' finishes the call. Then he picks up a small calculator from the desk and adds numbers with precise chubby-finger jabs. When he finishes, he stares straight ahead for a moment.

Without his aviator sunglasses, the dark crescent knife scar under his right eye looks like *another* eye - closed and red - under a normal eye. The scar doesn't look that old.

His fleshy face is grimly set, eyes focused on something meaningful in empty space a few meters ahead. Then he slowly stands, bringing with him the plastic chair molded around his Herculean butt until it's pried off. He lifts Chirp's case off the scales and sets it down with the other bags. The pilot appears to have made a decision that he's not entirely happy about …me either, whatever it is.

Talk about too-heavy planes and tropical storms stirs up a funky rumbling in the tummy. I recommend drugs, so I extract the two lorazepam tablets stashed earlier in my pants pocket, pop both, and swallow with saliva. I'll probably need more during the flight, so I fish out my last two tabs from my overnight bag and slip these into my pocket for later.

With marginally less dread in my gut, I grab my bag, step up to the check-in desk, and place it on the scales. Bob notices it weighs only a few kilos. All that's in there is a change of clothes, a bathroom kit and my field journal.

"Don't worry, Jack. Take it with you on board and stuff it under the seat in front or secure it in an empty seat," he says, adding, "There's no time to open the cargo bays, shift things around, and reload. We're on a wing and a prayer as it is with this weather."

It seems reasonable to press Bob for further information on the risk of perishing today, but he seems to read my mind, stating, "She'll be right, Jack. We'll be taking off with a stiff north-easterly blowing across us. It'll be bumpy for a while. But we'll soon get clear and ahead of the storms. If anything, the air mass will push us along in front, and we'll get to Darwin sooner. I'm sure an old hand like you has flown around in plenty worse."

Wings and prayers, overweight plane, inclement weather, fat patronizing pilot - I absently reach into my pocket, inch around, and seize my last tranquilizers, pop-and-swallow. My face must have soured, and he preempts the appropriately obscene comment forming on my lips by picking up Chirp's bag and saying, "I'll take the kid's bag on board and come back for you ...What's the kid got in here? Feels like a flagon of wine." Then he adds, "Ask that Sister Mary and see if the kid needs to piss, will you?"

He unhooks the security rope barring the exit, and leaves the terminal with Chirp's bag. His bulk takes up almost the whole of the door frame, and he walks away five or six meters before any of the shiny white, red-striped Lorina beyond comes into view.

I join the others, now seated together in a row under the air conditioners. Korda has two or three multicolored medicine capsules in a bony outstretched hand, and Mrs. Korda gives him bottled water to wash them down.

His condition seems to have deteriorated since our drinking session last night, and he's having trouble breathing. He bends forward in his seat, and Mrs. Korda sits beside him, patting his back.

Next to Korda, Chirp taps his sticks together slowly, persistently, seemingly oblivious to his surroundings. On Chirp's right, Sister Mary carries a concerned expression in soft brown Dumbo eyes. Sue Tran stares vacantly ahead, politely ignoring Korda's distress.

I'm about to ask Sister Mary about Chirp's bladder situation, but she sees me coming and steals the moment, leaning over and across the lad to speak with the Kordas.

"Is there anything I can do? I can't help but notice you're not well." Sister Mary's white nurse's uniform is doubtlessly comforting, universally symbolic of clean and caring - and virgins, notes the Rat.

Mrs. Korda warms to Sister Mary's concern and confides details about her husband's condition. "Mattius just had surgery for cancer tumors, and then there's the chemo. He's taking very aggressive antibodies, but he seems to have picked up a cold or something. He's a bit hot now. I think we might have made a mistake with this trip. But there's really not much to be done but get him home," she says, and doubtlessly noticing Sister Mary's large wooden cross, adds, "But thanks, Sister. Perhaps you'll remember us in your prayers."

Chirp's watching the wooden cross dangle from Sister Mary's neck as she leans across him. It's hanging over his lap, gotten in the way of his tapping, and he's had to stop. He's staring at it with dark deep-set eyes, brow inquisitively set, and doesn't seem concerned after my 'warning' about crosses. He gives the crucifix a tentative experimental rap with the clapping stick in his left hand as if testing musical percussion qualities or just to see what would happen or just because it's there in his face. Curiously, the cross and the old mulga stick are the same dark reddish-brown, like polished mahogany, and both look old, solid and used - never far from respectful superstitious hands.

Sister Mary sits back in her chair, taking her cross in both hands, caressing the smooth wood between her thumbs and fingers. Her lips don't move, but her open eyes seek the ceiling, and a frown of concentration creases her narrow brow - a silent prayer perhaps, or just farting on the sly.

I look left to Sue Tran, preparing to smile (with modest charm) if I catch her eye, but she still seems preoccupied. Maybe she's running through a to-do list for her banquet tonight back at the Humpty Doo restaurant.

Suddenly, I remember Chirp might need the toilet, but then Bob's back. He gets everyone's attention, audibly clearing his throat.

"Ladies, Gents …if you follow me out to the aircraft, we'll hop onboard and get away. Can I ask you to take your bags as we leave the terminal and keep your things with you? You can put them under the seat in front of you, or if there's room, you can put bigger items in an empty seat and fasten the strap so it's secure. Please sit in the forward seats so our weight's nice and balanced. Ok, let's go."

I remove my hat, stuff it in my bag, and put on sunglasses. Bob indicates to Sister Mary that she and Chirp should go first, so she gets the lad onto his feet and steers him slowly over to and out the exit door. Mr. and Mrs. Korda and the rest follow. Bob stays back momentarily; the air-conditioners shut off. He turns off the lights, closes the exit door, and everyone proceeds onto the tarmac, squinting in what is probably the last of the sunlight before the storm.

Sister Mary looks skyward, concerned eyes above chubby-cherub cheeks. Huge billowing storm clouds form a collar around the northern, eastern and southern sky, extending almost overhead. A sharp gust of wind pastes the long hair fringe back onto her blue headscarf, instantly fattening her face. Korda's GUMO cap flips off his bald skull, and he watches it skip away irretrievably down the runway toward the sea.

We move in a line past the left wing of the Lorina, its aerodynamic engine molded in seamlessly, and up to the open door at the front left of the long, sleek cabin. Bob has Chirp by the arm and helps him up three steps into the plane, and Sister Mary waits. Chirp goes in first with Captain Bob, then Korda and his wife, me right behind, followed by the caterer Sue Tran, and Sister Mary is the last on board.

There are five seats along both sides of the long, skinny cabin. Bob's secured the lad in one of the middle seats on the left over the wing. The last seats on both sides are occupied by Chirp's suitcase and Sue Tran's box of lunch, both strapped in by seatbelts. Korda sits in the front right seat, and Mrs. Korda is beside him next to the cabin door. Sister Mary sits directly behind Korda over the right wing next to Chirp. I'm behind Sister Mary and beside Sue Tran.

Bob stays in the back of the cabin as we find our seats, secures the larger passenger bags, and then moves forward, raising and locking the cabin door, which also doubles as steps up to the cabin, and he arranges himself in the right of two pilot seats in the cockpit. He's moved through the cabin quite smoothly for a man the size of a small troll. It's his lair, after all, and he glides into his seat backward like a huge octopus settling into a space that you'd swear at first was far too small.

Bob secures his lap and shoulder straps, removes his hat, dons earphones, and turns the plane's electronics on in one fluid movement. He presses buttons and flips switches, lighting up the instrument panel display. A small computer comes alive with a digitized map and a tiny arrow indicating the plane. Bob speaks low, officially to air traffic control, using call signs and running through normal preflight protocol.

The passengers are settling in, stuffing handbags and incidentals under the seats as best they can, but the space is too small, and most things end up half under the seat and half under feet. This plane's got plenty of cargo space, but the lardy pilot is too damn lazy to stow gear properly. I've half stuffed my bag under the seat in front, but it's very uncomfortable for my long legs, so I transfer and secure it in the empty seat behind me after first removing my journal. I'll make notes about the signing ceremony during the flight: who signed, who danced, who blackmailed.

Mrs. Korda has no seat in front, and after I solve my legroom problem, she hands me back her handbag before I sit down again, so I tuck my journal under my chin and buckle it into the empty seat behind Sue Tran. There's a body or a bag securely strapped up in all of the seats, ready for takeoff.

Bob half-turns in the pilot's seat and addresses the passengers. "Can I just make sure you've all got your seatbelts firmly fastened? There'll be a bit of turbulence, so keep them on nice and tight. We're going to take off toward the east into the wind, then bank hard around to the right or south, and then head west. The flight will be bumpy until we get above and ahead of the storms - for the first twenty minutes or so - and then plain sailing into Darwin by 4:00 pm. You'll find a bottle of water in the pocket of the seat in front, and there's a sickness bag there if you need it. Life vests are in the compartment behind me, but we won't need them."

We seem ready. I think we're all a bit worried that the Aboriginal lad might go weird during the flight, but he's settled into his seat well enough, albeit he still has those damn sticks.

Sister Mary takes up all the space of the seat in front and spills out a bit around the edges. She fidgets with her seatbelt, adjusting it to fit. A thought crosses that this might be the Sister's first light aircraft experience. I expect she'll soon be praying it's her last.

The left-hand engine comes to life whining and sputtering, the propeller makes a few tentative jerky revolutions, the engine catches power, and it's a blur as revs ramp up to a loud, steady snarl. Bob starts the right engine and gets both running at the same high droning pitch by making a few adjustments to the power control levers. He applies a little more power, and the aircraft inches forward, picking up speed. We taxi onto the runway and roll briskly down the airstrip, bumping along to the far western end.

I can see the Arafura Sea and the sky out to the northeast. There's a solid grey mass spreading from the horizon, arcing over us directly above. Except for a small bright patch in the west, the gloom grows all around, enveloping us like an immense, ever-closing shell. Now it catches up to the sun, leaving only dull lightness in the sky, and everything suddenly falls into shadow. The sea turns from bright, glistening aquamarine to dark green-grey in an instant. The churning surface rolls and breaks, and meter-high whitecaps spew wispy foam that's wind-whipped into thick grey mist, the ghostly prelude for a killer storm.

These must be what Bob said we'd be flying *in front of*, that would *push us along*. We get to the west end of the runway, and Bob turns the plane around and lines up for takeoff to the east - right into the black twisting guts of a *significant* weather event. I'm in Bob's hands now, a shocking idea at the best of times, now bordering on suicide.

The fearless fat man tosses back a final glance at his passengers, eases the engine control levers slowly forward, ramping up the power, and then jams them ahead as far as they'll go. The engines' low drone fires up to war-cry screech, the fuselage vibrates like bees' wings, and the aircraft seems to bend forward in excited anticipation like a sprinter set at the starting line, muscles tightly tensed for the pistol. Bob releases the brakes, and we lurch forward, pressed back in our seats, accelerating like a racecar down the black runway, broken white center-line a blur, aiming at stormy darkness dead ahead.

Mr. and Mrs. Korda hold hands across the aisle, but each looks out their own window. In front, Sister Mary seems to have settled, doubtless cross-in-hand. Sue Tran extracts the small bottle of water from the pocket of the seat ahead and takes quick sips, her eyes forward, expressionless. Chirp's glued to his seat with clapping sticks held tight and silent on his lap. He's watching Bob work the controls wide-eyed, face set otherwise idiot-blank.

The plane's gunning down the runway requiring my full attention, but for some reason, the thought strikes me that all the passengers today are from *very* different backgrounds: a rich South African mining magnate and his upper-class English wife, Sue Tran from southeast Asia, Sister Mary from Ireland, me from Canada, and

Aussies Bob and Chirp. And if we're all going to die in a horrible plane crash, at least most of us are Baby Boomers with two-thirds of our worthless lives already lived. We won't be missed, unlike our parents.

We inherited the last half of a century that belonged to them. They knew the industrial strength carnage and unimagined horror of mechanized warfare - twice in the space of one or two generations. Many died for God and country, and many who lived came home knowing that God was not able or willing to vanquish the evil of a violent monster. Or perhaps there was no God. And in 1945 when a tiny sun built by men lighted up the Los Alamos desert night, you will find a Godless place.

These men of science were mostly atheists, they gave us a secular world, and those who would inject their superstitious fear and loathing are not welcome in my world. And now, *I am become ATHEISTMAN*, the wrecker of lies and deceit, and bringer of no hope[16].

Let's not bring back a dead God. It would insult our parents' courage and sacrifice, and dumb down the quality of today's civic discourse. Emboldened weirdos would abound with many wanting to

---

[16] It is with the grandest of thievery that Levague has usurped from the father of the atomic age, his famous quoting of the *Bhagavad Gita,* the ancient Hindu religious text. Robert Oppenheimer used the words of the god Krishna *I am become death* …to indicate his angst at the thought of a final nuclear war. The level of irony used here by Levague can only be measured in terms of kilotons.

hunt yours truly and rational humanists to the ends of the earth.

Tip your hat to the Silent Generation. They gave many of us single-payer universal health insurance, Star Trek, and the confidence to send a man to the moon in real life and bring him back alive, albeit that moron Armstrong couldn't bloody manage to string together his *'It's a small step ... '* speech without blowing it[17]. All should have died much older than many. Certainly, they probably should have had far fewer kids. But we Boomers made cars and oil for everyone, quadrupled the population, and plundered, wasted and destroyed the environment along the way.

Our parents might have killed off God, but it is we who will kill off Earth. Well might we remember Nazis, ancient Romans, or Aztecs as world-class dickheads, but if our species survives another thousand years, our descendants will *surely* look back at the Boomer Generation and say they were the biggest assholes in history.

The passengers on this plane are all separated by years and miles, language and life experience. Yet circumstances contrived that we

---

[17] Undoubtedly, this is a reference to Neil Armstrong's historical comment: *It's a small step for* Man, *one giant leap for* Mankind. Here, the indefinite article is missing in action, and 'Man' is used in a collective sense that means *Mankind*. So, he is saying the same thing twice.

Levague feels that this is a gaffe of galactic proportions, and he noted somewhere mockingly that Armstrong *had two jobs – not crash and make the speech, and he screwed it up - It's a small mistake for an* Idiot, *one giant blunder for an* Idiot.

should all be right *here*, right *now*. In the end, of course, it's just a bunch of random people and seemingly unrelated occurrences following simple laws of probability and modest human design, and I suppose, ultimately, atoms and particles obeying the will of Gravity and Quantum Mechanics. But fifty years ago, if you placed a bet that seven individuals from precisely our backgrounds would now find themselves barreling down one of the remotest airstrips in Australia with a common purpose, you'd get astronomical odds.

Of course, the odds shorten over the years; Sue Tran escapes a war-torn Vietnam, and there's a reasonable chance she might settle in Australia, but perhaps slightly longer odds she'd end up catering in Darwin rather than in Sydney's 'Little Saigon' Cabramatta; Sister Mary is at shorter odds in ending up here - Australia is lousy with Micks; Mr. and Mrs. Korda were probably shorter odds on getting together, both are cosmopolitan types and Korda's mining career makes it quite possible he'd visit a place like Australia, and had I stayed out of bars in Amsterdam, *ATHEISTMAN* might never have been brought to the vengeful attention of excitable clerics in Iran, and I might never have had to join the delightful descendants of convicts in Australia.

And as time leads up to this moment, the odds of all that has ever happened to bring everyone to where they are now, alive and in one piece, shorten to absolute certainty. And we can all be dead certain that the odds start lengthening alarmingly fast with each inevitable tick of the clock[18].

We're rocketing down the runway but not taking off. The plane accelerates to just short of critical flight speed as we race past the five-hundred-meter mark on the tarmac. Bob has a tight hold on controls, nervously pressing forward hard on the power levers. Powerful gale-force wind hammers us sideways, veering us onto the edge of the runway apron. Only slightly farther, the right wheel will run off the tarmac, plow into loose gravel, and drag the plane smashing into the terminal building, the fuel pumps, or both.

Except for Chirp, all the passengers are forward in their seats and stone-still, arm-rests tightly gripped, adrenaline percolating around biochemical systems. I can't read Chirp. I expect he'll come

---

[18] This example of confounding philosophizing evokes recollection of confusing positions Levague has advanced throughout a career of poor scholarship, even concerning his foundational notions on 'life'. For example, in his doctoral dissertation, he states that *the emergence of self-sustaining biochemical replication from previously inanimate material 3.8 billion years ago on Earth is the most profound instant of time anywhere in the Universe throughout all eternity* (Notes on the Meaning of Life - Jacques Levague, age 20).

This can be contrasted with the following Journal entry: *the life force celebrated by science and philosophy, that we admire, adore, and worship narcissistically, originated by some incidental accident - in some moist, dingy fold of Universal skin - and left to simmer and fester with its dirty chemical business unimpeded for millennia* (Dr. Levague, age 60).

undone and start shrieking in panic at any moment ...or that might be me. The aircraft rattles alarmingly, suddenly hits a bump, and there's a sharp *snap* as the stowing compartment door behind Bob flies open and bright yellow life preservers spill onto the cabin floor.

The engines strain loudly, fully at operational limits, and still, we can't climb into flight. The end of the runway looms. Beyond is a solid dark-green barrier of eucalypts, the top branches dancing frenetically in the wind. As we speed past the terminal, a streak of lightning splits the darkening sky to the south; anticipatory seconds pass breathlessly, then deep rumbling thunder we can hear over the engines.

Thudding rain drums the cabin. Thick drops spear into the plane's windshield, splattering and blurring visibility ahead.

We flash past the runway's fifteen-hundred-meter mark, the point where safely abandoning takeoff is an option; we're committed.

The downpour intensifies, rattling into windows on the left and streaming down the fuselage. Cylinders of white mist jet backward as twin propellers carve through sheets of driving rain.

Just as it looks like we've run out of airstrip, I feel a sudden surge forward, and Bob eases the flight controls back. The plane takes a tentative hop and touches back down, then the engines seem to roar with extra power, and we're almost imperceptibly airborne.

It's one of my worst light aircraft take-offs, and the flight's no better. I expect to climb steeply, but we race ahead at a catastrophic land velocity only as high as the cab of a large truck. The plane labors to stay straight in stiff crosswinds, but then Bob raises the landing gear, and we rise slowly, barely clearing sweeping treetops. My stomach contents include four tranquilizers that haven't kicked in yet, and I'm fighting to keep them down. Puke-green bile spray-painted on the back of Sister Mary's head at any moment seems about even money.

Bob shifts his weight and pushes buttons on the instrument panel with his index finger. His head quickly swivels back and forth, checking out both sides of the cockpit windshield, making sure we're not plowing through trees. The minuscule digital image of a cartoon plane lights up on the small computer screen beneath the power levers. The navigational GPS is functioning.

The plane climbs slowly, straight into swirling clouds. Seconds later we clear land, flying low over grey rocking waves twisting and crashing together. Suddenly, thick mist envelopes the plane, a dull, formless white-out.

We fly on for long, blind seconds, and then the cloud thins, lightens and clears. Bob inches the flight controls forward and right, banking the aircraft slightly south. A ragged red coastline stretching to the horizon emerges from the mist. We're about five hundred meters high, at the precise point on the north Australian coast where the Arafura Sea melds into the far northwestern Gulf of Carpentaria.

Bob steadily banks the plane steeper into our right-hand turn. The passengers relax, no longer gripped by hair-raising fear. Sue Tran, in the seat beside mine, and Sister Mary ahead, gaze out their windows. I see what the Sister sees - a black line jutting into the sea off a spit of coastline at a geometrically perfect ninety-degree angle.

This mathematically precise straight line is the GUMO port jetty, a thin needle into the sea from this distance. It looks about two hundred meters long. Along the shoreline, I make out a concrete barge landing slanting down to the base of the pier, and several graded lay-down yards on the foreshore, a small silver tin-roofed storage shed, and idle steel-frame loading cranes. There are none of the ubiquitous white utilities anywhere near the port or on the track to the mine a few kilometers west. The port facilities are deserted.

Chirp slouches forward in his seat, still holding sticks, head down, seemingly back to staring at Nikes. Mr. and Mrs. Korda lean together across the aisle, perhaps sharing a tender confidence that I can't hear over the Lorina's engines.

The plane's flying steadily, smoothly cutting through heaving air, gaining height, swinging inexorably towards the west, closer to the direction home. Out my window, the main GUMO mining operations come into view. The flight takes us closer, and the accommodation village where we stayed last night is laid out in a neat little grid of miniature building blocks forming a large 'H'. It's about halfway between the jetty and the main mining area, well upwind of toxic dust and processing fumes.

We climb to a thousand meters, heading southwest. Below to my right are the nuts and bolts of the GUMO industrial layout.

The northern boundary is marked by the biggest item of

infrastructure, a dozen five-hundred-meter square tailings ponds lined with black plastic storing mine tailings under some sort of chemical liqueur that absorbs radioactivity. The neat squares of still, dark liquid, each contained in reddish-brown earth bunds several meters wide, are laid out east-west in a row of two, like a giant's ice cube tray buried in cleared ground. South of the tailings ponds are individual mineshaft decline entry points – several tiny mouths on the red face of the landscape.

Even in the storm, it's busy here. A steady stream of squat yellow bulldozers emerges from the depths, transferring mine-face ore to loaders and onto dump trucks with wheels higher than a tall man. From up here, they all look like bustling little dinky toys.

The Lorina sweeps southwest, banking further west, and we re-cross the coastline heading inland, flying higher. The mine's diesel power generator plant comes into view to the northwest with long silver cylindrical fuel storage tanks lining three sides. Evenly spaced steel frame pylons carrying high voltage electricity lines branch out from the generator in straight lines northwest to individual mineshaft declines and directly north to the accommodation village and jetty. Occasional lighting towers are spaced regularly along the power lines, each with multiple high-intensity metal halide bulbs capable at night of flooding a whole football field in an eerie uniform amber glow.

All the bits and pieces are connected by a steel lattice of pipes turning and folding around like intestines in a toxic chemical digestive system feeding on bare earth and defecating uranium oxide. It's all the apparatus and artifacts necessary to convert relatively harmless natural uranium ore into highly radioactive, dangerous yellowcake. Packaging it all up is a gravel-red ribbon network of vehicle tracks crisscrossing the GUMO facility and outlining the square perimeter around the entire mine lease.

The track marking the western edge extends south toward Minjininga community and north in a straight line to the airstrip. It's too far to see people, but tiny light utility vehicles traveling about the mine site appear on the tracks as slowly moving white ants. Away to the north, what looks like a small red speck darts towards the airport and might be Jacob Kunmubilpilguru's old beat-up sedan on the way to pick up a new four-by-four motorcar courtesy of RCC boss Mattius Korda.

We swing around south of GUMO, still banked at a slight angle, complete our right turn, and then head west towards Darwin, wings level. Bob's flying the plane with the prevailing wind at our back, and the mine shrinks quickly away behind.

We gain altitude, speed-on and the futuristic outpost of human industrial muscle is just a vaporous postage stamp now in the hazy distance. Within the mine lease, Western rules of organization, discipline and precise measurement allow extreme energy levels to be controlled, focused and converted to a substance with far more energy conversion potential. The difference is *profit*.

But only a few kilometers in any direction, order vanishes, replaced by a complex mythological landscape, a tapestry of totemic energy imprinted in Aborigines since the dawn of humanity, with ancient subtle laws. I'm an expert, but I'll never know more than Chirp Kunmubilpilguru knew when he was two …or possibly some other tribal kid.

We're about five minutes into the flight, still well short of cruise altitude. We climb steadily but *far* too slowly. Perhaps Korda asked Bob for one final low flyover to say goodbye to GUMO, but given the rush to beat the weather, this seems unlikely. *There's something wrong with this plane.*

Outside to the left, more blustery dark storms loom in the southwest; the mass of rain and wind is swinging, curving with unmistakable cyclonic spiraling, and the shifting turbulence is cutting us off ahead. Bob watches the weather, anxiety showing on his sweating face, the wariness of an old fighter waiting for round two after being beaten about badly in the first.

The others watch the gloom ahead and shift restlessly, double-checking already tightly fastened seatbelts. But my biochemical complex is assimilating molecules of benzodiazepine. These search out, find, and slot into myriad two-way connections in the BSI Interface Matrix, feeding sensory information into and around my nervous system. The cumulative effect: a reasonably convincing illusion that I'm snuggly calm and mentally peaceful despite the weather tossing us around. Secure in this pressurized metal flying machine - in neither one place nor another - and protected from the atmosphere outside, the slight vibration from droning engines, occasional rocking pitch, and gentle shake is soothing and relaxing.

I resist the urge to settle back and close my eyes and focus instead on the battered leather-bound journal on my lap. It's held closed with a thick red elastic band that secures the pages and the pencil I use for making field notes.

I remove the elastic band, wrapping it around my wrist. I intend to note specifically the matter of Jacob Kunmubilpilguru's new GUMO car in case it gets picked up by some do-gooder leftwing political journalist who writes a load of sanctimonious tripe about rapacious greedy underhanded miners making deals with slimy Aboriginal politicians to get a dirty uranium pit producing at full tilt - mining out not just *some* of the mineral resources, mind - but *all* of it.

It's enough that a report in the *Darwin News* last year accused me of drumming up Aboriginal support for the mine expansion and dared insinuate that I was angling for some 'special consideration' from RCC. The *News* article even made a scurrilous reference to the Social Impact Assessment I prepared in relation to a gigantic gold mining operation in East Kalimantan, Indonesia, on Borneo Island back in 1997. It bordered on defamation.

Sure, the Canadian mining company behind the development, Bre-X of Calgary, hired me (and paid a very handsome retainer including a few share options as is normal), and I did travel to and consult with most of the small communities that were to be impacted, but I was totally unaware that the head geologist was 'salting' exploration drill cores to show huge gold potential when, in fact, there was nothing special in the ground – all to inflate Bre-X's share price[19].

There is no record that I had anything to do with this massive gold fraud then, and I've stated for the record that the fully loaded, late model, RCC-owned Landcruiser parked in my driveway is purely for work purposes associated with consultations about the GUMO mine expansion. It's specified in the agreement between TALC and RCC and will be returned to the mining company *eventually* (although Pam has grown quite fond of it). Everything is on the up and up and fully fair dinkum.

I make an entry in the Journal critical of Jacob Kunmubilpilguru's side deal with Korda over last night's gifted ute with tongue only slightly in cheek. Secondly, I think I should make a quick observation or two about Korda's biochemical condition, in case he croaks during the flight, and somehow, I catch flake for that.

Just as I conclude the notes, lightning flashes outside the left cabin windows, and I watch Sue Tran's head quickly turn to look, startled by its proximity as a violent *crack* and deep rumble shake the plane. I follow her eyes outside and see expanding darkness below, to

---

[19] When the Bre-X operation came to the attention of people in the Suharto government, the matter of Levague's *fatwa* came to light and he was forced to flee the country. While still in Borneo, he was reportedly a passenger on a helicopter flight when the 'dirty' head Bre-X geologist somehow 'fell' out over Busang.

It was officially concluded that he jumped, but it was muted that he might have been pushed.

the side, and ominously, above.

I absently wonder if I'll get caught if the rain forecasted for Darwin and get soaked during the two hundred meter 'bolt' from the arrivals terminal to the uncovered short-term parking lot. But the blank pages of my journal stare up at me, so I pick up my pencil and jot down today's date: *7 February 2011*. Then I hesitate, mentally collating all the important facts.

I record copious amounts of anthropological and scientific data. I try to capture every raw gesture of native ritual, every subtle nuance of primitive ceremony, unchanged perhaps for thousands of years, and persisting as cultural accoutrement to savage belief systems, licentious gods and rampaging sexual mythology.

If I don't write things down, the event will likely never be recalled. I'd be lost without the Journal. It contains the inventory of contact between my biochemical complex and socio-culture that gives my life meaning, a coherent account of my reality, each entry a bite of critical information, a snippet of actual occurrence.

I need to make detailed notes because my short-term memory is virtually nonexistent. This might be caused by chemical adjuncts to my biochemistry, particularly the blending of copious amounts of alcohol and cannabis over about forty-five years, or it could be one of those wonderful things about old age that everyone can look forward to. Either way, it seems these days that only things recorded in the Journal can I later recall as having happened in real life.

I've kept the Journal all my professional life and earlier. The first entries record various adolescent business enterprises: *ATHEISTMAN* comics, failed attempts to sell enough dope so I could smoke for free, and details of planned field trips never taken along inland US waterways from the Caribbean to Chicago that a rowboat could use to run cocaine from South America. The Journal contains fieldwork associated with my doctoral thesis and notes on ground-breaking research leading to my BSI Theory.

It contains the complete, unabridged notes of my anthropological career, starting with the 1973 UN inquiry regarding the legality of possibly *too-young* bride exchange rituals among the Edo Tribe of the Amazon. These early recordings reflect youthful idealism and contain exuberant descriptions of raw ritual debauchery, and I made detailed participatory observations. Because of my status as a respected ethnographer and an official of the UN with *fiduciary* responsibilities, there was no question of impropriety when I adopted that orphaned Edo lass, and certain affidavits concerning the girl's traditional logging and mineral rights were placed into a legal trust for which I acted as executor. Decades later, during which the Edo Tribe rejected any logging or mineral exploration on their traditional lands, it came to light that the trust was still holding certain titles that were now totally useless (the reports that I tried to offload my niece's interest at a discount to the infamous American investment firm, Enron, are totally false - the company's massive Ponzi scheme was uncovered way before the bogus Brazilian court orders were served).

And who's to know just how old she *really* was? She was fully developed. and ladies of esteem in the Amazon are already made into mothers by sixteen years. I make no value judgments about such culturally relativistic matters. After all, I'm a scientist.

Then there's the data concerning the Bougainville Rebellion fiasco in Papua New Guinea and the first attempt to subpoena the Journal. The International Court in the Hague required that I photocopy all the Rebellion documentation and then certify the copies before Interpol stopped hounding me. Of course, all entries were completely innocent – scholarly, scientific accounts of structural-functional tension in social organization, mostly over the loot from a big mine - and I found the *kava* ceremony particularly symbolic of basic communal harmony that had been lost to the avarice of mining mammon.

All problems between people seemed lessened after a daily dose of ten or fifteen liters of the peppery narcotic punch, and the drug became central to the negotiation process. *Unfortunately,* my attempts to mediate peaceful outcomes failed, and I was accused of applying *'few rigors'* in finding acceptable reconciliation.

After spending a month around the *kava* bowl, often alone or with my young local assistants, I reported to UN headquarters that everyone was happy and left the island optimistic that all serious dissent was settled. Regrettably, as history records, the restive Melanesian brutes took after each other with spears, clubs and machetes the minute I left Arawa - apparently incensed that local *kava*

91

stocks were significantly diminished, and certain massage services involving my assistants had gone unpaid for - and after I gave away several cartons of Bundaberg over-proof rum to antagonists on both sides as a gesture of goodwill and to settle my accounts. Authorities were satisfied that the Journal recorded no crime, just *unfortunate* judgment in their *unfortunate* words

Only a few years later, I willingly handed over the Journal to outside scrutiny - the first and only time - and *only* because it was a matter of my life. It was 3 June 1989, to be exact; the day that crazy Iranian mullah, Ruhollah Khomeini, condemned me to hell with his deathbed *fatwa* - an invocation to the Iranian faithful to murder me – all because of a harmless cartoon drawing. The suggestion that it tipped the old fart over the line to his doom, I find hard to believe.

The Journal records the circumstances of the famous *ATHEISTMAN vs* Khomeini cartoon and shows incontrovertibly that it was not uniquely devised to insult the imam, that *ATHEISTMAN* had a long history of insulting the divinely inspired of *all* faiths. I wanted to demonstrate that I held no particular malice towards pious Iranians and that my assumption of privacy and basic values of free speech meant there was no insult because the miserable evil-bearded lizard shouldn't have known anything about it.

It's a typical *ATHEISTMAN* cartoon depicting my comical alter-ego, just a bit of irreverent fun. In 1989, I was still employed by the UN and in Amsterdam, developing a psycho-social questionnaire for the Dutch armed forces. Dutch soldiers were to join UN peacekeeping forces in the former Yugoslavia, and my profiler was used to identify subconscious racism and religious bigotry among rank-and-file troops.

I prepared the profiling questionnaire in my office at the University of Amsterdam, having to pass Hunter's Bar and Hoticulturalis Botanicus Park on the way to work each day. But I don't believe the efficacy of the *Levague Prejudice Profiler* was in any way lessened in Hunter's Bar or the lovely garden. The pejorative comments made against me following the Srebrenica Massacre (in modern-day Bosnia-Herzegovina) were all hyped up and totally irrelevant[20]. The Dutch troops who stood by and watched the Serbian army murder all those Muslims were total pussies and could barely tell the difference between one end of a rifle and the other.

But there's no denying Hunter's Bar is conducive to whimsy. The spring of '89 was unusually cold and rainy in Amsterdam, and most days, I parked my pushbike outside the famed coffee shop on Warmoesstraat early, and it stayed there all day. I drafted several versions of the *Profiler* in Hunter's, but usually, I'd just go through the previous day's messages and telexes from the office and then enjoy the coffee for the rest of the day.

---

[20] Dutch soldiers acting as UN peacekeepers were found by the International Court in the Hague investigation to be at least partly liable for the deaths of about 300 Muslim men massacred by Serbian forces near Srebrenica during the Yugoslavian civil war.

Court filings stated that the *Levague Prejudice Profiler* was largely *intellectual-sounding gobbledygook.*

In late May, I received a memo directed to me from Geneva concerning UNICEF educational grants to several mostly Middle Eastern countries where science funding was being used to teach children that the Theory of Evolution was wrong and the infidel Charles Darwin was burning in hell for his blasphemy.

Well, during my morning *white widow* joint, while I pondered the issue, the cartoon just came to mind ...*there* he was, or I was, in my usual *ATHEISTMAN* superhero guise: a shimmering black nylon bodysuit, skintight from neck to toe with dazzling-white full ninja head-mask and only my cold, piercing, appraising, judging, punishing eyes showing. I have matched white elbow-length gloves and a silver Velcro utility belt with several hardcover university textbooks fastened around my waist, slung within easy reach should I need to draw a scientific reference. Golden leather knee-high boots with flaming red hotspur wings emerging from heels complete the uniform.

A glowing, sapphire blue letter 'A' glued to my muscular Superman chest blazes forth from the black bodysuit. *I am ATHEISTMAN! My solemn mission: to boldly challenge religion with reason and truth and bring hope and enlightenment to the masses ...well, enlightenment anyway.*

In that day's musings, my fantastical super foe this time is the Iranian leader, Ayatollah Khomeini. It could have been any old Middle Eastern tyrant - Mubarak, Assad, or Yasser *bloody* Arafat. But having taken hostage the entire staff of the US embassy in Tehran ten years earlier, his heartwarming face was better etched in the mind than the other murderous villains.

The libations at Hunter's Bar are world-renowned. Imagination can get carried away, and *ATHEISTMAN* fought that day in a hot, dark, loud Mexican professional wrestling ring that somehow is all there is, the totality of the Universe, and everyone's there, not just Mexicans.

Smokey light from somewhere above floods an endless arena, bleachers reaching out and up to infinity. The crowd tonight is loudly expectant and restless. Latecomers jostle for seats, white-uniformed snack vendors troupe up and down the aisles shouting for business, and bookmakers furiously work pencils and pads, taking bets from outstretched hands before the feature bout.

Everyone who's ever been is talking and shouting, and the raucous din of 100 billion hominids around the ring is deafening. Modern living *Homo sapiens* hold tickets closest to ringside, and all the people who have ever lived and died are chronologically seated farther from the ring. Behind the humans are earlier but still clever hominid species in cheaper seats: *Neanderthals, Cro-Magnons, Homo erectus,* and a smattering of cute little furry hobbit-like *Homo floresiensis* standing on their seats with binoculars *way* at the back, trying to see the fight.

Suddenly, a shaft of dazzling light bathes the center ring from a powerful spotlight, or star, high above. The official announcer clambers through the thick leather ring ropes in a too-small tuxedo and steps purposefully to the center of the canvas. A microphone lowers from somewhere above. The crowd hushes.

"Good evening, Ladies and Gentlemen, and welcome to the main event on tonight's card …for the Heavyweight Championship of the *Truth of Evolution* …and now, introducing in the red corner …It's the Champion of Reason, *ATHEISTMAN!*"

ATHEISTMAN steps into the ring, and the crowd goes wild, whistling and roaring unanimously with deafening cheers. He shakes hands with the referee, waves to adoring fans, and warms up with squats, running on the spot, limbering up for the bout.

The announcer raises his hand for quiet, and the crowd noise diminishes in excited expectation. "And in the blue corner …it's the Tyrant of Tehran, *Ruuu-ho-la Kho-mein-i!*"

This time, the crowd howls with derisive jeers. It's heavily partisan, and most are here to witness a once-and-for-all knockdown battle where truth will triumph.

In Hunter's Bar that day, the bout went on round after bloody round, coffee after coffee, bizarre image after image; the assembled hominids from all of time, animated in a frenzy of excitement, with loud arguments and occasional jostling breaking out among the fans in cheaper seats. A few '*God is Great!*' chants are heard, and most of the punters respond with taunts of '*Imaginary Friend!*'.

At the end of the last scheduled mental round, the Champion of Reason reaches down to his silver utility belt, releases a Velcro tab, and extracts a well-thumbed hard copy of Darwin, C (1859) *On the Origin of Species by Means of Natural Selection, or the Preservation of Favored Races in the Struggle for Life.* A few *Neanderthals* who somehow snuck into ringside *Homo sapiens'* seats shout, 'Darwin's a Racist', but no one is listening or cares, mostly because they're extinct.

With only seconds in the fight left it's the instant when *ATHEISTMAN* suddenly leaps high - radiant in a simple, absolute black-and-white uniform - twirls full around with athletic precision, and smashes Darwin (1859) down hard onto the turbaned head of the wicked old mullah, sending him staggering and knocking him out cold on his feet ...It's frozen right there - *that's* the cartoon I drew[21].

Somehow, my doodling - on the back of a Hunter's Bar drink coaster - found its way back to UN headquarters with normal correspondence and was spotted by a Malaysian journalist who brought it to the attention of the Iranian Charge D'Affairs. I'm told Khomeini was shown the cartoon as he lay on his hospital deathbed. Apparently, set upon by a fit of apoplexy, the ruthless old bastard breathed his last, spitting out the *fatwa* in a final last gasp.

My protestations about *privacy* and *freedom* fell on deaf ears. I even tried to sue the Malaysian journo for copyright infringement. All I got from the UN was the Journal back, the sack, and a plane ticket to a destination of my choice.

Of course, the 1996 UN Enquiry into the *Levague Prejudice Profiler* was retribution for having the audacity to seek compensation for unfair dismissal - and not because of *lax research* that resulted in a massacre. As I say, I have never been *convicted* of a crime.

---

[21] A facsimile is found at Attachment A, pg.16 above.

As serendipity would have it, the Iranian *fatwa* enforcement budget for the next decade was taken up almost completely by the more notorious vendetta against an innocent author[22]. Thank goodness it was the old Iranian creep I fought in my mind - a real person - and not the Magical Guy in the Sky. The new and quite delightful Iranian leadership canceled the kill-Levague edict five or six years ago on the condition that I never again publish 'apostate literature' and stay out of the region and anyplace where people of the true faith assemble *forever* - a fair bargain.

But there's nothing like having millions of fanatic devotees howling for your blood to give the old stomach a turn, and it was about then that I first came down with Cyclical Vomiting. My psychiatrist recommends I should use the Journal to 'write it out of my system', to record troubling thoughts and dreams, especially nightmares that recur, and 'streams of thought' immediately at the onset of feeling nauseous. He believes they may contain clues to what 'deeper fears chill my subconscious', what 'bleak panorama of secret hopelessness' I stumble through day after dark day that makes me *still* want to puke at the drop of a hat. I need to find out the *real* troubles, face them, and learn they're *not* real - just irrational impulses intruding on normal biochemistry.

But I don't remember my dreams, I don't wake up in cold sweats very often, and there's nothing much of interest to a psychiatrist I can think of to write about except my marriage. So

---

[22] This is doubtless a reference to Salman Rushdie and the *Satanic Verses*.

instead of writing psycho-babble when I'm not recording new ethnographic information, I like to review previous journal entries, especially from more traditionally oriented indigenous communities and from days when a younger sensitive Levague actually gave a damn.

It seems I just have to flip open the Journal, and I'm instantly back in time and really *there* again. The vivid landscape comes alive, the people and colors, and the smells of food cooking in native villages at night. I casually flip through 1970s entries, for example, and I'm taken back …ah yes …*to the day I paddled a dugout tree-trunk canoe up the Amazon River in the hazy mists of a dry season dawn as the giant red furnace of the sun bulbs over a verdant blanket of rainforest jungle stretching forever into the horizon. The screeching welcome of rainbow-beaked toucans, the morning songs of a thousand species of insects, and a cacophonous chatter of squabbling howler monkeys in nearby trees greet a new day.*

Under a canopy of huge forest hardwoods, naked young Edo tribal girls barely past puberty line up along the sandy riverbank for traditional pan-tribal bridal exchange as I guide the dugout closer across the smooth calm river, my bow-wake gently lapping the shore and the girls' tiny bare feet.

Small smiling faces, fully tattooed reddish-purple below their innocent, shining brown almond eyes, are all shy as I push the flimsy boat up to the bank. The girls' small button noses are pierced with thin yellowing capybara rib bones, confirming their status as novices in the vigorous 'girl to woman' ritual that will shortly change their futures.

This jewelry adornment is the only distraction from their young nubile nudity: small ripening breasts with tiny puffy-pink nipples, lithe thin waists you could close large hands around, lean smooth, un-stretched hips, taut slim buttocks, and long firm muscular hairless legs ...the girl closest has a strangely familiar 'moon-crescent' knife blade that I never noticed before ...

...Suddenly, I'm wrenched sideways by forces unseen. The space around me shunts violently to the right, and my eyelids flutter open, and I'm in my seat on the Lorina, soaked in cold sweat.

I jerk my mind to awareness, and the other passengers are totally alert as the plane sweeps first to the left and then to the right, violently tossing us up and down like frightened human salad.

We fly in dark, swirling rain clouds solid enough that they cleave apart like bow-wake as we rip through thick black air ahead. Blasts of rain batter the fuselage with liquid shrapnel. The plane hasn't climbed high enough to escape the weather.

I glance down at my open journal. The only words are *late storms for Darwin*, the date, and a few sentences. Chirp has his clapping sticks on his lap and taps away irritatingly while everyone else grabs their armrests as if readying for a rollercoaster. No one else seems to pay him the least of mind; everyone's glued to seats, frightened eyes searching for light in roiling darkness and praying to break free of the storm's violent clutches.

But then an explosion of blinding light flashes on all passengers' faces, and a sharp *BANG!* rocks the plane. A jagged bolt of pure blue-white lightning crashes into the Lorina's port engine, instantly shattering forward sections of white wing-cowling, blasting the propeller to splinters, welding steel pistons to cylinders, vaporizing electronics, melting rivets, exploding and ripping metal like searing bullets tearing up flesh.

A half-instant later, the lightning-torn sky slams back together with a deafening *WHACK!* close enough to feel as a sharp slap to the ears. We're thrown immediately forward as half the plane's power dies.

Thoughts seem to flit across consciousness at the Speed of Light, and a part of me knows beforehand - *my biochemistry won't like this*. And I'm sure it's happening to everyone just as my adrenal gland injects its whole load of panic. But there's no escaping the *Pencil of Death*.

Chapter 3: Fearless Crew

The others' terrified gasps barely register. I'm trapped in private horror the instant lightning strikes. Paralyzing panic glues me to my seat; molten lead stirs my gut. Time itself is stunned still, but at least one violent vomit-hurling event is imminent. Mrs. Korda voices the cabin's collective sentiment, "Dear God, no …not now!"

All our biochemistries scream silently for physical action, an appallingly useless urge to run or fight. Mine clears the deck of anything not part of this second. I flash through sensory data, process facts, figure out the angles, and try to plan to save myself. This plane's crashing: *ball of fire, all aboard perish, tributes (brief), mourning, insurance payout, sadness mitigated, footnote in aviation history*.

But the plane's still flying. Captain Bob Palmer has strong, steady hands on the flight controls. The Lorina's not mortally wounded. The funk freezing my brain steps back from the brink of the black pit. I battle down the digestive gorge that's threatening escape. Four lorazepam tabs re-establish a semblance of order.

The pilot does several things at once: speaks clearly, calmly into his headphones, '…*13:45 hours, one engine struck by lightning, returning to GUMO Airport*', manipulates flight controls testing left-wing structural integrity, ramps up the starboard engine's power, and effects the protocol for flying a two-engine plane on one. He turns to us, mouth pressed firm.

"We have to return to the mine. In twenty years of flying,

that's the first time I've been hit …*Bloody Hell!* The plane flies ok on one engine, and everything seems to be working. Keep your belts fastened up tight. We still have a bit of weather to get through. Sorry, Folks."

The cockpit instrument panel flashes an alarming number of red and amber lights, rows of them, but Bob presses buttons and turns dials with cool certainty, unerring sausage-fat fingers precise in an emergency. He wriggles slightly, rearranging bulk flesh higher in his seat, at full attention. We're all sat forward in our seats watching Bob work the controls, and no one's voicing distracting questions like *'Are we going to die?'*

I look at Sue Tran and catch her eye, which is filled with scared bewilderment. I say what I'm thinking: "I wonder what the odds are … lightning hitting twice."

Her mouth is slightly open but assumes a thin line, settling her expression blank, clearing her face of fear. She sits back in her seat, glancing out her window as lightning flashes again but safely in the distance.

"We'll make it," she says softly, the words meant mostly for herself.

I don't find this reassuring, but the reliable tranquilizers have reasserted themselves, and I sit back, riding the wild wind, watching the storms on my side, seeing if I can spot a killer in the midst.

We fly through intermitted curtains of rain that play the fuselage like a drum, slow beats building up-tempo to rapid snare-roll and then petering out, repeating again and again. Passengers monitor storms out their windows warily, apprehensively; injured birds watching a hungry cat close in.

No one talks. My eyes track the back of Bob's head, trying to judge if the quick turns and nods mean he's in control or panicking.

Suddenly, there's a flicker on the instrument panel. The collective glow dims and then disappears. The grey gloom outside spills in thicker through the windows, absorbing all cabin light.

Bob's head doesn't move, but his left arm shoots out instantly in front. He presses buttons, raps the computer screen with a heavy index finger, then slams his left hand down on the dashboard above the instruments hard enough to raise a puff of dust - all to no effect. He lifts his hand and taps his left earphone again and again, each tap firmer, repeating call signs over and over, each call louder. Then he removes his headphones and tosses them onto the copilot seat to his left. The radio's dead.

Much of the cabin's illumination came from the GPS *Navaid* computer screen. When it winked out, so too did the little digital arrow airplane and map that knew where the blazes we were.

Mrs. Korda leans forward so she's closer to the cockpit and turns to her husband. She places her right hand on her husband's knee and pats it once or twice, a calming, mundane gesture, but there's desperation in her eyes. The couple exchange silent glances before Mrs. Korda addresses the pilot.

"What's up, Bob?"

Bob's locked onto a brighter patch of cloud to the west, and then he turns the plane north. The lightest splotch, indicating the sun's position, tracks slowly to the left across the cockpit windshield. Now Bob looks out his side, forehead pressing the window, scanning below, searching for a landform to get his bearings and only shapeless misty-grey out any window.

"Lightening shorted out the electronics. We've lost navigation ...and the radio. I'm taking us down below the clouds to see where we are. We'll head north, find the coast, and then follow it back to GUMO. Everyone hang on." Bob sounds a bit perplexed, his voice less steady.

The pilot completes the right turn, aiming the plane north towards the coast, easing the flight controls forward, angling the nose down. The right engine revs louder. Power and Gravity push the plane faster, steeper.

We streak down only seconds ...then suddenly, *stillness, silence*.

The blur of propeller spray winks out from the corner of my right eye, and I turn in time to see the other engine's life expire. There's a muffled sputter, the engine coughs, then nothing ...and more nothing.

A second passes while my heart punches me in the solar plexus. Bob's head jerks right, startled. He sees the dead propeller but the sound of silence, the suddenly stilled vibration, has already told him what's happened.

Sister Mary points out her window at the right engine, half-crying, half-screaming. "Oh no! What's happening?" Well ...*nothing* - except new, ragged-edged horror slicing through the background noise of today's ordinary horror.

"Fuel's ok ...generator? I don't know how ...must have been the lightning." The first sentence is loud and fast, as if he intended to speak over running engines but forgot, or maybe to sound an alarm. The second is soft, slower, to himself, confused, scared ...and alarming beyond measure.

But my aging biochemistry has spent its coin of fight or flight hormone; the drugs are still working. I seize and take a moment to calm down and take quick stock of the situation. All right... I see ...ok ..., and *ATHEISTMAN* can sense the fear of imminent death reeking in this plane, with useless whispered prayers for salvation forming in the mouths of some at the same time as bowels are loosening in the pants of most. But even he is not so tactless as to ransack the hope clung to by desperate people, save to wither any I might have held.

The others start shouting questions at Bob. Mrs. Korda sums up, urgency pushing the words, more plea than a question, "Is there somewhere we can land Bob ...*anywhere?*"

The Lorina's lost all power and transformed into a heavy glider. There's no reading on the dead digital altitude indicator, but I figure we're about three thousand meters high. At a glide ratio of ten-to-one, we probably have a radius of thirty kilometers, maybe more to

106

the west and less to the east with the wind, fifteen minutes to find a landing strip.

It appears we're streaking towards our doom, and still, we're bucketing about in a raging storm, tossed about side to side, jerked helplessly up and down. The rushing air expands from a deep, low whistle to a piercing, tortured howl. Bob holds the controls tight in both hands, occasionally wiggling fingers, fastening his grip.

"This is an emergency, folks. We might have to put down on a track or ditch on a beach. Hold on. I'm really sorry."

Bob's not just *sorry* for killing us; he's *really* sorry, not *imaginary* sorry …well, we're pointing down, so he'll splatter first. I'll have a thousandth-of-a-second on the fat bastard, a miserly *nano-gloat* …but I'm glad of it, a glad gamer[23] to the end.

One-tenth of a second, an instant of lightning, has altered our reality.

---

[23] Oddly, this is possibly a reference to the Pollyanna books by Eleanor Porter and the famous 1960 Disney movie starring a pubescent Hayley Mills. The stories contain the misadventures of an orphaned missionary's daughter who tried to find something positive out of sad situations by playing the Glad Game.

Levague would have been about 10 years old when the movie was released, and perhaps Hayley Mills was something of a first puppy-love crush. Also, contemporary movie reviewers noted the *Christlike* characteristics of the protagonist, which doubtlessly tweaked a nascent *ATHEISTMAN's* interest.

Nevertheless, that this allusion should pop into the mind of a 60-year-old lecher under the current precarious circumstances, I find both astonishing and disgusting.

Like a random arrow fired from the Moon or a tiny rock from the *bloody* Kuiper Belt, it could have hit anything or missed but chose to pierce the five cubic meter moving target of space that contains a plane with *me* in it - the killer out of nowhere. Working the odds, you'd have to figure your number's truly up.

But it's no bolt from the blue, no dark-alley attack - reasonable people don't fly in *metal* boxes through air charged fully with *metal-seeking*, high-voltage electricity. This shouldn't occur. For some reason, I feel I need to get this out for the record. I say to all, "I don't like you're driving, Bob. If we survive, I'll probably have to kill you."

Sister Mary seems to find this amusing. I hear a choked, sharp breath intake that's half-giggle, half-hiccup from the seat in front. Mrs. Korda tosses back a brief glare, frightened and stern at the same time. Bob says, "Rough road."

I take inventory of fellow passengers, surprised no one's lost it yet. Sue Tran is bent forward, all orange with a reflector-striped GUMO shirt, arms folded on the back of Chirp's seat, head resting on arms. She's rehearsing the emergency brace position and hasn't given up hope of surviving. I can't see her face, and I wonder where her thoughts are; if she's religious and making some sort of mental account of her life, balancing up good and bad, a tally of life leaving a final balance in the black or red ...maybe a Catholic, the daughter of parents who converted when the French colonized her country. Or perhaps, the offspring of Vietnam Warfighters who taught her that an individual's life is only a tool to pry open some bigger reality and to never give up no matter the odds - a dead soldier's daughter with a dead soldier's luck.

Sister Mary's a sickeningly bright raincoat in the gloomy storm of life, holding tight to faith and her seat. She turns toward Chirp, and a white hand reaches over and pats his arm. Her face is set *professionally* peaceful. In her eyes, there's reassurance that not all is lost, but it's very close to not-so-quiet resignation that all is ...*sensible girl*. Chirp doesn't respond or acknowledge the Sister's gesture. He's leaned back in his seat, clapping sticks now still and resting on his lap, face glued fearfully to his window. He seems to know 'what's up'.

I wonder briefly what made Sister Mary abandon a normal life to become a 'Bride of Christ' and now a minder of petrol-sniffing zombies. Was her father an abusive drunk, beating his family, driving young Mary towards more positive male role models in the Irish Catholic priesthood? Was growing up so awful that she traded hope for a normal family of her own for faith that sacrificing her hope could bring something better in the service of the Big Guy? That seductive promise of faith has a legitimacy that persists in Ireland like no other place ...but still, everyone thinks of nuns that there must be something wrong with them as *women*. They couldn't or wouldn't find a man ...yes, lesbians, *all* of them.

The Kordas have moved as close together as possible and still be fastened firmly in their seats. They lean into the aisle space between them, hold each other's hands, and lock onto each other's eyes, all glistening with quiet tears, and soft sad smiles reflect loving sentiment back and forth in these, the last moments of the miner and his wife. Perhaps it's a blessing that things should end this way. The 'G' force on impact, slamming the brain's frontal lobe forward, splattering inside his skull, and squirting out eyes and ears, will bring quick endings for both. Perhaps it's better than a prolonged agony as cancer eats away Mattius, leaving him in nappies and comatose, and a grieving wife to watch it all, left with only despair and desolate memories until eventually the devil catches up again. At this moment, they're consumed by something special between themselves, and neither appears to want an outsider like me or God. I look away before my eyes wander further down the front of Mrs. Korda's blouse.

I glance down at the black journal closed on my lap. My *Notes on the Meaning of Life* and the flimsy extension of my doctoral dissertation, my *Biochemical Socio-cultural Interface Theory*. Ironically, I should be ready for this very moment. Life has no meaning. It's just an illusion of biochemistry. What's so special? Well, the old BSI theory is no companion for a last drink in Levague's *saloon-de-vie*, and as long as my reflection peeks back from the mirror behind the bar, through whisky bottles half-full, I'll drink and rage, and goddamn it all.

And Bob Palmer's in the captain's chair, his attitude belying nothing but big fat determined concentration. *Good on ya, Bob!* He's fixed on the farthest distance possible in the formless grey ahead, searching for the first clue of land materializing before actually crashing into it.

I hope Bob sees no glory in ending in a blaze of fire, the justice of '*he lived by the sword and died by it*' blurring his focus on saving my life. But he strikes me as someone who'll see things through to the end: go for the jugular in a knife fight, serve out a tough jail sentence, battle down endless foes and demons; and for Bob, I'm certain the ends are never the *real* thing, it's the *getting there* - in youth with horsepower by Harley Davidson and mesmerism by the white line on the open highway, and later with the inspiration of self-interest, and wing power by airplane engine ...like a this damned Lorina's. *No good lousy stupid goddamn Brazilians, the useless progeny of Portuguese peasant riff-raff, the flotsam and jetsam of a thousand sleazy Rio nights ...building airplanes, what were you thinking?*

But it's no good blaming third-world workers for the mess we're in; it's no one's fault - just a bunch of stuff that's happened according to Laws of Chaos ...and probably, Lorina's engineers are really Germans, the children of escaped Nazi Luftwaffe engineers disguised as Brazilians.

So now is as good a time as any for my life to start flashing before my eyes, but the paucity of accessible memory inventory surprises. There are a few mental shimmers of tender moments: a child on my father's lap watching Walt Disney on an early black and white TV, maybe Alice in Wonderland; Chanel No. 5 perfume as my mother tucked me in; my first *terror* - at missing a school bus and getting lost on the way home; and the exhilarating clueless fumbling of sticky romance with a first girlfriend.

These and a few other images condense the meaning of my entire childhood. They might not be real, only idealized representations of a million unremembered experiences. Distillations of a life crystallized in a few clear memories, each one *too* sharp to be true recall.

In 1965, I smoked my first joint, listened to *all* of Bolero, started writing *ATHEISTMAN* Comics, and went out to look for something to eat that I found available in a rainbow of flavors as a UN ethnographer. Best job I ever had – all those opportunities to conduct meaningful comparative, world-systems analysis …naked Edo ladies' gymnastics, opium rituals with Berber chieftains in the high Atlas Mountains, something stronger a few years before in the higher peaks of Armanistan. Shame I got fired. I have no regrets about the drugs; none remembered anyway. Those who remind me of Hunter's Bar and the ill-fated Profiler, indelicate *ATHEISTMAN* cartoons, and *unfortunate* actions in Bougainville – *fuck 'em all!*

But there's no denying the Iranian *fatwa's* impact on my professional and personal life, all those years of jumping at every door-knock - every stranger, a deadly assassin. I kept a low profile, mostly working for TALC with Aboriginal lore masters in outback Australia, recording data in the Journal, and watching my back. It's a place where you can see them coming for more miles than anywhere else in the world – pancake flat. It's hard to sneak up on anyone in the desert.

I fed my boys *witchetty* grubs, and they swallowed red dust from a hundred dirt tracks. They learned a healthy respect for poisonous snakes - reptiles and humans. My wife put up with the desert in the summer, and we raised our kids.

Then there's Pam. I must admit, I can barely remember the first time we met. It was in the summer of 1989, a few weeks after my *fatwa* sentence, and Las Vegas was the first place I thought to hide for a while – thousands of strangers, cheap hotels and alcohol, hot buffets - and if you stay away from the casinos, your loot can go far.

Of course, I didn't, and recall waking in fright after a particularly destructive bout of martinis and blackjack on a Shoshone Federal Indian Reservation north of Vegas, where I apparently sought refuge from the jurisdiction of the Nevada State Gaming Authority over the trifling matter of a bounced cheque …And there she was, my dream princess.

I snatched my chance for love. With a million fanatics trying to kill me, it was time to have babies, and I took her from the Mohave to the Simpson Desert already pregnant with our first, and she stuck with me through fifteen long *fatwa* years, constantly complaining at the dearth of shopping options in the Outback - but always covering my back, and we battened down together and came through every desert dust-storm, every seasonal flood, every dead pet, every summer and winter …every *bloody* minute of every *goddamn bloody* day.

…But right now, it's the time to remember the glow of maternal love in her eyes when they were the first our babies looked into at birth, the deepest satisfaction imaginable on her face at getting through the pain of childbirth, at looking down into new eyes that are her own eyes reborn, with certainty that she has transcended death, that life is secure and safe for now …I'm sure something like that happened, but I wasn't there - nothing turns a gut to retching like the sight of a woman giving birth.

We have a houseful of photos from over twenty years that record our marriage. I don't have to remember anything and generally don't. She's the memory side of the family, and all the pictures of Pam and me, from our brief courtship (my agreeing terms with her father and brother), our marriage in Las Vegas (Clark County License - $2.50), and our entire life together in Australia and all around the world aren't pictures of us, but rather of *her* with me in them. Pam's in the light, I'm in the shadows, shady.

I think of our boys, almost men now. They're bright stars lighting up the Universe, holding my galaxy steady, keeping me from flying apart - cosmologically expensive for precious little return, testament only to ultimately aimless fertility, the tyranny of worthless Levague genes selfishly[24] hurrying to be passed on in the constant threat of Daddy's *fatwa*. And that's about it: my whole 8mm film fades to black, and there's still plenty of time to kill.

We're still flying blind, with wet mist all around, still too high to see the ground. Time enough for some practicalities: Iranian *fatwa* canceled …*check*; final will and testament valid …*check*; substantial

---

[24] Readers should not mistake this for an original notion – see Dawkins, R (1976) *The Selfish Gene*.

accidental death insurance payout pending ...*check*; favorite scotch ...*Johnny Walker Black Label*; favorite strain ...*Gorilla Glue No. 4*; favorite extinction event ...*Permian*[25]; pet peeve ...*Homo sapiens.* Perhaps a sliver of my brain will survive the plane crash. Cloned and somehow able to assimilate the staggeringly meaningless and pointless information I've recorded in the Journal, could *ATHEISTMAN* be reborn?

Suddenly, the fog thins and the cabin brightens. Light flickers through windows and plays across passengers' faces. We slice down clear of the lowest clouds and fly underneath. Visibility's restored ...only wide-open ocean dead ahead, a vast watery grave – *wonderful!*

But out my window, I see land to the east. We're one thousand meters high, gliding north in a controlled dive. The atmosphere's suddenly calm. Maybe there's still a bit of luck somewhere we can still spend; there's plenty of old airstrips all along the coast. Bob's in serious control, potential for a soft landing, new hope.

A fresh dose of adrenalin perks me razor-sharp. I search for

---

[25] Somehow, Levague switches from sensible and practical considerations (under the circumstances) to listing aspects of himself as if filling out a form on an internet dating app. What kind of people have both a favorite kind of cannabis *and* a fondly considered mass extinction event, except perhaps Canadian evolutionary biologists?

Of the 5 or 6 mass extinction events known to science, the Permian was almost certainly the worst. I found Levague's evocation of unprecedented death and destruction troubling. This highlights a *red flag* for the Australian Federal Police.

clues to where we are. To the left, the unmistakable southern peninsula of East Crocodile Island, a dark brownish-green patch on shifting grey seas. We're about two hundred kilometers dead west of GUMO, at the mouth of the muddy-red Woolen River.

Mrs. Korda shouts. "Look!" We all see it.

Heavy billowing clouds are exploding all around, roiling darkness towering five kilometers into heaving troposphere …and a golden shaft of glorious light blazes down from above, punching a small hole through atmospheric turmoil, shining, expanding and illuminating the southern half of the island, lighting a scene of hope, maybe lifesaving - a biblical vision, God's brilliant divinity casting a glowing promise of salvation on worldly gloom …but instead of *Jesus*, East Crocodile Island airstrip is in clear, blessed sunlight - and *it's* reachable.

…Curiously, a recent cover of *Watchtower* magazine pops to mind - that wonderful Jehovah's Witness Monthly, the only true comic book left. Maybe because mortal close calls prompt thoughts of regret - I've always delighted in perverse pleasure at tormenting these poor people when they come proselytizing at my door; they never get away scot-free. If Pam's not home, *ATHEISTMAN always* comes out. You'd think they'd have some sort of register of houses not to go to, a black list - yet they keep coming back.

This Watchtower cover had the stock *stormy-dark-clouds-with-ray-of-heavenly-light-shining-down* spotlighting Jesus, the shepherd in a pastoral setting with staff in hand and a lamb in the crook

116

of an arm. The theme was *'the light of God in times of trouble'*.

The Witnesses were a young husband and wife and their two daughters, maybe ten and twelve, all scrubbed up in 1950's Sunday-go-to-meeting dress, ribbons in the girls' hair. They approached from the street as I watered gardenias. Presenting me with this month's issue, the man asked, "Have you noticed that there's violence and strife everywhere these days, wars and refugees?"

ATHEISTMAN pretends to be a friendly old fellow watering his flowers, interested and smiling. I tell him pleasantly, "Actually, I thought last century was pretty violent."

If this is or isn't the case, it doesn't matter - the woman starts explaining that the *awful* things happening *today* are clearly forewarned in the Bible, and this month's Watchtower provides *proof*, a dire message indeed - but not to worry if you get on board with Jehovah.

Most times, I let them go through their prepared spiel and then see what they have to say about the *Unified Field Theory*. Usually, I end it by feigning sudden recall that these are people who'd let their children die rather than allow a blood transfusion. Then, I accuse them of child abuse and chase them off my property.

But this time, what with the young girls, I say, "Perhaps you can help me with a question I've been thinking about from the Bible. You know, the story in Genesis, in the Garden of Eden, when the snake talks to Adam and Eve …well, I wonder …does the snake's mouth *magically* change into a tiny human mouth with lips and a tongue so

117

he can make speech sounds, or does he just open his little snaky-mouth, and a human voice *magically* comes out?" I let them walk away peacefully when they didn't know, a rare example of the kindness and sensitivity of *ATHEISTMAN*[26].

Bob's head is fixed on East Crocodile Island, three or four kilometers ahead, slightly to the left. The cloud cover moves west fast, breaking up completely north and south. Sunlight flickers through the cabin and stays; the sun burns high in the west, blue sky patches expand above, glittering water below, storms slide off in the distance, and the wind is less a factor.

The plane banks left, and the island spreads out ahead, a flat spill of pale green and rust red on a shifting sea canvas, twice as long north-south as the four-kilometer width (see Figure 3, pg. 375). Beach erosion has serrated the coastline with crescents of white sand. A jumble of outcropping red granite boulders and a low, ironstone hill cap central portions, all glimmering bright and wet from recent rains.

---

[26] The Journal contains few entries where Levague speaks calmly with religious proselytizers (rather than terrorize them). For example, he reports an encounter where he philosophically asked, *Was there a God before language, before words were available to think divine thoughts? Is God just in the words of humans? When our speechless Australopithecine ancestors died, did they go to Heaven? Can you look an Orangutan in the eye and think, I go to Heaven but you don't?* Levague notes the believers' reply, 'Who's Anna Rangutan?'

A creek emerges from a shallow gully on the southeast flank of the hill and traces a line of ephemeral water for several kilometers southeast towards the main beach like a silver thread edged by dark river gums. It flows into a tangle of mangroves lining the margins of a narrow estuary on both sides, choking the creek mouth with fine, grey-black tidal mudflats.

Altogether, the island looks like a jagged shard of blood-red, patchy-green stained glass lying broken on a sparkling blue carpet - with a sharp, pointy end facing south and poised, two kilometers offshore, to stab the mainland in the back where it's already bleeding out the swollen Woolen River.

We glide lower, closer. From three hundred meters high and a thousand to the east, I make out tiny concrete slabs, broken walls, and collapsed building rubble, all forming a white crescent of five or six abandoned community buildings on foreshore dunes along the main beach south of the estuary.

The largest derelict structures front onto an old village square. There are a few solid concrete buildings still standing, but smaller timber and sheet-metal outbuildings were wind-dismembered long ago, leaving a patchwork of crumbling grey-white slabs and their respective piles of debris. The biggest living thing anywhere on the island is smack-dab in the center of the old village square, unmistakable even at this distance - the gigantic dark canopy of an ancient Morton Bay Fig tree.

The creek and the estuary form the northern boundary of the

historic ruins. The tidal mudflats are exposed, isolating the estuarine waters and forming a swampy lagoon with mangrove thickets crowding the margins. The creek flows into and is absorbed by the swamp half a kilometer inland from the shoreline. Shallow rivulets trickle from the eastern edge of the lagoon across the mudflat for fifty meters down to waves breaking lower on the sandy beach. Further down, a semi-submerged sandbank forms an arc across the mouth of the estuary to the next beach north. You could walk on it, from the south beach to the north beach, without getting bogged in mud - or cut across it east to west, from the open ocean to the mud; and then it's a warm, slippery haul into a lovely swamp - if you were a crocodile.

The historic remains are the abandoned Catholic Mission Settlement, set up early last century as an isolated home for Aboriginal *lepers*. Now, it's just a short string of discarded broken concrete shells on a lonely beach, lost in a readily forgotten past and long ruined by the elements. It shut down in the 1950s when the last inmates died.

The collective graves of those sent here from all over the Territory to live out their miserable lives are registered as an Aboriginal Sacred Site. Locals seldom visit. Only the most senior ritual *lawmen* come here for very occasional ceremonies. They alone have the power to withstand the angry chaos of malignant spirits interned in the cemetery; only they can placate the otherworldly malevolence of East Crocodile Island.

That's what they tell me anyway. I'm sure a good measure of the old fellows' ritual grit comes from not believing any of this spirit nonsense anyway. Demystification of reality is the final *rite-de-passage* in all cultures, but there's nothing like spinning a good yarn to keep women and children away while men get on with their secret 'sacred' business: clapping sticks, crucifixes, cricket bats - all the same.

According to the lore, it's not so much the fact of being *dead* and/or a *leper* that pisses off the spirits on East Crocodile Island; it's being buried *together* - in an intolerable state of proximity. A person should be buried *alone*, where he died - out in the bush, and the place avoided until grieving, the reliable work of carrion scavengers and the desiccation of time erase memories of life and sadness. A spirit could move on, alone and untroubled by demanding relatives, dead *and* alive.

But with so many packed in so tight, with no fence of distance, there's bound to be trouble between deceased neighbors: family insults flying, bickering, tempers forever fraying. Old scores among the dead can only grow older, always stirring up strife, never settled.

It's the usual social pattern of any Aboriginal community, no different in death than life but made scarier, I suppose, by rotting noses and bits of ghostly leper-bodies falling off. There's a TALC fine of $500 for being on the island without a permit.

East Crocodile Island was first described in 17th-century journals of Dutch East India traders rather than in any British historical records. Indonesia is far closer than Sydney. I read the originals in Amsterdam for myself, I think.

Interestingly, the generic name for *white fellow* among local Aborigines is *'Ballander'*, a distillation over the centuries of *Hollander*. Traditional Aboriginal cave paintings in Kakadu Park show European male human figures in traditional 'stick-man' motif smoking clay tobacco pipes.

I recall the main reason it was named *East Crocodile Island* - because there are just as many of the rapacious Jurassic monsters as on *West Crocodile Island.*

I look at Chirp, alert and sitting up straight. His wide eyes turn right and follow the island coast north, then dart back to Bob working the controls, then out his seat window and settling on the distant, endless, dark mainland to the south. He doesn't seem overly worried that his immortal soul will spill out of his dead, crashed body and have to fight flesh-dripping ghouls from a leprosarium's graveyard for permanent dead space; he's more excited than scared. He knows what's happening and apparently anticipates the plane will land safely *...the unshakable optimism of the especially stupid.*

Bob angles us in, gliding over the ocean, adjusting wing flaps, correcting our line-up with the island's gravel strip. "It looks clear! We'll make it! Bend down, hold your knees, or fold your arms on the seat in front and put your head down. Don't worry about life vests. Do what I *bloody* say when I *bloody* say it!"

No one moves. There will be no brace position until the last second. We're busy bending our collective will, all our most profound best luck to Bob - by gaping mindlessly at the hard ground looming, red-green earth rising, unable to blink or turn away, transfixed, waiting to be road-kill.

Bob takes his left hand off the steering controls, aviators glued dead ahead. He finds a red knob below the useless power levers marked *Emergency Gear Down* and pulls it full-out. …Nothing. There's no sound of the landing gear, no effect on the plane's glide, no evidence that anything's changed. Bob pushes and pulls the knob several frantic times, then gives up.

"Now listen! There's no gear. That means a hard landing. See above the door to the right, behind the co-pilot seat …the red fire extinguisher …if I can't, and you have to, pull out the ring, point, and pull the nozzle …See the door, just pull the lever to 'open' and push out from the top …When I say go, you go! Keep your belts on until we stop completely." Bob's voice is loud but matter-of-fact calm, strong, no quaking, commanding - as if he knows what he's doing, does it all the time.

The four tranquilizers I ingested almost exactly balance out the adrenalin; I'm able to register Bob's instructions with no new anxiety. I can handle the door if I survive the landing reasonably intact and Bob doesn't. There might be an expectation that I'll step up, what with Korda being ill. I rehearse the 'open door' steps once or twice in my mind, knowing that if it's me who has the detail, it's me first out the door.

We're almost over the white sandy shoreline but *way* too high. Bob adjusts the wing flaps, increasing the angle of descent and velocity.

We whistle down over the sea, over beaches, foreshore dunes, trees - *too* high, *too* fast. But then Bob suddenly pulls the flight controls back and turns the plane almost sideways to the left, exposing the right side fuselage flush against a wall of oncoming air, sacrificing aerodynamics to slow us down.

The airstrip is ahead out *my* window as if we're landing sideways, sideswiping the final few meters of solid air. Heat and humidity pervade the cabin.

We clear vegetation, sliding side-on into a thin corridor carved out of eucalypts decades ago when constructing the airstrip. The strip's mostly white, beach sand blown over red gravel. Low shrubs and brown grasses outline the runway and spill across in places. A plane hasn't landed here in years.

Bob has no control after touchdown; we'll skid and plow straight unless a tuft of grass or a termite mound throws us sideways or back up into the air; either way, it'll be a violent ending. At the end of the strip is a meter-high wall of earth graded up from the runway, topped by a thick tangle of dead uprooted eucalypts: old broken tree trunks, branches, roots – all scraped up in a pile the width of the runway - a final spiked, thorny barrier to snare the stricken Lorina.

Bob slides the plane into rushing air a few seconds longer. The ground closes in; the forest edges blur silently past, runway in sight, ripped-tree thicket barricade waiting to sink barbs into prey.

Suddenly, erupting from trees lining the runway ahead to my

right, a startled flock of red galahs scatters wildly in all directions as if panicked by the approach of a great, white-winged raptor. But following instantly from the same patch of trees, a small brown life form scurries onto the end of the runway and sits momentarily still, looking at us …at me, and I can just make out what I first think is a wallaby or small kangaroo. Then disbelief steals the moment. The animal has red feathers - in two *hands* - and its mouth. There appears to be a carnivorous monkey on the runway, looking directly into my eyes. Then it's gone, disappearing back into trees and shadows as quickly as it materialized. There are no monkeys in Australia. I keep silent.

The Lorina glides sideways, a meter above the ground. The split-second before crashing side-on, Bob rights the plane, pushing and turning flight controls fast and sure, and we *spank* the ground hard and stay down, dead center of the runway but *way* too near the end. We're thrown forward the instant of impact, and I have to push heavily against the seat-back in front.

The plane's fuselage plows through sand smoothly like a sleigh on icy snow. We scrape across patchy gravel, a series of screeching jolts ripping thin metal skin like a grinder on steel.

We skid through tuffs of grass, each a shuddering thud, knocking the plane sideways one way and then the other. Small rocks slam the floor like baseball bats …and the end of the strip approaches *too* fast. The plane's still level, holding together, but we won't stop before we smash into the plowed-up earth and tangle of skeleton trees

125

dead ahead.

We all see it coming for a long second, long enough to gauge that impact might not be catastrophic, more a robust parking-lot collision, a bump in the head, a fender-bender for the Lorina ...*survivable!* I brace myself by bending forward and down in my seat, leaning to the side, pushing myself back, hands on the seat in front, kind of crouching behind Sister Mary on the theory that what will happen to me will happen to her slightly before, possibly cushioning the worst.

"Hang on!" Bob shouts in the last rattling bumping moment. We hit the meter-high earth bund hard at a slight angle, low speed, but the jarring bump jerks the Lorina's nose sharply to the right, bouncing us slightly up, turning the plane forty-five degrees, and sending us crashing into the sharp tangle of uprooted trees. The last few meters of motion forward are accompanied by the loud cracking snap of dead wood giving way, the shattering crunch of splintered glass as sharp tree roots shred the windshield, and an awful human grunt as a broken tree branch spears through the cockpit window with enough force to drive clean through the front left passenger seat and before that, the upper chest of Mrs. Korda.

The sounds of her death are distinct from others: *crack* of ribs, a moist *squelch*, and her collapsed lungs squeezing out a last wheezy, bubbly gasp; a sound a person doesn't live through, a sound to haunt the ear. Her face is turned to her husband, frozen in jaw-dropped shock, wide-eyed, astonished ...but showing no pain; a final muscle reflex fastens both hands around the base of the smooth wooden spear shaft protruding from the center of her body, grasping even in death, to somehow pull it out.

I've seen plenty of dead bodies but always avoided people in the act of dying suddenly and close up. The difference between life and death is not so much seen as felt in the pit of your guts.

Amazed, sickened and ecstatic in the same instant, I register the most important thing. I have survived. But just before Korda manages his first high-pitched scream of anguished, a new sound emerges from the still, silent second after impact that I know means something bad: a loud hissing, pressurized gas escaping, *fuel*.

Korda lets loose his body-racking wail, the appalling wordless cry of the sudden end of everything - but I'm tuned to a muffled, baffled air sound I know, the awful *whoosh* of flames right outside my window. The impact of landing must have stretched and torn thin sheet metal, rupturing a wing tank; the friction of heated fuselage, rubbed red-hot by grinding gravel, likely the spark.

Flames quickly engulf the right wing. Liquid fire flows down its length towards the cabin. Wind fans the fuselage with deadly heat. Black smoke enters through the shattered windshield.

There is no time to appreciate the fine irony of surviving the impact only to burn in the fire; there's nothing like flames to give biochemistry a bit of hurry-up. Bob moves first, launching himself out of his seat, ducking surprisingly nimbly under the branch that's sticking through the shattered windshield and Mrs. Korda, and

127

levering and pushing the cabin door open in a heartbeat. It opens only a fraction, held fast by a wedge of tangled branches. Then Bob shoves his mighty weight against it with both hands, and it drops to the ground with a crash of breaking wood, scraping against the earth bund but clearing the main shatter of the Lorina's debris. He barges into the sunlight outside, turns, and leans back, shouting, "Fire! Get the hell out ...run to the trees ...don't stop ...out ...out! ...Jack, get that *bloody* kid!"

Passengers move now, some faster than others, forming a naturally selected pecking order. I'm surprised it's Sue Tran out first (rather than me). She's up, passed Chirp, under the lance sticking through the windshield and pinned to a dead body, and out the door in a blur of orange just as I clear my seat.

Chirp's trying to lift the clasp of his seatbelt but can't because he has a clapping stick in each hand and won't let go of either one. He's getting desperate, and because I'm there, and it'll take no more time to reach down and release him than it would take to hurl myself out of the plane, I do so. When he doesn't move instantly, I grab the kid by the hair and turn his face toward the fire raging out the right side until I know he's seen it. His skinny body now eagerly follows as I haul his hair to the door. He sees the sunlit ground outside and has enough sense to dive at the same time I *bowl* him under Mrs. Korda's branch and out of the cabin.

I should be out of this burning plane, but my eyes hook onto Mrs. Korda. The spearing branch has entered the point of her sternum almost exactly above her blouse cleavage, a circle of deep blood-red marking a bull's eye. I can't look at her face again, her dead eyes. Her left hand still locks onto the lance through her body. She could be holding it in now. There's a large pink diamond attached to a clinching finger. A thought pops to mind that his lump of carbon will outlast today's wreckage by a billion years and keep its brilliance for eternity after its last wearer is blown away dust. And then another thought pops - perhaps I should steal it, but there's no time.

Korda hasn't moved; he's frozen in grief, maybe death-wish. Acrid, silvery smoke from burning fuel and chemicals floods the cabin through the smashed-open windshield and flows thick along the roof like upside-down lava, poison fumes that incapacitate in seconds.

I ignore Korda and turn to Sister Mary, who also hasn't moved. Her expressionless eyes are glued out her window as flames lick and crack the glass ten centimeters from her face. Tiny yellow flames dance in her wide, unblinking stare. Her mouth is gaping, and she's in shock.

There's no time other than to save myself. The cabin's choking up fast; two or three more breaths before the next air is fatally toxic.

There's a drive for self-preservation capable of unconsciously taking command of biochemistry, of stepping into a busy intersection when the lights go out and directing mental traffic to prevent thoughts from careening around smashing into each other with resulting gridlock. Its decisions are final; once an order is given to go, there's no appeal for reconsideration. My drive is harder than steel to break. I'm a survivor. I'm out of here. *I don't move.* There's something else, some sort of biochemical catalyst, an awareness that's foreign, obtrusive, but oddly somehow familiar, a fossil memory of an old acquaintance or casual well-wisher - or adversary. It feels a bit like altruism, so I slap it away before it bites hard.

Maybe it's the drugs, maybe the realization I might get stuck with the fume-sniffing nitwit, but with seemingly little volition, my vision lowers, and I'm bending close to the Sister's ear, and I feel myself gather my last clean air, and I hear my mouth shout loud, above the sobs of Korda, above the crackling snap of flames half a meter away, "Mary Mary Quite-*Fucking*-Contrary!"

She turns toward the shouting, a frown pulling down that hair-fringed brow, seeing me with vacant eyes that quickly cast about the cabin for meaning. Perhaps the rhyme touches a childhood memory of hurtful taunts or echoes a madman from her earliest years, and she seems to come to her senses, locking into my blank stare, uttering matter-of-factly, "I think I wet myself."

The next thing I see is my black journal slamming into the side of Sister Mary's face with an oddly satisfying, crisp, leathery *whack*. It's in my hand as it happens.

I tell her, "Move or die!" She moves, scrambling on all fours around Mrs. Korda's feet, under the new tree-branch cabin infrastructure, and as her meaty white backside disappears into the sunlight out the door, like a small rugby player diving for a try, and even with the carnage of death and flames all around, I can't help notice a dark wet-patch on the seat of her uniform but *so sorely* wish I could.

My eyes scan once more around the cabin just as a sharp *bang* shakes the nose of the Lorina, splitting open the cockpit floor. The front tire has heated beyond tolerance and blew up the wheel compartment. I hear Bob swear. For some reason, he's near the front of the plane. More smoke enters through the new hole in the floor.

It's now or never. I can barely see. I crouch low, a hand finds the strap of a leather bag, and I scramble the few meters to the door on my knees, dragging the bag with one hand, the Journal held tight in the other. Just before I'm out, I spare one more glance at Korda and give final professional advice. "She's dead, you fool."

Only with inspiration from rare madness can a man allow his flesh to burn. As I'm out the door, running past the tip of the left wing, I stop, and Korda stumbles clear of the plane and falls, crawling after me. He's slow. I'm surprised that I noticed. And where the hell is Bob?

Then I see him ahead and halfway to the line of trees edging the runway where the women and Chirp are. While I'm rescuing passengers, he's walking backward, straining to drag two large white canvas duffle bags, one in each hand, feet digging in the sand, and his legs pumping hard under the load, heading to the cover of trees, face tight with exertion. He's rescuing the damn *cargo!*

Beyond, Sue Tran is in the shadow of trees with Sister Mary

and Chirp nearby. She's trying to use her mobile, but we're way out of range.

Just then, what must be the right landing gear explodes on the far side of the fuselage, shaking the burning plane. I turn back as a spray of flaming fuel forms a burning fountain over the crash scene. Korda scrambles to his feet, stumbling away, needing no more incentive to move.

My legs want me away faster, and I'm half the fifty meters to the runway tree-line when the last tire goes, shattering the wing closest. I look back and see, feel, and hear both right - and left-wing fuel tanks explode virtually in the same devastating instant. The first blast lifts the whole plane a fraction just as the second blows the left wing into several parts, launching the remains of the engine up into and through the tangle of dead trees.

The shockwaves hit almost instantly. I'm instinctively diving for the ground and caught in mid-air as the first explosion flattens me, and I eat sand. A microsecond later, the second shaves my back, and I see Korda tumble five meters past like a thrown doll.

Smoke, dust, white shards of shredded wing steel, ripped mechanics, splashing fire - all rain down in an arc that includes me. Solid flames cover every surface of the now unrecognizable airplane, and a final, orange-black fireball explodes high above the inferno.

The combined force of simultaneously igniting several hundred liters of fuel on either side obliterates the passenger cabin. Blackened sheet metal, broken burning seats, a bulkhead bent in half, charred, blistered pieces of torn Lorina, passenger bags, clothing, bottles - all the debris of crashed, burnt, twisted human artifacts falls in a circle around where the Lorina used to be.

In a heartbeat, it's gone, a pile of black smoking wreckage including the charred remains of a human body, and a dozen spot-fires I can't hear crackling with my loudly ringing ears. I stay face down and test my condition.

I'm in one piece, and nothing's broken. Some green liquid substance has splashed on the ground around my head and spattered my face. Droplets seep from my mustache into the corners of my mouth. It's not fuel. It tastes septic and smells of disinfectant and …stale urine. The back section of the Lorina with its upturned chemical toilet is two meters away and just missed me.

But breathing in dust and smoke from the blast, there's another taste in the back of my throat that tweaks strangely - of days long ago and far away - of youth and happiness; there's a feeling I know without thought, a hot tribal memory awaking from deep slumber and melting away decades.

Overnight bags are scattered around, most with their own little fires, including mine. Chirp's suitcase has fallen open near the remains of the tail section, pried open like a square blue oyster shell, a smooth football-sized stone nestled among clothes like a big black pearl. It's slightly kidney-shaped and looks suspiciously like what is described in the anthropological literature as a *TWO MEN* stone, a tool of ritual penile circumcision used in secret Crocodile Cult blood ceremonies. Chirp should not have this sacred, ritually powerful object. It's forbidden for women and boys to even *see* it, on pain of death. It's not something normally packed for light aircraft travel.

Just to my left lies another of Bob's white canvas duffel bags, smaller than the two he was hauling away. This one's split open, and its contents spilled out: individual, disc-like solid packages – twenty or so - each clad in tightly stitched yellow cloth with small black stenciled foreign lettering and a miniature dragon inked on one side. The disc closest to me has a torn corner. The cloth cover and clear plastic wrapping underneath have ripped open, and its white, powdery insides smudge the red dirt less than a centimeter from my nose.

Several physical things happen in quick succession. I blink once, and in that time, I reach ahead with my left hand, trap the torn disc under my journal, and snatch it back. Then I haul myself to my knees, my back to the others, and at the same time, gather both journal and disc and stuff them into the bag I have in my right hand, which I notice is Mrs. Korda's green Prada. I do it all secretively and fluidly and look around for the others as I stand up shakily, deliberately scuffing red dirt around and through a large white heroin spill, managing to look like I'm staggering a bit. Sister Mary's running up to help Korda. She's between me and big Bob, who's walking towards us, away from Sue Tran, Chirp, and the two larger duffle bags at the edge of the runway.

Mentally, I compute several chains of data at once, starting with totally forgetting the fact that the crashed remains of an airplane and a dead body are still smoking within spitting distance. Firstly, several ideas flash as a unit: drugs, lots of drugs ...*grab* the drugs. Secondly, the drug is heroin and belongs to criminals, probably including Bob Palmer, the knife killer. Thirdly, they don't like sharing.

Now don't get me wrong, I'm not a junkie[27]. But I marched through youth trucking arm-in-arm with furry freaks, and shared an ideology that drugs will get you through times of no money better than money will get you through times of no drugs. Our everyday drug was bulk Mexican or Columbian pot and occasional hashish, and special rare treats of everyone's favorite hash, the intoxicatingly pine-perfumed, legendary Lebanese Blond.

No one can't stay drunk all of the time; there's no such thing as a healthy, fully functioning alcoholic. But with eye-drops and mint gum, you can stay stoned on cannabis, and I learned - later than most - that if you want to stay high, you have to have money, you have to have a job, you have to raise a family, and you have to appear normal - so you can be left alone with your druggie business. Only hard-earned thirst is legitimately sated in our society; I picked that up from my folks; you don't need God to be good, just a good stash.

But like alcoholics, you can't function long and well as a full-time junkie - it's too expensive. As a once-in-a-while recreational indulgence, it's nicely unsociable, a bit of growing-up fun that, in my

---

[27] As evidenced in these pages, Levague *is* almost certainly at least, a part time junkie.

case, stretched far into extended adolescence and beyond. But the old poppy can sneak up and run amuck with your life if you're not prudent. It needs to be done sparingly - at Xmas and birthdays - not in the back alleys of every seedy third-world sleaze-bag country a UN anthropologist could possibly visit.

And I've waked in fright on a hundred strange carpets, spied lost-the-night-before, half-full plastic dope bags and chunks of hash under furniture so often, and instinctively made the grab; the conditioned response is unconscious reflex, even if the drug's a kilo slab of pressed heroin, and the furniture's a crashed plane on a deserted island, and even after twenty long years with Pam - the Oracle of Abstinence, the Queen of Cold Turkey.

I've ingested every non-lethal mind-altering substance imaginable: uppers, downers, moldy old mushrooms grown in cow dung, bits of bark, cacti, and the output of several psychedelic drug labs. But I've always had a particular weakness for the finer things. The brief snort I got from the burst disc as I lay face-down in what might now be a crime scene floods my biochemistry with warm fuzzy sensations of yore, and opiate molecules welcomed open arms in forgotten cerebral nooks and crannies, a celebration of returning heroes. I try to corral emotions into comprehensible thoughts but can't break free of *excitement*: the anticipation of *more* teased by apprehensions of danger.

I'm taken back to the pure simplicity of base reptilian desire. It's top-shelf primo *scag,* and I have a kilo.

Chapter 4: Desert Isle

I find myself standing, Prada bag zipped-closed, strap over my shoulder, slapping the dust off my clothes, scratching my nose, and wiping green piss off my face. Captain 'Drug Smuggler' Bob and Sister Mary are ahead, trying to get Korda to his feet.

I look skyward, half expecting helicopters, police, doctors, emergency vehicles, flashing red lights and sirens, but it's empty sky-blue in all directions. The sun's lower in the west. The atmosphere's grown quiet, stilled its rage. The storms have sucked away the afternoon heat and humidity. A light breeze coaxes smoke tendrils from smoldering plane wreckage to dance gently as they rise. The day has turned out to be fine. There's maybe three hours of daylight left but when I feel like I do now, I like it to be dark.

Testing my legs, I walk a few meters, and Korda is on his knees bent forward. Bob has his left arm and gently pulls him to his feet. Korda holds his right arm tight to his chest, and I'm not sure if it's broken or maybe it's just the cancer, maybe just his heart. Sister Mary takes over Korda's arm from Bob when he's reasonably steady and leads him away towards the edge of the airstrip.

Bob looks my way, aviators on me like mantis eyes. I realize I've lost my sunglasses. He's a few inches taller than me, and his sweating bulk looms silently in the space I intend to walk through. Then he speaks in words that seem far away from my still-ringing ears, "Your head's bleeding …cut on top." He points to the place on his

137

head that's bleeding on mine, his blue hat smudged with oil. "We need to get clear away …if you're all right, Jack, let's get over to the trees with the others. We still need to follow the safety protocol."

Blood trickles down the right side of my face into my beard hair and behind my right ear. My shaking fingers run across my bald scalp and zero in on a straight gash three centimeters long, starting behind my right eye and running straight back. Whatever did this would have hit me square in the forehead if my head wasn't firmly in the dirt when the fuel went off. I have nothing to staunch the flow. "Take this." Bob gives me his oily blue cotton hat, and I clamp it tight on my head. He's still pretending to be the skipper and concerned about passenger welfare.

Bob looks down at the small duffle bag and spill of heroin discs. *Fifty-two pick-up* played by increasingly bizarre circumstances. His dark reflecting glasses come back to me, eyebrows raised a fraction, lips pursed. He calmly states, "I need to collect up these mine-sample bags. If they burn or spill, it could be a chemical hazard. Go join the others …best just let *me* get these."

I try to find something in his voice, his face, anything in his manner to convince me that this statement is something that he really expects me to believe. Does he think perhaps I'm suffering some sort of post-traumatic stress, not thinking clearly, that I haven't noticed that the cloth-covered hazardous mine samples are dragon-tattooed with Arabic-style Armani lettering?

Bob goes about gathering up the spilled drugs and re-stuffing

138

the torn duffle bag as if they were Xmas presents, him a jolly Santa and me perhaps an undeserving naughty boy. He doesn't appear to miss the 'mine sample bag' now in the Prada. I decide it doesn't matter to Bob what I think. He's made a statement of *policy* about *mine samples*. He expects me to comply, and comply, I will - for now - without any *policy enforcement*, which I'm sure involves blade-sharp sanctions. It's a *safety* thing.

Sister Mary calls out Chirp's name loud enough for me to hear edged with startled concern, and I turn to see the lad sprinting towards me and Bob. I'm impressed he moves so quickly, tilting forward and then running fairly smoothly so as not to fall on his face. He catches up with himself every few steps and slows before plunging on again in an instant. It's jerky, a bit stop-and-start, but he's past me, deftly hopping around and over bits of smoldering wreckage, moving unerringly to his open blue suitcase.

He stops before it, looks down, and then raises both arms in front of him, hands opening. He seems momentarily puzzled that they're holding his clapping sticks. Then he squats down, drops the sticks, and with two hands, lifts the ancient kidney-shaped stone tool. Leaving everything else he might have packed, he comes slowly towards me, deliberately, his eyes on the stone he holds forth like a young man (or any man) hesitant with an infant.

With outstretched arms, he offers me the stone, speaking in rapid-fire *Yolngu*. He's scared, petrified. The words come out too fast, and I have to mentally translate what first seems only gibberish, trying to find coherence and relevance. He doesn't meet my eyes, but something in his voice tells me he's intending to do something extra idiotic.

The kid's got himself all worked up; his head jerks up-down, left-right, eyes dart sideways, backward, like he's expecting an attack. He's straining his senses to catch something in the corner of his eye or hear a whisper in the breeze, anticipating something terrible only he knows about.

Curiously, the weirder he gets, the more his eyes - their positions on his face - seem normal, the sagging left side seemingly squaring up to the right as his fear takes hold. There appears to be less and less *physically* wrong with the kid, and it occurs to me he might be running some sort of government disability services fraud, though to what end?

Then the meaning of his words sinks in, and I'm struck by his direct communication of what appears to be some actual information, utterly stupid though it certainly is. He's just crashed and almost burned, and yet he's moving around autonomously and speaking reasonably clearly. Perhaps the near-death experience has shocked a few solvent-pickled brain cells into sparking.

Without thinking, my hands - one caked with red dirt and the other holding Bob's bloody hat - form up in front of me to accept the stone. At the same time, I say in English, "Don't go anywhere. There's *no* spirit. We'll put the rock back proper-like. We're all fine ...*stay ...right ...here.*"

Then Sister Mary arrives, her white stockings scraped and torn at the knees, one scuffed and bloody, the front of her uniform streaked with red dust from crawling in the dirt, and crucifix-less now - she's lost the damned thing in the scramble. She reaches for Chirp's skinny arm, but he's off like a hot tarred jackrabbit in blue trousers, scampering fast a few meters in flopping white Nikes until he's sure Sister Mary's not in pursuit. Then he pauses, retrieves the clapping sticks near his suitcase, turns back to me, and looks searchingly into my eyes. Evidently, he thinks he's found something, and next, he turns to the nun. They lock gaze for an instant, the woman's insistent, kind, personal ...and amazed - it might be the first time she's actually seen sentience in Chirp's eyes.

The kid's still nervous, but his head's stopped jerking about, and he says in clear English, with a softness that's unusual for an Aborigine, especially a lunatic, and with sadness and...*affection*, "Don't come. Stay with this old man ...*Gee-Like-In-Veggie*."

Then he bolts - straight across the wreckage-strewn runway, around the far edge of the ploughed-up row of dead trees, and disappearing into the shaded forest west of the airstrip. I watch him go, suddenly too dazed and tired to worry about naught but old *Veggie* himself.

When Sister Mary speaks next, I'm surprised I've worked Chirp's heavy stone tool into the bottom of Mrs. Korda's Prada bag and zipped it up. Her demeanor hardens, her face twists about from puzzlement to anger, and a brave bush-fly in the corner of her open mouth looks like it's thinking to make a go for it. It's gone when her mouth starts working, "What's going on, Jack? What did he say? What spirits? Why has he got that rock? How long before we're rescued? Where's he going? Is he coming back? Oh, why is this happening? …Where's my bag?"

She becomes more animated with each question, each sought-after bit of information seemingly more urgent than the last, her face transforming, blooming in desperation, her voice rising in a screeching interrogative crescendo, all in one breath …*pitiful*.

A waft of smoke from the burning remains of the Lorina reminds us both where our bags are, and Sister Mary drops to her knees, covers her face, and all the mental weight of a crashing plane and someone dead spews forth in a river of wracking sobs, and the Sister gives in, losing herself to tears. "Oh, that poor woman …the poor, poor woman …Oh …no, no, no …" There's no one about to give the poor girl comfort; she'll need a moment to tire herself out.

The smoke stings my eyes, and I face away, tracing down the length of the runway. My gaze stops at the point where the Lorina first touched down, the start of a dark furrow in white sand leading to a blackened mess of disaster. My eyes cast themselves over the still smoking chunks of a crashed plane, looking towards where Mrs. Korda's remains are. There's *something* in the air: seared flesh mixed with acrid chemicals and burnt plastic - but distinct - sweet and sickly, like half-assed pauper's cremations at Varanasi on the Ganges in India, and yes, it *does* smell a bit like meat, the hot sizzling Schezwan pork at Ling's *does* come to mind.

A few spot-fires crackle and burn here and there, but the main blaze quickly consumed all the plane fuel, leaving only a smoldering husk - the tangled snare of broken trees too wet from rain to catch. The blood flow from my gashed head seems to have stopped, and I don Bob's oily blue and red hat to keep the sun off. My hearing's back to normal if the Sister's blubbering is any gauge, just as her emotion finds language again.

She's still on the ground, mumbling between sobs, "You have to help me find him. I'll get in trouble." Then a wagging finger comes up, and she spits the dummy again. "This is your fault ... Oh, what did you say?" And then her hands are back over her face for another round of sobbing. "Oh ...no, no, no ...Oh, what's happening?"

Inspecting plane wreckage suddenly appeals to me, and I walk over and find the little fire consuming my bag. I scoop on sandy dirt with my foot until it's smothered. There's nothing of my bathroom kit left, my hat, and clothes - all reduced to smoldering ash. Had the Journal been in there... well, there'd be no reading about it.

My sunglasses are nowhere around. Broken green glass spills from a cardboard box nearby. One of three bottles of Sue Tran's wine is intact ...amazing! It goes into the Prada.

I reach into my jeans pocket and pull out my tobacco pouch, which is almost empty. It's only been an hour since my last smoke, and although the need for nicotine is relatively immediate, I'd better save what's left. All the recent events are catching up to *me* now ...as

143

well as the girl. A simple short-term plan that will tide me over until we're rescued takes shape: find someplace a bit sheltered, snort some of Bob's scag, drink the wine, and about halfway through the bottle, I'll light up my last smoke. It'll be the best moment I can expect until rescue, and soon too, something to look forward to, work towards, and be glad about. I just need to ditch the people.

A dozen little bottles of water are scattered about, and I collect up a few. There's not much room left in the bag and nothing else useful close by, but as I turn towards Bob, Sue Tran and Korda, my eye catches the glimmer of a silver chain, and I follow it into the dirt, nudging Sister Mary's dark wooden, identity-defining crucifix clear with my shoe. And *ATHEISTMAN* can't help musing about the horror of the thing. It's elegantly simple: two pieces of wood fixed together on which to nail up a dying human to instill terror and manifest power. Adopted as the emblem of the church – bizarrely and with the finest sense of irony, and marketed skillfully over centuries – the practical *terror* function has changed to a symbol of hope and salvation for Christian believers. I sometimes wonder how Catholics would worship if Jesus had died in Rome, with a bigger Coliseum audience and higher production budgets ...perhaps in the *Screaming Bull*, the appalling cast-iron vessel shaped like a cow with a fire lit underneath, and victims are slow-roasted inside, howling their lungs to shreds, delighting the most discerning in the crowd. Today, girls might wear around their necks a little golden bull of Christ, the *Holy Bull*.

I'm sure the cross in the dirt at my feet would give poor Sister

Mary great comfort now. And I'm surprised a small part of me hopes that she finds it again.

Bob has taken his smaller, torn, drug-filled duffle bag the fifty meters back to the trees edging the airstrip clearing and joined the two others in the shade. He sits on one of the larger bags hunched forward, elbows on knees, aviators off, face in hands. I suppose crashing a plane, killing a passenger ...*the boss's wife*, and then rescuing about two hundred and twenty kilos of contraband from the burning wreckage can take it out of a big old fellow.

Korda's on the ground, on his back, using the other large white duffel bag as a pillow. He's still and might be unconscious ...*or dead*. Sue Tran is pacing back and forth behind the two men with her mobile phone in hand, still trying to find a signal.

I wonder what Pam will do when I'm not home for dinner. She'll expect my call, letting her know I'm back at about 4:30 pm. She'll start to get annoyed at about 6:00 pm if the authorities don't contact her before. *What authorities?*

A backlog of cerebral and sensory data needs urgent sorting. The smack-augmented tranquilizers holding back an avalanche of pent-up emotion are on the verge of running for cover.

I approach the others with a growing agenda of questions lining up on my tongue: *Has Bob set off the emergency beckon? How long will it take them to get here? Will they send a chopper today?* What's Bob going to do with the *mine samples* ...there's no way he could be hoping to have these rescued as well. What happens when

145

Korda asks, *'What mine samples?'* ...*mine samples* ...*mine.*

I instantly recognized the black lettering and dragon logo inked-stamped on the pressed slabs as Arabic-script Armani. From my little taster, the heroin is No. 1 Gauge Armani, the highest export quality. How did it get from Zamari Sharif to RCC's Gove uranium mine in Arnhem Land? It would require a sophisticated smuggling network, with contacts in Armanistan, Pakistan, and, depending on the *modus operendi*, possibly Indonesia. *Who's Bob working for?*

Suddenly, the struggle to get the Lorina airborne and our failure to climb quickly to a safe cruise altitude - and ultimately the cause of our crash - is explained. We were way too heavy when the kid and the beefy nun joined us. I walk towards the others, and Bob's still slumped on his duffel with his face in his hands. Sue Tran is pacing back and forth directly behind him, eyes downcast. She's given up on her mobile, but I catch a few angry words she appears to be directing at her feet. Some of it sounds oddly familiar.

I come up to Korda and give his foot a nudge, and he stirs. His face is a mess of burn-blistered red extending from his forehead to his shirt collar. Blood seeps from each ear. Tears flow from closed eyes; brows and lashes are burned off. His eyelids are scorched raw red, and when they open a fraction, his blue eyes are watery, unfocused, capitulating, dying-old-dog eyes needing to be put out of misery.

Sister Mary arrives and kneels by his side. I turn to Bob. His eyes train on me as if I'm about to say something or draw my weapon. I suddenly feel like an intruder, a problem. He's engaged in a dangerous enterprise that had nothing to do with me - originally. We've crashed *with* drugs *because* of drugs. A person has been killed during the execution of an illegal drug-smuggling felony, that's 'murder-one' in some jurisdictions. I'm worried if I ask too searching a question like *'What's really in the bag, and how dare you risk my life flying an overweight plane in an electrical storm?'* or *'How much is a gram or two of your excellent heroin?'* it might be interpreted as provocative.

No, it is best just to follow the safety protocol and allow Bob to volunteer the information that he thinks I need to maintain ignorance of any crime. I'll let him continue in his role as pilot and *commanding officer* even though he's lost his plane. I'll follow carefully what he says, filter each comment, each nuance, choice of word, and play an innocent, compliant, shell-shocked crash survivor …and try and figure out how all this could play out to my advantage.

And then it all seems to catch up - my life, my dear, precious life - under mortal threat in filthy Armani hovels from dirty-needle Hep B in '74, a year later in Algeria with AK47 bullets whizzing past my ears in the desert night and a savage angry Berber father on my heals, grave danger in Borneo in '97 as Bre-X 'cheated' Dayak maniacs sized up my head for shrinking potential, and fifteen long years of *fatwa* even if they didn't try all that hard …and now, an inch away from annihilation, crash-landed on a desert island hundreds of kilometers from civilization.

My mind swirls with images of a dead woman, fire and echoes

of Korda's anguish, Sister Mary's sobbing, and two hundred and twenty kilograms of quality narcotics. My pulse races, my head pounds, my heart throbs, and the blood pressure behind my eyeballs blurs my vision. My legs turn to jelly, but I manage to hold it together long enough to ask, with as much casualness as I can muster, "Did anyone see that monkey?"

I sit down next to Korda before I'm out on my feet. A long moment passes. The near-death crash and now the effect of accidentally snorting just a bit of heroin overwhelm my limbs. I let go, flop back on my side exhausted, and lay on the ground, propping my head up with an arm, feeling that old allover opiate itch of not-quite-enough. I'm facing Bob but watching the start of a little light show on the back of my eyelids.

From behind, I hear a series of high-pitched squeaks not unlike a pinched lap dog's yelping that I think must be Sister Mary ...giggling - a hair's breadth short of hysteria.

"It had a bird," she says, laughing more like a normal person. The monkey seems to focus her thoughts and she asks, "It was a monkey?"

"It was a monkey," Bob confirms. "It's *somebody's* monkey ...Who could have a monkey?" Bob's words move from puzzlement to suspicion, and I open my eyes to find him staring at me without his sunglasses - his knife-scarred right eye, my unavoidable focus. There's an edge of nervous urgency in his words, close to the first panic I've seen from the man. There's fear in those eyes, alarm that the worst of the day might actually be ahead.

I'm not really sure what Bob *is* anymore. He managed to crash his plane – he's no longer useful as a pilot. He's managed to smuggle two hundred and twenty kilograms of heroin *into* and then *out of* officially 'secure', 'sterile' legal status - from 'checked-in' at GUMO Airport, where it could be transported to and offloaded at Darwin Airport still 'sterile', and then be re-routed to anywhere in Australia without *any* security inspections. As a smuggler, he's failed spectacularly.

I wonder if Bob has any equity in the deal or if he's just a mule to get it to Darwin. Does he still connect with the biker underground and its commercial drug network? There's no neutrality in aviation and drug smuggling; if you're not an asset, you're a definite liability. The desperation in his eyes confirms his changed status. Such men can be rash.

My eyelids seem to be fluttering, wanting to relax the strain of muscles exerting to hold them open. My biochemistry courses with the warm, tender blush of inchoate opiate intoxication, caressing every nerve ending with velvet-soft loving hands and tempting me to surrender. I want more - *right now*.

"Who's got a monkey out here?" Bob demands, and my eyes reluctantly must deal with the reality of Bob glowering down at me. His voice is even, but the question is like an *accusation* - as if I'm privy to important information about this monkey's circumstances and holding back.

149

"I never heard of a monkey in Arnhem Land. It couldn't survive," I state more defensively than intended, declaring my ignorance, innocence, ruing that I even brought the damn thing up. "I don't know who owns it."

That's the truth ...well, most of it. It was a *macaque*, the most common monkey in Southeast Asia, often carried as semi-tame pets onboard itinerant Indonesian shark-fin vessels that sneak under the radar and raid the reefs along the north Australian coast. Released on a desert island, a monkey that's been fed *salt* will quickly sniff out surface freshwater or a natural spring if it's there, where no human could, allowing fishermen to stay out longer.

"It might belong to Indonesian shark fishermen[28] ...or it could be an Irian Jayan boat collecting trochus shells for mother-of-pearl... probably moored off the north of the island. It could be that they camped on the beach during the storm. They've probably seen the crash or at least the fire. I'm sure they'll want to check it out," I state.

Bob's face turns blank as he considers further complications. I think it's more likely the monkey's been here awhile and gone feral.

---

[28] Many such fishermen are the direct descendants of Macassar *trepangers* from Sulawesi, harvesters of *beche de mer* (sea cucumber) for centuries before the English ever got to Australia. From generation to generation, these people have retained and handed down intimate knowledge of islands along northern Australia's coast as far east as the Kimberley.

Shark fin 'fishing' is unsustainable, and Australian border patrols regularly arrest and deport them and destroy their vessels – if they can catch them. Mostly, they can't.

There's permanent water somewhere, or there'd not have been a leprosarium. It's learned to hunt birds. There are lizards, snakes, crabs, nuts, roots and maybe some old community fruit trees. The truth is, any illegal foreign fishermen seeing a crashed plane will quickly piss off to international waters before the authorities arrive and bust them. But it's given Bob something more to fret about and made me less of a worry.

"When will the police get here?" Sister Mary asks, cutting through monkey crap to the point - although the irony is that Australian quarantine authorities would be here in an instant with the army if a dirty foreign simian got loose in Arnhem Land; the response would be massive, far more robust than for crashed humans. "Mr. Korda has a broken arm. He needs a doctor. I think his eardrums are punctured. His face is burned. He can't hear. He needs a hospital."

Bob executes a few scary facial contortions and turns, glaring at the Sister. "If it wasn't for your useless white carcass ...and that dumb little bastard," he shouts, looking impressively terrifying.

Sister Mary gapes, shocked and confused, but holds his eyes, scar and all. Then she looks at me conspiratorially, as if reaching out mentally to a fellow *normal* person and seeking confirmation that it was a reasonable enough query given the circumstances. But nothing is normal.

I try to offer *nothing* in return but say, "Steady, Bob. We'll get through this. Just ...follow the protocol ...and just what is the protocol, Bob? You've set off the emergency beacon, and emergency services will be here in a few hours. Isn't that *how it is* …Bob?"

Bob takes a moment to decide how it is. His eyes narrow, mouth firms, nostrils inhaling deeply in and out, and he calms, gathering his wits. "Yeah, that's how it is, Jack …and under the protocol, I have to be in charge until the authorities get here. Now, the Sister stays here with Korda. Jack, let's see if anything's intact and see about …the body. Sue, see if you can find any bags. Does anyone's mobile work out here? Jack, what's in Mrs. Korda's bag? Here, let's empty it."

Instead of handing the Prada to Bob, I begin removing items, starting with the Journal, the water bottles, and the wine, and laying them on the ground between Bob and me. My hand is shaking when I get down to Korda's suit jacket, a laptop computer, a clear plastic medicine box, and Mrs. Korda's personal things, including her mobile phone. The ritual stone tool is last out, lightly dusted with a white powdery substance.

Only a one-kilogram slab of pressed Armani heroin - that I seem to be stealing - is left in the bag. "That's it," I say.

"Let me see the phone and yours, Jack," Bob says. "Let me see the medicine," says Sister Mary.

I hand over my phone, and Bob checks if somehow these might have a signal when his and Sue Tran's don't. Then he hands both back to me, and I start re-stuffing the bag, leaving out Mrs. Korda's personal things. The laptop, medicine box, water bottles, and wine go back into the Prada, and when I reach for the last item - Chirp's rock - Bob asks,

"What *is* that, Jack? And where'd the kid go?"

"It's a *special* rock …like a 'totem'. And I believe he's in the process of 'doing a runner'. The rock's sacred. He shouldn't have it. He'll be speared …and he appears to know it. I wouldn't worry about him. This is his country. He seems to be …thinking …sort of."

Bob knows enough about tribal ways to understand special rocks and that the penalty for what Chirp has done is dire – but it's just 'Blackfella' business.

"Why'd he take the rock, Jack?" Bob asks. But he's not interested in rocks; he's staring down at the thing, his voice conversational, his mouth quizzically pursed, his eye seemingly caught on something of interest. He touches the rock with his finger, and it comes away with some of the powder. He tastes it, and his eyes flash to mine.

"It's complicated," I say, seizing the stone and stuffing it in the bag while holding his gaze. It burrows into me like a sharp, accusing dagger.

I've learned well over years of *fatwa* that just because you're not paranoid doesn't mean that they're *not* after you. And I'm an expert at appearing normal, straight-faced sober, but I know this ex-biker is reading the bleariness, the slightly unfocussed, vacant waste-land of my eyes for what it is, I'm actually quite high - on *his* dope - and without my sunglasses, vulnerable. *Bob's onto me.*

Being caught stoned, whether by Bob, Pam, or the boss at work, triggers the same old adrenalin rush as being busted by my mother. It spoils the buzz.

I clamber to my feet, position the Prada on the ground behind me, hold the strap with my right hand, and try to look like I'm ready to heave it over my shoulder.

…Now, I'm a peaceful guy, a coward, actually. But as a young man, I didn't mind the odd blue, the occasional barroom dust-up. But I never put myself at any real risk. Mostly, I was the guy who snuck up behind and smashed a bottle over another guy's head …and ran away if he didn't go down.

I wasn't sure if I still had it, but I was reasonably certain that the ritual stone artifact would do the trick - probably the only good use it's ever had. I tense my muscles, mentally running through the exact mechanics of the next half-second, and see it perfectly in slow motion.

Suddenly, I wrest my eyes away and gaze searchingly, with exaggerated surprised concentration - past Bob at a vacant patch of sky just above the western horizon behind his right shoulder. I let my mouth gape a tick before pointing and shouting, "Look, it's a plane! …No! …it's *ATHEISTMAN!*"

At the same time, as Bob looks back over his shoulder, the Prada swings around from my side in an arc, hard and fast, and slams into the back of his head at about the instant I'm shouting '*ATHEISTMAN.*' I aim for the base of his skull.

The sacred stone inside the Prada catches him flush at the exact spot where the back of his head joins his upper spine – a wonderful, sickening *thunk*. He falls to his side, fat torso following the trajectory set by his fat head, sprawling face first over the duffel of drugs and moving no more.

Of course, the only good time to hit a big man is when he's not looking, and preferably while he's lying down. I'm mildly surprised he fell for the old *what's that? – 'one-two' punch* routine. But then, it's not the sort of behavior you expect from a sixty-year-old Ph.D. cultural anthropologist.

When the Prada swung, my focus was glued to the point on Bob's head where I figured I'd have my best chance, where I thought I'd do most damage without killing him. I know Sister Mary saw me do it when she yells, "A plane ...where? No ...stop ...Jack, what's happening?" Sue Tran, standing behind Bob, saw me do it, didn't fall for my ruse, and kept her eyes on me the whole time. She wears a perplexed expression, but for some reason, I sense she understands more - it's the lack of scared surprise in her eyes, the absence of shock. Her now hostile eyes flit to mine, to the Prada, to Bob. If she had had the time and means to stop me, she would have.

"You crazy man!" she shouts, animating herself and taking a step back out of Prada range. Sister Mary, immediately on her feet suspecting I might be just that, says shakily, "Oh no ...what's happened?"

I find a piece of thick white cotton cord next to the smaller torn duffel bag, and at the same time, on the premise that a picture's worth all the words, I grab two of the cloth-covered disc slabs and hand one to each woman saying, "Here ...calm down ...have some narcotics

…it's Bob's …he has lots today."

Removing the discs reveals a small aerial sticking out of the canvas bag that I recognize belongs to a GPS tracking unit. I fish it out, and it doesn't look like a remote area emergency beckon, and it's probably not indicting the location of stricken people needing rescue and being received by emergency services. It's transmitting the location of lost drugs that need retrieving - privately, stealthily …*with no witnesses*. I squash it the best I can under my heel, breaking off the metal aerial, but whoever's on the other end already has his fix.

The two women take what's offered on reflex, turning the discs over, feeling the taut yellow cloth, the weight, studying the Armani lettering, looking back and forth at each other, down at the duffel bags, at Bob, and then up to me standing over Bob with rope in my hands.

Sue Tran says quietly, "Here, better put it back." She tosses the disc to the ground at her feet and then stares down at it with eyes that appear to look deeper. She seems to care more about this moment than you would expect of a Chinese food caterer.

Sister Mary still has no clue, but I've got no time. I study her a moment, worried a repeat of her earlier blubbering abandon might be imminent.

When it isn't, I'm standing over Bob, realizing that although I have been tied up - by Borneo headhunters in '97, as it happens - I've never actually tied anyone else up before. He's too fat to maneuver his arms behind, and I figure out it's easier to tie the rope to one wrist, drag his arm around his back, and then wrestle the other hand into

156

position, wrapping the cord around both wrists, tightening with each loop.

The unorthodoxy of the moment moves the Sister, "I don't want to know about this. Why did you show me this stuff? I don't know anything. We just crashed in a plane. We almost died. Isn't that the main thing …getting rescued?"

In response, while I'm finishing with Bob, I manage to pant out between four laborious breaths, "Staying safe …getting rescued …yes …that's the plan."

When Bob's secure, I'm exhausted, and I sink down next to him, thinking …*what have I done*?

The probability of the linebacker-sized ex-biker knife-killer deciding unilaterally to dispose of witnesses to a sizable international drug smuggling operation is somewhat mitigated. But this scenario only plays out if those with proprietary interests get here *first* – before emergency services.

Bob could never have pulled something like this off by himself. He has associates and/or a boss. At least now, we'll be able to prepare for *their* eventual arrival without Bob's looming shadow hanging over us, unsure whether he's planning premeditated mass murder at a time of his choosing. He could easily do it with his hands. My plan is to hide, better than the others, and wait the danger away with some of Bob's dope - just a little.

If the authorities get here first, it's not likely even Bob could kill *everyone*. His plan might be to destroy the drugs at the first sign of rescue, get rescued - innocently - like the rest of us, and worry about accounting to his bosses later, or maybe disappear, or bury the treasure and come back later.

I can't believe Bob would torch all this valuable dope, especially after the really hard part - getting it into Australia. I wouldn't. No emergency services beacon has been activated from East Crocodile Island, or I'm reading this all wrong.

I try to remember our last communication with the outside world. It was when the plane got hit, just before the radio died, probably less than fifty kilometers to the south. Air Traffic Control in Darwin believes we're heading east back to GUMO Airport on one engine. We should have landed there half an hour ago. By now, they'll have figured out we didn't.

My bet is the authorities will contact Aboriginal communities first - to see if we've made an emergency landing at one of their strips - before sending out a search plane. It's likely that the search will concentrate on a one-hundred-kilometer straight line between our last radio contact and GUMO Airport and then expand out in a grid pattern. Then they'll be searching for plane wreckage. The forest undergrowth, at its thickest this time of year, will make the search painstaking …slow …might take days. When the grid pattern expands to include the coastline, a reasonable assumption will be that we've ended up in the drink; there's so much of it, and you have to play the odds.

Whoever was tracking the GPS signal knows exactly where the

158

drugs are. *How can they get here? Where are they now?* There's no way they'll chance landing a plane on this airstrip; it would be folly …maybe a helicopter.

The nearest big community airstrip is Milingimbi, an island just off the coast, fifty kilometers generally west. They may be able to rent a boat big enough to reach us, but not without someone noticing.

No one goes to Milingimbi, and no aircraft gets chartered legally in Arnhem Land without a TALC permit. That's why they needed the cover of a legitimate flight to GUMO and a willing crooked pilot like Bob, a rare treasure. Well, Bob's blown his chance.

The mouth of the Woolen River, two kilometers directly south, is the closest point on the mainland that's reachable with a four-by-four vehicle in the wet season. The track, along winding rough terrain - sometimes only wheel ruts - heads directly east to GUMO Airport. The three-hundred-kilometer drive would take maybe six to eight hours towing a boat and outboard motor in an emergency. A driver might know the way, might be someone who already has a permit, perhaps issued through his employment, someone like …my old mate, *Yousef!*

Bob's not secure enough for my comfort - just like him to wake up wanting to kick me to death - so I find the end of the duffel bag Korda's head's resting on, intending to use the cord to tie up Bob's ankles.

What if I'd missed? If Bob wasn't sure what to do with me

159

before, clubbing him in the back of the head could certainly make up his mind. Normally, there's no possible configuration of my biochemistry that could provide a stimulus strong enough to risk *missing* Bob's head and provoking a truly undesirable response from a desperate and mildly injured convicted killer - I just didn't want to give back the drugs; I'd had a taste. And I still have my kilo. Indeed, I have two hundred and nineteen more.

I've always had to consider the Second Law of Thermodynamics[29] in calculating the value of commercial quantities of *my* illegal drugs. Most of the dope I've ever had for sale was subjected to an insidious process of entropy ending with *me* proving the Second Law beyond doubt. My intention was always to sell just enough so that I could stay high for free, but almost always, I'd consume the whole lot and make no loot.

But two hundred and twenty kilos? I do the sums: at $10k per kilo easy wholesale, that's $2.2m. I do the logistics: a boat to get it to the mouth of the Woolen River and a four-by-four to get it to GUMO

---

[29] Elsewhere in the Journal, Levague refers to that *damned Second Law* in pointing out the inevitable consequences of the Universe (and everything in it) moving from a state of low entropy to high entropy. Simply stated, it means that the Universe is getting colder by losing heat. It also makes backward time travel impossible and the death of living organisms, including and especially *himself*, inescapable.

In the context of dealing drugs, it's just another example of Levague's fondness for confounding scientific nonsense. He is simply a drug addict who is a poor drug dealer. The reader should not be hoodwinked by esoteric jargon; it is just another example of the man's moral abasement.

and then Nhulunbuy, stash it until the dry season, then arrange a field trip from Darwin by road across Arnhem Land tracks, pick it up …might have to kill a few people including a nun. But afterward, I'd be rich and having martinis at the Waldorf with Pam …or maybe some shapely blond people.

The truth is, East Crocodile Island will soon be crawling with crash inspectors and cops, and even if I wanted to stash the dope here and come back later, I probably couldn't *kill* anyone. But *what if* everyone else had perished in the crash - happens all the time - and just me left alive, with millions in heroin? I'd see it as winning the lottery, the income I need until the end of days comfortably within grasp, likely the last chance ever for a fast buck.

What if only *one* other passenger had survived? Perhaps injured or near death, suffering the agony of burns, or dying of cancer – would I hurry him along to keep my treasure secret? Even if I got away with the drugs, I'd be looking over my shoulder twenty-four-seven, not knowing when Bob's associates would get me. They'd track me down soon enough, bust in my door …possibly torture Pam until I give up the drugs, force me to watch …I wonder how long she'd last. She's a savage but more used to dishing it out.

Oh, well. It's all just whimsy. My big-time drug dealing aspirations were dashed on the rocks of reality decades ago; a career in cultural anthropology was somehow my next choice. But as my musing fades, more modest, manageable possibilities don't disappear completely.

"What happens now?" asks Sister Mary.

"We just wait for the authorities. Keep an eye on Bob …just wait …maybe all night," I say.

"Bob's a dangerous man …you too," she says.

"Yes."

"Do crocodiles come out at night?"

"Maybe."

Sue Tran's face is still downcast, and there might be glistening on her cheek. "Are you okay?" I ask.

"No …not ok," she says, and there's nothing in her tone inviting any solace or comforting words from me, so I *shut the hell up*.

She starts walking towards the wreckage but first pauses, looking down at the prostrate Korda, seemingly assessing his condition. There's no sympathy in her eyes, just cold detachment, blank to his distress, uncaring - she might be back in Ling's kitchen sizing up a cut of meat. Sister Mary kneels back down quickly beside the injured man, placing gentle hands on his chest, maybe protecting him or holding down a frightened man so he doesn't run away.

Sue Tran moves off, her GUMO shirt flashing reflector strips like the bare ribcage of an orange specter. Sister Mary begins fussing over Korda, unbuttoning his shirt, inspecting burn damage, and as I too turn away – to find a good place for a private snort - Sister Mary says quietly, "I couldn't move in the plane …You saved me."

These are surely words I never thought to hear or ever wanted to…dangerous, sober words. I turn back to her, having no idea what

162

to say other than instinctual denial.

"It's not over yet …probably won't happen again."   I'm shocked and disappointed to find myself saying this without the absolute conviction I intended.

"My name's Ann," she says while pealing back Korda's shirt to reveal the extent of his neck burns. They're reasonably superficial, first and second-degree skin damage but not too deep, agonizing but not immediately life-threatening - until the infections take hold. "Sister Mary's the name I took with my vows …but my real name's Ann …Ann Quigley. I'm 'Ann' to friends and family."

"I think I'll go check on …the …Mrs. Korda," I say.

"Why *did* Chirp take a sacred rock?"

I'm walking towards Sue Tran, now fossicking about amidst still-smoldering bits of an exploded airplane, but I hesitate, considering whether and how to answer. She's just an ordinary girl …*Ann*: a nice short, no-frills name, one syllable, simple and honest, a name from my culture, a name I'd call a daughter but for the Levague propensity for swinging-dick kids. She seems to be becoming a warm, dimwitted young lady, not some delusional catholic nun …maybe not much in it, really.

"He did it …for *you* …took the rock …from the cave near Minjininga that he visited, if I'm not mistaken." Her ministration hesitates. I continue, "He thinks the rock will cure him …or change him into someone *you'd* notice, make *you* see him as a man of status, a man with ritual strength, with power over old death spirits at the hospice, an equal to the doctors and nurses, an equal to *you*. He wants you …for a *wife*. Go figure, eh? And the little bugger thinks we crashed because he stole the rock. Apparently, Mrs. Korda's spirit is trying to get into his brain."

She looks up. "He told you …*that*?" And then she goes back to work on Korda, gently fastening his shirt buttons, pausing, and then unbuttoning them again.

"Well, that's foolishness," she allows, not thinking about the plane crash or angry spirits. Her voice and eyes belie a soppy contrary view about what's foolish - perhaps the first similar thought she's had in years, maybe in her life.

"Absolutely," I say and walk away towards the plane wreckage.

Sunlight is angling from lower in the west, about the time I'd normally have a bit of a lie-down. The tropical sun sinks fast at dusk. We've only a few hours of daylight. There's no hope of rescue after dark. We're here for the night.

I approach the crash scene, and there's no plane recognizable anymore. The blackened ruin of Mrs. Korda, still strapped to her seat, lies on its side near the mangled roots of ploughed-up dead trees. Most of the length of Mrs. Korda's branch has broken off, but a meter of charred spear still pins her tight to her seat like a giant's burned cocktail weenie.

Repulsed and transfixed, I come closer and notice her clothes must have been synthetic. They've melted onto her corpse - a tarry skin of burnt plastic, blistered with blood-streaked yellow ooze as her fat liquefied and bubbled out of her body. Her hair's gone. Her nose and lips flash-fire burned to bone and teeth. A barely recognizable human form in a fetal-like position, there's nothing of a woman left. Her arms have had their endings - her fingers - completely burned off, only black ashes where her hands used to be. The wind swirls at my feet, fanning fumes rising from her body into my face, and I have to turn away.

Half a dozen yellow life preservers around the wreckage might be useful, and I collect one as well as a few more intact bottles of water. I spot a folded blue tarpaulin big enough to decently cover Mrs. Korda's body or for me to relax on after more of Bob's scag. It goes into the Prada for later.

I'm surprised to find myself nosing around for Sister Mary's, or Ann's, silver chain and crucifix, thinking I like her better without it. My shoe finds the cross but not the chain, and it goes in my pocket.

There's nothing else in sight to make me comfortable, and my eyes default to Sue Tran in her high-vis orange shirt. She's standing over a pile of ashes that might have been her bag, kicking around what looks like the burnt remains of some catering gear. She holds a large carving knife that seems to have escaped flames, inspecting it, turning it over, its clean blade glinting in the sun. She grips it with both hands, and Mrs. Korda's pink diamond ring sparkles on a finger of her right.

I'll steal candy from babies, but I don't recommend robbing

the dead. You might think it the other way - babies bite. What with dead people's relatives or business partners, you never really know who you're dealing with. Suddenly, I recall the words Sue Tran spoke in frustration earlier when her mobile phone wouldn't work. Dazed after the crash and my little snort, I paid no mind at the time. She was parroting a comment I made during the flight: *'Yeah, Bob ...I don't like your driving, Bob'*. I now realize that the utterance was exaggeratedly snide, oozing contempt *pour moi*. I should have read her cold and calculating reaction to me clobbering big Bob a few moments ago for what it belied. *She's in cahoots.*

"Find anything useful?" I ask, talking directly to the diamond on the knife-hand.

"My best knife," she says quietly, more to the knife than me. Then her head slowly turns my way, eyes wide open, radiating hate and fearlessness, locking on target. "I'll cut your stomach. You'll die slow ... You bloody Mister 'sweet and sour mud-crab'. I never cooked it fresh when you ordered."

"That's *Doctor* sweet and sour," I reply, tensing with adrenalin, ready to run or fight.

It takes a tick to catch up. "Oh, so better than me?" she spits.

"Probably," I taunt, deepening her scowl.

Never have I felt threatened by a petite fifty-year-old female caterer - I'm a reasonably large customer. And I saw her taking her chance, not primarily to avenge my attack on Bob, but to reclaim control of a situation that clearly didn't end well for *business* - and maybe, between her and me, a bit personnel - only a culinary heathen spoils the taste of steamed crab with sweet and sour. She won't stop until she kills me. There's no other *accounting* option.

Sue Tran closes the space between us, knife held forth, a weapon now advancing slowly, wanting me to anticipate pain and death, trying to induce panic. It would normally work.

But now I'm not scared. The early heroin has infiltrated my biochemistry, and it's edgy for the company of much more. And it's made me hungry-junky alert and rat-smart, a fighter who goes low for first blood.

I face her, steely calm, shaking out the Prada at my side with one hand like readying my mace. It's bulky now with all the additions, more unwieldy, but she's seen its work on Bob.

She circles now, wary but determined, trying to get the sun in my eyes. We're like gage-fighters sizing each other up. I know she'll lunge straight away, rightly judging I'm too slow for effective defensive. In the instant before she attacks, in passable Saigon slang, I shout, "Don't do it! I'll help you. I can get the drugs out."

The small woman hesitates, surprised as all Asians are when a white man speaks a bit of their lingo, and maybe interested in a deal, a bloodless way out. I drop the Prada, all disarming-like, and start explaining in English how I can arrange a boat and get a vehicle and that I know the country much better than Bob.

And she's steady in front of me, crouched low, knife-arm ready, feet apart, planted, preparing to strike. Then her knife lowers an inch, and she starts to straighten. And just as she's relaxing, I move in close, snake-fast, wind-up, and kick her hard enough between her legs to lift her onto tiptoes. It's straight out of Butch Cassidy[30], and she drops the blade, doubles over, hands to her crotch. Her face, showing more astonishment than pain, is *right there*, lined up for my fist. But I'm not fast enough, and she falls back just at the last instant, and my missed swing sends me off balance.

We dive together for the knife, and for a second, we grapple and roll around in the dirt, both getting hands on the hilt. But I'm much stronger, and as I sink my teeth into the small woman's thumb, she shrieks in pain, lets go of the knife, and my other hand comes away from her throat, clutching a silver chain.

She scrambles to her feet in an instant, backing away, shaking her stinging right hand. I clamber up with the carving knife as she turns, running fast and making for Bob and the duffels of drugs. I follow slowly, knife and Prada at the ready.

She gets to Bob, slaps his face, shouts his name, and gets no response. She tests the binding around his wrists, but the work's done well.

---

[30] The famous 1969 'Buddy' Western movie *Butch Cassidy and the Sundance Kid* features a crotch-kicking fighting event that apparently strikes Levague as an appropriate strategy for assaulting a woman. But I do not believe he is emulating a scene from a classic movie.

Rather, the maneuver reflects the natural inclination of a cowardly dirty fighter or the practiced mental defense he rehearses in recurring nightmares about his wife Pam and Mrs. Skinning.

When I'm too close, she turns to me, face contorted with hate, fear and frustration. She spits out words like venom, "Soon, you die." It's a bit rich coming from a woman who's just lost a knife fight, but I don't doubt the sentiment.

Then she takes off, running south down the airstrip along the tree line. It's a cute, girly shuffle rather than pelting away for her life.

About halfway down the runway, she pauses, shaking what might be blood droplets from a deep bite on her right hand. She looks back, sees no one following, and turns east into the trees, the bright orange fleeting in and out of forest shadow until she disappears; the shining, bouncing horizontal reflector strips, the last to vanish.

The woman *they-often-call-Sister-Mary-but-her-real-name-is-Ann* has Korda sat up, back to a duffel bag drug pillow, and he's conscious. His watery eyes - blistered red slits in a totally hairless head - look somehow obscene. They watch me hover over Bob, the wife's Prada on my shoulder now sporting bloody dirt stains, a silver chain in one hand, a carving knife in the other. There's apprehension there, or maybe that's his normal look now. The eyes go blank when the knife is stowed in the Prada. Ann's done a good job cleaning up the blood seeping from his ears.

I glance once more down the runway towards the sea, my eyes trained for orange, and then sit down next to Ann, handing her first a broken length of silver chain and then a dark wooden cross that looks smaller in my hand than hanging from her neck. A moment passes before she offers *her* hand as if she doesn't recognize the possession or its giver.

"It's broken," she says, inspecting the chain. "Can you put it away for me …in your bag?" she asks, and when *ATHEISTMAN* doesn't, adds, "It doesn't bite." I zip open the Prada for her to drop it in.

I lean back on the pile of pressed heroin discs next to Korda, exhausted, rubbing tired eyes. I make to remove Bob's hat, but it's stuck on my head with blood from my earlier gash. It stays on so the wound stays closed.

Not only have I been scrambling out of a crashed, burning plane, heaving around Chirp's sacred ritual stone, and wrestling in the dirt with a woman trying to kill me - only to have her get away and now loose on an island with her own personal *fatwa* out on me - I've missed my nap. Normally, that would make me grouchy.

Funny how the day turned out; I could be dead – *crashed*-dead, *pounded-to-pulp*-dead - had I missed Burly Bob's head, and the wiry little Vietnamese vixen could have killed me with that meat knife. Only a few short hours ago, everything was more or less *legal*, the 'less' being me. Now, just about everything's *illegal*: illegal drugs, illegal sacred artifact, illegal assaults …threats …stealing off a dead body, illegal monkey …Mrs. Korda's *illegal* death. Nothing much happens on East Crocodile Island, but when it does, it's shonky as hell.

My hand has unzipped and entered the Prada. Fingers search, testing objects until they find what I'm looking for. I work open torn cloth and plastic and break off a small chunk of pressed heroin about the size of a minty. I crush the hard-packed powder while my hand's in the bag, getting a snuffing-sized pinch between my thumb and index finger. I've been looking forward to this, but just before I transfer my finger from Prada to my nose, Bob starts moving.

His head starts turning side to side; there's a large navy-blue swelling at the base of his skull capped by a splotch of dried blood-black skin where it recently impacted with a large rock. A low moan describes the doubtless throbbing pain in the back of his head, and his eyelids blink open. He takes a moment to see what condition his condition is in.

When he sees me in the picture, he speaks softly at first, "You're a dead man, Levague." When I look at him, he adds louder, "You know that, Jack? …You better kill me, Jack," then louder still, "I'll kill you, Jack …I'm coming for your family, Jack …I'll kill your wife …your children …your …"

He's shouting now, his ire rising his blood up to the boil. He has to stop mid-threat, grimacing as head pain throbs him into silence.

"Dog?" I offer.

And then he starts up again, all calm and reasonable.

"Look, Jack, I've known you what …twenty years? We can make a deal. No one needs to get hurt. No one knows where we crashed. They'll be looking for us way to the south. We'll get this shit off the island tomorrow …and you too. You didn't have to do this?"

My finger has found my nose, and I sniff up what I consider just another little taster, not too much - I still have work to do with

Bob. He tries a different tack.

"Sister, please help me. Don't listen to Jack. He's mad. He'll get you in trouble. He'll end up killing me, you, everyone …He's tied my legs too tight …help me …please. You have to let me move my legs. They're cramping up in this position …Help me move, will you? I've got cramps in both legs …if you just untie my legs …just loosen them a bit, there'll be less cramps. Please, Sister, don't make me suffer."

Well, my heart's beating a slow, strong timpani drum, each shaking thump echoing loud in the ears, pounding blood beats coursing through my biochemistry with a good measure of glowing orgasmic opiate well-being - but '*less*' cramps?

My thoughts tinge all red and angry just as I'm peaking with my high. Why did he have to use the 'less' word?

"You want *less* cramps, Bob? How about *less* broken bones? I'll give you *less*, Bob! Here, have more *less* …"

I'm in an adrenaline rush, reacting to deep impulses that move me before I can apply a test of reasonableness - before my mental cop blows his whistle.

Suddenly, I'm standing over Bob, winding up again with the Prada; this time, his legs are in my sights. I'd been thinking of leaving him crippled anyway, reasonably impotent as an adversary in a drug war without actually murdering him, but now he needs to say 'fewer', or I'll break his ankles for spite.

Just as I'm committing, two strong hands grab my shoulders

firmly from behind, interrupting the Prada's backswing, and Ann turns me to her with fear in her eyes that steals away my resolve to break a man's legs for bad grammar.

But it's the weak, injured Mattius Korda who rasps, "Stop …Levague," and I'm not sure if he's talking to me, Ann, or gasping out a last invocation to the faithful.

Chapter 5: Castaways

The alarm in Ann's eyes fades, the fear of a man's violence pushed out by something like a glare for a man on his hops, sour eyes saying, *'Oh no, he's stoned'* in a language known to women across all cultures and usually picked up at an early age. I'm an expert linguist and know the lingo.

The Prada slips from my hand and falls harmlessly near Bob's feet. His legs pull up of their own accord to maintain distance.

Saying my last name made Korda's burned mouth move. He probably found *Levague* more painful to get out than *Stop*. His tongue scrapes across dry, raw-red lips, and he manages more, "Just destroy the heroin, Jack. Get rid of it all."

It took courage to get all that past his blistered lips. It was the drugs that killed his wife, sort of, and cold fury usually trumps pain. Destroying the contraband would be revenge, kind of.

Fresh blood seeps from Korda's ears after his effort. He grimaces in pain, finds that this hurts too much, and he groans, forcing his face back to blank. Uttering the words was no mean feat, but the skin-breaking expression of agony stretched and cracked his burned cheeks, leaving a face plastered with little red lesions like grinning clown makeup.

Ann gets back to work on Korda's head. To him, she says, "I think you're right. Better not talk. Oh, just look at your ears." He's spilled blood over his nice, clean face, and now she'll have to mop up again.

    'That's crazy talk,' thinks Jack-the-Rat. Bob stops squirming and listens to Korda's recommendations. Our eyes touch, and on this, I'm sure he's with the Rat. Bob and I don't care what the girl thinks, either. Bob's zeroed in on me, and I watch him back but say to Ann gently, thoughtfully, reasonably, "It doesn't matter."

    Ann's listening, Bob too, probably not Korda. I continue, all the while locked onto Bob. "Bob's got a partner in all this. It's not just him and Sue Tran. I think that someone at GUMO is involved …some sleazy foreign weasel named Yousef. Smuggling runs in his family, or he's no Armani[31] …probably got tired of smuggling his people out and turned to heroin - his country's next main export - smaller volume, more profit per unit …makes good business sense."

    Bob looks away, a gesture I take as confirming my account. I continue, "Ole' Yousef. He'll be here before the police or emergency services or the flying doctor …probably tomorrow. He's very interested in what's happened …*what's happening*. He might have a gun." Ann's eyes narrow at this comment and her lips are firmly pressed. Desperate men with guns is a theme Irish girls know all about. She's not old enough to have experienced much of the Troubles, but the wondrousness of religious sectarianism still potters about a modern Emerald Isle.

---

[31] This scurrilous slur against Armanistanis requires condemnation and heartfelt apologies on behalf of the Anthropological Federation…*again*. We are all aghast and disgusted. For the record, carpets and dried fruit are the main exports, and much of this is not smuggled out.

"Ann …we're in danger. Even if we burn it all up or break open all the little packages and toss the powder to the wind, we still *know …what's happening.* If Yousef gets here and there's no heroin, he'll shoot us so we don't talk to police. Probably chuck us in the mangroves for the crocs. He'll have nothing to lose. If we hide - and the drugs are still here - there's a small chance they'll just retrieve their property and not waste time looking for us, especially if we're all spread out and hiding in sand dunes. They'll have only a day or so for a get-a-way before emergency services arrive and the police get wind of all this. They'll be in a hurry."

I turn back to Bob. "Now, I've looked at *what's happening,* this way and that. We can't keep old Bob here all tied up and just wait for some psycho killer to arrive, and then we'll have two bad guys, two angry, awful men after us, maybe one with a gun. And Sue Tran, she wants me dead, probably you too." I pause and then conclude my perfectly reasonable discourse.

"Even if the police get here first, it might be days, and it's cruel to keep him like this. The most humane thing to do is un-tie him …but *look* at him; he's an overweight grizzly bear; he could kill you like swatting a fly, hug you to death if he gets hold …Best thing to do is break his legs, or at least his ankles or feet, even a few toes - just so he doesn't want to walk too far too quickly."

I've pitched this all calmly and rationally, and for a second, I think Ann's seriously mulling over the issue. Bob's probably thinking he'd do the same in my place or worse. But a thought takes shape.

Not normally found in the day-to-day conceptual arsenal, it takes a tick for the words to form in my mouth. "Let's ask Bob. He can decide …rope …or Prada …or incapacitating dose of today's contraband narcotics. Which way will we go, Bob?"

"You're the fucking *foreign weasel*, Jack …you *French junkie asshole*. It'll be the trifecta, I know it …overdose first …then the legs …and the ropes stay on. That's *what's happening*. Isn't that right, Jack?"

"I was thinking the other way round, but we can have it your way," I say evenly, my tone thick with menace, the soft words of a calm and considerate breaker-of-legs. "And …time's run out! I've decided. Let's have a big old snort of very strong Armani heroin; it's un-cut, mind - if I'm a judge. It'll be poetic, Bob - wonderful irony. We'll even use my personal stash. I just hope you don't OD. And, oh …I'm not French …I'm Canadian …you can trust me …*eh*?"

"I won't do it," he says. But it's not an option.

"Right, then," I say. "It's the legs first …or how about the crotch? I'll wager the old sacred stone in the Prada has seen more than a few willies."

"Fuck you," Bob says, and his face turns from defiance to resignation, proving the old adage about balls, hearts and minds.

"If you make him take …that *stuff*, and it's too much, you might kill him. That would be murder, Jack," Ann says, dabbing Korda's dry lips with what looks like Mrs. Korda's denim shirt from last night.

"Ann, I'm a *scientist*. We'll follow the heroin safety protocol," I reply in a sane, even tone. Ann's kind of shading into *liability* herself if she keeps nagging.

"Right! Now …Bob," I say, sitting down next to him, resting back on his white duffel bag. The slabs are packed tight; it's like leaning against bricks.

"First, let's make sure you're going to be ok by being *here* for a while. Look's all right: there's shade, no ants, crocodiles won't come this far from the water …I don't think anyway. You can nod off for a while, all nice and cozy."

I remove my lacerated discus of heroin from the Prada, turning it over, studying the Armani script and the little ink-stamped 'dragon' symbol in more detail. It looks remarkably like both the dragon on the front of Ling's lunch menu *and* the 'Rainbow Serpent' motif on the front of Chirp's TALC T-shirt. It's a *Chinese* dragon with no wings.

I break a reasonable nugget off, surprised at how hard the powder's pressed together, like rock candy. The chunk takes the pressure of both hands rubbing together hard and crumbles into two or three grams of powder, enough to kill an elephant but not one who's a regular user.

"You look like a beer drinker, Bob. You don't …partake of the poppy, do you? Maybe in the old biker days, eh? …You're carrying too much weight, Bob. You need to take better care of yourself," says the smoker to the fat man.

There are two 'pinch-of-heroin' measures: one, a pinch

between the tip of the forefinger and the tip of the thumb; the other, between the *flat* of the finger and thumb. A 'light' pinch of the former is about one hundred milligrams and will get you nicely high; a 'heavy' pinch of the latter is about five hundred milligrams and will easily kill a man Bob's size.

"Me first," and with that, I transfer a *very* light fingertip pinch to my nostrils and snort, not loudly so as to make a big production and get the girl all fretting again. I take it way-in though, evaluating its strength and purity – a man's life could depend on my judgment - but I give up after a second, and I allow myself to be mentally carried away from this ridiculous situation as all my aches and my cranky-old muscle joints, all deep with fatigue, are washed clean of malcontent. It probably takes too long.

"I'd be having my wits about me, I think," Ann mutters to herself, presumably.

But my wits do roust, and now there's a thick finger-tip pinch under Bob's nose. "I'll count to three, Bob, and you take a snort. Make it a hard sharp sniff, with both nostrils, mind. It'll sting, but you have to be brave and snort it all back without sneezing, like the old trooper I know you are. If it doesn't work, we'll keep trying. But we don't want to try too many times …I'm worried about a heart attack."

Bob makes a good fist of it, not his first by a long shot. He snorted like a pro, though a bit rusty like me. I watch as the drugs take effect. He's still on his side and facing me. There are no convulsions, no cardiac arrest, no bleeding nose or frothing mouth. But it's the eyes

179

that confirm the dose: all glassy, pupils at pin-points, eyelids at half-mast.

"How's that, Bob? Good gear, I'll tell ya," I say. Unfortunately, Bob is still able to speak.

"You know, I always figured you for a druggie, Jack," he slurs, chewing the words, jowls barely moving. "All those times we flew around the desert. I always thought you smoked a joint before getting on the plane ...or took something. That hippy ponytail, all that slinking around the Outback, you always seemed on edge, Jack, always looking around behind ...And then sometimes I'd watch you talking to the old men, listening to the songs, writing in your book. But when you danced with them, stripped down naked and all ochred up ...well, I reckoned, 'This bloke's high as a kite.' I was right, wasn't I?" *Yes.*

"Sue and I have a half-share between us," Bob whispers, thick but clear enough. "Everything we've both got is tied up in this deal. We don't have another way to get it to Darwin. We'll have to take it all back to GUMO or Nhulunbuy and stash it until I can arrange another charter or the tracks dry out. Then, we could use four-by-fours. You could help us get permits. You know the tracks, the people. You don't have to do anything, no handling, no distribution, no work ...and you can have half a million bucks."

His eyes start fluttering madly, seemingly alarmed at the strength needed to stay open. Slouching down on the large duffel bag on my side like Bob - except my hands aren't tied behind my back - I respond, "What about the Sister here and the mining boss? What's their cut?" I pause, then say, "You know Bob, I don't think I've got strength left today to break anyone's legs, yours especially. I'd have to wield the Prada more than I care to now, just to be sure of your ankles. It might take me an hour of pounding away on those thick legs of yours."

Bob's face relaxes more - if that's possible; he's barely conscious but still able to make sense. "So, what do you reckon? By the way, keep the hat." The words are slow, his tongue lolling about, kind of just loitering in his mouth. He closes his eyes, and I watch him, more curious than concerned. But there's one more thing on my mind before Bob's completely gone.

"Bob, why did you bring all this dope to GUMO? I mean, why bring it ashore so far from civilization?"

"No one was looking," he mutters, still apparently with us. It takes a few minutes of Bob-watching to feel he's safely passed out, but he surprises me. "I broke my leg riding my bike when I was a kid. A car hit me. Hurt like hell," he says low, barely a whisper, swallowing dry and hard, throat muscles working like a grotesquely fat worm. He frowns slightly, then his face settles peacefully, his breathing slows, and he's winking, blinking and nodding off so far away he might as well be unconscious.

"That's fascinating, Bob ...which one?" I ask, adding, "It might be easy to break it again," hoping it's the last thing he registers.

With the GPS locator signal sent before I stomped it to death, Yousef now undoubtedly knows that his shipment has gone astray, but no one's going to drive from GUMO tonight; he'll come at first light tomorrow. I figure Bob will be fine for a while. Sue Tran will be sneaking about, probably now wise to her orange high-vis problem and waiting for darkness. She'll be thinking of freeing Bob as soon as the Prada and *my* carving knife are gone.

Truth is, Bob's not coming after me for a *long* while. And even when he's …better, he won't leave the stash, not if he thinks some thieving Indonesian fishermen - the owners of the rouge *macaque* - are in the vicinity and curious about the plunder potential of a crashed plane. I wasn't sure about the unhinged Vietnamese caterer, but I thought she'd also stay close to the dope and Bob until he's back on his feet, to which I really should apply the Prada.

There's nothing to be gained by staying at this plane crash scene; the spot's seen enough violence for a day. I've got enough energy to walk half the length of the runway and follow the old pathway down to the beach, maybe build a fire, spread out the blue tarp, drink the wine, light up a smoke, and snort some more scag. So, I turn to Ann, stating, "I don't think we should stay together. I'm afraid it's every man for himself now. You'll have to make the best of it. But I wouldn't stay here. Might be best that you hide in the sand dunes near the beach. Bob will be harmless for five or six hours at least. Depending on how long it takes to rescue us - and that could be a day or even two - we aren't safe. These people are hard-core villains.

I can't really see how they'd want to leave anyone to talk to the police. When Bob's associate gets here, probably tomorrow, the best thing they can do with the heroin is stash it somewhere until they get another chance to move it. Maybe they'll try another charter, maybe wait until the dry season and drive it out, maybe hire a yacht in Darwin and go for a sail in the beautiful tropical waters of the Ara-*bloody*-fura Sea. There won't be another chance if *we* tell the police. The best outcomes for *them*: Yousef picks up the heroin and secures it back at GUMO until the coast's clear, and Bob and Sue are the only survivors of a terrible plane crash when the authorities get here. You need to find a hiding place and lay low until the police come."

Ann's looking at me with those big brown Dumbo eyes: fearful, ready again to abandon herself for tears. The poor woman's really out of her depth with the drugs, but maybe not with *desperation*. After her earlier sobbing, she's held herself reasonably together. Tending to Korda has given her purpose after misplacing Chirp, but she needs to worry about herself. She rallies and sets her face firm.

"I should get some salt water on Mr. Korda's burns," she says evenly. "He might be more comfortable lying on the sand. Can you at least help us get to the beach?"

I'm scooping heroin discs out of the smaller split duffel bag, transferring about half to the Prada, sculpting a plan out of uncertain circumstances, but pause. "Yes, but I'm taking this heroin as evidence, and enough to bury in the sand as a bargaining chip, in case we have to …bargain. You'll have to give *me* a hand as well." It's

183

intended as a statement of Levague *drug policy* and includes the criterion that has to be met before I'll help a nun with a dying man.

I spare Bob a final glance. Suddenly, a fluffy pink feather – possibly plucked recently from an unlucky galah by a monkey - floats close in on the breeze and catches in Bob's short grey hair. It nestles for a second near the swollen black bump on his head before another puff of wind swirls it away. Bob is breathing deeply and steadily, and his eyes dart about behind closed lids, having adventures elsewhere. He's a bit lucky not to be dead from an overdose.

The rope cords tied around Bob's wrists and ankles are redundant and potentially useful to me, so off they come, freeing the big man. I shiver again at the thought of Bob stalking around when he regains mobility, and although most of the island is sandy - easy on bare soles - I remove his shoes and throw them thirty meters behind the tangled wall of dead trees that spiked the Lorina.

Ann struggles to get Korda onto his feet. When he's up, she fashions a crude but effective sling with his dead wife's long-sleeve shirt. He's fit enough to walk and talk. "I have to see to my wife's body ...I can't hear."

I'm able to stuff four slabs of pressed heroin along the sides of Korda's broken arm in the sling. The elbow's swollen up badly. The drugs make a snug fit. A little moan escapes when I wedge in the last disc hard. Ann has the damaged smaller duffel bag, still with six or so kilos of smack, as well as four small water bottles, Korda's jacket, medicine box, a few un-inflated life preservers, and the blue tarp, and

I insist she carries the wine.

I've squashed ten heroin slabs into the Prada after removing everything except the Journal, two useless mobile phones, my hard-won carving knife, Korda's laptop, and Chirp's sacred kidney-shaped stone artifact. Ditching the rock would lighten the load. But not so close to Bob ...*what goes around.* And swung in the Prada, it's a tried and trusty assault weapon. I'll manage the load.

We set off and walk fifty meters to the crash site. There are several sizable chunks of blackened debris: the starboard engine still molded into a meter of scorched wing, the tail section with its bits of chemical toilet, and still recognizable seats with the fabric burned off.

When we're close enough for Korda to see his wife, she's the only piece of wreckage attracting flies. His eyes narrow to red weeping slits. "I'm sorry, Julie ...I'll be with you soon." Fortunately, the pain of speaking stills any inclination to say more or further unburden his grief with a round of skin-splitting, broken-heart facial contortions and wailing. He's seen his wife ...and his future. Time to move on.

"It's awful to leave a ...her like that, all gruesome and ...uncovered," says Ann after a moment's reflection. I agree, but the tarp stays in the Prada. "She doesn't mind," I reply.

We walk away from the crash scene, heading south down the cleared airstrip corridor cut so squarely out of the wilderness decades ago. I keep my eye on the tree line to my right, thinking maybe Sue Tran's gone topless to easier sneak about unseen, and certain she's watching our progress - the lady killer - sleek, silent in shadow, deadly in skintight black jeans and black lace-fringed bra. During fifteen years under the *fatwa,* my imagination often conjured phantom lady assassins: lithe, scantily clad fem-fatales, hiding grim purpose behind pink silk veils and ambiguous baby-blue eyes. They were mostly fair-skinned and too blond for Iranian chicks, dressed more for the harem than blood-letting. They were the sweetest of nightmares, but none of the girls was a match for a Shoshone Indian princess, and my dreamtime musings invariably ended with a dripping-red Mrs. Skinning and the poor girls' filleted livers sliding around in pools of blood on the floor.

As we trudge slowly along in the late afternoon sun, it occurs to me that up until Bob regained consciousness after his early unfortunate encounter with the Prada, and even after my scramble in the dirt for the knife with Sue Tran, Ann had no *objective* evidence that *I* hadn't organized this whole smuggling business. And apparently, no thought that the drugs might really be *mine* all along and that I was acting out my innocence and setting up dominos for Bob and Sue Tran to take the fall. Even after I revealed my shady side: the violence of a ritual stone, the cool menace of *ATHEISTMAN,* and the self-interest of Jack-the-Rat, Ann still sees staying with me as preferable to perhaps a more rational plan to hide somewhere by herself, as far away possible from the likely target of deadly wrath - *me.* Even to save her life, she seems rather to need and trust the oldest man, the one with a long white beard.

And I must say, it wasn't an anguished gasped entreaty from Korda that stayed the Prada from crippling the fat man's legs; make no mistake - diminishing his mobility *was* the right thing to do, the smart thing. Call it drug-induced inability to seize the moment or a failure of nerve - it was none of these. In that split second, a truly old-school Levague didn't like the idea of a nun witnessing me at this dirty work, especially if she survived to blab. But now, I'm tempted to go back and finish off Bob, but I don't. And I shudder for a moment, feeling an icicle slide down the spine of the fool who perishes from untaken opportunity.

Korda moves slowly, and by the time we walk one hundred meters along the runway to where the plane first slammed down, we all need a rest. So we pause at the exact spot where our lives ...*my life*, could so easily have ended.

Looking back, I see Bob's prostrated form is still sprawled motionless on the pile of white duffel bags, and there's no sign of Sue Tran, orange or otherwise. I scan the wreckage and follow the deep, straight groove plowed out by a crashing plane backward to the depression at my feet. It's been a dangerous day, and not over yet. The lightning strike was an act of God, and you can't prepare for those; they're less scary for being beyond control. The danger now is calculated, premeditated – the danger of desperate men. As much as I'd like to do *nothing* except enjoy more scag, all the wine, and my last smoke, I need to prepare for manmade menace, more predictable than an act of God and all the more troublesome for it.

187

And now, the baggage of these extra people: a girl with limited cerebral apparatus in an easily spotted white uniform, a pitifully injured recent widower wallowing in the sorrow of his appalling situation, and the love-sick superstitious kid, currently being harried by ghosts, guilt-riddled at breaking his clan's ancient sacred-stone taboos and at-large somewhere on this goddamned desert island …It's just not part of the Levague plan for survival. The plan is about *me* and keeping a very low profile, nimble and unencumbered in case I have to run.

These people are not assets, can't be used as weapons, and are of no help getting off this accursed island. We started with seven; one got killed, and now six stranded castaways are here on East Crocodile Isle. Destitution on a desert island; there's nothing funny here.

But while the nun and the injured man are expendable - in the greater scheme of things - a bond of sorts has formed: the togetherness of those who suffer common strife and deadly struggle. It might be strong in their minds, reinforced by the intensity of the shared impending threat. I'll be in the fellowship …for now. It'll be broken soon enough when it comes down to them or me - *cometh the hour, cometh the Rat.*

We struggle down the airstrip for half a kilometer and find the track that leads to the old leper Community and follow this generally northeast until the outlying remains of several old buildings come into view. When we can just hear the waves breaking on the main beach, we leave the track and head directly east into patchy tree shadows. Breaking waves can be heard as slow crashing echoes through the trees, louder as we approach the sea until we emerge onto dusky foreshore dunes. After several hundred hard meters, the open sea comes into view, a flat, uniform grey in the twilight of a setting sun. From here, the ocean swell rises, folds and spills onto the shore, leaving white foam along hundreds of meters of crescent beach to the south.

Teams of gulls strut along the edge of breaking surf, stickybeaks checking for easy washed-up pickings, shrieking and squabbling over each tidbit. A loan sea eagle banks high in the early evening sky, spying alone, silent on the wind, searching out unwary prey.

It's taken a dozen rest breaks to get twenty kilograms of heroin and the injured Korda this far. Along the way, we shared one of the small water bottles and now have one left each. We might find fresh water along the creek that runs west of the derelict community. If not, we won't be the first to die of thirst in Australia.

Finally, we shuffle through fifty meters of dunes, each one edged with long, sharp grass. Between the high sand dunes are smooth concave blowouts and swales several meters deep, offering respite from the ceaseless onshore breeze and shelter from hostile view unless random eyes - lucky or careless - stumble upon us unexpectedly.

The going's tough in soft sand, but we press through, arriving at the beach about the same time as the sun sets on the other side of the island. The western horizon behind us is all aglow with layered sky-slashing purple-reds. Bob's got a better view, and it's possible, but not likely, that he's conscious and able to marvel at the splendid celestial event.

We're at the northern end of the main beach, and the derelict remains of the historic leper community are on higher ground immediately to the west. The full dark foliage of the Morton Bay Fig soars higher than any of the old buildings and marks the heart of the village.

The beach ahead ends in a tidal estuary that edges the community on the north. It's cut off from the sea at low tide, leaving wet silt mudflats extending down to breaking waves lower on the shoreline. Beyond the narrow, muddy mouth of the estuary, another beach starts up on the northern side.

We walk down to the wet sand and head north along the beach. The most energetic waves reach up far enough to wash our footprints away. A stupid tracker could think we'd walked into the sea and disappeared. A smarter one would see us heading north along the waterline, intending to turn up the beach and make for the derelict buildings, someplace out of the wind, maybe an old community building still with structural integrity to be defensible. We'll do neither.

Walking Korda along is easier on hard, wet sand, and we make quick progress. We pause once, and Ann uses her headscarf to bathe Korda's face and neck with salt water. A large safety pin, apparently critical to keeping the blue scarf in place on her head, is now attached to her uniform lapel next to a red stitched crucifix. Her uncovered short hair stirs and lifts in the sea breeze. In dull twilight, her face seems smaller, darkness scaling back those chubby cheeks, lessening their impact and making her prettier for it. But maybe it's just the night and the drugs when everything's a bit shady and uncertain.

As darkness grows, a half-moon materializes and early stars stud a cloudless blue-black sky. We arrive at the far north end of the beach that edges the mouth of the estuary, still isolated from the sea by low tide and basically, a brackish black tidal pool swamp. The sand ends in moon-glistening mudflats which extend for a hundred meters across the mouth of the estuary to the next beach to the north. Here, the sea is relatively calm and the distant sound of waves breaking over reefs to the east can be heard on the breeze.

On the margins of the estuary, mangrove thickets extend inland, eventually giving way to occasional river gums at the point where the principal creek drains into the estuary on the far side of the old community. The eucalypts queue up and follow the creek line inland to the island's main landscape features: large granite boulders around the base of a prominent smooth-flanked ironstone hill capping the center of the island and casting a round black silhouette against the low twilight-purple horizon.

All the old buildings are on the southern side of the creek and estuary, and it makes sense to have a community next to significant drainage at the point where it spills into the ocean. The creek's a source of fresh water, and the tidal swamp and foreshore mudflats and sand can be dredged for landing shallow-draft ocean barges; you'd probably have to cull out the crocs from time to time. The ruined concrete and stone walls are pale-white against the dying light, some in regular configuration and others at odd angles, all half-covered by banked-up windswept sand and needing a fair measure of imagination to see as having once been purposeful constructions.

The ruins are on high ground just beyond the foreshore dunes immediately to our left. A straight pathway, cobbled with smooth dark river stones, runs between two of the larger buildings and cuts through dunes down to the beach almost to our feet.

"I don't think we should camp anywhere up there," I say, indicating the old buildings. "It's where they'll expect us to be when emergency services arrive - but also Bob and co. They'll follow our footprints in the sand. No one is coming tonight, but we can't risk it."

The tide was low when we first stumbled onto the beach. Now, waves reach a bit higher up the mudflats. Soon, as the tide rises, the ocean will swell sufficiently to assimilate the isolated tidal swamp and push up into the creek to the point where mangroves stop, and the line of river gums starts. It's prime crocodile habitat, likely home to at least one monster-sized alpha reptile. At this time of year, the beast might be nesting if it's a female, maybe four or five meters in length and weighing up to a thousand kilos. If so, it's likely to be well ensconced further up the tidal pool guarding a patch of creek bank on higher ground above the water line where up to fifty ready-to-hatch eggs are all warm and cozy in a mound constructed of mud, grasses and leafy litter. If it's a male, it'll be much bigger, about six or seven meters, and fifteen hundred kilos of monster.

It would be ill-advised to go *there* now. It is not likely we'll encounter crocs where we *are* going, or Bob; asked which I'd prefer, unless he's packing a flame-thrower, the cute tiny-teddy drug smuggler any day.

Lower down the beach, below the waves lapping up the estuarine mudflats, the sea ripples gently over a semi-submerged sand bank, forming an arc from this beach to the next. I draw Ann's eyes down the flat, muddy shore and trace with my hand where I'm certain the shallow sandbank connects to the beach on the other side.

"If we can walk across …about like that, we can reach the next beach and camp in the sand dunes on *that* side. It'll be too deep to wade across when the tide comes in. No one is going to follow us or see where we went. Don't worry about crocodiles right now."

"Why not?" she asks reasonably.

"No time," I say, planning wine, tobacco and smack.

I leave the girl and Korda and walk about twenty meters to the base of the stone pathway up to the community, turn, and walk backward, scuffing my feet in the sand as I go. When I've returned, to an unpracticed eye, it might look like three people walked one way up to the broken old buildings.

"Right, let's get wet. Keep your shoes on so we don't step on any poisonous fish, jellyfish, octopus, or God knows what slimy horror. And keep together in an Indian file. We'll go slow …piece of cake."

Getting a hundred meters to the next beach takes half an hour. Halfway across, in moonlight, we have to feel for the sandbank with our feet, shuffling in black knee-high water, deeper with every step, unsure legs feeling the pull as the tide comes in. I thought once or twice we might lose Korda but we manage to keep all the narcotics dry.

Finally, we arrive on the southern end of the next beach and collapse in the first deep sand dune blowout on the foreshore. It forms a wide saucer-shaped depression rimmed with long, whip-thin dune grass that catches the breeze, stilling the air where we intend to spend the evening. The blowout's deep enough to conceal three standing bodies. The fanning grasses set occasional rustling whispers on the breeze and a chorus of nearby bugs swells a growing humming undertone to the early night.

I've walked with a dying man, lugging a Prada bag full of hard drugs, and arrived at a place where I'll stay the night. I'm uncomfortable as hell right now but with good prospects of a painless evening's repose until the madness of tomorrow arrives with first light.

It's been a long, stressful day, another ahead. But now I have no more miles to go, no promises to keep - except perhaps, an implied promise, as husbands make to wives, the promise to come home. I'm sure Pam's moved on from annoyance at my lateness (stopped off for tobacco and/or liquor store), through anger at my not calling (flight postponed, got drunk), through breathless creeping fear as the phone rings confirming a missing plane and husband. By now, the grieving widow's checking the insurance policy, making sure her tears don't smudge the fine print, and looking for my will.

"Where do you think Chirp is? Should we be calling for him?" Ann asks, fishing out little water bottles and wine from the bottom of her duffel bag. The tarp comes out next, and I spread it at the lowest point in the swale, wide enough for all to lie on.

"He's gone to higher ground. He's safe tonight …and probably thinking about you." One of these, I was pretty sure about, and Ann falls silent. He's probably caught a lizard to eat, cooked or raw, and thinking thoughts best filed under *Shit*.

The thought occurs that Ann likes her tucker and might miss a regular meal or two. But tonight, all we're serving is drugs: a fine entrée, main and dessert for me, and I dare say Korda, but nothing a young hefty lass can take hungry teeth to. She might have to follow the monkey tomorrow and see what it eats.

The sick, injured Korda takes a bit of jockeying with his sling, but he's soon on his left side with his jacket as a pillow and stretched out in a position that least exposes him to the pain of his injuries. The nun empties one-kilo slabs of heroin out of the torn duffel and hands me life preservers.

I manage to fish them out of their plastic covers and inflate them by pulling the cords. One goes under Korda's head, and his coat

195

becomes a blanket. He moans with the fussing; the burning on his face seems to glow red in the moonlight with its own heat, looking like agony.

Ann is speaking nonsense and apparently to no one. "He *talked* to me …and his disability, you know, it's not so bad. Sometimes I catch him *looking* at me, and he seems calm …and then he gets kind of embarrassed and shy, and he always looks down, and then he's *gone* again." She has the presence of mind to pass me water and start checking Korda's plastic pillbox.

I roll the last of my tobacco, light up, and Ann's got three different pills in her hand. I smoke and savor the nicotine rush. It might be one of the best cigarettes I've ever had, top five.

"The capsule is an antibiotic, I think, but I'm not sure about the two tablets," she says, catching the glow from my lighter. Mr. Korda, can you hear? What pills do you need to take?" She shouts in his face and gets his attention.

"My face is burning up. My arm's broken. I can't hear," Korda rasps out, mouth dry, words barely stirring vibrations in the dark, still air. He seems to be responding to different questions and pointing out the challenges that a conversation might pose for the other party. But he sees Ann's intent and can prop his head and take the medication with sips of water.

"These don't help with pain," he says painfully, weakly, lamentably. "I had the last of my morphine before we took off."

I empty the Prada and I've got the small laptop out. It's got power. The screensaver lights up. A photo of Korda and his wife in front of the El Alamein fountain in Sydney casts enough light to see that the keyboard is covered in heroin, strong morphine indeed.

So is everything in the Prada; the ritual stone has ground away at the broken disc of pressed powder, leaving only half a disc, like the moon tonight. The stone, the wooden crucifix, the pile of heroin slabs - everything is coated white.

When I tip the empty bag upside down, about half a kilo of fine white powder spills onto the tarp in the space between me and Korda. We could bake half a dozen cakes if it was sugar, four or five cups when I scope it all together, enough for all our reasonable morphine needs tonight.

Korda is aware of the huge mountain of heroin; his blistered, raw face shows intent, resolve, or resignation; it's hard to say which. He struggles to muster some words. "Might help …what do you think, Jack?"

"It's pure, very strong. Your face is burned to shit. It'll hurt your nose to snort, and more if you haven't done it before. I don't think snorting will work. I can use some of the antibody capsules, empty a few out, and repack with …effective painkilling medicine at wholesale prices. And wait, there's more. If you're not completely satisfied …and then I stall, talking to a deaf man, unable to find a sufficiently witty or profound punch-line to amuse myself.

I go about my pharmacological task with half a dozen antibody caps. They're reasonably large, like .22 caliber bullets. But I haven't a clue how much he'll need; oral ingestion delivers no rush – one or two to kill his pain, more to kill his anguish, this latter measure likely equating to a fatal dose.

Korda decides to try two caps after Ann recommends one. I take another light pinch in the nose and lay back, an inflated life preserver for a pillow. A few draws on my smoke, and I'm drifting nicely as the drugs kick in. I've got the measure of this batch of uncut smack and know if I took just another light fingertip snort, I'd be as stoned as I've ever been on opiates and remained conscious. My natural inclination is to go for it, and I'm about to as the laptop goes into power-save mode and the 'Happy Couple' screensaver blinks off.

I check reality first. The half-moon is high in the sky, and the brilliant galactic wheel of the Milky Way paints a swath of twinkling lights, bright heavenly glitter as if God sneezed out a great snort of his infinite crystalline stash, unfailingly awesome, the majestic sweep of the Universe, of Forever …*blah, blah, blah!* Of course, the shining star clusters, vast glowing nebulae, and interstellar gas clouds are mostly in a small rural portion of only one galaxy. Our sand dune is a mere Hicksville along the lonely lanes of the Milky Way's Cygnus spiral arm but I'm too high to think of myself as anything other than the star of the show.

As always in the Southern Hemisphere, my eye seeks the greatest of the constellations: Orion, the bright giant star Rigel marking his right leg. The Hunter - with shield and club or bow and arrow - is a favorite of all cultures, spawning mythologies in ancient

Greece, early civilizations far and wide, and half a dozen indigenous cultures in Australia alone. Amazingly, many are associated with the myth of the Seven Sisters.

I learned smatterings of Aboriginal Seven Sisters mythology from Dolly Kunmubilpilguru, Jacob's senile mother. The bent old buzzard's still hanging on in Minjininga and never shuts up.

The local version of the legend focuses on the local landscape. The mythological Dreaming Sisters traveled across a flat earth, *dancing up* blank, featureless terrain into hills and valleys and bringing forth rivers and forests, forming the landscape with their 'Dance of Creation'. The islands along the Arnhem Land coast emerged when the Sisters vomited the Arafura Sea into existence after eating too many honey-ants, as you might. The mythological story ends with the Sisters' ravishment and death, both at the hands of the Hunter. Then they're transformed into the stars of the Pleiades constellation, east of Orion in the low night sky: the Seven Sisters of the Pleiades, always within the sights of Orion's arrow and ardor and pursued forever by their psycho heavenly suitor across the immensity of space.

It's exactly the same story as the heroic Greek tale but told around Arnhem Land campfires millennia earlier …if you believe Jacob's mum. I can't find any way that the ancient Greek version could have polluted the Australian story (or *vice versa*). But it's too much coincidence for my liking, and I've always smelt an early Arnhem Land missionary rat with a penchant for the classics.

I like Orion, not because of any ridiculously Freudian myth but

199

because Betelgeuse is his left shoulder: my red, super-giant star favorite, burning so hot, it twinkles red to the naked eye. It'll burn up any day. It might already have gone supernova hundreds of years ago. I hope so. Maybe it's not there anymore, and I'd dearly like to look up before I die and see her blow.

I finish and lament my last smoke for a while just as the screen saver lights up again on the little laptop. Korda's managed to sit up and use his left hand on the keyboard to produce a video image.

It's a man being *crucified*, and for a horrible second, I think Korda's going to pray for his wife or his own sorry ass with inspiration from a computer. But he pushes a button, and it's the black and white movie of the book by Nevil Shute, *A Town Like Alice*, and it's poor Joe Harman, the main male protagonist, being nailed up on a Banyon tree by Japanese soldiers for helping Jean Paget and the rest of the English women, all stranded in World War Two Japanese occupied Malaysia. I know the flick. The ruthless Captain Takata crucifies Joe for some insult; Jean thinks he dies, but he doesn't; they reunite after the war in *a town like Alice* - as if Alice Springs is romantic, a place to fall in love, symbolic of someplace or thing other than a dusty, drunken oasis for cattle ranchers, destitute Aborigines, those with no sense to be anywhere else and, of course, at least one desperate, hunted cultural anthropologist.

It's not a favorite movie, but as a reluctant inmate of Alice Springs for fifteen years, give or take, I felt obliged to read the book and see the flick. I could never marry up the love Joe Harman felt for this town with emotions that could be felt by anyone who wasn't an idiot.

The performances are wooden, and let's be frank, the British characters start grating early, many deserving their plight at the hands of the Japs to my mind. But it's the very end of the movie that redeems it for me. Jean and Joe have found each other after the war, and it's the moment of their reuniting. Jean waits all aflutter as Joe walks up to her at the airport after getting off a flight from London. When she speaks his name, it's the last dialogue. She says, '*Joe ...Oh Joe.*'

I forget about it being his name or anyone's; I don't hear just words in a language. What I hear is a beautiful young woman aching for love after war. I hear her make a sound with her mouth, with joy melting her heart, and the mere words kissing and caressing the air with her lips, '*Joe ...Oh Joe*'. I named my first son *Joseph*, not after an Aussie bloke who gets crucified or some fictional, new-testament cuckold stepfather of Jesus Christ[32], but because I wanted a son to have a chance in life for a woman to make *that sound* to him.

Here in the swale of a sand dune, the evil Japanese officer is

---

[32] A favorite blasphemy that unfortunately seems to delight Levague concerns the *Virgin Birth*. The following Journal entry exemplifies: *Boy meets girl, girl screws a different boy, baby born and worshipped as God by over a billion people?*

Perfidious wife or bulk gullible twits? I say both.

I'd have checked down there to make sure all her virgin bits were still intact as soon as she started showing.

scolding Jean and the English women for stealing food or some such crime, and Captain Takata growls, *'You very bad people. You do bad thing'*. Then, it's Matius Korda speaking low and seemingly with little difficulty, "Julie brought this movie for the trip. She was going to finish it on the plane home. It's *A Town Like Alice*. It's about Alice Springs." He says 'Awlis' *twice* …very irritating, and continues, "It's some sort of classic. She never liked Australia. I suppose it's a place you either *really* love or *really* hate. A woman gets a sense of a place …more than a man."

I watch him in case he overdoses, and the heroin takes his brain so completely it forgets to breathe, not that there's anything I'm likely to do. He's had nothing to eat all day, and the drugs come on quickly. The molecules are a close enough match to the morphine he's been taking, and he seems to like it. He stills, taking an introspective moment. His eyes stay open but vacant, perhaps looking backward into memory inventory rather than out on an empty real world. His breathing's slow and deep and unlabored. But if it weren't for that fact, he'd look dead and wearing a Mona Lisa smile to meet the devil.

Suddenly, his eyes widen, and he clears his chest with a few hoarse coughs. Then he leans further over on his left side toward me and starts dry-retching, heaving his guts in great convulsions, trying to puke into the space containing my face. I note all this with the detached interest of extreme distance, perhaps a little scientific curiosity, but with absolute certainty that it's nothing much I care about right now.

Korda retches on until some involuntary reflex convinces itself there's nothing substantial in his stomach to throw up. He settles himself a moment and then knocks back another four capsules of heroin with sips of water. He manages all by himself, one-handed, eyes wide open. If he'd taken this dose intravenously or nasally, he'd be a dead man now. They'll sneak up soon enough, and his intention seems clear: he'll endure pain no more, not ever. I wonder casually what a man says after committing an act of suicide, but it's unlikely either of us is listening if he speaks. *Better not let the nun catch him.*

On the other side of Korda, I see Ann's head tip back, a bottle attached to her mouth. She's asserted proprietary interest in the wine and shows little inclination to share. But I'm passed any interest in cheap plonk; my biochemistry's gone all posh.

She breaks the peace, "'*We're all God's children regardless of our superstitions. To find Him, all you have to do is open your heart*' …I told him that," says Ann, taking another long quaff. Maybe I should have opened *my* heart …and *my* mind," she continues, voice quavering. Another round of tears and 'Oh, no …what's happening,' seemingly even money.

Meanwhile …Jean is pleading with a Malaysian village headman for help. The English women have marched from village to village for weeks, the sick and old dying along the road, with nowhere to go, nowhere to stay, and no end in sight. Hito, their Japanese guard, has died of fever. Jean explains to the local village headman that they will *all* die, and she pleads with him to let the women stay in the village. But the old fart seems reluctant. *'It is written that the Angel said everyone who lives will die,'* says the headman. Jean counters, *'Is it not also written that if you be kind to women, God is well acquainted with what you do?'* A bit flabbergasted, the old fellow asks, 'Where is *that* written?'

Ann interrupts the negotiations, slurring with drunken resolve, "I'll have to find him in the morning …when the sun comes up …before Bob or that …Yousef." She tosses back the last of her wine: a toast to a new day, a plan for the future. She drank quickly, on an empty stomach, the only way.

Korda rallies. Apparently, more needs to be said …right now. I was hoping the drugs would fool him into thinking he was dumb - as well as, or rather than, deaf - as if his inability to hear himself talk meant he was unable to speak, so why bother? I'm sure he'll make it brief, keep it profound and reflective, as befitting the solemnity of what should really be a silent moment. It's hard work staying with real events when Jean's in dire straits and a snow-dusted mountain of smack lies waiting to scale.

"She didn't want to just watch me get weak and die," he says, still disappointingly lively and surprisingly lucid.

"She wanted me to fight on. She said if I didn't *try* to live, she wouldn't stay and just watch me die. She was going to leave me. She said she couldn't last …didn't want to last."

"So, I let her make plane and hotel bookings: Manila, Mexico City, Bangkok, the Vatican. Every miracle surgeon and faith healer,

204

every way-out treatment ...I didn't want these straws to clutch, to spend my last months in a desperate, exhausting, humiliating ...useless sprint ...it's all fantasy ...but she wouldn't have it. She wanted me to be like ...like ..."

I've followed this. Hoping it might end the conversation with a deaf man and bring closure, I'm able to breathe out, "Steve McQueen."

"Yul Brenner, the bald guy," he says.

That's it for me. I tune out. I allow my senses their own reign, and they start crossing over, melding with each other, and coalescing into pure *feeling*. My biochemistry becomes a uniform fuzzy hum - seeing, hearing, smelling and feeling as a single sense, a unified field.

The space around me, the people close by, and the stars overhead all start vibrating and glowing, and the blood in my ears echoes a uniform background rhythm for a heavenly light show. Irregular lines blur solid shapes, things and people become insubstantial, energy captured in familiar configuration dissolves into kaleidoscopes of flashing color, pulsating back and forth between dreams and vision.

I can see and feel and smell the pure forces of nature, shining and singing in chorus and as separate melodies: the *electromagnetic* force forms a glowing red lattice of familiar forms, shimmering with power and brash ringing fanfares of trumpets, smelling of cordite and coffee; the *weak nuclear* force, somewhere between piss-yellow and puke-green, coats reality with radium glow, tapping out a slow funeral march on quiet single snare, exuding a faint, sickly sweet stench of distant rotting decay; the *strong nuclear force* radiates blue-steel grey, thundering timpani-rolls, smelling of hard work, sweat and cut timber; and almighty *Gravity*: glistening gossamer filaments stretching forever in an ocean of soft sighs and ethereal strings, smelling of something very subtle, barely there, the background smell of creation …kind of like *gardenias*[33].

A sharp irritation spoils my reverie. The seemingly indestructible and increasingly annoying dying man next to me is making noises again, dragging me back to these miserable sand dunes, souring a perfectly happy, drug-induced symphony of pleasure. He should be dead by now, an opinion seemingly shared by an itch in my Prada hand.

Reluctantly, I tune back in as he speaks, slower and softer than before - words stealing a ride on deep breath rather than enunciated. "She didn't want to see me die slowly …until at the end, it wasn't me on the deathbed, just an empty shadow, the residue of a man. She wanted me to end as the same man she always loved. It broke my heart knowing I'd be less and less each day …as she watched …and waited …and hated me in the end for killing the man she married,

---

[33] This sentence is longer than the GUMO airstrip, and it may be that cannabis, lorazepam and opiates have caused his addled brain to hallucinate wildly. Levague is clearly close to the edge of insanity. But does this mitigate criminal culpability? I think not. If one peels away his professional university degree and checkered career, what's left is a psychedelic maniac with pathological proclivities tending to the bizarre - another red flag for authorities.

putting her through hell with a stranger, and making her stay. I bought a shotgun – for me, not her …I was going to end it while I could still shit without help and pull a trigger."

Despite myself, I can't help but wonder if Pam feels the same way, that I'm putting her through torment by not quitting tobacco, for DIY grave-digging - each joint, cocktail and smoke, a shovel closer to death? And I wasn't sure about who Korda was shooting until the clarification.

But what he's talking about happens to everyone, and usually, it's the husband who goes first, the natural order if you take a young wife. And both Pam and I come from the same old-school values about marriage: a *real* man doesn't leave while he's breathing; so too, a *real* woman, and *her* making them both suffer for it until *his* last miserable lungful. If I were unfaithful, she'd cut my dick off - to smite me despite spiting herself - and still, she would never leave …*ever*. She'd lose face and break her vows; it would be a *sin*.

Meanwhile …Jean and the women are happily planting paddy rice in the fields alongside villagers. *'If a Malay can do it, I can do it.'* It's the indomitable Mrs. Frith.

The dying man continues. "How can *all this happen*?" indicting the night sky with a glance, "How can it be …an accident, just chance? How did *we* get here?" Korda's laying on his back now, head flat on the tarp. Surprisingly, he's been able to maneuver the life preserver under his broken right arm, and it's propped up next to Ann. The stars above have trapped his eyes, sticking them open wide, and

207

his face is set as philosophically as any man with facial burns and a blood-blister smiley face.

Now the chatty dying man has awoken *ATHEISTMAN*, "Big Bang, Evolution" pop out of his mouth …and then Ann is moved to elucidate her considerations on the nature of things.

"I always thought God made a mistake with me …that *I* was an accident. I was born a boy …*Andy*, but then *He* gave me strength to make my own destiny …and when I had my sex-change operation, I thought it best to dedicate my life to …"

I get stuck on her first comment, sufficiently bogged down to miss most of the blithering nonsense that followed. Mental adjectives string themselves together of their own accord: *Irish, Catholic, post-op transsexual, sort-of-nurse-nun. ATHEISTMAN*, Jack-the-Rat and Dr. Levague all fail to comment, tipping their hat only at the increasingly bizarre Sister Mary/Ann. The Rat is marginally intrigued …and she's still talking, "Chirp and I liked to watch nature documentaries at the hospice," she says thickly, drunk conversationally. "Last week, we watched one that had a little gecko changing color to blend in with leaves. It walked in slow motion on a twig and caught a beetle with its tongue …I didn't like the one before, though …wild African hunting dogs …a pack of them. They all jumped on a poor buffalo and brought it down near a waterhole….and the dogs started eating it while it was still alive, feeding from bloody tears in his stomach, even before it was dead. The buffalo just stares in terror at the dogs as they eat it, making terrible cow-lowing cries that sounded so horrible …like a huge human baby, like …"

"Beef," I offer.

"Oh, why is nature so awful?" Ann poses, and in summing up, "How could Evolution be so cruel …but it's just a theory. I can't believe we're descended from monkeys."

The Rat and *ATHEISTMAN* are thinking about stealing two hundred and twenty kilos of smack again, and that mass murder might, in the end, be the best thing all around. I see merit in both.

Korda's not interested in a B-grade movie for his last thoughts. "There must have been a Creator, Jack. Somebody *made* all this," he says, weakly; and with the certainty of a dying man on opiates, and chiding himself for ever doubting, adds, "I mean, look …*at everything.* And here we are …You'd say: '*Big Bang …and here we are!*' It can't be that simple. It's not *chance*, Jack. Do you know how stupid that sounds? …I'll miss looking up at the stars …what do you see, Jack?"

"I see lots of hydrogen gas squeezed by Gravity so tight and hot it ignites, and energy gets wrung out of its guts. I imagine that this hurts like hell, and all the stars scream in agony as they light up and burn," I respond to nobody.

Meanwhile …the moment's coming! Jean's waiting at Alice Springs Airport, and Joe's arriving in a DC3 after flying all the way from England (where he was looking for her – he thought he might just run into her in London, as you would in *Alice*). It's the big post-war reunion love scene finale.

209

"I've had a life, Jack," Korda breathes and needs a few more breaths before he continues, barely audible, "How could there be just *Evolution* …and then we have *human* lives, and then we're here having a *discussion* about it all for Christ's sake?"

A shiver takes Korda's body. He sucks in quick, gasping breaths and then exhales long and slow. His eyes lose focus, flutter and close. It would seem the second lot of caps has kicked in. He manages one more comment, though, and then passes into a deep sleep or coma.

"I think I'm going, Jack …must say, don't like your chances with that brute of a pilot."

"I'm hungry," says Ann, previously Andrew, yawning.

'*Joe …Oh Joe,*' says Jean.

Chapter 6: Best of Things

8 February 2011

The Amazon is calm. I step onto the riverbank, and young, naked Edo girls haul my dugout onto land.

The girls are to be exchanged among old men in a society ruled by an autocratic male gerontocracy. Women from the grooms' families must itemize, detail and assign a bride price for each girl.

The work is taxing - every minute portion of each girl's body must be inspected, and various physical traits, compared and evaluated. Arguments and disagreements, occasional fights, some ending in nude mud-wrestling and splashing in the river, leave me exhausted from recording in the Journal.

The shade of a coconut tree I've been watching crawl across the line of nubile brides beckons ...And now I sit under the tree, sliding down the smooth trunk, far too tired, and I'm reclining on a blue tarp from somewhere with my head cradled in the lap of one of the smaller girls. Tiny fingers gently remove my hat, which seems stuck to my head. They tickle, finding old scars on my scalp to trace with sharp claw fingernails.

She lightly licks my head like a kitten lapping milk. I begin to feel a slight pricking on my skin, and it slowly grows painful, like a pin pushing into my scalp. The girl's tongue is now teeth, impossibly sharp needles biting my head. I reach back with my left hand to grab

211

the bloodthirsty mini-cannibal ...Ouch! Ouch! Goddamnit-mother-lord-jesus!

I'm zapped semi-conscious by a blurry rush of adrenalin-driven incomprehension, a sharp pain in my left hand, and my arms and legs flailing about wildly. I seem to have a furiously squirming ball of fur and bones in my right hand, and it's attached to my left by its teeth. Its mouth is clamped viselike into the joint of my little finger and won't let go. I scramble to my feet, kicking heroin all over the tarp and the body, or corpse, of Mattius Korda, and I'm dancing about and howling in pain and shaking my hand like a madman trying to dislodge the locked jaws of the awful little terror.

At first, I think it's a deranged feral cat until I see its fierce, beady little eyes, and an image of yesterday's pre-crash bird murdering rampage by a similar beast clears away my remaining opiate befuddlement. The creature doesn't let up until I slam my hand, with him attached, down onto Chirp's ritual stone hard enough to crack a few of its tiny ribs, slowing it down sufficiently for my right hand to find its scrawny throat. It takes a long minute of hard exertion and insane shrieking from both of us before I throttle him one-handed, and even when it's still, I have to pry its dead, needle-sharp jaws off my hand with Sue Tran's knife. It's another bloody monkey, or more likely, the same one as yesterday.

I've been bitten by a few macaques and the odd rhesus - a dry wit might observe the metaphorical simian on my back - but mostly the attacks were my fault, over a matter of stolen peanuts or some shiny trifle, and my involuntary reflex to snatch back. If you grab back, you get bit. It's understandable and justified monkey behavior. But they never latch on to something ten times their size and fight it to the death. That takes a very sick monkey.

It's not a perfect start to the day, which I notice hasn't really arrived yet. The pre-dawn horizon is tingeing red along the line of the sea; stars are fading above. I fought this morning's unhinged monkey in the early grey light and have half an hour's head start on the sun.

Squawking gulls already parade the shoreline. Andy-Ann is sleeping next to Korda. Only a meter from the previous man-now-woman, the monkey and I were consumed by a few moments of ferocious mayhem, both of us snarling and shrieking like a shaken box of Tassy devils - and he-she snored on right through the entire drama like a soused white pig.

And this dead monkey has swollen, weeping eyes and excessive saliva around its mouth, mixed with *my* blood – *rabies*. Its last behavior was clearly the bizarre affectation of what's commonly called 'furious' rabies, doubtlessly set off when I grabbed the disgusting creature while it was biting into the bloody gash on my head. It stinks of dead monkey, *diseased* dead monkey, and fresh blood seeps down the back of my right ear, and now my left hand's bleeding from dirty tiny teeth-marks.

On some flash of lunacy, I scrap a handful of spilled heroin off the tarp and rub it hard into both wounds, thinking that it might make any rabies virus somehow overdose to death. A bit on my finger finds its way into a nostril, then the other. The 'snortette' calms me down just enough to restore a bit of mental equilibrium: a gentleman's nip to rekindle a light biochemical glow, diminish the ubiquitous all-over body itch, and relieve the stress of rabid monkey madness but keep my wits within reach.

A thought scratches around in my head and, with a bit of dogged persistence, transforms into cerebral information. A monkey dies within about twenty days of rabies infection. The stage of hyper-aggression immediately precedes, by a matter of hours, the paralysis of limbs and throat muscles and eventual fatal respiratory failure.

There is no way this monkey could have been infected on East Crocodile Island or anywhere in rabies-free Australia. It must have arrived here sick and no more than a few weeks ago, three at most. I wonder if it was tossed overboard from an illegal Indonesian fishing boat when someone saw rabies symptoms or escaped when the crew camped on the island, sheltering from the weather, hugging the coast with their sneaky secret business. The monkey's death grin melds and morphs into the hideous smiling countenance of Yousef, the GUMO Armani drug smuggler, and my spine chills at the thought of more bloodthirsty poisonous vermin after my scalp, possibly within hours.

A lighter blue sky grows above the red horizon, and sunrise is minutes away. Before long, the mid-morning sun will blaze down on our shade-less sand dune, and I'll have to move.

I kick the monkey carcass a few meters off the tarp; then I kick Korda's leg. He doesn't stir. I kneel beside him, place my ear next to his mouth, and find his limp left wrist and a weak radial pulse. He's alive but appears to be in a coma. He'll not last the day with the tropical sun beating down on him and no water. It could be a long, slow death, but painless.

He's being kept warm right now, and maybe alive, by bulk heat coming from the amply fleshed Ann lying next to him, his broken arm somehow freed from his sling and resting on her left tit. I find myself feeling ambivalent about Ann's tits now, needing time to sort through how I should feel about *all* her bits. Somehow, knowing her male genitalia's been removed doesn't change very much, and I conclude the brief time allotted to consider the matter with the observation that *ATHEISTMAN* prefers 'Ann' to 'Sister Mary', the Rat has a penchant for lesbian nuns, and Dr. Levague is wondering whether Ann keeps her dick in formaldehyde as a souvenir from her previous life.

I find Bob's oil and blood-stained 'captain's' hat I lost in a dream and/or a scuffle with a monkey and use it to wipe new blood off my hand and head. The hand hurts, and I might be imagining the redness, the slight swelling, and a deeper poison flooding my biochemistry with rabies virus, but probably not. The bleeding turns to a slow trickle, then to an ooze of tiny blood beads drying almost to scabs.

The sun is just moments under the glowing horizon of a dead-calm sea, and birds in foreshore eucalypts trill, squawk and chirp in a frenzy of joy at being able to see again. I search with all my senses for the rescue chopper, but nature is too big and loud. I inch over to the southern tip of our sand dune depression and stick my head over the rim. The tide's receding. The estuary mouth we crossed last night is a mudflat again, and water leaks from the mangrove swamp in shallow, thin rivulets down shiny-wet silt banks to the line of lightly breaking surf lower on the shoreline. Our sandbank from last night's crossing, then partially hidden under the rising tide, is now fully exposed below the mudflats, a hard, wet pathway south to the main beach.

There are no signs of human life anywhere along the five hundred meters of beach to the south, no flash of orange, no incredibly large, tan-uniformed Bob skulking about. But it's a bit early; Bob's almost certainly still indisposed.

I've got an opiate hangover, like thick treacle blood and mattress stuffing for brains. I have no tobacco. My shoes are wet. I rested throughout the night, nodding off from one vivid drug dream to another, but it wasn't sleep. I'll likely be a bit cranky today.

At least Pam's probably not slept well either. She'll be driving emergency services to distraction all day with useless phone calls every ten minutes instead of patiently waiting for word. As far as she's concerned, until I'm found, they're working for her. If someone is not sufficiently helpful each and every time she calls, she'll get his name. She might even look up his address. Pam usually manifests anxiety and uncertainty with some form of aggression. She'd be intending only to intimidate by asking for a name...*probably*. It might take the other party a while to realize this and then dismiss her as just another hysterical woman, a sleepless wife stressed to the limit over a missing husband and snapping indiscriminately but harmlessly at the end of her leash. When he goes home after work and finds his front window broken or his cat missing an ear, he might realize his misjudgment, but it's unlikely – only a Shoshone princess and her disturbed husband would associate this as cause and effect.

It's been twenty hours since my last meal. I haven't had nearly enough water, and our little plastic bottles are empty. As much as I'd like to hole up right here until we're rescued and apply the heroin in heroic measure, I'm very likely to die of thirst or at least suffer permanent brain damage from dehydration before anyone helpful manages to show up.

It's a reasonable bet that the creek skirting north of the old community buildings contains potable water after yesterday's storms, at least further upstream away from the brackish creek mouth and mangrove thickets closer to the shore. All I need do is follow the margins of the mangroves inland, and eventually, the dark, stagnate swamp will give way to cleaner, fresh creek water. I could then follow the course of the creek to higher ground and keep an eye out for Bob and two for a small boat. I'd likely find Chirp up there as well.

The urge to do nothing won't leave. I have a few agenda items tossing around in my head, competing for inclusion on the list of things to do today. They're mainly concerned with my drugs, other drugs that aren't mine yet, and people who aren't me wanting all the drugs, people who probably want to kill me as well - people I will have to stop from killing me. I can't see me being that busy. Just fighting a rabid monkey has exhausted me.

Suddenly, the Rat's plans for wholesale drug dealing seem overly grandiose; the body count is too high, and the energy required is unavailable. I'd have to best Bob and Sue Tran, possibly in mortal combat - and the evil Armani weasel from GUMO, who might have a gun - and avoid detection by rescue authorities who might not be smart enough or lucky enough to find me for days. If they never show up, I'd have to use the boat Yousef brings (after I deal with him), steal his vehicle on the mainland, 'stash-the-hash' safe for a while, and somehow contrive a story accounting for everyone's demise but mine.

And I'm afraid the two souls I'm with right now will not be able to keep my secret …and live …well, maybe one and a half. But even if we don't count Korda, I'd still have to dispatch the nun. Knowing she used to be a man makes her look far stronger. I'd have to use Sue Tran's knife or Chirp's stone and strike when she wasn't looking …like right now. But even the Rat's no murderer, and I'm too tired anyway to wrestle and scrap around in the dirt with a beefy young man/woman if the stone missed her head or the knife missed her heart. I decide to check out the old community ruins first-up, before anyone else, and the creek in the immediate vicinity for water. I'll let desperate needs dictate the order of today's agenda and see how things pan out. I don't think I can kill innocent people, but let's wait and see who dies of their own accord.

The sun breaks clear on the ocean horizon, providing an

impetus to worry about shade. I was thinking of fashioning the tarp into a kind of lean-to using sticks and piled bricks of heroin in the construction, but it would take too long, too much effort, and I wouldn't be here to enjoy it. I'll leave it for the girl to figure out when she wakes, and soon, Korda won't need shade or anything except burying.

My reconnoitering will be quick and quiet. I'll travel light. With no human danger imminent, I leave the sacred stone and take the empty Prada, packing only Sue Tran's knife, the plastic water bottles, and my solid half-moon of smack. The Journal always stays with me, as I later record. The sleeping nun and comatose mining executive mind the stash of narcotics.

The sandbank route to the main community beach takes me back along the path we took in knee-high water last night. Exposed now by low tide, I leave information that might be valuable to deadly pursuers as footprints to our camp. Until I'm back, the worry will wait.

Along the way, I see several dinner-plate-sized crabs scuttling about like jerking shadows on the mudflats quite close to the shore. They find puddles of seawater left by the receding tide and excavate depressions in a swirling cloud of muddy sand, becoming all but invisible when it settles.

I find the old river-stone walkway from the beach leading up through the foreshore dunes to the derelict community. A light on-shore breeze and little surf leave the air clear of morning mist, and the sun warms my back. I follow my long shadow up the pathway, eventually having to plow through soft mounds of sand blown up high between two reasonably intact concrete structures before I stumble onto clearer ground and what might have been the main square of the old leper colony.

The principal community buildings, most with at least one wall missing and none with roofs, front onto the community square, still clearly outlined by a few hundred meters of sand-blown red gravel track on each of the four sides. Occasional copses of small native shrubs have taken hold of sandy ground here and there, but no significant vegetation has reclaimed land originally scraped clear for the village center.

Amazingly, the large Morton Bay Fig tree, introduced from the mainland perhaps a hundred years ago, still grows dark, green and strong in the center of the square. Thick curtains of aerial roots droop from lower branches around the meter-thick trunk like melting silver-grey candle wax, dropping down to and into the earth, searching deep for groundwater. The process has been going on so long that the huge tree has several anchoring root systems, and it would take more energy than a cyclonic direct hit to topple it over.

Green-purple fist-size figs bunch at the end of branches and scatter on the ground below. I try a few: dry and tasteless but edible, and a dozen go into the Prada.

To my right, at the northwest corner of the square, stands the most substantial building by far. It retains all its creamy-white concrete walls, reinforced and inlaid with darker river stones, and part of a rusted sheet-metal roof with a cross affixed at the front above the doorless entry - the community church.

The overgrown cemetery is on the western side of the church and extends to the banks of the creek. Individual grey gravestones stand in rows and randomly, a few erect but most at odd angles and some leaning on each other as if old, weathered dominoes have been knocked around. The unnatural straight lines and regular geometric shapes of these human artifacts cast the same early morning shadows over a smaller area as the buildings.

A line of large shady river-gum eucalypts on the creek's margins marks the graveyard's northern boundary. Following the creek northwest leads to the low black ironstone hill in central parts of the island. The other way, the river gums vanish, and you're soon wading down into a stinking mangrove swamp extending two hundred meters to the sea outlet - the ideal natural habitat of the estuarine crocodile.

Directly opposite on the far side of the square is another formidable stone-inlaid concrete structure still with four walls but no doors, window or roof. The shadow of my head pokes above the sun line, falling at the foot of the door-less entrance. The interior is roomy, like a warehouse, with stacks of old mattresses and broken bed-frames here and there. It's likely the clinic or hospital, and being next to the church and cemetery, conveniently located.

The hospital and the church occupy the western and northern

sides of the central square. Facing onto the eastern side and backing onto the beach, with hard-to-avoid sunrises from likely bedroom windows, are two lesser stone-concrete structures that might have been the staff residences. The river-cobble pathway from the beach passes up to the village square between them, both buildings having to bear the brunt of never-ending weather from the east, and both with seaward-facing walls almost completely buried by banked-up wind-blown sand, and both roofless, probably since the first storm-season after the community was abandoned. The sides facing onto the square have long ago lost their front and interior walls, and piles of collapsed roofing timbers and the debris of a thousand monsoon storms litter what might have been living rooms.

Next to the beach-side staff quarters, extending for another fifty meters, and all along the southern side of the old square to my right, is a collection of derelict wood-frame tin-clad houses with posts still set in concrete slabs. These have all but collapsed and been blown about into heaps of broken timber, shattered window glass, and folded rusting sheet metal.

The gravel track along the square's southern side continues roughly southwest, probably to the airstrip, and the scattered remains of occasional out-buildings - workshops, sheds, and community stores - are strewn about for a few hundred meters on either side. Further along are distinct square patches of weeded-over ground outlined by long, low rows of stones and pebbles. They're too regular and green for nature and might be historic vegetable gardens still with actual soil that hasn't eroded away. Long dead tree stumps in two or three larger rectangles might have been citrus orchard trees.

There's still a definite order to the place: gravel track around the town square, the towering spread of introduced Morton Bay tree-shade, substantial buildings, and regular even plots for gardens. It's all turned to useless junk with decades of wind, rain and the hammering tropical sun, but time and nature haven't erased the picture completely. The damage looks more recent than its true age, but as if bombs went off here and there and not too long ago.

In its time, it was probably a nice, peaceful island setting. But it's a paradise with an appalling past: a virtual jail for Aborigines unfortunate enough to be leprous in the lucky country, a life sentence for criminal biochemistry, and all mustered here from every corner of the Territory, not speaking a common lingo or English, and being minded by a religious authority convinced that if it weren't for the fact they were savage uncivilized heathens, God wouldn't have made them sick in the first place.

These Aborigines were trapped here by disease, their traditional beliefs were demonized, and their tortured souls were confused by a hazy notion of some magic dead guy named Jesus - foreign and incomprehensible at a time when only the comfort of their own superstitious nonsense can ease a miserable ending to a miserable life. But I suppose it was all for the best back then, and there was nothing for it. You can't allow lepers to roam free, infecting and freaking out whole communities, and it's probably better to collect them all up in one isolated spot even if the price is a good smothering of Christian oversight. I expect it was a bit like Chirp's home at the Darwin Catholic Hospice – a hopeless situation for helpless folks.

It's truly a lovely place, though, and I see a bulldozer as the first step to putting things right - with Club Med, a golf course, and ubiquitous paying Chinese tourists to follow. There are plenty of stories and interesting history here, and I'd like to have a good-old squiz, but I have no time to potter about now; I'm expecting company and have to put on my face. Of the whole affair, I observe that the church alone seems to have withstood abandonment and the weight of time, and is still a defensible structure for desperate people.

The figs I ate left my throat dry and a woody taste on my tongue, and now I have heartburn. I head north and pass the open church, pausing briefly to search the shadows inside for anything useful. There are rows of wooden benches and bits of sheet-metal roofing and ceiling debris that could be stacked from inside to barricade the doorway and windows, but nothing is immediately apparent as a weapon.

I walk across the shadowy west side of the church and around behind into the cemetery, straight north to the margins of the creek, and look down a shallow embankment. To my right, there are two hundred meters of swampy tidal pools and mudflats with mangrove thickets crowding the margins all the way to the beach.

The creek is several meters down a gentle grassy incline to a lower muddy bank that marks the estuarine high tide. This grey-black mud continues flat for five meters, then drops off sharply, revealing the rocky bed of the actual creek, maybe two meters wide, and then more muddy banks and grassy slopes on the opposite side. Here, a steady stream of clear creek water trickles over stones and cobbles and drains into the swampy mangrove tidal pool.

Tall silver-bark eucalypts line the shallow gully and run away with the creek to the northwest, shading it inland to the granite boulder outcropping and ironstone hill. In a few hours, the rising tide will push up the creek and assimilate the flowing water a few more meters upstream from this point. I'll go further up the creek for a drink.

My way passes a few graves, including those farthest from the church and hosting the most recent leper residents, judging by the readability of epitaphs etched on still-standing, less-weathered headstones. There's 'Lefty Williams', 'One-Eye Bob', 'Paddy Kunmubilpilguru' – I'm pretty certain that Paddy brought his real name here with him and, unlike his sicker neighbors, kept it to the grave.

Finally, I arrive sufficiently upstream and scamper down the creek bank to wet rock and a steady trickle of water several meters wide. I find a narrower section with faster flow channeling down a small stony incline like toy rapids, fill a plastic bottle, and take a sip - warm but fresh. I drain the bottle, then another.

Fumes of old man's smell and junkie breath cling to the morning air, holding still and close around me. I take the opportunity to rinse out my mouth and the blood from Bob's 'skipper's' hat, splash water on my face and under my arms, and wash my head and hands. The monkey bites are redder but don't sting, and when I complete my modest ablutions, I feel half alive.

I find a flat rock and sit down at the edge of the little rapids, sipping more water. I have another of the semi-ripe figs, this one covered with heroin powder from the inside of the Prada, and I resist the urge to reach in with my fingers but confound the effort by thinking about tobacco. I have none; therefore, it's best I have a snort of heroin. A tiny piece of my pressed-powder rock candy makes a small snort, and I take five to admire a slightly elevated opinion of the day.

The warming sun has climbed to midmorning in a clear sky. Tall river gums, their leaves glittering in a light breeze, provide dappling shade from my perspective. They trace a green line across plain red ground stretching featurelessly up an imperceptible incline to the base of the black hill two kilometers away. Downstream, the creek disappears into stagnant mangroves, never quite making it to the clean sea. There's primordial danger for unwise humans in the thick, murky water. It's watching …and waiting …and ready to feed. There's a *fatwa* feel to the swamp, and a nascent unease sneaks up on my pleasant opiate glow, a warning of ancient mindless violence lurking in the shadows.

But upstream, a menagerie of birdsong floods the soft morning sunlight and tree shade: parrots, cockatoos, woodpigeons, cormorants, crows – I hear each different tweet, whistle and screech and know its source. I feel smart and alert, and the mild smack buzz I'm wearing

226

urges me to focus on ...*more* – but only when I'm safe and after I've earned it properly and finished the day's hard yakka.

My world becomes crystal clear. I'm certain of my senses - that I'm reading my environment with the best, cleverest eyes. I can sense crawling insects and slinking reptiles behind the whispers of grass along the creek bank and feel the scuffling of leaf litter when a raven walks lightly by, lurking close as if I wasn't there. In the distance, I hear the occasional snap, crackle and pop of ridgeline rocks expanding in the day's early heat, and everywhere, I see the shimmer of slightly thicker air warming on the surface of bare red ground in quivering, liquid mirage.

I know this awful country well. I'm at home here. I speak the language. I'm old. And I'm wise. Each natural sound, each creak and rustle on a breeze, and the play of light and shadow across the landscape: a symphony of senses enticing memories, experiences ...knowledge.

I wonder briefly what the old Aborigines would take in and process from this environment: plants that are food and poison; dark, small places where lizards can be trapped and caught; stones and rocks that can be flaked into blades sharp enough to butcher any animal. I know if I hunted along the creek bed long enough, I'd identify stone artifacts possibly twenty thousand years old. Knapped spear points, scrappers, and knives – simple, effective tools made from the silica-based rock: silcrete, quartz, and jet-black chert so glasslike as to be indistinguishable from the finest midnight obsidian. This basic technology - along with controlling fire - separates us from animals. Being able to pass down and improve on knowledge of stone and fire through *language* is what makes us human.

An ancient Aborigine I talked to years ago in Alice Springs - an old fart who claimed to have seen Halley's Comet *twice* - told me he was the last Aborigine to manufacture a stone tool as part of normal domestic life. He said that after the first time he saw a steel knife, he never made another stone tool.

It was like an epiphany; the new tool was infinitely superior. And that was that - the end of the million-year-old, uniquely hominid, stone tool technology ...and it passed into history in a second, not too far from here and not too long ago – disappeared in a final single event: unmarked, unlamented; a most important date, a singularly significant, melancholy, Universal moment that just seemed to melt away unnoticed. I'm not normally the sentimental type, and this morning, I take great comfort that I have a 21st-century razor-sharp Vietnamese caterer's knife, and the knowledge of where to stick it.

And I've lived in real danger - hideous villains driven by insulted national honor and no sense of humor dogging my heels for years, and I've practiced certain skills - not just hiding - skills I can use in places just like this. Zealots are unwary, and I always took comfort that even the most dedicated resolve wilts quickly in the ruthlessly persistent wind, the blistering hot red sand, and the fatal wildness of the Australian bush.

I've recorded decades of data on hunting and traditional

weapons in the Journal, and I recall situations I *feel* as real and personal, with important meaning and information about *this* moment but that I know are from a thousand other books and movies. It's the knowledge of a lifetime of watching, reading, and not-so-make-believe stories of how people in dire straits were plucked out of normalcy, challenged and made stronger by strange events, triumphing over adversity, natural and manmade. And I'm mindful of the easy descent into the mindless violence of our true nature, using terror as a tool, *the* tool: the terror of a strange, harsh place and monsters that call it home. I'll be that beast today.

My eye catches shifting white, and Ann's uniform flashes in and out of sunshine between downstream river gums near Paddy Kunmubilpilguru's headstone. As she approaches, stumbling along the rocky incline of the creek, my senses lock onto the shadowy mangroves behind her at the base of the cemetery, prying for any subtle changes in the play of light and shadow as she walks by, the gentlest of rippling in the still, black swamp, the smallest indication that something massive might see Ann as an opportune meal, and inch ever slightly closer. There are a few thick half-submerged logs here and there, but only a uniform darkness and nothing moves in for a kill.

Ann arrives. "Mr. Korda's not moving. I raised his eyelid, and it stayed open. It's not supposed to do that. He's only *just* breathing. He's dehydrated. There's a disgusting dead monkey with a bloody mouth covered in flies near the little computer. Maybe it bit Mr. Korda and overdosed or something. There's drug powder all over the place. I think I breathed some in. I feel sick," says Ann, taking a bottle of water and draining it despite her illness. I hand her a second. "Bummer," I respond.

The water lubricates her mouth, sliding the tongue into gear …high gear - straight away. "How can you *just say that* …so unfeeling, cold, matter-of-fact …like you don't care? I'm not sure what you're doing, Dr. Levague, but I don't think this is right. You shouldn't have hit that man. If the rescue people get here first, I'm sure Bob will destroy the drugs …or we should - like Mr. Korda said - and then it wouldn't matter what we saw or said – there wouldn't be any evidence. That would be it. And if we never took any notice of his …stuff, I'm sure Bob would have gotten us off the island when his partner arrived. No, *you* caused all this! This is not my problem. I've got nothing to do with drugs …I'm a nun! No one's going to kill a nun and a young Aboriginal boy. We've got to get Mr. Korda to a hospital. You just go and apologize to Bob and convince him that everyone's lives are worth a lot more than some measly bunch of drugs! Tell him I don't know anything, and Korda needs a doctor, or he'll die!"

I must say, she lost me when I got stuck on the image of a dead monkey - all 'lord of the flies' - and Korda's semi-corpse, maybe keeping his stuck-open eye on the filthy little carcass in case it springs to life hopping about and banging together toy symbols. The man will be starting a slow-cook process under that grilling sun, especially on that dark blue tarp. He'll need flipping soon.

Ann's emphatic advice so early in the morning - and the last bit delivered with glaring eyes, raised voice, and fists on hips - is too confrontational for my biochemistry right now, and I feel the Rat rising. But I keep him on a short leash. Perhaps Ann's just not a morning person.

An inclination to go fingering about in the bottom of the Prada finds my hand opening the bag. It settles on the handle of a carving knife. But instead of snorting more drugs and walking away - or murder - I set a stern, intolerant glare on her until the feisty fierceness in her eyes passes, and she resets her face to a sullen petulant expression, which I note is its usual disposition when she's not in shock …or when she's not lurching about in panic over crashing planes, dead bodies and missing hospice patients …or when she's not latching angrily onto someone to blame for any small part of her current miserable predicament, which seems mostly to be me.

"Good morning, Ann," I reply, intending a cheery greeting. "Yes, shame about Korda. In fact, *dying today* is his intention, I believe, and I'm a bit surprised he hasn't managed it yet …and incredibly, we're maybe in the only place in the world right now where a bookie would give 'odds-on' that an *actual* nun will *actually* get murdered …um, that would be *you*. I'd be more worried about myself right now if I were you." And *ATHEISTMAN* can't help it and butts in with, "How's your faith today, *Sister?*"

Ann bites back, "Why are you always like this, Jack …always

knocking religion, as if faith in God is bad …a weakness …a mental illness? Am I so bad if I believe in God? That I want to share His love? More people are believers than not, Jack …including the greatest minds. I'd be lost without something greater than myself to believe in. I pity you. I'll say a prayer for you."

The last bit sounds like a threat, like '*I'll tell God on you*', so I hand her two of the water bottles and start heading back downstream toward the graveyard. But it's a nice day, the drugs feel *right* …and so I slap down my anti-theistic alter ego, thinking, what the hell, and I pause while she takes another drink and I allow kindly, "You can eat the figs under the big tree if you find any without little worms." It's just nature that doth provide.

But *ATHEISTMAN* insists on saying more so I put it bluntly, "It's personal for me. I think religion, and yours especially, has set back the quest for scientific understanding by several hundred years, and it is during these specific years when the discovery of a cure for the disease that will probably kill me might have been found. I'll die younger because of religion and I'm sorely aggrieved."

There are other words that an old man can say to a young boy/girl about religion and dying, and the eloquence of my voice fills my ears with claptrap, sounding even to me a shade short of sincere, along the lines of "I'm sorry for Mr. Korda. I didn't know the man well. He was probably good in many ways, but I thought him mostly arrogant and greedy. Truth is, I won't miss him. He wanted to end his life last night, and who can blame him? It was an act of utter lucidity and, in his condition, probably the most reasonable, rational thing a man could do. I thought I was watching a pre-eminently logical self-mercy act, quite courageous and bittersweet. You might have missed it getting pissed and fretting about your ...*boyfriend*."

Ann is trying to scrub red dirt off the front of her uniform with her damp blue scarf. The scrubbing turns to abrading when Chirp comes up. Her resolve to strike out at first light this morning and search for the pathetic love-stricken imbecile seems to have drained away with the dregs of last night's wine.

"Did you *kill* Mr. Korda, Jack?" she asks softly, apparently getting to the nub of what seems to be pitter-patting troublingly in the dim recesses of what passes for her frontal lobe. But it's a fair ask, I suppose. Mind you, what's she expecting – an admission of guilt to homicide - and evidently, the fellow hasn't even snuffed it yet, albeit there's probably not much in it from moment to moment.

I let a tick pass as I recall the times people have asked me that before. Over the years, I've had to state publicly a number of times that I *did not* push a Bre-X geologist out of a helicopter to his death in the jungles of Indonesian Borneo back in '97. The chopper made an emergency landing, and we both made it out alive, right into the clutches of Borneo Dayak natives, mind - who never quite gave up their notorious proclivity for hunting heads.

The notion was rhetorically put to me long ago by UN investigators following the Bougainville Rebellion. And there were the accusations following the Srebrenica massacre in '95, the

233

sickening TV images of huddled shot-dead bodies of boys and men still skulk about my memory. But my conscience is clear. Was it due to the limited efficacy of the *Levague Prejudice Protocol* or the bloodthirsty religious hatred of Serbians - and Dutch peacekeepers displaying all the military precision, martial excellence, and true grit for which their armed forces are famous?

"I did nothing to prevent a man from easing the burden of his awful last moments," I reply, and believe it or not, she starts weeping - just a bit, a respectful tear for a dying soul …or maybe for herself, the sad introspection of a strayed lamb of Jesus who's trapped by circumstance and now thrust into the company of guy on a desert isle who might have murdered another guy with an overdose of heroin last night, and the another-guy who might have committed suicide during the same act and then abandoned himself to eternity with a dying arm draped over her drunken left breast. I guess murder and suicide involving guys she just met and got drunk with - spent the night with on the beach - may set twists of ethical uncertainty churning in a young nun's empty stomach.

"What's all this about *ATHEISTMAN*? Mrs. Korda told me you worked for the UN …insulted a *whole* country …Iraq …or Iran …and you shouted it when you hit Bob with Chirp's rock, like some crazy war cry. What is all this business …sounds like childish silliness, and insulting and mean-spirited," she opines, continuing her wash: arms, knees, feet, toes.

I've had no coffee, no smoke, but my biochemistry is

multitasking reasonably well on just heroin, and I gather in the local environment with all senses, setting the sounds of insects and birds, the wash of the sea on the beach in the distance, the gentle breeze flapping and slapping eucalypt leaves, and the low occasional gurgling, deep-gut bubbling of the muddy estuary downstream – all as a kind of foreground noise, or musical accompaniment to reality, such that the minutest change in the elements, one tiny discord to the song - caused by fat and/or Vietnamese drug-smugglers - will instantly be noticed.

I gather a breath and elucidate, "You're way too young to remember ...it was in the 1960s...drugs and sex and rock-and-roll. Before I became an anthropologist, I was known for creating *ATHEISTMAN* superhero comics and cartoons ...it started the whole satirical underground comic movement ... the old hippy days. It paid for my university education.

But I kept it up ...maybe I shouldn't of ...as a kind of science superhero to counter age-old acculturating and socializing in American churches and schools, the religious *brainwashing* of kids. I don't like models of reality that contain *magic*. Magic isn't real."

"God isn't *magic*," Ann protests.

"The cartoons were harmless enough, with *ATHEISTMAN* holding up a banner reading *'Jesus is your Pretend Friend'* or *'Good ...but Godless'*; it was kind of like 'the Easter bunny brings chocolate' or 'Santa brings toys', and *ATHEISTMAN* bringing nice, new shiny nuggets of truth ...Don't worry; nobody wanted any."

235

"Alas, a misdirected cartoon drawing - the first one that pops up on the computer when you search - is *ATHEISTMAN's* fight with the old Iranian leader, Ayatollah Khomeini ...over Evolution - you're even too young to remember the Iranian revolution ...Anyway, it was that one that resulted in my *fatwa*, an invocation for faithful Iranians to assassinate me on sight as an enemy of Islam[34].

If you search the internet long enough, you might find a cartoon of *ATHEISTMAN* relaxing on a photon of light beaming across the Universe and having martinis with my wife ...and there's the drawing of *ATHEISTMAN* spray-painting the front window of the Dover, Pennsylvania School Board Building with '*Creationists Suck* '[35].

"*ATHEISTMAN* sometimes appears in his superhero uniform at atheist organizations' functions, seminars and annual conferences. I was a guest speaker at several events, then handed out agendas, and finally manned the refreshment stand as a mascot when they tired of my jokes. At the National Atheist Association annual general meeting in Melbourne last year, they stuck the ice cream stand in the car park

---

[34] See Attachment A, pg. 16 above.

[35] The Dover Panda Trial of 2005 foiled an attempt by the Christian-dominated Dover School Board in Pennsylvania to force schools to teach 'creationism' as an alternative theory to evolution and the origin of life in high school science classrooms. It failed and the court found that the theory of evolution was science and creationism wasn't.

The pro-creationist school board members apparently were set to appeal the court's findings but reportedly changed their positions after receiving anonymous phone calls threatening the mutilation of family pets.

236

next to a vocal group of bearded anti-atheist protestors – all men and mostly newly arrived Pakistani immigrants – and each icy-pole *ATHEISTMAN* sold moved the customer to wish me a long painful death. *ATHEISTMAN* is semiretired; occasionally, he climbs back into control for short missions but rarely involving anything more exciting than the watering of gardenias and the scaring of Jehovah's Witnesses."

By the look on Ann's frozen blank face, all these words have remained childish silliness, drug-fueled nonsense, and probably insulting of reasonable sensibilities if she cared to think about it. But she's got a peculiar glint in a guarded part of her eye that's maybe reserved for the truly delusional - old eccentric crackpots of indeterminable actual threat but probably harmless. And it's there for me, showing no interest in exploring the sociological implications of imprinting children with systems of belief, morality and philosophical epistemology that are demonstrably false ...at least not at the moment, not when it's time for a nun to figure out how not to get killed today.

"So, you were a cynical young man who didn't believe in God ...and now you're a cranky old bastard who still doesn't believe in God," Ann observes. "Probably should have left it at that, huh?"

I leave Ann to her ablutions and cautiously retrace our steps back downstream to the graveyard and the church. A large river gum marks the high tide line where the creek spills into darker, swampier waters. I stop at Paddy's gravestone on the creek embankment above the start of the swamp. From upstream, I watched this very point as Ann walked by, peering intently for signs of the smallest movement, for a gentle up-swelling of swamp water as a crocodile braced to launch for Ann's legs, and for amber-diamond eyes blinking on the swamp's surface, glittering amid dark greens, wet blacks and shifting grey mangrove shadows.

Suddenly, Ann appears behind me, startling my concentration, "What's down there?" she asks.

"A swamp, basically," I say. "This is where the creek runs out, and it's the start of mud and mangroves that go all the way to the beach."

"So what?" asks Ann, not unreasonably. Then I find what I'm looking for, and even with the expectation that it might be there, the proof of it brings the old gorge lurching up my belly and a flutter to the heart. I point to the mud bank just below Paddy's gravestone in the shade of the last eucalypt before the mangroves, where the creek assimilates into the swamp at high tide. She also points, whispers, "Crocodile nest?" and promptly freezes.

Australian marine estuarine crocodiles routinely grow five or six meters long, much of it toothy jaws. I've seen two 'salties' rip the rotting carcass of a water buffalo in two and swallow a whole half each in two or three massive gulps. But you don't tend to get the really big ones on the islands. Although at home in the open ocean - and I've spotted plenty while flying around island communities – it's usually only young males on island beaches; the larger crocs are more at home near the mouths of the very large rivers on the mainland, like the Woolen River estuary two kilometers to the south. Monsters on coastal islands are more occasional and opportunistic.

Only five or six meters down the grassy slope from our feet, the unmistakable mound of dead leaves, twigs and muddy-grassy debris marks the nest of a female marine crocodile, the largest lizard alive and the only routine man-eater. The nest sits on the highest level of mudflat, and the full tide will gently flush around the base. It measures about one meter long and wide, and the grass and plant litter emerge half a meter above the muddy surface and probably extend another half meter underneath. It looks like a small pile of hay surrounded by a mote of muddy grey water - Mum's wallow - surrounding the whole nest. It's her bed while she's curled around her precious eggs, maybe vibrating her throat at the base to entice the faintest ...*chirp* ...*chirp* ...*chirp* from the incubating bevy of little horrors after they hatch.

Her claws leave deep prints along the margins of the wallow, and a smooth, muddy trail shows the way she hauls in and out of the swamp water and where she crawls up onto the top of the creek bank and into the cemetery, perhaps taking the afternoon sun from time to time with the ghosts of old Lefty Williams and One-Eye Bob.

Suddenly, the sharp snapping of wood breaks the background calm, and a half-submerged eucalypt log slides silently down the muddy bank on the opposite side of the creek embankment, seemingly of its own accord. I press my senses deeper, and they train onto yellow-brown, red-streaked eyes, diamond pupils shining blacker than coal. Then the log loses all harmless pretense, and the real, deadly menace appears as if molding itself from wet mud: a five-meter mega-lizard on the far side of the creek, spitting distance from our transfixed eyes. It becomes quiet and stock-still against the dark mud bank, virtually the same deep green-black as anything in the shadowy swamp.

It would be invisible if I weren't glued on its impossibly amber eyes, perfect malice oozing from those bottomless black pupils. The spiked tail ridges extend the length of its back, and the tops of its legs are like bent, wound-up tubes of steel ready to spring; and finally, its head, a meter long and mostly industrial strength viselike jaws, closed now thankfully, and just peeking out the sides - a dozen creamy-white, dentally faultless teeth looking like they belong mounted on a large wall in a natural history museum.

The awful lizard starts a slow mud-crawl towards us, suggesting we're too close to her nest and/or she wants to kill us …for food …or for something to do. My instinct is to use either Paddy's gravestone or Ann as a springboard to climb into the river-gum if the croc's slow gait decides to shift into *rear-leg-lunge-run-on-tips-of-claws-gapping-jaws-grab-the-prey* gear, or just shove her down the bank as an offering to the monster to keep it off me as I bolt. Now that I think about it, Ann could easily lose her footing and slide right down.

Instead, while keeping Ann between me and the crocodile, I whisper, "Let's very quietly … and quickly, but with no sudden moves

…just take a few steps back into the cemetery and keep going. If the croc goes for you, run for your life …away from the croc, mind …make for the old church. I'll be just in front of you."

We start inching backward across the cemetery, occasionally tripping over toppled grave markers but showing no historical interest in names and dates other than to casually wonder if leftovers from a croc's meal back in the leper days might have been substantial enough to warrant its own headstone, maybe Lefty's.

I'm not much on lamenting the passing of a living species of anything – life's evolving and extinguishing fairly routinely - and as long as beef, pigs, chickens, blue whales, elephants and myself survive, I'm not too fussed about what goes extinct next. And to *my* mind, crocs look far better as leather products, footwear accoutrement for a fashionably rugged look, and as exotic steaks and kabobs, and when the Australian species was all but shot out last century, I wasn't crying - crocs have a horror that is assessable with superlatives normally reserved for the fossil remains of dinosaurs. It's the crocodile's *smile* that does it for me - the toothy edged upper-jaw resting on the bottom, with dagger-sharp teeth spilling over the lower lip like some kind of bizarre reptilian slack-jawed yokel, but at the same time possessing a primeval, cagy canniness - and always the happy, mindless smile - the last thing a meal sees before the maw of death opens. Of course, it's precisely this toothy smile that somehow ingratiates the awful beast to indigenous cultures; the facial expression of a grinning terrible demigod that can be appeased with gifts and

241

rituals: afterbirth offerings gifted to Amazonian alligators among the Edo tribe come to mind, and bloodletting circumcision rituals closer to home.

But in our *mac.disney.dot.com* culture, there's no getting past that image of a smiling, cartoon crocodile - the stereotype of a mindless monster - lurking silently and searching for the rest of a wicked Captain Hook pirate - just deserts for a particularly villainous rascal.

I watch in horrid fascination as the giant reptile eases itself into the muddy wallow around its nest mound, not unlike some nightmarish roosting alien, and then she flutters her neck muscles too fast to see, sending a spray of muddy water over herself and her soon-to-be babies. Surprisingly, Ann has moved with speed and stealth that would normally belie a running nun in a knee-length nurse's uniform, but she may have previously played rugby, and she's fifty meters over near the old church when I finally look away from the settled primordial monster.

The shadow of the church's roof-mounted crucifix seems to have stuck on her face as she sprinted towards the building's entrance and glued her stone still in sunlight a few meters in front. When I approach, I think maybe she's been taken suddenly by the mood to thank God for not being eaten by a crocodile, but then I see she's fixed on something on the ground: a thick brown-banded yellow snake with a black-tipped tail, one meter long and curling itself into pre-strike posture - a northern death adder, deadly poisonous.

She's frozen in fright with the snake near her foot, and it too seems to have stopped moving, possibly put off by a large white, motionless thing that wasn't part of the environment yesterday. We both watch it move again, slithering around Ann's feet, making for shade inside the church.

I don't know how I survived to this point today without puking: impending drug war, rabid monkeys, irritating accusations of murder (or, at best, assisted attempted suicide) from a transvestite nun with a crush on an Aboriginal kid who might have a slight mental disability (or equally, be defrauding the Commonwealth of Australia), a crocodile I've been far too close with, and now deadly snakes …not one, but two - a second now slithering around the southern corner of the church, following its comrade to the darkness inside.

It's very odd to see two snakes in a year, let alone within seconds, and there must be some aspect of previous human habitation here to account for a veritable plethora of the damn things, maybe introduced mice that ran amuck. As they disappear, a new source of fear - and of *possibility* - crawls across my skin, into my brain, and settles in a corner usually occupied by a large rodent …*one snake* …*two snakes*.

I'm *way* too old to have learned my letters and numbers on *Sesame Street*; I'm *Howdy Doody* vintage. But I've always loved Count Dracula, and while Burt and Ernie annoyed me with their never-explicit but always implied *old guy - young guy* gay routine, I thought the Count was a wonderfully perverse way to teach preschoolers about the difference between quantities of things: an aged bat-creature, dressed for the morgue with an ill-defined east European accent always ending his dialogue with *blah, ba-blah, ba-blah, I vant to drink your blood!*

I was just old enough to wonder what the toddlers made of the Count's fangs as he counted out six lollipops and seven whatever. Doubtless, many of these kids ended up on the boards of America's biggest bankrupt companies, never having thought a counting puppet vampire the least peculiar or portentous. And I can't help put on my best Count Dracula imitation for Ann – to lighten the moment.

"One snake, two snakes …maybe more snakes …*blah, ba-blah,*" I say, breaking the silence and apparently the grip of fear preventing the girl from breathing.

"Jack, let's sit in the shade of the big tree …and you can tell me all about numbers and snakes," she says, not unreasonably and slightly exasperated but resigned to receiving information from me that will sound like a dissertation on the bleeding obvious but possibly contain a snippet that might be important, might come up during final exams.

I'm seriously considering asking Ann what she knows about talking snakes in the Bible, but as we walk across the old square into the shade of Morton Bay, I continue with my original thought.

"The important thing about snakes *right now* is that they exist, that instead of having a situation of 'no snakes' – we actually *have* snakes. One snake is proof that there is no such thing as 'no snakes' in a correct model of reality …just as the fact that 'something' in the Universe is proof that there is no 'nothing', although theorists might argue that almost all of 'something' is really *nothing* and if you look close enough at 'nothing', it's teeming with zillions of quantum bits and pieces that pop into and out of existence at the drop of a hat."

"Are we going to eat those snakes? They're getting away," Ann says, trying to anticipate my point, any point. She's gathered a number of Morton Bay figs and experiments with various options for peeling and eating them, and I'm surprised the possibility of a barbecued snake breakfast could be on a nun's menu. Occasionally, her face sours in disgust as the maggot of some insect sticks its head out of the fig she's about to consume, but with a little never-mind shrug, she gets seriously stuck into half a dozen figs without being picky.

There's a particularly useful shape to one of the lower Morton Bay Fig branches, and I cut it off with Sue Tran's knife and whittle a staff-length that ends in a two-pronged fork, like a 'V'. The other end, I sharpen to the sort of point that makes sense to a hunter.

My left hand hurts after being used in a bit of carpentry. I note that the skin around the monkey bites has turned slightly grayish with red swelling on the edges and looks sickly. My finger runs over the skin, and all I feel is numbness, like the caress of a feather. Perhaps a scientist should know, but I have no idea how long it takes for rabies to attack the brain. I should probably apply some opiates as a priority.

I continue my discourse, "The *point* about 'having snakes' is like 'having crocodiles'. Knowing the point, you can be careful where you tread. Those snakes are slow, but if one bites you bad enough - or maybe two bite you at once - you might just have time enough to make a fire, skin the snakes, roast them on hot coals, and eat them before the muscles that make you breathe completely paralyze and you die. I don't like eating snakes…how about mud crabs…possibly with roasted, slightly caramelized figs …to give it a certain *je ne sais quoi* kind of sweet and sour flavor?"

Chapter 7: Uphill Climb

Ann and I gather up enough insect-infested figs for several desperate people and return to the beach along the river-stone pathway between the derelict ruins of the old leper community. Before clearing the staff residence buildings, I hold us up to be certain our way through the foreshore dunes will not encounter lurking threats.

The tide is still on its way in, and the main beach to the south is smooth, hard, and free of footprints. An unnaturally white object, however, lies at the margins of dunes directly east of the airstrip at the south end of the crescent beach, five hundred meters away.

It looks to be one of the large drug-filled duffel bags from the plane. Bob and Sue Tran have been busy if they've hauled one hundred kilograms from the airstrip through the trees and dunes to the beach. It must have taken hours. They've both probably gone back to the crash scene to fetch the other one.

When we get to the exposed sandbank and the mudflats at the mouth of the estuary, it's time to try out the Morton Bay Fig spear. I find the location of a large mud crab, hunkered down, all comfortably camouflaged in a sandy depression with maybe a patch of him the size of a quarter showing above the sand. It's a simple matter of positioning the spear at just *that* point and thrusting through the crab's carapace, pinning it to the sand so it can't dance away. If you get it right, the poor animal's two huge front claws reach back and grab your spear, literally holding it in its own back, and the crab doesn't slide off when you transfer it to your tucker bag – in this case, the Prada. I can't quite suppress an image of Mrs. Korda holding onto *her* spear - it's a similar autonomic reflex.

I catch another this way, enough to my mind, but Ann insists we get a third, theoretically one each (including Korda). So, I make her catch it, and she manages well, only once slipping ass-over-end in the slippery mud and coming up smeared well down her entire front and back with fine-silt, grey-black clay. For anyone not wanting to stand out like a large white kitchen appliance on a desert island, it's not a bad look.

The sun's at an angle in the eastern sky, suggesting about 10:00 am. Search planes leaving Darwin at daybreak for East Crocodile Island would be arriving soon. But they'll be flying fifty kilometers south of us and looking for wreckage on the mainland today ...and tomorrow ...maybe all week. An inexperienced bush driver towing a small boat from GUMO could be expected later today if he had all his gear ready. I don't think rescuing the stash from East Crocodile Island after crashing the plane is something you'd plan for, so I figure my grinning Armani friend won't realistically arrive until late tonight at the earliest.

We arrive back at our camp, the place where we keep our comatose, heroin-overdosed colleague, dead fly-struck monkey, about twenty kilograms of illegal drugs, and an empty bottle of cheap wine. I kick together tufts of dead grass, gather up dry branches from near the watermark on the beach, and soon have a handy fire blazing away in a swale just downwind from Korda.

Ann has Korda's head propped up on her lap. She drips water onto his lips and tries to elicit a swallowing reflex, but what water she gets into his mouth just dribbles out the corners. Now, she's content to bathe his facial blisters and cuts with her damp headscarf and doesn't believe she's wasting water or time. He's barely alive.

When the fire burns down to coals, the also barely still-living crabs and a dozen figs go into the fire with a great deal of hissing, shell cracking, and crab-writhing in what is likely to be unimaginable pain for a crustacean, and instantly, I might add, steaming out the most delicious smells of barbequing seafood. Ann watches all this, and I expect her to grimace in sympathy when the crabs go onto the coals, but the hungry feminine fly-half covered in mud has only drooling anticipation on that chubby-cheek face.

"Maybe Chirp will smell these crabs and come running," she posits as I flip things over on the coals, applying Sue Tran's knife to my *fresh* crabs, possibly for the first time. "Do you think he's ok?"

"He's an idiot. For an idiot, he's fine. I would imagine that sooner or later, he'll get tired of hiding out and come around to the idea that maybe the plane crash wasn't his fault and that he didn't actually *kill* Mrs. Korda. He'll still have to cop it from his relatives for inappropriate use of a sacred ritual stone. But who knows what's rattling around in his brain …although I must say there seems to be a few semi-normal things going on there."

"Does he really believe in ghosts?"

"Do you?"

"I believe that Mrs. Korda's *soul* has gone to heaven."

ATHEISTMAN is too tired to take on a nun, and Dr. Levague says, "Well, there you go …for Chirp, ghosts include some notion of actual corporal reality – they're *really* there …in a kind of spiritual layer of the world that you can't normally see but sort of brushes up against everyday layers of reality; and the spirit world can overlap and interfere with everyday real events. And sometimes it's possible for living people to enter the realm of the spirits in a dream or through ritual and ceremony, and make things happen, redress imbalances, right wrongs. In a nutshell, Chirp is dealing with two problems: Mrs. Korda's spirit shouldn't be here; she's *way* out of her depth, what with one-legged nose-less vindictive male ghouls from the old leper days swarming around, perving on a new woman's spirit - fashionably attired in modern, green skirt and blouse, mind - and all that lecherous ghostly slobbering …Chirp feels responsible …and secondly, how to get that damn special rock back where it belongs. He might feel that his theory of the transmutation of power from the stone into a love potion to trap you for a wife might need a bit more research. Yesterday, he was in a mad panic because he thought he caused the plane to crash …or rather, the stone caused it because it wasn't happy about being stolen. He had some ridiculous idea about the Seven Sisters Dreaming Spirits holding Mrs. Korda in protective custody somewhere on the island, and that's where he went. He still might think the only way to fix things is with complex ceremonies and rituals. He believes that only the '*TWO MEN*' - the strongest magic of all, the ritual blood-rite of the '*Mother's Brother-Sister's Son*', the all-powerful male cult spirits - can put things right, but the magic is beyond him. He doesn't know the correct spells. And he's still going to have to front up to his Uncle Jacob, his 'ritual boss', who'll almost certainly want to spear him when he catches up with the little bugger …probably in both legs."

Ann takes this in with an expression I can't see, mostly because her face is full of eating roasted crab and figs. I'm not that hungry, but I enjoy the meat of two claws I crack open with Sue Tran's knife and a bit of toasted fig. Korda passes. She offers to split his share of the food, but I decline, and she gets stuck into a second crab, ignoring the sandy grit she also consumes by not chewing too much and washing it all down with water. "Do you know the correct rituals …the correct spells?"

I reckon I've recorded more rituals, ceremonies and religious data in the Journal than you can shake a stick at. I reply, "I know *of them*. I know *songs*. But I have no authority to sing them, to metaphorically enter the Dreaming, use powerful words, or cast spells. I'm not ritually pure enough to participate. I haven't allowed my genitals to be mutilated. And remember, we're talking about the *make-believe* world …stuff that's going on in a young man's mind – which almost invariably gets back to overactive hormones and a juvenile infatuation …with you."

Her mouth sets in a firm line, an appearance suggestive of

251

some sort of thinking process, and softness creeps into her eyes, an expression that kills any inclination I might have had to elucidate on the relationship between the *sacred* and the *profane*, probably for the best at the moment. In Chirp's case, it's a most peculiar crossover between strongly held precepts of traditional religion, a biochemical imbalance involving primarily his testicles, and his unique, solvent-sodden imagination. Basically, he needs a psychiatrist and a girlfriend…probably both.

"Is Chirp in danger? Do you think Bob and this Yousef fellow would …"

"…murder Chirp to keep him quiet about the drugs?" I suggest adding, "I don't think Chirp figures much in their equations. If he blunders back to the airstrip or runs into Bob and Sue Tran …or Yousef, and if we're not there, he might tweak that something's amiss and keep his distance. Alternatively, Bob might just kill him as soon as he can get his hands around his neck, but he might think Chirp doesn't know about the drugs, and Bob should be aware that the police would have a big problem with Chirp as a 'witness'. They won't likely take him seriously about anything and might not ask him any questions at all. I don't think Bob would kill Chirp just to tie up loose ends. Yousef, on the other hand – and Sue Tran, I imagine - have no such qualms. But Chirp reckons Bob's still pissed about the special rock crashing his plane, so he'll probably be steering well clear."

"You have to go find him and bring him back so he's with *us*," says Ann. "By the way, does Chirp's family *own* the island …the old community?" she asks, re-endearing herself in my estimation.

"Might say the land owns *him*," I say.

"I'm going to go and have a talk with Bob now …like you said. I'll make a deal with him about the drugs - as long as they leave us alone. You can't come with me in case the negotiations are unsuccessful. If you want to find Chirp, just follow the creek from this morning. He'll be up near the black hill – watch out for that big croc."

"What about Mr. Korda? We should move him to the shade near the old community buildings. Someone needs to be with him …to give him water if he comes to," says Ann.

"Suit yourself," I reply. "I recommend you use the 'fireman's grip'. Or you could drag him through the sand. You'll need to get across the sandbank before the tide drowns him. Alternatively, you might be able to use the tarp for shade and keep him here. Either way, you're on your own. Bob has seen the smoke from our fire, and he'll think we're somewhere near the old buildings. That's where I'll be waiting for him. …Can I borrow you're safety pin? I need to pin a message somewhere Bob will find it."

Ann's looking at me with a *what-a-heartless-jerk* glare again. I get it a lot. But I've no time, strength or energy to help shift Korda's body several hundred meters just to find a dead man some shade, even if he's not technically dead yet. I look up, following the now faint smoke trail from our fire in the breeze, and hear myself add, "After Bob and I come to an agreement, I'll go and find Chirp," even though

I rate the chance of either event becoming a real occurrence as low to moderate.

I do help fashion an area of shade in our sand dune using a few bits of wood and a couple of small logs that we didn't need for the fire. Ann makes Korda look comfortable, and after she gives me her headscarf pin, her muddy and crab-juice-smeared hands come together, and she kneels beside him, looking heavenward. Just before she prays, perhaps wary of *ATHEISTMAN*, I catch a sly glance to see if I'm watching and likely to make an obnoxious comment. I don't, and what she has to say to God is thankfully said in silence. But I can't help but wonder exactly what particular divine intervention Ann has in mind. With Korda, she's starting with fairly dodgy material: a massively drug-overdosed, aggressively cancerous, suicidal, currently comatose, burnt, broken, dangerously dehydrated mining executive that a number of people will likely try to murder today. If she's asking any more than swift heavenly removal for a deceased soul, the odds of success are probably several hundred orders of magnitude to one.

My focus turns to useful things, and nineteen idle kilograms of Armani heroin are assembled and packed into the Prada as well as the sacred stone, the small torn duffel bag, Sue Tran's knife, my broken disc of drugs (now a thick crescent), the Journal and a few other items. I have my two-pronged Morton Bay Fig spear, tips now fire-hardened, and I'm ready for Bob.

"I recommend you keep your head down …and keep quiet," I say to Ann, perhaps unnecessarily, but I truly can't say if, upon seeing

Bob and Sue Tran strolling up the beach, she might up and shout *'Over Here! Mr. Korda needs help!'*

Beyond voluntary castration, something else niggles about the girl's judgment, her disinclination to consider that illegal drugs - the ownership, control and clandestine movement thereof - are uppermost considerations in the minds of all the people she's likely to come into contact with today; and she's preeminently a liability, not only expendable but a definite loose-end.

And, no matter how you cut it, I'm coming to a view that she's as cerebrally challenged as the Aboriginal kid she's minding – the stupid leading the *bloody* stupid; it's not only they both seem to think magical forces have a bearing on what happens today on East Crocodile Island, they're both under twenty-five and thus by Levague definition, about as smart as the first two clay pigeons at a skeet shoot.

I trudge down the beach with my load of narcotics and across the soon-to-be re-submerged sandbank below the estuarine mudflats to the main beach. I spear the dead monkey as I go. The fire-hardened point works as I expect, and I take the diseased carcass with me. There's someone he just has to meet.

There's no sign of the others anywhere. I'm reasonably certain Bob's seen the smoke from our fire, but his priority will be to keep the duffle bags together, and he and Sue Tran will still be hauling the other one away from the crash scene to join its mate on the southern end of the beach, ready for pick-up by boat, maybe later today.

Nevertheless, I use extreme caution and stalk slowly up the stone pathway and into the space between the two old staff residences. I pause, my back flat against a wall, and my long shadow, its head in the village square, becomes still. I turn my senses to any sound, any sign of movement, any change in the patterns of nature.

And I wait, getting the rhythm of the old broken community: the background squawks, buzzes, and trills of birds and bugs; the different sounds of different breezes, one moment strong and stirring giant foliage in the Morton Bay Fig, another now caressing grasses on the margins of the main square; the play of light and shadow in and around the collapsed and ruined buildings; the shifting shade of the big fig tree; and the tiny, crystalline flash of individual sand grains when a wind-gust sweeps low on the red gravel track around the square.

Everywhere is unthreateningly normal, and my slow breathing is the only human movement. I walk silently to the square, leave the Prada under the fig tree, and take the emptied duffel bag and my spear on a tour of the old buildings. I start with the church and validate my theory that snakes like it here because it's shady during the day, and the old stone and concrete walls trap heat and stay warm during the night. What I need I easily find here and in a dark corner recess of the old hospital under folded sheet metal. The two-prong end of the spearing tool I fashioned earlier is crude but effective.

Stage 1 of my welcome for drug smugglers is completed in about an hour, and next, very cautiously, I sneak into the shade of the old church and edge myself along the creek gully, through the cemetery, and up to the grey stone slab marking old Paddy's grave. I flatten myself against the trunk of the big river gum nearby and check out the crocodile's nest only five steps down the creek embankment - about a half-second lunge for a five-meter crocodile. It's unguarded. And I'm riveted to the tree, as still as its bark, and again, I wait.

It takes a long time for someone with the intestinal fortitude of a Frenchman to be certain Mother Crocodile is off sunning herself …or eating something, and with a dead monkey, a crucifix, and some heroin, I complete Stage 2. It involves sinking the point of my spear through the center of the crocodile nest and seeing if anything gooey is stuck on when I pull it back out. I find blood, *not* the amniotic fluid of young eggs, and I'm almost certain I hear the feeble *chirps* through about half a meter of the nest when I ease out the spear. Knowing that if Mum also heard, she'd be onto me like a torpedo, I hastily complete arrangements and almost trip over my feet as I bolt back through the graveyard to the shade of the Morton Bay Fig.

Stage 1 arrangements are rechecked, and then I wait in the shadows of the church doorway for my visitors to arrive. From my vantage, all approaches to the village square are clearly in view. The Prada's back with me, and I apply a small pinch of heroin to get in the mood for quests. Otherwise, I'm likely to find them boring. But not much; the snort's just enough to tighten a loose flapping of biochemical sail and take the edge off - an edge I thought age might have dulled, but that's keen as ever.

257

I resist the urge to repeat the measure and take up the Journal. Recent events haven't gone to script, and I need to record extraordinary details while they're fresh.

I review what I've written during the last twenty-four hours, especially my description of pilot Bob Palmer and Sue Tran. I've misjudged her and inaccurately recorded elements of our previous encounters.

For example, I appear to have mistaken Sue Tran's attitude during previous professional consultations over Ling's lunchtime menu. I always thought her friendliness and seemingly easy familiarity in response to my charming, personable food ordering was a kind of innocent flirting instead of the condescension of a hateful Vietnamese caterer with an inferiority complex. On the other hand, I had Bob pegged as a lawless road warrior the first time I met him, and if ever there was a bent rascal, you can't go by yesterday's smiling Armani GUMO driver. But there you have it; I've never been able to judge the true disposition of a woman.

Of course, as a male, I have pondered on the subject with enthusiasm from about age thirteen. But try as I may to penetrate the mystery of femininity, I've normally been more absorbed by trying to find a path to the rolling hills and valleys of a woman's topography. And, in truth, I've not really managed to make much progress toward understanding what really makes a human female tick beyond what it takes to address the immediate needs of my lust.

But let's be fair, for almost precisely 99.99% of the time that

Homo sapiens have been on this earth, the division of labor in social organization has been based exclusively on biological factors, specifically age and sex. There have been jobs done by young men and others done by old men, and there were jobs done by fertile women and jobs for non-fertile girls and women. I don't think my brain has made it into the most recent 0.01%. I still divide them up the old way, perhaps as nature intended. 99.99% of anything should not be taken lightly, and it might take a bit more time for a few of us older blokes to finally come around.

Practically, I know little about the female mind, and I was never proud of this. But analytically, my nimble mind concluded early on that love is a natural process easily undifferentiated from others, such as *weather* or *rust*. Somehow, most people did not share this fundamental scientific insight - and almost all girls. And although I've been married to the same woman for twenty-two years, I only gradually became aware of the depths of her own superstitious nature, the mild but definitely feminine psychopathology in getting her way, and her deviously imaginative depravity in hatching plots to change my behavior, to whip me into good health, and then *spiritual* shape fit enough to join hands with and walk together into the little philistine's Shamanistic influenced Pentecostal Paradise. I should have seen the signs from the start. The bride price demanded by her father was very modest and appeared to be *means-tested* – and I'd lost my bundle the day before in a Las Vegas casino. He practically gave her away.

Looking back, Pam's seen me all along as a work-in-progress

and, in the bargain, from time to time, made my *actual* life a bit like I imagine Hell is intended …as a warning, a little taster to prompt along the mending of my ways. As the whiskey-sodden Shoshone Chief's temperance-driven daughter, she was probably just as insufferable before I settled matrimonial terms with him and her older brother.

But fair go, waking up to the maladjusted biochemical responses I manifest each day that cumulatively appear as my behavior - slightly eccentric to *my* mind but I concede are borderline schizophrenic by some measures - have worn her down a bit, dampened her expectations, and we've reached a kind of truce. Our relationship was always kind of about the exploration of limits. I know what is an adequate level of alcohol and drug-induced contentment - and she has a clear idea about what level will result in the consequence of everlasting damnation.

I accept that it's a matter of her principles, but she also accepts that I'll keep trying to push boundaries, and metaphorically, it's reached a stage where we define each other in terms of a never-ending but quietly acceptable relationship of cat and mouse. She plays with me, and to my bloodied, clawed, paw-swatted, cruelly-gnawed mousy self, I keep applying the medicine necessary to keep me alive and content - and she can keep doing what she likes to do.

Ironically, Pam has never been motivated to destroy *ATHEISTMAN*, although she's occasionally clashed with the Rat. The fuzzy machinations of her thought processes do not gel well with scientific and geopolitical information, and she's as interested in cold, hard reality as she is in yesterday's weather. If asked, she might describe *ATHEISTMAN* as a *professional anthropological teaching tool developed to demonstrate certain scientific precepts in a comical and thus student-friendly fashion* - basically what I told her - and not a mascot for deeply held philosophical beliefs. As far as Pam is concerned, no one in their right mind can believe in *nothing*, and such wrong-headedness can be driven out of its sufferer by persistent badgering, torment, and sinister application of unadulterated nagging.

She's never seen an *ATHEISTMAN* comic book, and I never actually explained to her specifically about the 1989 Khomeini cartoon or that seventy million Iranians were trying to kill me and that until the *fatwa* was lifted in 2005, I was raising a family without being eligible for life insurance...and that the reason I dragged her off to central Australia and Alice-*bloody*-Springs was not, strictly speaking, professional. But then again, I didn't know about Mrs. Skinning until *after* we were married – *quid pro quo*, I suppose.

Although I clearly misjudged Sue Tran and, embarrassingly, didn't correctly process Sister Mary's fly-half rugby physique to all possible conclusions, I don't make any revisions in the Journal. To do so would change reality, tantamount to traveling back in time and interfering with events, potentially causing a temporal paradox.

But I don't seem in the mood to make relevant entries, and it's not the anticipatory excitement of impending visitors or the dulling of said excitement by all the narcotics I've snored recently, but instead - visions I can't prevent forming on the Rat's multiplex screen in my brain - of Sue Tran and Sister Mary in *sexual* embrace.

In my half-drugged, daydreaming state, I'm stranded on a tropical desert island, and Sue Tran and Sister Mary morph into, respectively, a tallish, glamorous, sultry goddess-siren and a petite, slim, almost tomboyish country gal - both naked. And now I'm recording furiously in the Journal, making notes of extraordinary power and insight, capturing ideas that under every conceivable epistemological system are as real and legitimate as the laws of physics. To wit, who is hotter?

I write non-stop for seven pages, rest with another minor application of smack, and then review my entries: beautifully written, my finest prose, possibly Pulitzer quality. But although the Journal is private – the personal domain of privileged scientific and anthropological data, including secret/sacred material exactly like I've just written - I'm unsure whether the words might not have been, if not written before, certainly *thought* and considered from many angles by just about every man in the last forty-five years. Accordingly, I resolve that the entries are *drafts* until I make sure I haven't plagiarized copyrighted material. Also, I need to edit the entries when I'm completely sober - the words might turn out to be hackneyed garbage under post-opiate consideration, and for the first time, I may have to use the eraser.

Setting environmental background noise as normalcy pays off after an hour of crouching in the shadows of the old church. I hear the shuffling of heavy feet well before Bob comes lumbering into the village square from the beach. He has to walk slowly to keep the too-small pink flip-flops on his feet that were on Mrs. Korda's last time I saw them.

Right behind comes Sue Tran, still adorned in a bright orange reflector-stripped GUMO shirt. She moves stealthily, pointless in the high-vis shirt and with big Bob loudly dragging his fat feet across the sand and gravel like twin pink mini-dozers.

As anticipated, with the sun now approaching high noon, Bob hauls his sweating bulk into the shade of the Morton Bay Fig without too much study for potential hazards. It's clear he's had better mornings. He plods along laboriously, breathes hard, and when he becomes stationary - bent-over, hands on knees - he has trouble using his bone-dry mouth.

"I know you're here, Jack …Sister Mary," he gasps. "I need to get to a hospital. I think there's swelling in my brain. I'm having blackouts."

He gets no response and continues. "It's all up to you, Jack. We accept this is your turf …and now that we know, we're happy to pay whatever it takes to fix it up. We need you, Jack. You almost killed both of us …so this is *your* turf. There's a cut for everyone. What's the tax? …and we'll pay …just help us with this deal …please, Jack."

Sue Tran makes a quick silent reconnaissance of the community square, including a circuit around the gravel track. She hesitates at the northwest corner, peering in my direction until perhaps she sees the old cross over the entrance to the ruined building, and the meaning of the place sinks in. Then she turns away, walking back to Bob and the shade of the big fig tree. "He's in the old church …there," she says, pointing exactly at my location, setting my crab breakfast scuttling about my guts.

She spots the small white duffel bag before Bob. "Look! Our property …there's some paper on it. It's got writing …here."

Sue Tran rips off the note I pinned to the bag, reads it quickly, and hands it to Bob. He takes a few doubtlessly painful moments to focus and reads out loud, '*Dear Bob, There's nothing but death in this bag. Yours in Jesus, Sister Mary.*'

"What does this mean, Jack …Sister?" He speaks so low and sadly, dejectedly, that I can barely hear, but he looks directly at where I thought I was hiding. "Do you want me to destroy the drugs? …Jack, I know that's not what *you* want, but if that's what it takes …sure. Jack …Sister, if you agree not to dob us to the police, I'll destroy all the drugs …if that's what it takes. Fair dinkum, Jack, I'll do it. All this is killing me. I'm too old to go back to jail. How about we …talk it over?"

Well, elements of the situation - Bob's apparent change in disposition regarding drug ownership policy since I concussed him with the sacred stone, and his half-dead, less threatening body exhausted now from carting around bulk contraband - appeal to both Dr. Levague and the Rat. One of their hands reaches into the Prada

264

and seizes a carving knife, and the other slips the bag onto my shoulder. I inch out of the church shadows, knife at my side, not concealed, not in offensive posture - but ready.

"I'm really sorry about your head," I say, all sincere, and I walk into the sunlight at the edge of the village square and stop fifteen meters from Bob. The day's heated up, and there's a light, balmy sea breeze from the east. Bob's hat keeps the sun off my bald head.

"I must have lost *mine* there for a second," I continue. "But let me tell you, I'm kind of partial to …your product, and I guess I just got carried away. Tell you what, just let me keep the kilo that split open when we crashed …it got in my nose, for goodness' sake… consider it as *spillage*, and I don't care what you do. Korda's in a coma, the Aboriginal kid doesn't know …anything, and the nun's really young …and stupid. I'll tell her you decided to destroy all the scag before emergency services and the police arrive, and you left with Yousef on the little boat he's towing …to get help and rescue your passengers."

"It's kind of …what's the word …*ironic*? You reckon, Jack? Ending up here, like this, with someone like *you*," Bob muses lucidly. He points to the torn duffel bag on the ground next to the Morton Bay Fig. Sue Tran's standing next to it, perhaps reasserting ownership by being the first person who could grab it and run. "Look's a lot less than you took. Is Sister Mary returning this? Where's the rest of it? Why did you break it up?"

The deal I offer is the best Bob could expect from me under

the circumstances, but I trust the fat man, not a whit - and his accomplices less. I keep a diligent distance. Like a crocodile, Bob needs to be close before he attacks, and if the first lunge falls short, the prey could easily escape.

"It's a *taster*. I need to be sure we can make a deal. Then you can have the rest," I say, reasonably hopeful but not sure what for.

Sue Tran picks up the duffel bag by the torn end so nothing falls out, and she judges the weight by lifting the bag up and down like a large bag of onions. "There's less than half," she advises Bob, and she places the bag back on the ground and bends down over it, preparing to play *how-many-discs-of-heroin-are-in-the-bag*.

I'm not too sure if I can stop what I think will happen next. It comes down to this: if I do *nothing*, certain events will probably occur; if I do *something*, well, maybe …but Bob seals the deal. His manner changes from calm to injured badger in a heartbeat, and he inches towards me, his face assuming a hateful glare.

"Where's the Sister and Korda and the kid and the rest of our property *right now?*" he rasps, and clear menace emanates from demon-red, blood-shot eyes. He's breathing heavier in preparation for …*rage*. I don't think he's gotten over my smashing a sacred rock onto his head, tying him up, making him almost overdose, and stealing his drugs. Despite the seeming accord over my kilo of spillage scag, he's thinking of killing me straight away, and I'm sure, *horribly* in the bargain, just as Sue Tran tips out the contents of the duffel bag in front of her crouched body.

At first, in the tumble of ten Frisbee-sized discs of compressed heroin, all individually stitched-up in yellow cloth - and before they settle still on the ground - I swear I can't see *any* death adder snakes …nor, apparently, does Sue Tran. She moves her right hand near the pile of dope, still sporting reddened bite marks on her thumb, and commences pointing at each of the discs as she counts them up …*one* …*two* …she gets to *three* before the first snake strikes: a lightning-fast streak of thick brown-striped yellow tubing, its small jaws latching onto her hand, pretty well where *I* bit it yesterday.

Instantly, she jumps up, shaking the snake free, scrambling like a scalded cat, but she steps on a heroin disc, slips over, and her feet go out from under her. It's at *that* moment - when her left arm extends reflexively to the ground, bracing for her fall - that a second death adder springs with blurry speed, intercepting her hand and sinking fangs into the left wrist, into bare skin just below her GUMO shirt-sleeve.

One snake, two snakes …a third death adder is making a getaway, frantically wriggling back in the direction of the church, apparently choosing discretion over snaky valor.

Sue Tran is on her feet, successfully this time, and she's staggering backward, spinning and dancing around, wiping herself furiously to eliminate any excess snakes. Her eyes are in a panic, darting first to equally panicked death adders slithering here and there for all their worth, then to her hands, then me, then Bob, and back to me. Her face contorts with pain and then gapes in startled fear and

267

amazement as the baffling circumstances of being bitten by *two* highly venomous snakes sink in, and the dreadful truth that in all probability, *she's dead*[36].

Curiously, it all happened in a series of microsecond events, each of which would normally be accompanied by a terrified scream or howl from most Western women ...but not a peep out of Sue Tran, and I find myself wondering what Pam's reaction might have been. With a pang of affection, I posit that she'd have snatched the snakes right out of the air way before they got to her, even as they extended their fangs in mid-strike; quick as lightening, she'd have them by their throats like an excited Jack Russell seeing it all in slow-mo.

Bob is struck still as a statue, his fleshy face aghast with horror. It happens so fast that it's over before he understands what's just occurred. While they both process information likely to significantly affect their personal and business affairs, I prepare for Bob to go berserk.

I have little data about whether Sue Tran is physically capable

---

[36] It is difficult to conclude that Levague is not a psychopath from this account. It is clear evidence of a premeditated and gruesome murder.

Authorities should make little of the note from 'Sister Mary', nor can opiate intoxication or some notion of self-defense be considered as mitigating factors. Killing a person with death adder snakes is not normally what you'd expect from a nun or a cultural anthropologist, and it appears that this maniac is almost always high on some kind of illegal substance, with jungle law seemingly on his everyday mind.

of participating in a vigorous assault right now, but I'm worried she could still out-sprint me, possibly bring me down in a last, life-draining burst, and grab hold long enough for Bob to get his beefy meat-hooks on my throat. The carving knife in my hand seems to shrink to Swiss Army size, no longer holding deterrent value. It's time to split.

"You did this, Jack," Bob states quietly, for the record. I say nothing.

"Are you a *real* doctor, Jack?" Sue Tran asks with remarkable calmness in her voice. Standing still, she studies her right and left hands. I detect a slight slurring. Then she clutches her chest, takes short, sharp breaths, and adds, "Can you help me?"

"I think you could have survived *one* snake," I allow, surprised that I'm a bit sad for her predicament of having the monumental misfortune of seeing only Dr. Levague as a last useless hope.

"If emergency services arrive in a helicopter exactly *this* second …and if they have anti-venom, there's a fifty-fifty chance you could live, even with *two* snake bites."

That's probably the truth, but it would be professionally inappropriate to give the poor woman any false hope, so I add, matter-of-factly, "I think you'll find it harder and harder to breathe – over the next ten minutes or so - before your respiratory muscles paralyze completely."

To brighten the moment, I add, "But I don't think it'll be too painful. It might make you feel better to drink some water, and it's

269

actually quite lovely in the shade of the river gums upstream from the old cemetery. You'll find clean water just past the last grave, Paddy Kunmubilpilguru's, actually. It's not far...but you'd have to leave soon, or maybe Bob can carry you. You'll find the rest of the heroin over there as well ...if you're still at all interested."

Bob hasn't moved during the dialogue, his eyes glued on Sue Tran. He's unsure whether to go immediately to her aid, take her into his strong arms, succor her, and cradle away the last moments of his partner's life ...or throttle me. Finally, he chooses the former ...the big softy. He moves to her quickly, grave tenderness in his bloodshot eyes, and takes the small woman into his arms like a baby, saying to me, "I don't care, Jack. Look what you've done. It should have been me ...because I'll spend the rest of my life hunting you down."

"I know it's a small comfort, Bob," I say, "but my thought was *you'd* go for the bag."

Sue Tran's gasping. Her tiny body's gone still. Her right, twice-bitten hand hangs limply at her side, a pink diamond ring too heavy to lift, and she's using all her strength just to gather in air enough to keep from suffocating under the weight of her own lungs.

"You're one sick puppy, Levague ...a real psycho," advises Bob, and there's a depth of hatred in his glowering eyes I've only *occasionally* seen directed my way, and emanating from the huge, ex-biker - previously locked up for manslaughter - it's enough to set the old legs itching to bolt.

"Still want to make a deal, Bob?"

270

But just at that moment, Sue Tran goes completely still in his arms, and a final, wheezy sigh escapes her dying body, and Bob turns gentle eyes on her ashen face as *her* eyes close - and just before - perhaps the slightest of smiles …the last love for her big man. Gee, that *was* quick.

"There's no deal …just you and me," he says quietly, and he shuffles unsettlingly briskly to edge of the village square with a small corpse in his arms, gently laying it on a patch of ground that might have been a flower bed years ago and as he turns his back, I can see ugly purple swelling under the short grey hair at the base of his skull but I dismiss the urge to attack again while he's momentarily not looking - I'm just not fast enough to get to him.

He slowly stands, turning my way. In his meaty right hand: a jet-black dagger - a stiletto switchblade knife - that looks to have recently been in a fire. He's calculating whether he can close the fifteen meters between us fast enough for a successful fatal lunge.

Now, a bookmaker - or an actuary - would probably give you even money in a race to see who collapses first: a taller, fat fifty-year-old in too-small ladies flip-flops or a thinner, sixty-year-old smoker in normal shoes. But factoring in, respectively, blind rage and fear - it's easy money backing the cowardly old fellow every time. I slink away as he readies to make his move, sparing one more glance at the shrunken orange bundle of dead flesh and bones on the ground behind him, with reflector safety strips glinting softly in the dappled shade of the giant Morton Bay Fig.

I know he commits when his bulk tilts forward in preparation for getting those fat legs pumping, and this I barely register as I turn and hightail it between the old church and the estuary mangroves, making for the creek. He only manages a few meters, and I suspect he realizes I've gotten away when an explosion of pain so intense I almost lose consciousness spins me around on the spot like I've been hit across my right shoulder with a two-by-four.

I stagger backward, noticing Bob's still coming but seems to have lost his knife. Somehow, I manage to keep my feet as I turn, and a new rush of adrenaline sends me bolting into the cemetery, past the first row of gravestones, then Paddy's, and up the creek with nary a glance back towards Bob, or sideways down to the crocodile nest. All the while, the Prada is bouncing up and down on my right shoulder with ten kilograms of sacred stone, each step a stabbing-sharp agony and getting worse. I trudge down the gentlest of declines into the creek bed and keep increasing the distance from Bob's fury-oozing hate.

Throbbing pain radiates from my shoulder across my back and down my right arm as I stumble another two hundred meters upstream, and I'm spent out, puffing and coughing so hard I'm spitting. I cast my eyes back and spot Bob shuffling through the sunlit cemetery like a zombie. With footwear of marginal utility, he has no choice but to take it slow. For every ten meters he manages, I stagger twenty. His resolve will not falter, and I'm a condemned man having his execution stayed in blocks of ten minutes or so. Evidently, he's not worried about leaving his main stash unguarded on the beach.

He stops near old Paddy's grave and appears to look my way, and we're face to face for a moment. Now would be a good time for a crocodile to snap Bob's legs from under him and drag him into the swamp, and when I catch some breath, I find myself shouting down to him as loud as the pain permits to better the odds of that occurring.

"Let's stop and rest a bit, Bob. We both need a break. By the way, your dope's just down the embankment to your right. You can't miss it …Just down from the last grave…near the dead monkey staked in the mud. I'll wait here while you check it out."

He glances down to his right at the unlikely sight of a monkey stuck on a spear but he's not interested in retrieving lost property. He remains silent, glaring eyes back on me, and he recommences the hunt. He won't rest while rage is driving him, and he smells blood. The nest of horrors down from Paddy's tombstone remains still.

With only moments to spare, I fall to my knees on the grassy creek bank in the shade of river gums and try to let the Prada's strap fall off my right shoulder, but it seems to be stuck on, and I have to reach back over with my left hand and pull Bob's dagger out of both the leather strap and about three centimeters of upper back muscle, ligaments and my right scapula bone before it slides loose. I have to wiggle the knife a bit to pry it out of the shoulder blade, and while excruciating, the panic of finding a steel blade sticking in your back is usually incentive enough to get it out as a first-order imperative.

Now, Bob's twenty-centimeter flame-blackened stiletto is in my left hand with cold steel edges stropped sharp enough to slice through skin at individual cellular definition, and I can't help wonder if it's been in anyone else's flesh recently, hoping they didn't have AIDS. I seem to have dropped Sue Tran's carving knife, and likely Bob's retrieved it near the point where ownership of the switchblade changed back near the Morton Bay Fig.

I rotate my right arm once or twice to check the mechanics. It feels like a stake's been driven into me with a sledgehammer, but I have reasonably full movement. I shudder thinking that had Bob's throw been only a fraction either way, I'd have a stiletto blade stuck through the back of my neck, poking out the front of my throat near my Adam's apple or between my ribs in a lung or my heart. As it happened, the Prada's thick, two-ply leather strapping prevented the blade from slicing clean through my shoulder blade to the hilt, which probably saved my bacon.

The creek pools nearby, so I wash my hands and scoop water for a drink. My white T-shirt sticks wetly to my back. When the blood flow staunches and dries, it'll be scabbed onto my skin like Bob's hat to my scalp. Struggling back to my feet, I have to balance myself as blood drains from my head in a red, dizzy rush. When it passes, I reach back over my right shoulder with my left hand to assess the rate of blood loss from what I'm sure is a raw, gaping wound. My fingertips seem numb, not as sensitive to touch as normal, but they come away covered in blood, and when I wiggle my fingers in front of my face, they tingle painfully, and the monkey-bitten little finger won't flex at all. Before the disgusting animal had its teeth in me, it

274

was chewing on a pink galah and likely the stupidest, slowest bird in the flock as well - the one suffering most from some incapacitating filthy avian form of fast-acting lupus, I'm sure. My luck, I'm sick with that on top of the rabies.

The burned stiletto goes into the Prada, and then I hoist the strap over my left shoulder, holding my right arm tight against my chest to minimize movement. My eyes find Bob shuffling along behind, and I also notice I've climbed far enough up the almost imperceptible incline of the creek to have an uninterrupted view of the community ruins and all along the beach to the south, where bright-white duffle bags, two now, make an impressive pile of drugs even from six or seven hundred meters away.

My scan draws north again, searching for movement near a small patch of blue in foreshore dunes on the other side of sandbanks at the mouth of the estuary. There's no sign of a large white nun anywhere near the tarpaulin.

I also have a beautiful view of the glistening Arafura Sea, all the way to the grey-muddy mouth of the Woolen River two kilometers south of the island. Mid-afternoon sunlight falls from the western sky, and I search sparking, shifting sea hues of aquamarine, the endless glints and flashes of whitecaps in a gentle easterly breeze - and no Armani drug smuggler appears to be sailing our way …just yet.

Before I start hauling my ass further from Bob - a job-of-work suddenly all the harder for the knife hole in my back - I peer into the sky as far south as I can, tuning sixty-year-old eyes and ears to maximum sensitivity, and at the extreme limits of my vision, a tiny glint of reflected sunlight twinkles like the faintest early star in the corner of my eye; and when I zero in on the farthest horizon, I spy a white plane seemingly on a low flight-path back to Darwin, possibly searching the ground for a crash site. If it's following an expanding grid pattern, I should probably think about setting a fire tomorrow morning before its next run, or perhaps ten fires, or maybe set the whole damn island ablaze.

The creek and the line of river gums continue directly northwest for another kilometer or so and then disappear in the darkness of a skinny gully that the creek has eroded in the western base of the ironstone hill. I press on, exhausted and panting, already having walked farther than I normally do in a week. Although presently, I'm running away from Bob, I'm incidentally closing in on Chirp's likely location, and I start to wonder if he'll be a help or a hindrance…or perhaps bait.

For a seeming eternity of agony, I trudge along the bank of the creek. Each step brings the weight of the Prada pressing down on the button of pain consuming my upper back. My breath comes in sharp, rapid gasps, and I count the heavy slog of each meter by the rhythm of my racing heart, the thudding excruciation in my right shoulder, and the pounding in my temples. Knowing I'm still outpacing Bob, I let my gaze default to the flat ground immediately ahead of my feet, on guard only for an odd rock or unevenness that might trip me up, and I try to set my mind to wandering somewhere that doesn't hurt. I'm reasonably expert at pain mitigation, and happy anticipation of opiate relief at the end of this long march sets thoughts free.

...As far as I know, I haven't been actively pursued by an agent of malfeasance since 2005 – the official lifting of the Iranian *fatwa*. I took appreciable comfort in believing I was skulking unnoticed in the deserted wastelands around Alice Springs - and I was. But this time, there's no sense that any of this is *my* doing or fault ...and there's no hiding. No one could have ignored Bob's 'mine samples'. The circumstances were always - *he tried to smuggle drugs, and he crashed his plane; the attempt failed - and people who shouldn't know have found out*. Simply, the issue is - *how does Bob manage this problem?*

Keep trying is what I'd do. Or *start* trying ...But is that the *real* me? After surviving a crashed and burned airplane - at least for a while there - my expectation was that I'd get rescued in a reasonable timeframe, have a hell of a cocktail party story when I got home, and apply scotch whisky, tobacco, tranquilizers and pot - at will, for the 'stress' - and all in quantities rarely permitted by the pleasure-quelling wretch at home. I should be there with her now, regaling heroic tales of dogged survival, even as she scrambles to put away already-filled-out life insurance claim forms. But my accidental exposure to Bob's high-grade wares and repeated indulgence since has shifted my perspective. I'm more self-centered now.

As I slog up the creek to the dark headwaters and the foot of the black hill at the heart of the island, I think of three dead bodies I've

seen up close and personal - two if Korda's still technically ticking –
all in the space of hours, and already I've come close to being next,
and before the day's out, it's reasonably certain either Bob or me will
be dead or close to it.

I suppose I could keep ahead of him until we're rescued, but
somehow, a confrontation has become certain, and given this, I find
myself again pondering the equation - *what's actually in the way of
claiming $2.2m for the Levague pension fund?*

I could easily bury the stash and come back discretely - to do
further anthropological research and expand on points I've noted in
the Journal – when the heat dies down and in the fullness of time. And
why should I have to put up with this suffering and anguish: plane
crash, rabid monkey bites, stabbed in the back - all for nothing?

And who says cold turkey is inevitable? I could sell half the
consignment for enough ready cash to comfortably see me out forever,
and it would take the rest of a reasonably long life to get through a
hundred and ten kilos of uncut primo scag - at a healthy pace, mind -
never overdoing it and letting the drugs rule me rather than the other
way around; and when some cancer or wasting disease catches me
eventually, I'll be ready – the old Earnest Hemmingway
superannuation plan but with a less messy, more sophisticated illegal-
drug overdose rather than a shotgun …and the black-hole of fear I call
my wife can be damned.

The only thing between me and my *options* for the future is
Bob. Now, it's him or me, but after - when it's just me - *what's in my*

way?

I can easily avoid one Armani on this island - even one with a gun - for as long as it takes emergency services to arrive, if they're reasonably competent and comprehensive in their search, and if they haven't written us off as crashed into the sea and already sunk. With no Bob and Sue Tran, Yousef will never know what happened - or he might have an accident trying to get here ...*or after he does. Then, what's to stop me?*

I find myself composing words for a letter to a Mrs. Quigley in Ireland, and I try several drafts before settling on a version that gets to the point quickly, with the fewest somber words to prolong a creeping, fearful expectation of bad news - *Dear Mrs. Quigley. I'm sorry to report that a crocodile has eaten your daughter ...*

Every step along the creek is a test of physical endurance, and I drive my legs on and on, and the black monolith capping the island's heart looms. That's my destination, my dark destiny. Anticipation of quality drugs gives me the strength to keep going.

My lungs heave in great rapid gulps, barely gathering the air necessary to lift a leg, and my heart pounds a base drum in my chest. I can no longer carry the weight of the stone in the Prada over either shoulder, and now I'm dragging it behind me, hauling the strap with my numb, monkey-bit left hand, and I fall into a trance of pain with the stone in the Prada, jerking along with each step.

Suddenly, I stop, and I'm staring down at what takes a tick to emerge as meaningful: a bright new Nike running shoe, and just ahead, the other; and further on, a yellow TALC T-shirt with the Rainbow Serpent motif that brings to mind both the dragon on Ling's lunchtime menu and my favorite brand of Armani smack. It appears that Chirp's been here, stripped down, and gone native, although I note he still has his darker blue pants, which are harder to see at night.

His mode of thought has gone crafty, joining mine and Bob's. I can't leave the shoes for Bob; they go into the Prada, and I also take the T-shirt.

Finally, just as breathing is more agony than the stab wound in my shoulder, I'm approaching the base of the ironstone hill, coughing, gasping, drooling and panting like an old dog.

The huge monolith looks to have erupted out of the raw, flat earth and pushed its way up between two red granite boulders, both the size of small houses, and a tumble of lesser boulders, rocks and stone debris forming a ring around the base. Up close, it's more a huge black protuberance; a smooth-flanked stone mound, bereft of vegetation, rising low above its surrounds rather than a steep-sided hill, a gigantic black mushroom cap pushing up through the red ground - or the exposed buttocks of an Aboriginal giant buried face down below the surface. A fit person could easily clamber up the gentle gradient all the way to the top.

The granite boulders rest against the base of the hill's incline as if they've rolled down the side of the mound as it rose out of the earth. They offer shadowy hiding options. One lies at the entrance of a small gully cut into the base of the western flank of the hill, the smallest of butt-cracks in the huge black ass sticking out of the ground. It's possible to clamber on top of the boulder with a Prada bag full of rocks should I choose, and I'd have range to rain down death on anyone following the creek up into the gully. But if I missed, I'd be treed when my ammo ran out, and with Bob pacing back and forth below like a hungry grizzly, I'd be trapped up there until one of us starved to death, and Bob wears at least a month of fat.

Save for the top of the ironstone knoll, I'm at the highest point on the island. When I finally catch my breath, I glance over my shoulder down the creek line, and it takes a moment's peering to spot Bob's khaki-clad biomass shifting in and out of lengthening river-gum shadows, maybe six hundred meters behind.

The sun is about 5:00 pm in a cloudless, darkening blue sky. He'll take an hour to catch up. If I disappear and stay unfound a little longer, darkness and surprise could give me an edge. I need a plan.

Just as desperately, I need a smoke, and the pain in my shoulder won't let me think. Doubtless, I'll take frustration at the former out on Bob, and the latter means …well, there's nothing for it, so I find shade near the mouth of the gully, sit on a rock near the base of the granite boulder nearby, and unzip the Prada.

There's heroin powder all over my right hand when I finish in the bag, and I apply a reasonable finger-tip pinch to my woe: the tormenting pain, the impossibility of outlasting both Bob *and* Yousef and the general angst of trying to fit a truckload of heroin into a reality that rarely includes more than a few ounces of skunk weed.

Rubbing against the sacred stone inside the Prada has ground most of the rest of my slab to powder, and I remove the tatters of yellow cloth and plastic covering from the bag and discard them at my feet. Bob will find it I'm sure, and know that one-two-hundred-and-twentieth of his dope is gone now, and it might help refocus his priorities - he might come to his senses and retreat. Maybe not - after ingesting narcotics, it's possible to anticipate many impossible things.

There's no sign of the feral little petrol sniffer, but I spotted bare footprints near the creek at the narrow entrance to the gully. For the moment, I slouch forward with elbows on my knees while the junk stings my nasal cavities, watering my eyes, even as calm and well-being rush to my back, coating the agony in my shoulder with blessed narcotic tranquility. I take five, and the warm glow spreads throughout my whole miserable being, and I find myself drifting in a moment of bliss but with my gaze locked and tracking Bob, and I take heart when I register longer pauses in his pursuit. With any luck, fat-clogged arteries will deal his final hand before I have to – *or he deals mine.*

Precious time is used to recover from the long march - as much as I can afford *and* keep Bob a half hour behind. When I stand again, I notice the blood from my shoulder has soaked the right side of my white T-shirt and spread under my arm but stopped before my waist. Apparently, I'm not bleeding to death.

The creek disappears up the narrow gully. The entrance is twenty meters wide, and late afternoon sunlight funnels between high, straight walls of solid rock and deep up the crack of the black giant's ass. After about thirty meters, the walls come together, pinching off space just about where a sphincter would be. The narrower it gets, the tighter the walls form a natural trap.

As I enter the gully, the creek runs up against the northern rock face on one side, and a bank of sandy earth on the other forms a shallow, meter-wide channel. Sunlight glistens off a line of trickling water until it disappears up the gully into shadows behind ancient pandanus palms with dark green fronds arranged like peacock feathers, weeping coolabah willow trees with leaves all aglitter on low-bending branches, and occasional taller silver-barked eucalypts. But finally, the gap in the rock closes, and the darkness deep inside is rarely disturbed by the sun.

Chirp's tracks head up the gully, and I follow his path along the creek. Steep ironstone walls grow closer together, butt-cheeks clinching, squeezing Prada-swinging space. Just before the two walls join at the base of the gully, the creek ends in a stony water pool with wet sandy margins, the surface welling up with pressure from an underground spring. I fall to my knees and re-fill an empty plastic bottle from the Prada. Bare footprints are trampled all about, but Chirp's not here.

Late slanting sunlight filters its way up the gully, and trees draw sparse, thin shadows shifting across the waterhole in the gentle breeze. It's a lovely shady spot. The spring water is cool, and the sandy margins are soft and inviting. I'm exhausted.

The hole in my shoulder has sapped the adrenalin from my biochemistry, and my legs are cramping and almost useless for anything except standing up. But I can't afford to get caught in such a closed space, and when I notice Chirp's footprints leading back towards the mouth of the gully along the southern rock face, I flog a final briskness into my step and follow.

About halfway back, the ground rises slightly, and I stop near a small sand pile at the rock wall's base. Judging by the jumble of footprints, Chirp came to this point and stopped. The rock face is too steep to scamper up, and it's as if he got swallowed up or flew away.

But then I hear the faintest of muffled *tinking* - the sound of two ancient mulga wood clapping sticks striking each other, and it's coming from inside solid black rock.

285

Chapter 8: Like Robinson Crusoe

The source of Chirp's tapping appears to be a small pile of excavated sand on top of a mound rising several meters up the base of the gully wall. It's as if a few dozer blades of dirt from the immediate vicinity had been pushed up against the rock face and then weathered to look natural.

I lower myself gingerly to my knees, looking for a clue as sharp pain runs down my right arm from the knife hole in my shoulder. Just about my whole being is in one form of agony or another, but more a worry is suffocating weariness clutching me close. The trudging march of pain up the creek is more exercise than I get in a month *without* carrying hospital strength injuries. My legs are seconds away from seizing up with cramps. I didn't sleep last night, only nodding from one restless opiate dream to the next, and I haven't had my afternoon nap for two days running.

The thought of *angry-Bob-in-a-boxed-canyon* takes hold again, and my toes twinkle feebly in useless preparation for a dash out the gully and beyond. I'm all out of running.

There's something definitely different about the ground here. The recent disturbance looks like a wombat's excavation - a grotesquely obese gopher's diggings - and a forty-centimeter hole in the ground looks like it tunnels down and under solid rock. I scoop out the hole wider and deeper using both hands, ignoring howling protest from my right shoulder and the unsettling numbness of monkey-bitten fingers.   With each handful, the *tinking* becomes louder, closer.

Soon, I push away enough sandy dirt to see someone has tunneled a passage into a large cavity under the base of the rock. After a moment or two more digging, I break through into the darkness of open space and slide down a meter of sand, swimming on my belly to the rocky floor of a large dark cave, dragging the Prada in with me. I struggle to my feet and remain still while my eyes adjust.   The clapping sticks are silent.

Late afternoon light falls in from the passageway I've opened, and a curve of smooth black rock is dully illuminated.   It's a cavernous, circular space measuring about ten meters in diameter and five high. The base of the rock-face outside is actually the top of the low narrow mouth of a cave. It seems certain that years ago, earth and sand had been purposely piled up here to conceal the cave entrance.

"Mother's Brother," Chirp states my name in lingo, low and soft, going for formality rather than calling me *Veggie*, and his words seem to come from everywhere in the closed space, spooking the hell out of me. But I hear calmness in his voice in place of his usual panic, and he believes he recognizes the harmlessness of a classificatory close kinsman. He's somewhere at the back of the cave, and before I see details, all that's visible is a line of white teeth revealed in Chirp's familiar, especially idiotic grin.

"Shut the hell up," I whisper back hoarsely in English, trying to be even more formal.

He complies, and while he seems less unhinged than last time, I'm sure he's still reasonably tooled up for fear and panic and understands the urgency in the wise old fellow's words: danger from something *real*.

I strain my senses, trying to judge the merits of this place as both a hideout and a bastion of defense. The entrance can be walled up again with sand that's spilled inside, but there's now a major excavation at the base of the gully that Bob can't miss if he follows our tracks. There's no hiding here and waiting him out.

Perhaps it's better to sneak behind the boulders near the mouth of the gully and wait for Bob to come bumbling along, and maybe he'll spot the recently excavated sand and think he's trapped me down a hole. When he charges down into it all kamikaze-like with carving knife flashing, I'll see about setting something big on fire and tossing it in after him, and Chirp can use all his strength to scoop and plow sand over the entrance and keep it closed long enough for big Bob to suffocate. But compared to the old ruins of the church in the village, with too many windows and open bits of roof to guard effectively, the cave is easier to defend. I can't run anymore, and it's two against one, reasonable odds to get your chips all-in; and being a non-smoker, he probably won't have a lighter or matches to set a log ablaze and chuck it into the cave. As a smoker, I always hold the power of fire.

In the confined space of the cave, I determine that Chirp will be more useful as a shield for Sue Tran's knife - a fly to feed the spider when he comes barging through the entrance - rather than as an offensive weapon. I'll stay behind him, a shadow pushing forward, lunging with the switchblade while Bob's carving hand is busy with the kid. But I'm not sure of even modest uses for Chirp. He'll more likely react to threats only to himself, and now that I think of it, I've not had a chance to firm up in my mind exactly what's wrong with the kid and if he's any use at all. Sane people are all the same - predictable, but crazy people are each crazy in their own way, harder to stimulate a response you can reasonably anticipate and employ to sane ends.

"Sister's Son ...where's Sister Mary?" I ask in lingo, thinking *Yolngu* is better for judging true disposition. I'm expecting a puzzled look or the drooling continence of a lecherous mutt and a bit surprised when he replies, "She's with you."

"Right ...she's fine ...on the beach ...we ate crabs. She's taking care of the mine boss," I continue in even tones. "He's not well. He got burned in the plane crash ...Seen his wife lately?"

"She's over there," he says matter-of-factly, pointing with his head toward nothing but space and the back of the cave.

This isn't getting us anywhere, so I cut to the chase, changing the facts only marginally, "The pilot is very angry about you crashing his plane. I think he might be coming here to kill you."

My hand's on his shoulder just as he makes to scramble to his feet in doubtless preparation to bolt out the cave, out the gully, and as far away from this point on the island as possible. "Don't move. Stay here. I'll protect you," I say, patting his shirtless shoulder.

I'm trying to calm him but still sharpen his wits for the best chance he's got to save me and possibly himself, but I'm not sure he'll follow the script if the plan's any more complicated than *There he is! Get him!* I reckon the best thing is to leave him where he is, even tapping his sticks to get attention, and I'll be ready at the side of the cave entrance with a ten-kilo rock to crush the first bit of Bob that comes through the passage, and a stiletto handy to stab the next bit, hopefully, his neck or spine. Failing that, I'll use what strength I can muster to haul him all the way into the cave and bolt back past him for freedom or form a rugby scrum with Chirp in front and barrel my way out and through the gully, pausing only to set something ablaze behind me.

So I kneel down next to Chirp and say, "We'll wait for him to come through the hole. You sit here and tap your sticks, sing if you want ...keep an eye on the white boss's wife. I'll smash the sacred stone on his head if he comes in and stab him with a knife. Then we'll find your girlfriend and return the sacred stone to Minjininga."

"We have to bring the *TWO MEN*," he replies anxiously, and it takes a tick to credit he's still worried about phantom gods and spirits, but then I understand he might be thinking of *praying* to his supreme male-cult ancestors - to come to the rescue, to save his sorry ass - and he wants me to join in. Normally, it's Dr. Levague who deals with Aboriginal religion, and I might be expected to make a respectful comment, but now it's *ATHEISTMAN* who ignores the lad, and I realize I might be stepping over some final professional line, mocking beliefs I've tried to record dispassionately all my life. It might spell the end of anthropology for me, a sea-change to Jack-the-Rat - heroin dealer.

"Come here often?" I ask.

"The cave *called* me …so I came," he replies, offering up the uniquely indigenous notion of *talking* landscape. "It's my father's older brother's secret place. The Seven Sisters dance here, and the *TWO MEN* are in the big black rock."

I digest this nonsense and open the Prada, removing the kidney-shaped ritual stone - powder white with its dusting of narcotics - Bob's dagger and a length of rope sufficient to tie someone's hands and feet. I toss Chirp's runners aside. I use my cigarette lighter to find handy positions near the cave entrance for each tool. The glow illuminates brightly anything within a meter, and it's enough to catch a glimpse of markings on the cave wall that don't look natural.

Chirp's eyes fall and stay on the sacred stone, and he mutters, "Mother's Brother - Sister's Son Stone." He states, "We'll fight the big whitefella and then bring the *TWO MEN*." That's as close to a plan as I've heard from anyone lately, and the half that makes sense is all that matters. I set the stone, the knife, and myself near the entrance and await the endgame.

There's no sign of Bob after a while, and a sickening thought occurs that maybe he's lurking just outside the cave right now, possibly enjoying the sunset with a bottle of water next to the freshwater spring nearby and waiting for me to come out or darkness to fall. But all I've heard outside is the steady increase of bird-squawk as cockatoos, swallows, and others I don't recognize take roost in the gully trees for the night, and I would have read any variation in birdsong for its likely cause: a heavy-breathing, blundering human with murder on his mind.

I'm hoping to get this over quickly and relax for the night, knock my socks off again with a good measure of the excellent scag, and maybe sing songs with Chirp …or maybe dwell on the tragedy of a malicious drug dealer who savagely stabbed the lad to death to keep dirty drug deeds a secret.

I'm not at all sure how long I can keep my finger out of the Prada, but it's odds-on certain I'll not be sharp enough to manage Bob after another hit, and I can easily convince myself he'll miss the cave entrance in poor light and I'm safe in my hidey-hole until morning. It's a bit of a stalemate now, but the longer Bob takes, the greater the chance that a snort will just happen, probably in a split second – the situation escalating to a hair-trigger Mexican standoff, and one side blinking. It's not 'Miller Time', but it's taking Herculean effort to resist the urge to apply more medication. Discretion wins out, and I drag myself away from drug thoughts and set my gaze across the cave wall, searching for the unnatural markings I noticed earlier.

The narrow low cave opening squeezes out the last daylight as the sun sets. My cigarette lighter flame bends, folds and flaps as heavier, humid air pushes into the cave at ground level. Held up to the rock face, it returns the shifting image of a one-meter-tall band or strip of artificial lines and colors stretching from the one edge of the cave entrance in a circular sweep of twenty meters around to the other, about waist high, as if drawn by someone sitting on the ground and moving in an arc around the base of the cave wall, creating an extremely long canvas. The artist used light ochre colors: chalk white, soft yellows, light browns, and rust-red pastel hues to contrast with the blackboard of smooth ironstone rock.

Believe it or not, my first thought is *there's a scientific paper here*, previously undocumented Aboriginal cave paintings, maybe World Heritage-listed *Aboriginal Site - Levague EA01*. But as I move closer, the dull heaviness in my shoulder pushes away thoughts of getting out the Journal. And, oh yes …there's Bob to deal with.

Chirp taps his sticks lightly and slowly, and my heartbeat washes wave after wave of opiate-masked throbbing pain as I've rarely felt. But the lighter is in my hand, and my eyes get pulled back to the ancient drawings as if magnetized.

I start at the right-hand wall from the cave's mouth as I face it and move around to my right in a circle. Immediately, I see the drawings become more detailed, complex, and elaborate as if telling a story, moving from simple individual ochre and river-stone chalk marks to clusters arranged in order, suggesting a tally of some objects, animals or people. When I hold the light close-up, the single lines have tiny arms and legs and become human stick figures, the simplest recognizable renderings in the art of human form.

Further along, the tiny people assume poses suggesting

293

fighting and dance: Kangaroo-men, Emu-women, and Crocodile Cult figures with exaggerated genitalia, holding spears and digging sticks; and I'm reading a symbolic language, a pictorial record of great Ancestral Beings imprinting order on primordial black nothingness, creating the mountains and seas, the islands, plants and animals, and the dances and rituals to keep it all safe; the official, immutable account of how and why things are the way they are - chaos tamed, ordered, made predictable - a book of Aboriginal Genesis.

I move around the base of the cave on my knees, past Chirp, and I recognize the Aboriginal Dreamtime motifs of a dozen themes and dramas. Here is the story of Dragonfly men dancing the monsoon up so they can emerge from swamps to initiate the wet season. There is the Dreaming Story of the incestuous Owl Woman sentenced to fly only in darkness for her sin.

About two-thirds along, I make out white scratching, unmistakably representing a European sailing ship and tiny figures with hats smoking pipes. I've seen similar in Kakadu National Park - figures of Dutch sailors, *Ballender* to the locals, in cave paintings dating from the 17th century. All the little figures in this painting are clustered around a sailing ship and lying horizontally, meaning they're dead - except one, who seems to be isolated and on land, evidently on an island.

There is a temporal dimension to the drawings: the cyclical nature of Dragon-fly men regulating the cycle of the wet and dry seasons - the circle of life and death, and a linear timeline leading from the ancient Dreamtime up to and beyond first European contact - and *conflict* if a ship-full of dead Dutchmen is any guide.

The next pictograph is a swirl of female figures arranged in a circle, arms raised and legs caught in mid-leap, twirling and dancing up landforms into features: sand dunes, hills and waterholes. It's the story of the Dreamtime Seven Sisters. I read the drama, and Chirp is tapping his sticks faster, and my heart beats in tune, and savage imagery swims before me - a tale of sexual conquest and death. In the next scene, the Hunter arrives, a stickman with a huge penis, and the Sisters are dead, the killer standing amid his rampage of rape and bloody murder. The next frame ends the epic myth. Etched into the black rock at standing eye-level, bright stars in the heavens: shining yellow ochre dots unmistakably configured as the Orion and Pleiades Constellations - the Hunter forever chasing the Seven Sisters, the Sisters forever evading further ravishment as the wheel of the night sky turns.

Despite my pitiful condition, I find myself itching to record this material. The mythology is connected to the world-famous *Minjininga Cave Ethno-Arch Site EA01* paintings, and I've discovered a place that could be equally significant. I'm pondering academic glory, staring at the stars of the Seven Dead Sisters, but my eyes and brain seem slightly at odds, a tickling of *not-quite-right*, and I peer closer and count not seven stars but eight. There's definitely a dimmer star I initially missed, a star, not yellow - but green, like the Prada bag …like the eyes of a dead woman. I gather in a slow breath and my pulse thumps twice as meaning takes hold - Chirp's added Mrs. Korda to the seven other stars, the Eighth Sister. There's anthropology and psychiatry aplenty here at *Levague EA01*.

Instinctively, I search the cave floor at the foot of the new green celestial Sister to identify the material he used, a source of green pigment, perhaps the sap or resin of a coolabah tree mixed with crushed-up leaf. I find only bare rocky ground.

Chirp's tapping matches the quickening of my heart, and an unsettling disquiet creeps into my brain. My eyes have locked on the last painting, my jaw's dropped in disbelief, and my lighter goes out when I vaguely notice it burning my thumb. I'm standing still in darkness, blinking and shaking my head to be rid of an image that can't be real, only the reason-cheating fantasy-of-the-poppy delusions of sleeplessness and exhaustion.

So, I flick the lighter and look again - still there - and I look closer in amazement: two huge stickmen stand elevated on a hill - one sketched yellow, the other dark red. A dazzling golden light emanates from the two figures, an explosion of yellow ochre chalk lines shining brightly and radiating in all directions. Both figures point to the heavens with one arm, the other pointing to their feet at a scene of human wreckage. I've seen it before. It's imprinted on my brain until I die - clever, thin white lines etch a tiny airplane out of the black rock, crashed and broken in pieces, fire-red ochre flames in the midst of the carnage. The yellow ochre radiance of the two men is their Divine Power shining down. They are the *TWO MEN*. And they have caused destruction with their omnipotence, and five dead stick-people lie around the crashed plane and flames at their feet …and final details send shivers up my spine: there's no mistake - the larger of the *TWO MEN* has a white beard, he's holding a book with 'J' on the cover and a fag dangles from his mouth. Most horrifying, his humongous dick is daubed at the tip with bright, wet looking, blood-red ochre.

I let the lighter go out after it's been burning my thumb for indeterminable seconds, and still, the *tink-tink-tink* of Aboriginal clapping sticks beat out a fast drum roll from everywhere in the cave, machinegun beats in tune with my heart, and I'm taking steps backward, recoiling legs are lifting of their own accord but not smart enough to first turn me around, and something catches my foot. I stagger backward, and my other foot comes down heavy on a large round stone that crushes like a thick Emu eggshell, and kernels of bizarre meaning are firing in my brain like uncontained popcorn.

With drug-crazed *TWO MEN* hallucinations still swirling around my vision, I try to connect the crunching sound my heel is making and the light-pinching it's feeling to something real. I crouch down with my lighter and pry off what's caved in around my foot: unmistakably an adult male human skull, and despite wit and reason fleeing me like scattering rats, one notion carves itself sharp enough in mind's eye to tweak a vestige of professional interest - I might be desecrating an Aboriginal burial, and I'll have to blame it on someone else.

I hold the skull up close and bring up my lighter to see the detail. We're face to face as the lower jaw drops off the skull and falls, clattering onto the cave floor, but teeth in the upper jaw show decay, cavities, and general wear typical of ...*what?* My conceptual apparatus drops a gear to find traction in slippery opiate conditions. I know that skulls of Aborigines dating from before European contact had fine, healthy teeth. Meat, potatoes, starchy bread, and teeth-rotting sugar were regular fare for this chap. He's a European.

How long has he been here? Who put him here? It might be possible for a skeleton to remain un-desiccated and relatively intact if isolated from light, humid tropical air and water, say if entombed in a cave and walled up in darkness by a ton of sand.

My mind seems to want further clues concerning this skull, the comfort of a bit of logical deduction, a puzzle to solve, to be rid of the hideous *TWO MEN* image, especially the *MAN* with the red-tipped dick. Dr. Levague takes control, formulating important scientific forensic questions like *Where's the rest of him?*

I cast about hunting for bones, and my light falls on a bundled form, half-covered by sand that's spilled in from the cave mouth during recent excavations. A bony hand protrudes from under some sort of dark fabric shrouding a human skeleton, its right index finger crooked up, beckoning me closer. It works, and I fold back a sheet of what appears to have been oiled canvas or heavy sailcloth that flakes when handled, like the crumbling of an ancient brittle newspaper.

The skeleton underneath is complete – except for the head. But for his extended right arm with inviting finger, it's in a position of formal funerary repose, rather than the fetal position of natural death, or limbs all askew as if tossed dead into the cave unceremoniously. The clothes he wore have long ago disintegrated and been absorbed by the canvas covering, leaving brass buttons, a belt buckle, and a single coin where a waste pocket might have been. It's a silver Dutch guilder, still holding a minted date - 1699, and a king's head seeing its first light in three hundred years. I appear to be rooting around the final resting place of an early Dutch sailor, evidentially an unlucky one.

An old musket gunpowder horn, originally a rather large bull's and still finely finished and lacquered, lies by his right side. There is a steel cap sealing the sharp end and a silver sheath, like chain mail, wraps around the rest of the horn - decoration rather than serving function. His left hand is rested on his breast, above his heart, where he once had one, and clutched in his bony grasp, finger on the trigger, is a 17th century, dark wooden blunderbuss pistol, and it looks remarkably intact, as if ready to fire at ghosts and grave-robbers.

I know my blunderbusses, and this one's a *Dragon*, British-made. I stared at an exact replica for months in Amsterdam, mounted on the wall at Hunter's Bar in a glass case, just above the scotch bottles behind the bar. The comically flared barrel and impossibly wide bore always suggested swashbuckling pirate movies or a weapon perfectly suited for hunting the cartoon rabbit. But it could take your head off, and I see why - a single musket ball near the powder horn, five centimeters in diameter, grey-white with age and oxidization, but when I feel its heft, I know it is solid lead.

Both hands are needed to convince the Dutchman to give up his gun, and finally, I have to break off most of his fingers in the dark. I hold the pistol up close to my lighter, turning it over and checking the impossibly huge bore. It's thirty centimeters long, twice the size of a modern revolver, and weighs as much as a rifle. The dark wooden handle is cracked and split at the butt, but the barrel cradle is solid and molds around the age-blackened steel cylinder, still holding it firm. The other metal components are corroded and discolored by age. The flintlock mechanism: hammer, flint and trigger are rust-frozen in the 'cocked' position and nonfunctional, and the frizzen protecting the flash-pan is missing. Nevertheless, the spark passage is clear, and the whole barrel's integrity seems sound, and it should be possible to muzzle load gunpowder, a lead ball and stuff some wadding down to hold it all in, and then set it off with the open flame of my lighter held up to the flash-pan, like a little hand-held cannon.

Of course, there's no guarantee that the black powder is still potent - or if it is, that I'll get the measure right, but I can think of no chemical reaction that could change the powder's constituents in an airtight container in an airtight cave, and any outcome from *nothing* to *blowing me to bits* seems equally likely. To test the former, I jimmy off the rusty cap of the powder horn and inspect the contents.

Part of me goes about checking this and that. I test a small pile of the black powder with the lighter, and it sizzles and sparks with a little *whoosh* of smoke that puts murder in the mind of the Rat.

Fashioning a deadly tool is work that comes naturally to him, work he knows by finger touch, monkey bites notwithstanding, and I can leave him unsupervised, worried only his notion of *adequate charge* might be less prudent than mine. As a rule, the Rat likes his bangs bigger.

Chirp holds the lighter up and watches closely. My sense is he understands the Rat's hands.

Dr. Levague refocuses on effective tactical uses for a centuries-old blunderbuss pistol, but I get carried away in a new wave of optimism. *I might yet get through all this* …And I fall to musing how it is that your very life can sometimes come down to a few random objects in a clever instant of time: a gun when someone needs shooting, a sacred stone, a normally locked door opening in desperation …someone else's motorcycle with the key in the ignition when it's time to flee. And I took a chance or two in my youth - let's be frank - a Berber Sheik, or any father, Arab or otherwise, really shouldn't have to see his favorite daughter bent over the hood of a broke-down Chevy Impala, black *hijab* pulled up past her chubby, naked waist - and a bare-assed, hairy white infidel, pants around his knees, humping away at her from behind with dirty purpose …stupid risk to be sure …but when the first bullet zinged past my ear, her little red Honda 50cc *Cub* was *right there*, started first kick, and took me from Oran to safety in Algiers through an entire Saharan desert night on one tank of fuel.

But testosterone-driven aberrations of youth aside and ignoring a lifelong inclination to always strive for yet another bowl of kava, I've held the coin of my life clinched in tight fists. With the frugality of an old atheist bastard, I keep purse strings drawn, slow and tight in risking the preciousness of life, mine anyway.

Yet, here I am again, up the fucking creek - and the things to save my life: a heroin-coated sacred stone, a stiletto switchblade I recently pulled out of my own back with rabies-infected fingers, a nitwit kid with a fondest for post-op transvestites and high-octane fuel, and a three-hundred-year-old, dead Dutchman's blunderbuss. *I'm not through anything yet.*

Sudden squawks, the squeaky thumping of startled bird wings, and someone's at the entrance to the gully only meters away - *Bob!* Shuffling feet scrape the ground, closer, faster; narrow ironstone walls amplify heavy breathing, and a gasping steam engine heads my way. Chirp stills the sticks and chanting, and I shush him while I read the sounds. There's silence …then Bob speaks.

"If you're in there, son, better get out. You in there too, Jack?" he asks the darkness outside, and the glow of low, flickering light appears at the cave entrance.

Chirp's on his feet, crouching low at the back of the cave, conflicted between flight and fight instincts, and hyperventilating like a raced greyhound. It takes a sharp rap to his head with my knuckles to focus his mind.

Then the light grows: dancing, glowing, yellow-orange flames, as crackling leaves, dry twigs and grass catch fire in an instant at the mouth of the cave. Thick blue-white smoke tendrils feel their way up along the cave walls, flooding the chamber's ceiling, and burnt eucalypt oil fumes choke the air from my lungs. Bob had a lighter all along, a single object, and now, his clever moment.

"I didn't know you were a smoker," I say, wresting up a modicum of calmness. "Wouldn't have a spare cigarette?"

"It's Sue's …you know, the woman you murdered a few hours ago," he says.

"She started it. She took a dead woman's ring. I bit her thumb. Then she threatened to kill me - slowly, mind …did she have any cigarettes?"

"I believe in God, Jack. I'm an Anglican, and Jesus is my savior …and all that," Bob says conversationally, and I hear 'but' before he speaks again. "But I've done …*bad* things. I thought they were behind me. I'm not talking *bad* like running drugs or cutting throats. I mean the kind of evil God hates the most, the pleasure of inflicting pain for no reason other than pure recreation. The *bad* feelings are back, Jack. It's a kind of *rage*, Jack, and I thought I'd mellowed, grown too old to want revenge so bad, but now it's all there is."

Flames have taken over the entrance to the cave. A raging curtain of yellow-orange light reflects heat and crimson glow off ironstone-oven walls. Sweat glistens off Chirp's skin, and he's crouched at the back of the cave, wide-eyed in fear but not yet keen to dive through fire to get out. Bob's still talking and, I'm sure, building up to something awful.

"I heard something about revenge being best served up cold …or the last revenge is the coldest …or something. But I've got a nice fire going out here, Jack. There's plenty of fuel. The big stuff's a bit damp from the rain, but it'll burn all night. And I truly reckon the best kind of revenge is served *hot*. I like the idea of you burning to death *slowly*. I like it a lot. We'll have a *bon*fire. That's French for 'great fire' …but of course, you know that already."

Frenetic shifting flames across the cave entrance make it hard to find any solid form beyond, even something tall and obese, but I can see movement, and the regular showering of sparks and crunch of charred wood tell me he's stoking the fire high. I need to keep him talking to track the target.

"You'll have to speak up, Bob. The fire's too loud," I say truthfully. "Sounds like the *Screaming Bull*, Bob. That's horrible. What about the kid?"

"The way out for him is the same as you. Crawl out through the fire …like a burning rat …and I'm here waiting. I'll cut the kid's throat for him quickly. But I'll just keep tossing you back," he advises. "That's no bull, Jack."

Clearly, Bob's not up on ancient Roman torture devices, a bit surprising for an ex-Hell's Cheater - but I suppose today's acetylene blowtorch really has all your modern horrendous torture needs covered. I must say, it *is* getting warm in here.

Time to end this, and I move low to the mouth of the cave with the blunderbuss, trying to pick the target between shifting flames and wavering heat mirage, a shot into a fire-bright bush-TV image. And I make him out, semi-solid behind flames and peering into the cave, arms held forth, carving knife in hand, dancing yellow-orange reflecting on the blade; an angry brown bear on hind legs, waiting beyond fire with open arms and a butcher's knife.

"I don't think God's looking, Jack," Bob opines, "and even if he is, there's something about a witch-burning that's a holy duty to all that's decent in the world. And look, you're already in your grave …You're a *bad* man, Jack. And now, you're a dead bad man."

"You're not related to anyone *Iranian,* are you, Bob?" I ask, and then say to Chirp, "Sound's like he's pissed at both of us. Let's shoot him."

And I only have one shot. Best to aim at the general mass, about midriff; a gut shot won't kill him outright, but it'll refocus his thought smartly - on the gushing river of blood from the hole through his stomach the size of a small fist. I steady, light up my lighter, raise the flame to the flintlock flash-pan, and remember to close my eyes as I bring the flame to bear down on the blunderbuss, expecting an ear-splitting *sizzle-ka-boom* and sharp recoil. Nothing happens. I try again with my eyes open - same result.

It's probably a bad idea to bet your life on a gun that hasn't fired in three centuries. Nevertheless, I can't help but feel cheated. Look what happens when I leave the Rat in charge.

I've grown accustomed to ingenuity, caution and blind luck

providing effective buffers to sticky situations, and failure of even unreasonable expectations leaves me perplexed and angry - for about a second - and then the horror of imminent death in the most awful agony sufferable sinks in; and I feel myself shrink down into a quivering blob of terrified jelly.

I can go smaller. According to the Heisenburg Uncertainty Principle, it's possible for all the subatomic particles that cumulatively form the infrastructure of my consciousness to pop out of existence and reappear spontaneously somewhere in the Universe light-years away. I begin calculating the odds of this happening; I would think one in ten to the power of several googols of magnitude might be about correct.

But reality is punching me back toward this awful moment - there's too much noise, and I can't escape a vice of pain gripping my stabbed right shoulder and everything else. My eyes open to stinging smoke, and my lungs gather choking fumes. Someone is shouting, "Here, chuck it in the fire." I search for a meaningful shape in blinding smoke. It's some dumb-ass Aboriginal kid speaking to me in *Yolngu*, his hand on my shoulder. He's squeezing. It hurts. Now, he's poking me with a clapping stick, and I move to grab the damn thing, but there's a blunderbuss in my hand.

His intent hits me with a sudden jab of clarity. In an instant, I'm back, and sanity gives me sense enough to know that if the thing blows, it'll take out the radius of a quarter stick of dynamite, a hand grenade's worth of indiscriminate destruction.

With numb, poisoned fingers - convinced to be nimble and quick by the direst straights - I place the pistol, still charged with powder-and-ball, into the fire, pointing in Bob's general direction, and as best I can, jamming the butt against the outside of the cave wall to ensure it doesn't blast back in my face. Now, the just-about-full powder horn, clad in silver chain-mail shrapnel, goes right in the middle of the fire, as Chirp suggests - a marvelously brilliant idea for a dimwit, sheer genius by any measure, really. At the same instant, Chirp dives right, flattening himself at the side of the cave entrance, and I come crashing down onto the Dutchman's ribcage to the left, burying my face in the sand and getting my hands over my ears.

And it happens almost the same as yesterday's plane explosion, a double blast, virtually at the same instant, one just discernibly before the other. First to go is the blunderbuss, and I hear its loud, sharp *bang* a split-nanosecond before the very air explodes: a deeper, shaking *boom*, deafening even through fingers; and rushing air slaps me down, the rock around me shivers, and a storm of sand and burning splinters blasts through all the space within sensing distance.

It blows in half a heart tick, and I'm laying still on the floor of the cave, the Dutchman's bones poking my stomach, part of me taking roll-call for various bits and pieces, the other part worrying about the disturbing trend of almost getting blown-up, seemingly day after day; and I'm wondering if anything else is likely to explode as I notice new agony in my shoulder getting ridiculous - that I didn't feel above my normal, background, excruciating pain - and suddenly I'm up on my feet, slapping a glowing red-hot, brick-sized block of burning wood off the small of my back.

Miraculously, I'm again in a post-apocalyptic one-piece. My eyes wade through smoke and dust to the mouth of the cave. The fire's gone, or rather, it's everywhere *except* the mouth of the cave, which is now a mini-cratered ground-zero, and beyond - a half dozen little fires, smoking logs, and tuffs of burning grass outline the fallen form of big Bob Palmer, stone still and flat on his back. Two or three meters behind him is his right arm, a carving knife still clenched in its fist.

Before I know it, I've scrambled out the cave entrance, ignoring singed hands and knees as I crawl. I manage to drag the Prada out with me, but it's the only thought I had, and no part of me worries about Chirp - it's every man for himself when the bombs go off, and I'm on autopilot, my legs charging for the mouth of the gully; and I'm bolting past Bob - the big piece, thinking it's the glare of death in his eyes, and his left-hand shoots up snake-strike fast and catches my right ankle in mid-stride, latching hold tight as a policeman.

I fall to my knees, but I'm up in a hurry, and it's like dragging a beached whale. I'm falling forward, straining all my weight to escape his grasp, before I suddenly realize he doesn't have his other arm to squeeze or throttle me with, and sooner or later, he'll bleed to death. I can't wait, so I steady and come around over him, hopping on one foot, and I'm tossing up whether to stomp his nasal bone into his brain or grab his other arm and beat him to death with it. His relative harmlessness registers now, and my panic subsides. And I say to him,

"Let go, Bob. Your right arm's blown off, for Christ's sake. It's over *there*. Your blood's all draining out. Have some …*grace*."

I don't know if he's hearing the words or if he can sense anything, but he won't let go, so I shout, "Let go or I'll kick your balls up your throat," which I notice has a piece of black bull-horn sticking out of oozing bloody fat where his Adam's apple used to be; and I watch Bob's eyes go from gapping-in-shock to gapping-in-death wondering if the impending indignity of having your balls kicked as your life drains away is the thought he carries to oblivion.

Lightning flashes in the distance, and I find a half-moon's dim glow high in a cloudy, starless night as gentle rain starts to fall on little fires in the gully and the play of tiny flames dapple in Bob's blood, pooling and glistening black on the red earth of Arnhem Land. And still, he won't let go of my foot.

I'm prying a dead guy's fingers off something I need - the second time in an hour. Chirp has made it out of the cave and stands watching Bob's right arm, possibly worried it might slash out with the knife on its own accord. Then he quickly bends down to snatch the blade and finds Bob won't let go of that either, and we're both separating items from a dead man, still showing remarkable resolve.

Chirp finally wrestles the knife free and tests the blade with his thumb. His is the fourth right hand that's held it in a little more than twenty-four hours. A blood-sucking Muppet keeps counting: *one* dead body, *two*, *three*, *four* – well, three if Korda's made it through the day.

Had it not been for the happenstance of a random nun and the kid needing a lift, I'd be here alone on East Crocodile Island with $2.2m in contraband and the only one in the Universe who knew it. But then again, without the hefty post-op tranny, the plane would have lifted clear of the storms and made it to Darwin without incident.

Nevertheless, the Rat thinks *four down, two to go – three, if you count Yousef.* I remind myself that the girl has a name - several in fact - and the kid showed remarkable presence of mind in the cave - raging flames blocking the only way out, a murderous lunatic waiting to kill him if he tried to escape - and *he* thought to blow the Dutchman's powder-horn. Ironically, it's his *disability* - his mental incompetence - that makes him useless as a testifying witness to malfeasance – there is no *business* case for anyone to kill him ...or there *was*.

My live eyes fall back on Bob, and I bend down, close his dead ones, and I'm not sure for a moment how to feel about the body at my feet, the bit at Chirps, and the other bodies now dotted all over the island. Or, rather, all of me *is* certain, but different parts hold different views that are slightly opposed. A psychiatrist might say *Multiple Levague Syndrome*, and if I dwell too much on it, I might disappear up my own ass, and I'm thirsty, and it's raining, and there's really only *one* thing on *all* our minds - it's been a hard day. It's *Miller Time!*

Chirp looks up from the knife, then back at the knife, and there's intelligence and *purposefulness* in his dark eyes that don't look quite ...*sane*. Sue Tran kept the blade keen - for chopping meat. So far, it's managed to stay out of *people*.

"You ok?" I ask in English. "We don't have to stab Bob. He's not pissed off anymore. Let's go back to the waterhole."

"I think his spirit's still angry," says Chirp.

Light rainfall continues, but the air barely stirs. It's not the usual squally rain, but it's just a matter of time before the wind whips up a bit of weather. For the moment, it's not unpleasant, and Chirp and I follow the line of steep ironstone rock back to the water spring at the deepest point of the gully.

The remains of the exploded fire burn a few spots here and there, but the flames won't catch the damp grass. There's enough flickering light behind us to see our shadows spread darkness across the rock face beyond the waterhole as we approach, and I crumple onto my knees near the pool.

Soon, the rainfall is persistent, and I'm worried the half kilo or so of powdered heroin in the Prada might get damp, diminishing its snorting quality. There's no thought of struggling in darkness back down to the old community buildings. The old legs and my esthetic appreciation of fine real estate aren't going anywhere, and I'd like to wake up tomorrow to wonderful ocean views from this well-appointed, elevated residence. From this vantage, I'll be able to see if a boat's been hauled up onto the beach and whether my two white duffel bags are still there. My gully residence has running water, central heating, and a sheltering cave when it rains. So, knowing I'll be safe and dry, I drag myself and the Prada back to the cave, thinking only of my immediate comfort. Chirp follows. It makes all the difference to have cleared the agenda of imminent death.

Bob's body is virtually on my doorstep, diminishing the *feng shui* of the place. He won't start attracting flies until daylight, and when the birds set about him, the racket will wake me early from even the deep opiate dreams I intend to induce - I still have to deal with an Armani and the seemingly increasing inevitability of disagreement over drugs. I don't want him getting to our appointment before me.

I kick together a burning log and enough dry fuel to make a jolly little campfire near the mouth of the cave, big enough only to shed a bit of light and make snakes think twice about moving in with me, although with Chirp around, any game enough to try will meet the edge of a carving knife soon enough and end up toasting on coals.

"What happened to the orange Asian lady?" asks Chirp.

The dust and smoke have settled, my eyes adjust, and I'm on my side near the cave entrance. I claim my own little spot, mentally erecting a curtain between the other residents: the Dutchman and the unreal Dreaming Beings on the wall. My eyes sneak a glance towards my *TWO MEN* stick doppelganger with the red-tipped penis, but I soon relax. The sacred stone is where I left it, covered in ashes and sand. I tumble it closer, find the switchblade, get out my lighter, and scoop a handful of drugs from the Prada, making a little pile on top of the stone. A twenty-dollar banknote rolls into a straw, a stiletto point of smack - a centimeter's worth - goes over the flame of my lighter, and the inhaled opiate fumes go straight to my brain.

The rush is instant and orgasmic, but instead of lying back to savor it all, I manage to breathe out in answer to Chirp's query, maybe loud enough, maybe not, "Snakes got her, Sister's Son ...bulk snakes."

Another knife point worth of powder goes directly up to my snorting nostril, the last voluntary movement I make for a while.

The physical component of getting wasted on the highest quality opiates is usually described in sexual and pyrotechnic terms for the initial rush and, for the nodding stage, velvety-warm words suitable for the mother's womb. Cerebrally, there's really nothing much happening; all the springs and pressure points of a junkie's brain lose tension and unwind in a kaleidoscope of random images that cut through madness and pain, bullet-fast straight to the best of possible worlds - and this is different for everyone, everyone's unique heaven.

I don't have the writing skills for *heaven*; I'd be forever with the maybe-ifs and but-thens. For now, I'll take leave and just say it's a time of vivid imagination, and *my* mind becomes a mental casino full of whirring slot machines: flashing lights everywhere - sirens, bells, tinkling electronic jingles, the clanking of coins; the whirl of a thousand spinning reels: dollar signs, playing-cards, lucky horseshoes, leprechauns; a blur of brilliant colors, spinning too fast for meaning.

My mind is swimming in sounds and flashes as slot machines are paying out by the dozen: three kings run together in a five-reel poker game, and my senses produce an image - a dream that sticks around long enough to attract words and meaning but then disappears as another machine next to it pays out four of a kind and produces a more vivid landscape, a longer tinkling of coins, with time enough for words to tame the wildness of images into meaning. Now, a slot machine produces three lucky horseshoes and pays out an image of Korda's burned face, and Mrs. Korda is standing over a white silk-lined casket in a dark funeral home, all weepy in tiny black-chiffon nightie, and the Rat's beside her, comforting hand on the small of her back. A monkey jumps out of the coffin banging cymbals, but it's just another slot machine paying out. Now, a full house and the image of *ATHEISTMAN vs* Pope Frances in a Mexican wrestling ring pop into my mind. All the detail crystallizes, blurs, and suddenly the Pope's flowing white robes turn into a fully-filled white nurse's uniform and it's Sister Mary-Ann holding a glossy full-color travel brochure printed with high production values, a tour guide for the Creation Museum[37] of Petersburg Kentucky, with its diorama of full-size plastic dinosaurs cohabiting with extremely Anglo-Saxon looking, not-so-Paleolithic, blond-haired blue-eyed cave people - who then shrink into themselves and become animated stickmen on a blackboard. And there's Dr. Stick-Levague, wielding a green overnight bag and dispatching Dragon-fly men …and now he's sneaking up on Seven

---

[37] The 'Creation' museum is a Christian theme park that is a favorite bit of foolishness for *ATHEISTMAN*.

Levague has described the wooden arc, apparently built to biblical specifications, as a *bus loaded with clowns going over the cliff of lunacy*.

314

Stick-Sisters making ablutions near a waterhole, all bending down to drink on hands and knees, and Orion-the-Ravisher approaches up a narrow gully, and Levague darts in, fornicates with all seven, furtively, ejaculating prematurely each time, the selected advantage of quick 'in-and-out', and Orion and the women don't notice.

Whistles, spinning purple lights, and a slot machine matches four '7s' on five reels, and Pam fans a thick wad of cash in my face with her thumb. The banknotes have pictures of my children. It looks like a lot of loot, but they're all single greenbacks.

Now, there's a slot machine paying out a royal flush: blinding, flashing red lights, bells, whistles, and a deafening siren starts wailing. Big jackpots are routine at *Casino de Scag*, and this one will take a while to pay out: familiar Brazilian jungle, *me* reclining in the shade of a coconut tree, Journal open; and naked Edo girls, an infinite line of them, presenting themselves to Dr. Levague for bride-price assessment.

I know it's not a dream, or rather, it's an *opium* dream, an old favorite too, but I'm aware that I'm conscious, I'm in a cave, and I can marshal my senses and point them at what I choose, coordinate the scene here along the Amazon River or click my heels and see reality.

For example, the Edo girls go through their *dance-of-secret-revelation* - a gymnastic work-out, really, and featuring several apparatuses: uneven bars, balance beam, trampoline - but I'm also aware that Chirp is in the cave, and the girls prance their innocent routines to the beat of ancient Aboriginal clap-sticks and the soft throaty chant of the Crocodile Cult.

And although I'm principally focused on capturing minute details of the girls' incredible elasticity - as is the want of the anthropologist - I become dimly aware of and tune into a soft female wailing, spoiling the party. It drifts on still air from the shadowy interior of a grass-roofed hut just beyond the naked girls - a keening, sad song that's not the crying of sentimental tears for a formal rite of tribal passage, not the sad sweet weeping of celebration for the *girl-to-woman* ritual.

I know this girl! Oh God! ...it's my adopted 'niece', *Juliet* - and the baby beside her looks horridly familiar, *Levague* familiar.

My Juliet cries in pain that's real enough; her pelvis is stretched and broken from giving birth, a child-mother with fistula-uterus, chronically inflamed, raw, and untreated; and the poor girl sickened by the foul smell of her own fecal incontinence ...*This can't be right!*

A wave of fear washes over the scene. I'm powerless. My legs move in dream reflex, and I'm fleeing through the Amazon jungle, the woman's crying only growing louder, her baby's cries echoing my own.

The space suddenly shifts, and I'm flitting through a moonless Saharan night; a bullet sizzles past my ear before another one enters my shoulder, spinning me around, and now I'm slogging injured across the endless red expanse of the Simpson Desert, Iranian death-squads wearing me down, catching me up.

Chirp's clapping sticks sap my strength but drive assassins faster, and the tapping grows staccato-fast as I struggle on through opiate-fog mirages, running for my life but exhausted and resigning myself to pain; and now I'm crawling up a creek-bed, my legs are too heavy to walk; and finally, I'm trapped in a cave with flaming walls, pinned down by weight that settles on my thighs and I can run no more.

Now would be a good time for another jackpot image at *Casino de Scag*. But the royal flush is still paying out, and there's no break to the dream, the nightmare.

And now a fire-orange, reflector-striped woman shapes herself out of the flames raging around me in this cave, and she speaks a kind of drug-lingo, and sexy assassin-words slip from her pursed lips as she holds a butcher's knife close to my nose, with tiny fire-flashes sliding along the blade, *'Wakey wakey, little snaky'*. And the weight on my thighs solidifies into Sue Tran. And now the knife vanishes, and she's naked below the GUMO shirt, and me too – my jeans, seemingly in Quantum Entanglement with hers - and she's astride my hips, the orange ball bouncing a low quick basketball dribble – *this is more like it!* ...and her almond eyes sparkle in firelight, harmless in the darkness.

But it's not, and a cold chill freezes up my spine - good thing I'm dreaming. The bouncing ball slows, her eye-sparkle darkens to sly-twinkle and then sharpens to *savage-beauty-beyond-belief*, and it's my wife's lips pouting out Shoshone words, *'Oh, dear ... look what's happened. My husband's with another woman!'*

And Sue Tran has morphed into my wife, in the guise of her totemic sister, her alter-ego: *cougar-woman!* The core battery of my very being drains flat in an instant, mad-feline eyes hold me prisoner, a vicious animal sits on my naked thighs, and a dagger-claw swipes my face, ripping my beard off, and I'm frozen in anesthetic limbo, unable to stop time or move; and the carving knife's back, now in Pam's delicately deft, surgeon-sure hands, and it shrinks before my eyes into a thin, cruelly curved moon-crescent blade. *I know its name by what it does.*

I'm pretty sure my eyes are closed. If not, I close them again to be sure. Better still, I leave. I step outside myself. I bring company: a ridiculous black-suited superhero, a large cunning rodent, and world-renowned cultural anthropologist Dr. Jacques Levague. We know each other already; no intros needed.

From outside of myself, it looks like a bizarre Aboriginal blood-ritual ceremony. It's a good thing Dr. Levague's here with the Journal; he can record what happens. The Rat's edgy for blood, and *ATHEISTMAN* looks on in panic and disbelief.

A young Aboriginal man - *my* Sister's Son, *Brother's Son* to senior Crocodile Cult Lawman, Jacob Kunmubilpilguru - has already been fully initiated, and he kneels beside an old snow-bearded white gent who looks to have lost a few kilos recently. His aging eyes are thin slits as the weight of his eyelids presses down. He's in some sort of drug-induced psychosis or the psychological trance of a religious novice entering symbolic stasis on the way to the rapture of

318

enlightenment. His lips move, and deep, soft, hypnotic chanting, low in his throat, drones out words of the Crocodile Cult.

The old fellow leans against the obsidian-black walls of a cave in a low magnetite hillock. Firelight flickers on his face. He's naked from the waist down. His shirt is bloody and stained with the red earth of Arnhem Land.

The Aboriginal man – our Sister's Son - also sings, and as he does, a kidney-shaped ritual stone on his Mother's Brother's lap cradles the old white man's pale uncircumcised penis. The artifact it lays on has a name: *Mother's Brother Sister's Son Stone,* and a scientific reference: *Minjininga Cave EA01: Arch. 6211.*

The old man extends the foreskin of his penis and presses it flat and firm against the smooth sacred stone with his right index finger. It's normal to apply the slicing edge of a ritually-knapped flake of special stone, but the ceremony is completed by the Aboriginal man using what seems to be a domestic kitchen knife, the kind used for carving meat.

And this, it does, and in the instant, I feel a searing pain like a pierced ear - but in the dick, several pierced ears' worth, and blood pools around a severed penis-foreskin on the surface of the ritual stone, and traditional clapping sticks start a slow, steady *tink ...tink ...tink* echoing close against black cave-rock.

The Father and Child are ONE blood. The Mother and her Brother are ONE blood. These words seem to emanate from bare rock. *We say that this Mother's Brother and this Sister's Son must be*

319

united in ancient blood ritual. We say they are the TWO MEN and they sing secret words ...and they dance.

Casino de Scag is closed and silent. I'm banging and clawing at the door to get in. The tip of my dick is red and sore. I appear to be circumcised. The kitchen knife that did it lies in the sand, still sporting blood from the cruelest cut of all. How will I explain this to Pam?

My left hand tingles painlessly, feeling *nothing* at all. The fingers don't move much anymore. I don't think rabies is the cause; it's some other filthy simian virus in all likelihood, possibly avian in origin. I seem to be running a temperature - it might be a monkey bite, an infected knife wound, or maybe both.

And, oh yes ...someone will likely want to kill me tomorrow ...or later today.

There's a rolled-up twenty-dollar bill in my hand. Chirp's nearby.

"Sister's Son, be a good lad and pass me that green bag."

Chapter 9: Primitive As Can Be

9 February 2011

Awake in fright again. Seagulls squawk close by. A moment's befuddlement passes as I seek out the certainty of fine green Italian leather, the Prada bag. I check. Lots left.

Then I notice I'm not wearing my jeans. A shiver of realization cringes with horror and humiliation. I'm diminished. Like Bob, in two pieces.

My boxers used to be red poke-a-dots on baby blue. All the dots in the front have joined up in uniform blood, matching the back of my T-shirt. My jeans and shoes were a pillow last night. Big dead Bob's hat, also covered in my blood – from the bite of a rabid macaque – lies at the base of the cave, near Aboriginal etchings on the black-rock walls.

My feet are hard to find, and they hurt – from dancing. It takes a tick to get used to standing and longer to figure out why I got up.

But I'm collecting things: fire-blackened switchblade knife, my pants, the Journal, a dead Dutchman's silver 1699 guilder; and when I pick up Bob's hat, star-constellation drawings on the cave wall capture my eye like black-hole Gravity. But *ATHEISTMAN* allows no preternatural premonition and doesn't want to look too closely. So, we take it on *faith* - there's no eighth green Sister of the Pleiades and no Stick-Levague horror *TWO MAN* scratched on the rock with red ochre-daubed dick, and no crashed-plane havoc. I *know* all that was drug-induced imagination. If these aberrations were real, *ATHEISTMAN* would be insane. I'm too afraid to look.

I collect my things and stuff the Prada. The Mother's Brother Sister's Son Stone stays behind. My pants stay in the Prada. The circumcision wound needs the air of boxers only - for quite a while, I imagine. My dick will be useless for a month. A little purple-yellow wormy thing looks to adhere to that damned sacred stone with dried black blood. It was formerly the tip of my cock, the blood, formerly mine too.

Although *ATHEISMAN* is appalled, I'm ambivalent about the whole genital mutilation thing. Being initiated into the *Yolngu* religion is a dream for any anthropologist, but normally, to escape such a ridiculous, barbaric practice, I'd kill any man standing in my way. The man who did it, I'd kill several times. Where *is* the little psycho bastard?

But I suppose it's a bit like leaving the Rat in charge of my body when I'm prepping a three-hundred-year-old blunderbuss to save my life – leave an unhinged lunatic indigene in charge, with a meat cleaver and a sacred circumcision stone, the coincidence of our classificatory Mother's Brother's Sister's Son kin relationship, with One-Eye Bob, Lefty Williams, Mrs. Korda, Bob, Sue Tran, and goodness knows what other spirits marauding about the local netherworld, and this whole bizarre fantasy of mythical *TWO MEN* charging to the rescue of everything – well, my own fault for abandoning myself at *Casino de Scag*.

If you stand back and take the culture out - drain off the meaning - just like *crucifixion*, having a bit of your dick cut off is a truly horrid notion, unsettlingly Freudian. Perhaps I should be thankful his cut was accurate and clean. *Sister* Mary-Andy-Ann could have had company. Sure, it's a testament to acceptance by the indigenous community, but I'm native enough as it is, and I'm not sure Pam will buy the truth; she'll want to check down there for teeth marks.

I leave the cave purposefully, looking for Chirp, steer around most of Bob, noting birds have already started on his eyes, and stride past the smaller piece, making my way to the mouth of the gully. Fire-blackened tuffs of grass and logs, bits of wood, and strange pieces of metal that might have been a blunderbuss and chain-mail from a powder horn are scattered here and there as I go. My *ritual* Sister's Son - the petrol-sniffing bonehead with my blood on his hands - is nowhere to be seen.

A low cloud glows red on the eastern horizon, a warning of storms for sailors and those smuggling narcotics along the coast of Arnhem Land today. It's already a *red* day. Everything's red. My pencil bleeds.

The old community buildings are dark and still against the shifting grey ocean. Beyond, the Australian mainland stretches hazy, low, forever flat, and *red* to the south. For a second, I think I hear the faint buzz of an outboard motor and peer closely across the choppy

323

sliver of sea between the island and the mainland. I see nothing. It seemed *just* at the edge of hearing, then disappeared, and I chalk it up to the blow-fly rage party kicking along on Bob's carcass back in the gully.

I note that the white duffle bags at the southern end of the main beach below the village ruins are bright in the predawn gloom. They'll act as a beacon for anyone arriving by sea.

There's no sign of Ann tracking up the line of the creek. Had Korda died in the night, I'd expect her to be plodding along our way, the whiteness of her uniform still bright despite all the crawling in dirt and mud. My gaze trains down the line of river-gums to mangroves near the old church scanning for any movement at all.

The aroma of barbequing flesh, lizard's ...hopefully, wafts on air from deep in the gully. My nose leads to the waterhole. I follow the creek in; overnight rain has dissolved almost all of yesterday's footprints.

Early morning light has been sufficient for Chirp to find edible roots growing on the edge of the spring, and he's caught a small goanna. They sizzle on hot coals near the waterhole. The skinny reprobate tends fillets of the beast with a carving knife. Each flipping of the lizard sends a shiver up my spine, and I cringe as phantom pain bites into the phantom tip of my dick.

"You cut me," I say, and consider whether to wash some of the blood off by kneeling at the edge of the waterhole or wade right in and sit a spell. The part that's deep enough is the size of a child's blowup pool, and the water spring wells up from little fissures in rock at the bottom like gentle Jacuzzi jets, a hydro-massage for hands, shoulders, and freshly mutilated genitals.

I decide on the latter, and I'll deal with the kid, the Armani drug dealer, and whatever horror comes with the new day after I spend some time with my poor old willie in the cool, clean water. If I didn't have pressing business, the Prada and I could easily stay here forever.

The food's cooked. Chirp dishes out a portion of lizard's tail and toasted succulent root bulbs on a plate-sized piece of pandanus palm frond and passes it to me in my bath. Then he converses.

"Mother's Brother Sister's Son Stone *called*. We were in *the big black Rock*. You *sang* the *Crocodile Blood Song*. We were the *TWO MEN*. The dangerous spirits are finished. This is my country. I'm the boss. We made it *Clean*. *You* sang the Magic Words," he explains, as to a fellow initiated Crocodile Cultist, one believer to another, bringing me up on recent events in some otherworldly Dallas soap opera. If my dick wasn't the star, I'd find it tedious. But there's enough meaning in the generally schizoid thrust of it to suss out he *owes* me – for magical services rendered.

Despite the nonsense driveling from his lips, there's nothing of the lopsided features in his serious dark face, no spastic jerky-leg gait of a chronic petrol-sniffer. His clear, young eyes, strong forehead, and firm mouth are set with purpose and confidence. He's expanded his repertoire beyond extremes of vapidity and hysterics, filling in the space between with reasonable normality. For a solvent-sodden

325

teenager, when he sobers up, he has a surprising number of uses.

"There's nothing wrong with you," I state in English from the pool, leaving him to confirm or otherwise.

"I like to sniff petrol. But once, I forgot how to talk, how to walk from here to there. They put me in the Darwin Hospital, then the Catholic hospice. I like it there. I sniff too much at Minjininga. I want to be a *big man*. I took the Stone," he allows, and expands, "I like to sniff. When I sniff, it's good …I don't worry."

"I know what you mean," I say. "I think the white girl likes wine."

"I like wine. I like the girl," he confides to his Mother's Brother.

"She can't have babies. 'Sister Mary' is her name at the Hospice. Out here, we call her Ann. She's sort of married already…to Jesus …sort of. But Jesus isn't real, so she's free to be with you. But I reckon you don't need the Mother's Brother Sister Son Stone. You're man enough already, and she likes you. A bottle or two of cheap plonk, and Bob's your uncle," I confide in return.

"There are lots of girls for making babies."

Yes, there are. And I'm mildly interested in how he's intending to tackle the Jesus issue, but there's no more time to waste.

"You need weapons today. An Armani is looking for Ann. He's coming in a dinghy. I think he'll rape her. You might have to kill him. He'll probably have a gun."

"We'll rescue the girl and take the dinghy," he says. It's

326

another of his half-a-plans.

As we leave the gully, retracing yesterday's path along the creek, sunlight floods golden-orange over dark cloud layers building on top of the eastern horizon. The onshore breeze quickens, bending the tops of river gums and smudging whitecaps on the open blue Arafura Sea. A bit of weather's about.

A small aluminum boat with an outboard motor is hauled up the main beach at the southern end. He's arrived in the last hour.

Two hundred kilos of smack are piled on dunes nearby. The dinghy's just big enough to hold all of it or four people and no drugs.

No one is in sight. He might be lurking low in foreshore dunes anywhere along the beach, hiding in the shadows of the ruined community, or following a GPS to the original drug coordinates at the crash scene. With twenty kilos of dope missing, my bet is the latter. He'll walk up the airstrip to the remains of the Lorina, shout around for Bob, and poke about the wreckage for his smaller duffel bag, finding only Mrs. Korda bloating up with putrefying biochemical gases and attracting scavengers from all over the island.

After that, he'll not stay long, and most likely, he'll follow the track from the airport to the old community - it's the most direct route. There, he'll find some of his heroin under an old Morton Bay Fig in the central village square, near the dead body of Sue Tran. At that point, he'll know something's much more seriously amiss than a crashed plane and a random dead victim. He'll cut his losses and bolt back to the main stash and his dinghy, neither of which will be there if the Rat has his way. The clock of the day's events is ticking.

When we left the flies and birds to their smorgasbord of decomposing Bob, two eucalypt saplings were at the mouth of the gully. Their stems have now been severed near the ground. As we follow the creek line southeast down to the old community, Chirp strips off branches and bark and expertly applies the carving knife, and the saplings become serviceable spears as we walk.

The Prada is light on my shoulder with just my pants, the Journal, stiletto dagger, and five or six cups of powdered fluffy heroin. The sacred stone and those damn clapping sticks are left in the cave. Chirp chooses bare feet, and we leave his Nikes for the Dutchman.

We make good time retracing yesterday's slightly up-slope march of pain. The distance is shorter going downhill and friendlier to old legs. My T-shirt and boxers are blood-stained, the same rusty red as the ground-in stains of Arnhem Land dirt. Neither will ever come out. Normal daytime sounds fill the air, nature shifting up a gear with the morning heat. I keep my senses peeled for unnatural Armanis.

We stay on the eastern side of the creek, and when we reach the start of the mangroves, the leper graveyard and the rest of the old community are on the opposite bank, fifty meters across the muddy embankment and a short stretch of swamp water. I spot the river gum marking old Paddy's tombstone near the end of the creek. The crocodile's nest a few meters below is unattended.

Chirp picks up his pace and leaves me plodding through deep sand dunes skirting the northern margins of the estuary. Walking through several hundred meters of swales and blowouts leaves me panting, and my head's down when I stumble into the lad in foreshore dunes close to the beach. Before us, Mattius Korda lies on the blue tarp, much as I left him, but now his head's resting in a dark pool of blood from his cut throat. There's no sign of the nun, but I find the footprints of one person leading up and down the beach to breaking waves and a long, shallow, dinghy groove in wet sand.

For some reason, the South Armani weasel seems to have first landed his dinghy north of the estuary. Maybe the nun was the first large white thing he spotted from the sea, and he mistook her for a large bag of dope, understandably. I can't see *her* body anywhere. Seems he just stayed long enough to slit a throat, and then he moved the dinghy down the beach adjacent to the main stash. When I study the footprints around the tarp, it appears that she may have run off before he got her. I'll wager she powers over short distances but falters after half a rugby pitch or so, about the distance to the old community buildings.

"Help! ...Help! ...Jack! ...Someone! ...Oh, what's *Hap-Pe-NING?*" The *'Ning'* comes out like a fire alarm. It's a hysterical Ann, broadcasting louder than a boiled Scotsman from somewhere in the community near the Morton Bay Fig. She follows her interrogatory (to God, I suppose) with a truly gruesome series of wordless shrieks and screams that put a shiver on the morning air.

The awful hollering is enough to set Chirp pelting through sand dunes across the sandbank now revealed by the low tide to the beach below the community. He crouches low, spear in each hand, fast but stealthy. I can't see him avoiding disaster and expect to hear a duet of yelping directly. Never mind; his rashness might buy a bit of chaos and more time for me to get away.

Before I head off, I take in the death scene of Mattius Korda one last time, my eye drawing along the line of the tarp - and sure enough, peeking out of the sand where I'd previously constructed shade for an overdose case and a hung-over nun, is the top of a yellow-cloth clad, one-kilo disc of hard-pressed smack that seems to have been left behind. It goes into the Prada to swim with the powder scag and my pants.

I can't help but rest my eyes on the man I knew vaguely and not much liked. The paleness of death and his slit throat have drained the red from his burned face. Well, he got what he needed: a quick ending to a drug-induced coma he'd never wake from, and given his cancer and death of his wife, the best thing all around, really. And I can't help but notice his throat's been so cleanly sliced, a penetrating cut that's severed the windpipe, jugular and esophagus neatly - and little else - and maximizing the amount of blood available for him to drown in it. I suppose it's a bit petty to kill a man who is already mostly dead, but it's the work of deft hands. Many Armanis know a thing or two about knives and necks, but this shows the skill of someone to whom a whole village might turn for *all* their throat-slitting needs. It'll be over just as quickly for Chirp, or maybe he'll be lucky and get a well-aimed spear away before he's filleted or shot.

My eyes focus on the dinghy at the southern end of the main beach and the pile of heroin nearby, and the world shrinks. Along the shoreline, rolling waves rise like smooth tubes, fold over, and spill a wash of foam along the hard, wet sand. Gulls chase receding water after each wave while the ocean breathes and heaves again. Steady wind builds from the east, clouds overtake the sun low in the morning sky, and dark rainy squalls sweep towards the island across a pitching grey sea. It's time to get to the dinghy, collect the drugs, and decamp post haste.

I follow the lad's footprints across the sandbank spanning the narrow mouth of the estuary below the mudflats. His path leads to the right, up the stone pathway to the village – mine, straight ahead to the end of the beach. I see him crouching near the old beachside residences, carving knife and spears in hand. Crashing waves are not loud enough to stifle the nun's incessant caterwauling from the village square beyond, but I know if she's screaming, her attacker is gainfully occupied while I steal his drugs. Chirp looks uncertain, caution tempering his heroics, but each ear-peeling, semi-female howl from the village square shifts his weight, and he's barely restraining his legs. He needs to get in there and cause some chaos while I slip away.

I take a few steps towards my goal and away from the old community. The desperation under the Morton Bay Fig continues to filter through the rolling break of waves.

"Dr. Levague! Oh, where are you? Oh, no …*Help! Help!*" She's clutching at straws now.

Chirps stands between the walls of the old residences, spear held high overhead, his back bent, ready to throw. He prances up the final slope of the stone pathway and disappears on the other side of the old buildings. I pause, listening for the gunshot.

A light curtain of rain sheets along the beach and over me. The last blue sky shrinks away to the west. I find myself searching there desperately for a rescue plane.

My eyes don't leave when there's nothing to see. *ATHEISTMAN* looks too and sees blue-sky as *black*; he peers beyond the light-diffusing atmosphere, hiding endless darkness in lovely shades of blue. But he knows the Darkness beyond, and the pain and horror in the broken village square is just the meaningless conversion of energy, biochemical reactions in the Scum-of-Life - that tiniest portion of the cosmos that broke out like a rash in self-replicating chain-reactions of life, ever-more complex molecules evolving naturally, selected for sheer virulence, and running rampant for 3.8 billion years of Darwinian evolution.

It'll be over eventually. Extinction, the end of life, the Sun, stars, light, the black energy of Eternity diminished to nothing - *ATHEISTMAN* knows that place. There is no significance to life - amoeba or human. It's all the bizarre circumstances of biochemistry that's very temporarily got totally out of hand. I know it too, and according to my BSI Theory, whatever subjective, personal, moral or ethical dimensions there are in ignoring the desperation and hurt of a nun and an innocent kid - they don't amount to nit shit in greater schemes.

...But when *ATHEISTMAN* reaches into my mind for the certainty of our BSI Theory, my tinnitus seems to get louder, and it grows deafeningly. Then the buzzing starts to slow as if time was running down, and individual buzz-clicks become discernible, and I find no familiar comforting scientific knowledge to soothe a heartless dark moment, and I'm left with nothing except silence, broken only by the unmistakable *tinking* of Aboriginal clapping sticks, slow then quickening, faster and faster, and forming a new background buzz much louder than insects, and giving me a splitting headache. I can't think.

And the Rat - he's in a bit of a funk now, notes the shifting seas getting angry and unforgiving and becoming altogether a bridge too far for a fair-weather junkie-rat to risk drowning...alas, the woe begotten sea. Drug smuggling will have to wait, and the image of a panting, lecherous Armani forms on the Rat's multiplex, with hands underneath a dirty-white nurse's uniform, grabbing hold of meaty fly-half's buttocks and trying to find a lusty way forward into ...the *unknown*. The barbarous villain has a cigarette dangling from his lips as he roots around. *ATHEISTMAN*, the Rat, and I - all three of us - would kill for *that* cigarette.

Stay and help the nun and kid, or run off with the stash? Maybe I want to do both. And the idea of nicotine appeals right now, so I fish the dagger out of the Prada and clean up a bit of heroin dust with my nose. I feel my best rat smarts rising and the old hungry junkie disdain for commonsense, so with drug-hardened nerves, I turn up the stone path to the village square, knife in non-monkey-bitten hand, blood and tobacco on our collective mind, rain pelting my back, shrieking-nun howling on the wind.

I reach the rear of the beach-side buildings fronting the village and slip behind the old residences, exactly as Chirp did. The final section of the path rises steeply between them up onto the track skirting the square. From my position, the top of the big fig can be seen, but what's happening below the canopy is still blocked. Unlike the lad, my plan is to move to the ruins of the old church *behind* the buildings, unseen from the square, and slink into darkness near the doorless entrance. Somehow, I'll try and lure the Armani inside and jump him with the stiletto. Maybe I can get the snakes working again.

Before I move, there's a voice in the square that isn't Chirp's or Ann's, but I know the sound. It once hoped that I'd *'beat the rain'*.

"Where's the rest of it!" it shouts, in an educated southern Armani accent. "Where's the pilot? Jack? …Levague? The anthropologist …where is he? Did he take my property?"

"I *told* you! I don't know *anything!* I haven't got *anything!"* hollers Ann.

I inch ahead a fraction, low and silent, peeking my head up, and the square comes into view. A man of normal height, dressed in jeans and a tan long-sleeve shirt, has his back to me. A small handgun, a .22 caliber, is tucked in the back of his pants.

He's about the same height but not as wide as Ann, who's tied up, back against the Morton Bay Fig, arms stretched back around the wide girth of the trunk. If it wasn't for the rope around the tree's truck secured to each of her wrists, she'd look crucified, like poor Joe Harman from Alice Springs.

Yousef's pressing up against Ann, left hand clutching her neck, forcing her scarf-less head hard against the tree trunk. Clutched in his right, a thin blade sadistically held up to her eyes. He leans into her, his face inches from hers.

"You will feel little pain when the blade goes into your eye," Yousef says conversationally but loud enough. "It'll sting when I pluck the eyeball out of your head, and interestingly, you'll still be able to see out of it. I'll show you. When it's on the point of my dagger, I'll turn it to you, and you'll see the bloody hole where your eye used to be. When I pull the optic nerve away from the socket, *Ouch*! I'm told that's what *really* hurts. You can tell me again."

Ann's jaw has dropped, her face gapping in shock, wide terrified eyes locked onto the knife. Yousef taps Ann's nose with the flat of the blade and she goes cross-eyed. Then he traces the knife down her face and throat, and it finds the top button of her uniform, and the second and the rest, and he rips open the white dress, revealing Ann's underwear: white - top and bottom – with torn stockings up to her solid white thighs. He steps forward, planting his knee between her legs, and the knife comes up and underneath the bra strap between

335

her breasts. He toys with the fabric, the blade like another finger.

"Next, the nipples are severed," he continues, like a practiced chef, tapping each breast in turn. "Again, there will be an initial *sting* but little pain, at least when the first one comes off. The blade is very sharp. But the initial surge of adrenalin in your veins will quickly pass, and the second nipple *really* hurts. Again, that's been my observation."

He tickles the point of his knife down Ann's naked stomach, all the while holding her terrified eyes. "Then we'll move *down there*. You'll be able to watch with your remaining eye before that one comes out too."

This appears to be as much incentive as Chirp needs to play his hand. I hear him moving inside the same building I'm hiding behind, and the next thing I see is a spear hurtling through about twenty meters of space in the general direction of Yousef and Ann, and missing both, as well as the meter-wide trunk of the Morton Bay Fig. He must have been off sniffing the day they taught spear throwing 101 in Minjininga, but it got Ann's attention, and it caught the Armani's eye as it whizzed past, missing by two meters and skidding harmlessly into the dirt.

The instant these things happen, before Yousef can react by turning around to see where the spear came from, Ann tilts back her head and crashes her brow down into Yousef's face, cracking into his nose - the head-butt of a true Irishman. Yousef staggers back, spins around, blood streaming down his smashed face, and Chirp charges in, remaining spear held low, carving knife in his other hand.

He closes fast, but the Armani is faster, and Chirp spots the gun pointing his way in time to slide to a stop, turn, drop both spear and knife, and bolt back towards the path to the beach, and he's sprinting like a frightened Jamaican right towards me. He's through the gap between the old residences and falling forward down the slight decline onto the stone pathway, and I slink back behind the old residence, shrinking down low. He flashes past me at full pelt, making for the beach. I expect to see Yousef running past my position in hot pursuit and steady to pounce with the stiletto.

Bang! A sharp loud crack pierces the air and echoes like a tunnel between the old residences. The gunshot originated from just around the corner of the building I'm behind, maybe a meter away. Chirp screeches in pain and goes down clutching his upper right leg, growling and groaning like an injured dog, wounded but alive enough to complain loudly.

Ann lets off a new round of screaming. She can't actually see he's only been shot in the ass, more or less. Plenty left for Yousef to shoot again or take to with a knife, and I'm waiting in a kind of breathless limbo for him to walk past and finish Chirp off. He won't notice me crouching low against the stone wall. I should have his whole back to work with and a full second and get Bob's knife into his spine two or three times before he can even think of the pistol, and I'll be wrapped around him like a coat of paint, and he won't know where he stops, and I start to get off a shot.

He doesn't appear; seconds tick, and Chirp's low groaning

down the beach starts to become annoyingly persistent above the breaking waves while Ann's intermittent screams continue to assault the air in every direction. The wind dies and a steady patter of rainfall increases. My pulse races two to each pattering drop, waiting to jump the gun-toting killer.

In anticipation, I can almost smell the menace of Armanistan permeating the space around the corner of the old building, and I know it's ill-advised, but I have to see where he is, and as low as I can crouch, I inch myself forward, exposing only the top of Bob's hat, then peek my eyes around, and instead of seeing his feet and legs, I'm staring down the barrel of a .22 caliber pistol attached to the hand of a low-crouching murderer; and a toothy grin forms from the red mess under his broken nose, and a glint of surprised recognition stares out of his close-set manic eyes, and then his mouth tightens in a sneer of hatred, and the calm anticipation of blood-sport settles on his acne-scarred, horridly vicious gore-smeared face.

A knife's little more than provocation at a gunfight. It slips from my fingers behind me, and I freeze.

"You must be *'Jack'* ... *'Dr. Levague'*," he says, spitting blood with the words. "Tell me ...*what's happening?*"

Ann's roaring anew like a branded steer, and Yousef's expression turns to a kind of painful annoyance, surprised at the decibel level achievable by a white woman and probably making up his mind which of our throats to slice first. The gun follows my face as I stand.

There's little connection between my brain and my mouth or any other part of me. I know I'll probably have to say something or get shot, but all that's in my ears is the nun's desperate, incessantly noisy vocal distress. I'm thinking of suddenly pointing up behind the weasel-with-a-gun to the western sky shouting, '*It's a plane!*' but there's no out-sleazing a South Armani. He wouldn't fall for it; I'd just piss him off. I say what pops next to my mind.

"Is it not written that if you be kind to a woman, God is well acquainted with what you do?" I ask in Armani, using the dialect common in southern Armanistan.

First across his hideous countenance are surprise and suspicion, then puzzlement. He might be searching his memory of Koranic verse, doubting that such a thing could be written, or amazed at hearing his language spoken by a white man. Either way, it seems to lower the Armani's level of immediate malevolence.

"How do you speak my language?" he asks in English. "What happened here? Who killed the Vietnamese? Where's Bob?"

"The plane crashed," I continue in Armani, my accent shaping up as my mouth remembers the right sounds, practiced and perfected in only a few months over thirty years ago but imprinted forever in memory. I carry the experiences of my Armani assignment - every wretched day, every opium den and scag dispensary in Zamari Sharif - as words in the Journal, but I learned to *think* in Armani, and I can think it again. Thinking like an Armani is much the same as thinking like Jack-the-Rat.

"Bob got hit in the head. He thought the police would find ...the *mine samples*. He wanted to hide them here and there on the island, and the Asian women tried to stop him. They had a fight; the woman stabbed the fat man, and the fat man throttled the woman. Bob staggered over through the cemetery by the old church, all bleeding, and disappeared up the creek toward the center of the island. He kind of ...went to pieces. He's bled to death or had a heart attack by now."

"I understand you have heroin to bring into Australia," I press ahead. "You'll have to hurry before the rescue people and the police get here." Yousef's bloodlust, the first emotion most Armanis default to when things go awry, is subsiding - time for *commerce*. "I know about the consignment. It looks like the product of Ali Masoor, just off Shadian Rd in Zamari Sharif."

The rainfall has settled into a pattern of regular squally sprays, and I know my soaked blood-stained boxers and T-shirt detract somewhat from the businesslike seriousness of my pitch. But if I know this rascal, he'll see that his venture's prospects need improving now, and murdering me can wait 'till later.

"Your partners are dead. You need help to get it to Darwin. I'm Dr. Levague. Drug smuggling is my middle name."

Yousef gestures with the gun. "Come out of the rain. Walk to the tree."

Despite the lack of venom in his words, the Armani's gun is pressed into the small of my back the whole way to the village square. Ann has silenced her incessant bawling, but down the beach, Chirp continues to moan and whimper, the damp sand stained red near his right buttock.

We walk into the square, and Ann's tied up against the fig tree, her arms spread-eagled, the front of her dirty-white uniform open to the world, head down, obscenely-white torso looking like a small-breasted half-back in the lingerie football league with white-stocking legs thick enough to rush for short yardage against the best pro-defense.

I stop when I get under the wide canopy of the fig tree. Ann lifts her head, terrified eyes lock with mine, and then I turn to face Yousef. Ingratiating myself to this sleaze-ball Armani - appealing to the essential wickedness of his countrymen - is my last hope. He's looking at me quizzically. The dull pain in my shoulder, the sting in my crotch, and my cold, numb, poisoned left hand all throb in tune, the biochemical background beat to what will have to be some of the highest quality bullshit I've ever shot.

"I only have sympathy for your smuggling enterprise. I can help. I would like to join with you in business. I can get anything you want across Aboriginal Land to Darwin …God willing." The Armani words enunciate on my tongue and stream out clearly, without lumps.

"I lived in your country long ago. I was the UN representative for the Amat Darba River bridge project when you were a child in 1974." I continue, "I purchased my heroin from Ali Masoor."

Dropping the name is a calculated risk. Ali Masoor, a businessman and local warlord, was friend or foe to thousands. The duplicitous thug owned the only civil engineering company in town and received UN money to build the Amat Darba bridge on my recommendation. He also owned all the local poppy fields and micro-managed heroin production to ensure consistent quality.

His bridge-building skills were substandard, and he stole the UN grant as he always intended. The bridge never got built, but for six months or so, he favored me with consistently top-quality, export-grade scag, not at all different than today's *Dragon* brand.

Everyone knew Ali Masoor until his son shot him in the head and took over the business, thus keeping it in family hands according to normal local tradition. The Masoor name is dropped only in the finest heroin dealing circles. Doubtless, a member of Yousef's family has, at one time or another, either killed for a Masoor family member or suffered at his hand.

"Ali Masoor's son shot my father and raped my mother. Then he shot her too," he states with little emotion. That'd be right. Funny, when the words are said in Armani, they sound mundane, like something only slightly out of the ordinary.

"And may they rest in the Glorious Peace of the Almighty," I extol.

I press on regardless. Gesturing to the pile of ten heroin discs near a dead body at the edge of the square only ten meters away - that came tumbling out of the small, snake-filled duffel bag when Sue Tran tipped out the contents - I ask, "Why worry about such small treasure when the fortune is awaiting on the beach with the means to get it away?"

But I know the answer before his lecherous pervert eyes fall behind me onto Ann tied against the Morton Bay Fig tree in her major underpants and granny bra, and the front of her uniform flapping in the breeze. Well, there's nothing like *white meat* to the average Armani Hordesman. Such fine sport is not easily found in Australia, a rare treat for a connoisseur, worth the risk.

"What's mine is mine," he explains, making perfect sense in Armani, and he's looking me up and down: Bob's bloodstained hat, bloodstained T-shirt, bloodstained boxer shorts.

"Why are you bleeding …everywhere?" he continues softly, indicating my blood with his gun. His eyes come to mine, squinting, and he brings his pistol up level with my head. "Where's my heroin?"

"Would you have a cigarette?"

"Tell me where!" He's raised his voice, and the pistol comes closer to my face. Evidently, it's still him against the world rather than him and his brother, Jack-the-Rat.

I'm conflicted - naturally eager to part with information at the first hint of duress, as if I possessed no spine at all, but knowing as soon as I do, I'm probably a dead man. The gun's at the side of my head, pressing hard against my temple.

"Tell me, or I'll shoot the girl and the kid …again," he shouts, and Ann shrieks. Yousef points the gun at her, and she subsides back to less audible blubbering. The gun hand trains back my way, and he jabs me sharply in my right shoulder with the damn thing.

"Who stabbed you?" he demands, his experienced eye recognizing the ins and outs of knives-in-the-back and indicting the Prada over my other shoulder, "What's in the bag?"

A shudder of pain and weariness racks through my back and spreads a growing dread to my whole being, shattering my strength to deal with this day and weakening my resolve. Why couldn't I have just stayed luxuriating in my natural spring bath this morning with the Prada close by?

Ann and the lad start up again with the dismal wailing, and I'm sharing the general sentiment, about to join in, but I rally. "They're …small potatoes. They mean nothing to me. The kid attacked me. He cut my dick. I'll see him dead myself. Use the girl …as you please."

Yousef glances again at Ann, nose-blood still streaming down his cruel sneer, evil anticipation in his eyes. She's been listening to all the Armani exchanges with growing apprehension.

He says, in English, so we all understand, "Tell me where the rest is, then *you* can kill the girl and the boy …so I know I can trust you. Now, where's the other ten kilos …and what's in the bag?"

Well, there's nothing for it, and I'm scrambling for an answer other than *'some of your heroin … that I'm stealing …again.'* I feign difficulty opening the zipper of the Prada, a tricky enterprise with such high-quality leather haberdashery.

Ann suddenly shuts up, and I feel big Dumbo eyes peering through the back of my head, looking into my skull, willing me to turn my eyes to hers so she knows if I would do it. It's the last thing I need to see right now, so I maintain my focus ahead on the Armani.

"The rest is buried beside a grave in the old church cemetery," I say, indicating the direction, and I add in a growing funk, in a desperate moment careening out of control, "You need my help to save this situation. I have drug contacts and can arrange permits. We should keep hostages *reasonably* unhurt, one for the Aborigines, one for the police."

Of course, hostage-taking is generally a pointless way to conduct business in Australia. It's seriously against the law. In Armanistan, it's routine, the ethic being *'I could have killed the hostage, but I let him go. Therefore, I didn't commit any crime.'*

"They have to die. Open …the …fucking …bag!" he shouts, raising his pistol to my head, and with each word, rapping the barrel against the darkest part of the blood stain on Bob's hat, coinciding with the monkey bite on my head, the patch of scalp that's gone numb and feels nothing.

I kneel, and the Prada strap falls off my shoulder. Now, effortlessly, the bag unzips, and my right hand extracts a heroin-powdered black journal, a pair of equally coated blue jeans, and an intact one-kilo slab of pressed heroin clad in yellow cloth and dragon stamped, placing each item in the wet dirt next to the bag.

I'm expecting to be shot on my knees any second, and I find my eyes closing and heroin-covered fingers find my nose of their own accord. A second passes, and I'm not shot. A wave of warm opiate relief I'd like to dwell on betrays an introspective moment I might have used to prepare for death, as I suppose I intended. A ridiculous urge to feel *nothing*, be *nothing* in the tradition of the old gentleman adventurer Ernest[38], takes me, and in the rain, in my boxers, in my bone-weary old body, world-weary old mind, and at the end-of-the-line, I reach into the open Prada, take a fatal-dose pinch of smack between thumb and forefinger, and raise it to my nose for one last time.

"Stop ...Jack, please!" says Ann softly. I hesitate. Yousef begins a cackling sound that grows to a hysterical belly laugh. I stand slowly, my back to him, and blood rushes to my head, but through the red fog, my eyes clear and lock onto Ann's.

A deep sadness looks back. Her fear's gone, and goddamn it, if she doesn't look unsettlingly like Joe Harman from a town like Alice Springs nailed up on a tree in women's underwear.

God's looking. I'm a coward. Most of the heroin flies away in the wind before I take my snort, but not all.

The mad Armani is talking again. I face him as my eyes glaze over, at least from my side, and I notice he's leafing through the

---

[38] This is likely a reference to the famous writer Earnest Hemmingway, who seems to be a kind of literary hero for Levague.

He famously killed himself with a double-barreled shotgun blast to the head, apparently for no reason other than a litany of medical issues associated with his lifestyle and age. It was a celebrated act of rationality; there was nothing left to live for – he'd done it all. Clearly, the would-be writer wishes to emulate the famous writer. As I expected, he failed to live up to his idol by any measure.

Journal.

"'*The professional journal of cultural anthropologist, Dr. Jacques Levague*', French Canadian ...eh?" he says through his smile. He reads a few lines; his smile diminishes; he probably met *ATHEISTMAN*. Now he's frowning, and his lips move as he reads silently. I can follow, I wrote the words, and I watch his lips form into '*oozing malice ...intemperate thugs.*'

He focuses increasingly wild eyes back on me but says calmly, "You think you're so much better than me? I'll tell you what a *savage* Armani thinks. You're just a junkie who thinks he's a scholar, and now you're just a dead junkie." Coincidentally, I *am* savoring this last little opiate rush, but it's not enough to enter *Casino de Scag*, and I already know what's on his mind, and he's on a roll.

"This is what the *savage mind* thinks - you're going to live long enough to tell me where the rest of my heroin is and then watch your friends die ...you piece-of-dog-shit ...you drug-addicted fornicator of donkeys. Here, put your clothes back in the bag ...and the kilo. When the authorities get here, the only drugs will be in the bag they pry from your cold dead junkie hands. I'll burn your journal when I burn the girl. Now, where *exactly* is the rest of my property?"

A weak trickle from my adrenal gland is all that I can muster in response to this latest and likely final death threat here on East Crocodile Island – the end of *live* biochemistry, end of the Levague Journal. It's enough to kill my little opiate buzz and probably my last one in the bargain. Going to death with a clear head was never my plan.

I notice it's turned eerily quiet. The wind has silenced, and the rain has stopped. Ann sobs softly as the gentle drops of rain trickle through the giant fig's canopy. Distant echoing waves punctuate a growing stillness from the beach, and there's no sound of an injured young man's moaning.

And, I've got nothing left; my cleverest linguistic gambit has failed, and no commercial deal with this bloodthirsty villain seems possible. My only bargaining chip is knowledge of a few kilos of drugs, the only thing I have that he wants. My arm raises, pointing, and the words are on my tongue.

"In the creek, just down from the last gravestone."

"What's the name on the grave?" he asks.

"Paddy Kunmubilpilguru," I say.

He scrunches up his lips, trying to make the sounds. He can't, spitting the sounds out of his bloody mouth in distaste. "How do you spell that?"

I begin to say it slowly, thinking it might be the last word my mouth forms. The old linguist savors the last pursing of lips, loosening of jaw muscles, and slight opening of nasal cavities to make the name resonate in a deep, growling, throaty voice, like the song of the Crocodile Cult. *"Kun mu bil pil gu ru. That's K U ... "*.

"Never mind," he says, waving his gun. "Show me."

Suddenly, I'm aware of low mechanical droning, barely perceptible, wafting on the air at the edge of hearing, and I look skyward to the southwest. The cloud cover splits and a shaft of sunlight glints off a distant light aircraft flying low along the coast of the mainland - finally, a search plane. It's late. Yousef follows my gaze, the direction of the sound, and swaths of baby-blue sky grow across the heavens, breaking the weather up like Watchtower-worthy divine sunlight and setting a sparkle to the calming Arafura Sea.

The plane gets louder. He makes me take the Prada. It'll be my only legacy, evidence of a heroin smuggler who died violently in a 'drug-related slaying'. My darling wife will be aghast - for about two seconds - and then a pan-cultural, instinctive *'live by the sword, die by it'* sense of just desserts will settle her in resignation that despite best efforts, the devil always had the upper hand with her worthless old husband, time enough for the little tart to find love with another poor bozo.

Before we leave the square, heading north between the old hospital and the church towards the creek, I look again into Ann's face, red and swollen with anguished crying and tears, and hold her big brown eyes a last time. She smiles. I don't think there was a time in this account when I might have *really* wished her dead - until now - so she isn't humiliated and abused beyond belief before she's murdered. Well, maybe she *was* at a little risk from the Rat - when he stacked her up on his mental weighing scales against $2.2m in contraband drugs. But the Rat couldn't have run amuck sufficiently to kill *everyone*, and there was never time enough for snakes or other natural misfortune to take so many lucky courses …not so far, anyway.

I walk at gunpoint, slower than dignity might afford a braver man, and the damnable Armani keeps prodding my right shoulder with his snub-nosed pistol, and I stumble along ahead to keep out of reach. The search plane's droning mechanical hum is getting louder, heading our way. I wonder briefly what tweaked its curiosity. Searching eyes with binoculars may have spotted a piece of bent, scorched Lorina aircraft wing catching a glint of sun on East Crocodile Island - more likely, a four-by-four parked at the mouth of the Woolen River and a silver dinghy pulled up unexplainably on a nearby deserted island beach - a little irony to mull on as I stagger into the sunlit cemetery. Yousef will have about three or four hours before a chopper arrives; maybe it'll hurry if the plane spots carnage still ongoing. Either way, enough time to escape in the dinghy and get well away on the track back to GUMO before authorities arrive …and there can be no witnesses left alive on this desert isle.

Feather wisps of clouds drift slowly westward, and the shade they offer follows me through a lepers' graveyard - some tombstones fallen over, some leaning at odd angles, some perfectly upright - and past the final resting place of old One-Eyed Bob and Lefty Williams, and down to the edge of the little creek gully. And just as the sun shines down again, I'm stepping under the shade of a large river-gum tree, and Paddy Kunmubilpilguru's grave is at my feet. Under his name, it reads '*Born – unknown, Died 1938, Age – unknown. Resting with Jesus* - of this last epitaph, there's happily some certainty.

"Your property is down there," I say, indicating a mound of

leaves, twigs, and mud with a stick stuck in it, all covered over with yellow-clad, Frisbee-sized slabs and surrounded by a little moat of wet mud, about five meters down a grassy embankment. The tide is in, the estuary is flooded, and dark still waters soak around the pile of heroin. The nest is unoccupied.

Urgency has taken the Armani, and nerves are taking hold. Perhaps he's spurred on by a growing list of people who need murdering and running short of time to fully enjoy the sport, or it's the proximity of a rescue plane, regardless that the pilot won't chance a landing on the local airstrip.

"Go get them," he orders. "Toss the packages up here."

"An animal bit my hand. I can't use it. I can't dig up the discs with this shoulder …If you're going to kill me, how about a final smoke?" I reply.

And blow me over if he doesn't toss the Journal down onto Paddy's grave at my feet, and keeping his eye on me all the time, he takes a pack of fags out of his jeans pocket and tosses a cigarette down on top of the Journal. My fingers shake as I open the Prada and fumble in my pants for my lighter. Just as I fish it out, and I take my eyes off Yousef, holding the flame up to my smoke, *Bang!* … the gun goes off, and my immediate thought …hope …prayer is that he's shot at a crocodile, and the foreign numbskull has grazed the monster's hide or bounced the feeble .22 caliber bullet off its skull, tickling the beast at most …and maybe pissing him off.

But way before I can register this thought, even as the first words take shape in my mind, I know my right foot's got a bullet hole in it. I can see the black puncture in the brown leather instantly turn red when he pushes my chest, and I fall back on my ass, sitting on Paddy's grave, my back against Paddy's upright tombstone. And a vicious rage of pain builds, the kind that can be too intense to remain conscious, and it charges up my right leg, spine, and into the main cerebral biochemistry. There, it battles with opiates. They need to win to keep me focused on my smoke; the tobacco's burning, I inhale, and despite just being shot in the foot and about to die, it's the best damn cigarette I've ever had, the best that's ever existed in the Universe.

"Stay here," he orders. "If it's all there, I'll kill you quick; if not, your other foot …then we'll move up," he adds, indicating my recently slit dick with his gun.

The battle to stay conscious is touch and go, but I manage to register the Armani turn and walk slowly down the slight incline of the grassy embankment, and as he gets closer to the mound of drugs, he slows, or time does. As I fight the newest agony, he steps deliberately down into the muddy grey ditch, circles the nest, and studies what's stuck on the end of the spear in the middle. And he comes around facing me with eyes glued on the flyblown carcass of a stinking dead monkey that might be any piece of rotting flesh so totally crawling with flies it looks like macabre bees swarming on a branch.

I watch intently, and for a moment, no birds squawk in river gums or mangroves, the wind dies, the distant surf fades, and the

352

crackles and whispers of nature are smothered by the growing drone of a plane flying low over the island airstrip to confirm a crash scene. It'll be back directly, flying over the old leper community searching for life.

But now, it's just *this* moment. I'm spent out, and all the world-weary care and pain disappear in a rush of melancholy that floods my mind with memories of life, both good and bad. I see my smiling Pam as we first set out on our journey and our baby Joe ...*oh Joe*, and through a hazy, druggy fog, an image of Joe Harman from The Alice being crucified on a Banyan tree forms in mind's eye, but now it's *ATHEISTMAN* nailed to the Cross. His body looks broken and seems to hang lifelessly; the fire in his eyes is clouding over, and his piercing insight is failing. I don't think I can save him.

I'm shriveled and diminished. Without *ATHEISTMAN*, my Universe is shrunk into shades of grey, and I can't separate what's real from what's not. I'm no longer the best man I can be, but neither am I the worst. And against reason, as my last refuge, I cast forth all my thought and senses, passed the decrepit ruins of the Catholic Church and the old graveyard, and concentrated all my mental energy on far older foundations, and I *call*, and I'm praying words in my mind and synchronizing my heart to ancient rhythms, and I cry out quietly, song-words forming on my tongue in a language of First People, and I set them on the air, the dancing magic words of the Crocodile Cul.

As I watch Yousef's face, his gaze is set with curiosity, and then his jaw drops in shocked, baffling confusion. An expression of terrifying realization and pain freezes all features as he finds coherence and the horror of understanding …And at his feet - at the edge of still, piss-yellow swampy water - an ever-so-slight upswelling…as if a small submarine was gently pushing up the sea, and I hold my breath in hope …and *faith*.

Yousef the Armani tosses his pistol up onto the grassy embankment in my direction but a few meters out of my reach. Then he reaches down with both hands, grabs the spear shaft sticking out of his pile of narcotics, and pulls it free. The instant he does, a faint weak *chirping* is barely audible to a human and muffled by half a meter of rotting plant debris and occasional kilos of smack. He shakes the spear and dislodges enough of the flies to see the diseased furry remains of a macaque monkey underneath.

It's impaled on the spear, having had it shoved up its ass all the way to its head. *Vlad the Impaler* couldn't have done better, and at another time, I'm sure that the Armani would tip his hat in appreciation of fine work. This impaled monkey carcass holds a Christian crucifix in its hands, a dark wooden one about four inches long and two wide. Its tiny monkey face, black holes where its eyes used to be, is set in a happy rictus grin. "Jo-Jo? Oh …Jo Jo," he mouths, barely stirring the air. I had a hunch they'd met before, close old buddies from a drug-smuggling Indonesian fishing boat seeking shelter from late storms. It's a nice pan-cultural name.

While he quietly stares at the filthy remains of what was once his pet, I use my cutest, high-pitched, squeaky monkey voice and cast it down as best I can from Paddy's grave, like a ventriloquist: *'May the Grace of the Crocodile go with you'*[39] - and these are probably the last words he hears that have any semblance of meaning. The rest of his life is almost certainly incomprehensible.

The water's edge explodes in a vicious spray of splashing water and mud, and the great grey-green primordial monster lunges from the swamp, launching a meter into the air, amour-plated ridges down its back like metal rivets holding together an amphibious machine made deliberately for horror, a thousand kilograms of muscle, fury, and teeth, as if from nowhere, in half a heartbeat, with the blurry speed of a perfectly evolved killing machine. There's a flash of its pale-yellow underbelly as it twists in mid-lunge and the creamy-white of massive gaping jaws with ten-centimeter-long teeth lining the steel-trap maw like rows of little daggers, all looking sanitized and dentist-clean.

The steel trap snaps shut around Yousef's waist, and he's instantly flipped on his stomach, flat in the mud, held firm in a locked vise, and the adrenalin rush probably spares him the piercing pain of

---

[39] Even here at the end of Levague's field notes, I must apologize again on behalf of the Anthropological Federation. In hindsight, I should have redacted this deliberate and dastardly distortion of the final sentence of the Bible.

Of course, the words are *The Grace of the Lord Jesus be with all*. In my view, *ATHEISTMAN* should have stayed crucified instead of abusing the holy words of over a billion believers. I'm afraid that the shame of Levague must be worn now by myself, and I intend to resign my Chairmanship of the Ethics Committee forthwith.

sharp teeth spikes that have entered the small of his back on one side and his lower abdomen on the other.

He's in shock. His eyes flit around their sockets wildly, and his lips try to form a scream. The top half of him is sticking out one side of a crocodile's mouth, the bottom half out the other side like a nightmarish T-bone steak, and he's still clutching the spear with Jo-Jo stuck on the end.

Both predator and victim assess the post-attack situation, each in their own way, from their separate perspectives. And although it's poor Yousef in its jaws, those cloying amber crocodile eyes, with bottomless black diamond pupils, are focused directly on me. Yousef flinches first; his arms and legs start flailing about, and Jo-Jo's spear goes flying. He manages to find his voice for one bloodcurdling horrified shriek, loud enough to shame the nun.

I'm sure there's another one or two, but he makes no further comment as the gigantic crocodile pushes its thick, powerful forefeet into the muddy bank and, with several vicious, splashing shakes and shimmies, reverses itself with easy purpose back into the dark depths of the swamp, dragging the hideous Armani, kicking and scratching in mud and blood, to his hideous doom, probably drowning him before he's chewed into two, more manageable chunks.

Time is relative. The awful violence is over in the short time it takes to smoke a delicious cigarette, a moment quite longer if it's your last and spent in the jaws of a crocodile.

A few muddy swirls, ripples, and bubbles along the surface of the murky water point to dark mangrove thickets closer to the beach. She may prefer to wedge the corpse in a tangle of old waterlogged roots and trees in the depths of the estuary and let it rot there for a while, softening it up a spell to ease digestion.

The search plane flies low over the airstrip, confirming fire-blacken plane wreckage at the northern end, possibly noting at least one fatality when the birds scattered from their perch on Mrs. Korda's seat. I followed the Doppler effect as the engine noise grew in approach from the east, peaked, and then diminished, and it's coming around for another pass, this time from the west, over the ruins of a historic leper community where searchers might have spotted a woman in white underwear tied to a fig tree in the old village square, something they'd likely want to confirm before radioing ahead to Darwin.

Sitting back against Paddy Kunmubilpilguru's headstone, shaded by a river gum from the growing morning sun, I wonder if I should try to hobble to the square. But then I hear Ann screaming again, something about a snake slithering around her feet, and I hear Chirp shouting, "I'm coming! He shot me!" And I know they're fine, and both can stay where they are for the moment.

My foot's throbbing after the excitement, so I open the Prada again, but I'm frugal; although the apical lizard is otherwise occupied, the apical hominid needs to be mindful of the nest of baby snappers only five meters away. But the Journal's near my shot foot, and I have my Prada, and serendipity has saved, once again, the undeserving back-bacon of a blind-lucky Canuck.

I enjoy more scag, and Paddy and I enjoy a bit of peace. But then a loud engine drone builds to a roar, and the giant shadow of a low-flying search plane zooms over the old village, the beach, and out across the Arafura Sea, skimming at a hundred meters. I expect it'll turn west towards Darwin and fly back over us one more time to confirm GPS points. Vaguely in the background, I hear Ann shouting at the plane.

"Over here! …*Here*, damn it!"

I fall into marveling about the good fortune of a ravenous dinosaur-sized prehistoric monster appearing at precisely the correct moment. I was *hoping*. I was ritually circumcised. And maybe it's the drugs or my injury-torn sixty-year-old bag of tired bones and biochemistry, or the lack of food and sleep, the delirium and desperation – whatever, I had *faith*, and I prayed, and the *call* was answered. And I wonder – have the slow, low base syllables of the Crocodile Cult song I sang - vibrations that have resonated on the air of Arnhem Land for tens of thousands of years - become associated in the tiny brain of a crocodile with an easy meal, and it came to me as a conditioned response? Or is there something else, some deeper truth?

And in the end, there's a certain raw, savage satisfaction in hanging religious belief off the natural product of two hundred million years of Darwinian killing evolution. It has a ring of *legitimacy*. No psycho's nightmare can match what natural selection can conjure up. And it certainly beats the pedigree of two-thousand-year-old considerations written down by profoundly insightful goat-herdsmen, with their talking snakes and penchant for filicide, murdering a firstborn son seemingly always on their weird old biblical minds.

The search plane is approaching again, but utter bone-weariness, the lovely nicotine coursing through my biochemistry, and the build-up of opiate molecules over recent days, and I'm at the doors of *Casino de Scag*. They're wide open, and I know the establishment closes in about three hours when the police get here.

It's bright, merry, and noisy as usual. Colored lights flash, bells jingle, slots spin, reels whirr, and the clanking tingle of a hundred small payouts rings everywhere. But not for Jack-the-Rat; he's busy on the two-hundred-and-twenty-reel smuggling slot machine. The odds of lining up all the little golden dragon-stamped discs are astronomical, but still, he keeps pumping in coins.

Dr. Levague plays the Crocodile Cult slot. It has fifty reels and doesn't pay out often. He watches cute baby hatchlings line up, each icon bringing a loud chirp from the machine, remarkably like a real crocodile. Five baby crocs, ten, forty, all chirping like hungry baby birds …and fifty little green lizards, all lined up—*Jackpot!*

But over in a corner near the row of ATMs, a figure dressed in his absolute black-and-white uniform is playing the reality slot machine. It's the Hero of Reason himself – the wonderous *ATHEISTMAN* - resurrected and real, as if risen from the dead. He wins a jackpot with a million airplane reels, and the poker machine flashes a blinding divine magical light, and the mechanical roar is that of a million real planes.

He's back, but he's useless in a world where real and not real are horribly, glaringly and absolutely clear, and I'm thrown out of the Casino's door on my ass and have to open my eyes to yet another awful reality - a new flash of pain, now made more disturbing than normal because it involves my *un*shot left foot *as well as* my shot right foot. It is a truly regrettable occurrence because several baby saltwater crocodiles, twenty centimeters long with prickly, tickly, scratchy claws, are crawling up my bare legs to join a few chirping cuties already crawling all over my lap. One seems to want to slip up and under my boxers, maybe smelling its first blood.

Interestingly, the mother has firmly taken both my feet in her jaws, clamped down hard with a ton of pressure per square millimeter, possibly breaking my left ankle, and she's slowly tugging me down to the swamp, backing herself up into the dark mangrove estuary where Yousef disappeared; and instead of picking up each of her wayward hatchlings one by one, and exerting the energy to do this fifty times, she's figured it's far easier to drag *me*, and carry them all away in one go, my weight is nothing at all.

I try and sit, sliding down the grassy creek bank on my ass, and unfathomable amber eyes are staring at me *again* - cold, emotionless, no *intelligence* - just pristine clarity of purpose, unencumbered by *right* and *wrong*, cunning, and calculating only whether I'm likely to move suddenly. I'm frozen stiff and her babies are doing fine, heading in the right direction, riding on another big meal.

The croc's behavior strikes me as odd and curious. It appears like *reasoning* behavior, and I wonder if it's the effect of a bizarre, environmentally conditioned response ...

...Of course, this scientific consideration occurs in one of those instances I spoke of earlier, a thought that flits by faster than the Speed of Light, an idea that occurs before sensory information has a chance to interface with biochemistry and precipitate an appropriate mental and physical reaction to being hauled into a swamp in the jaws of a crocodile.

Well, not *actually* faster than Light-Speed - that would be crazy (LOL) - but in a slice of time only one Planck unit long[40], the *shortest* possible instant - the time it takes a light photon to go somewhere that isn't the same place where it is.

I live on that photon now, and these tiny time units are an eternity.

Surprisingly, or perhaps not, the old Levague adrenal gland is able to squirt up a last cocktail strong enough to bring me back to useless, quivering fear-paralysis - but in real-time, and the immensity of my folly, and the insidious seduction of *Casino de Scag* (and the nicotine high from *that* smoke), washes through me, spreading the darkest blackest moment of my life, the utter awfulness of *now*, to every fiber of my being ...*again*. And I slide closer to the muddy edge

---

[40] A Plank Unit of Time is 5.391247 seconds x 10 to the power of -35. It is meaninglessly small – about the same size as the point Levague is making with this drivel at a time when you'd expect him to be a bit more focused on imminent demise.

of the swamp, joining the pitiful Armani, clamped in a monster's jaws, toothy and smiling in subtle mirth, low grunting rumbles from deep down her throat, and her kids *chirping* a chorus in raucous approval. What can *ATHEISTMAN* do about this ...eh?

The air above me shakes with low roaring vibration as search-plane engines approach directly overhead. My outstretched arms drag uselessly at my sides as I slide down the embankment. My left hand catches the hard, smooth metal of Yousef's discarded .22 caliber, but my fingers don't work, and I know, even as my hand brushes over it – that if I could get a numb, monkey-bitten finger to the trigger, I'd only use it on myself.

I'm dragged down to the swamp's edge, only the crocodile's huge metallic grey-green head now visible above water with my legs sticking out of its mouth, and hauled helpless, paralyzed, past the dug-out remains of her former nest, now a scattered mess of dead leaves, twigs, muddied heroin discs, and a few recalcitrant hatchlings.

The shadow of the search plane flashes over me a pulse-beat before the thunderous engines grow deafening, shaking the air directly above me, and I lie back and watch the underside of the plane's fuselage fly over me, heading off west, and the wings tip up and down a few meters, and it's waving to acknowledge us - our ordeal is finished, rescue is imminent. It's not a conscious action, and I'm mildly surprised to see my right hand rise into the air and wave back.

...And the roar of the plane becomes slow timpani pounding in my temples, diminishing with each heartbeat as it flies away, and between each heavy thump - as time hangs between then and now - the soft lilting strains of an old Beatles song rise-up clear and beautiful, and soft weeping drifts on warm still air above these pristine tropical wetlands, and a precious, last image of my darling wife ...well, she can take that damned chest x-ray and ...

...They're not quite the very last thoughts that find words. Annoyingly, my body is starting to hyperventilate. Slave that it is to life, the damnable autonomous preparation for holding my breath as I disappear into a swamp is sabotaging a more reasoned approach favored by *ATHEISTMAN* - to quickly gulp in breaths of the dirty, stagnate water and drown my sorry self as fast as humanly possible. Just as we rally to enforce commonsense, to tame the final folly of life, and at the very instant when all that's visible above water are my white hairy legs, a giant crocodile's bony snout and upper jaw, and those diamond-slit, black-flecked golden eyes, mesmerizing with their horror...there's a sudden loud cracking *KAPOW!* from close behind my head near Paddy's grave - high-powered rifle-fire, and I seem to hear, a millisecond before, after or during - a thick wet *THWACK!* as the top of the crocodile's head, amber eyes included, vanishes in an explosion of boney flesh and brains, and a misty spray of blood.

The dead great animal is motionless; a cloud of gore and red bits spreads on the swamp from a wide hole in its massive skull, and immediately, the steel vise locking my feet relaxes, and the pain of one recently shot foot, another with broken bones, and both chewed to a bloody mess of torn skin and muscle, on top of not-forgotten background agony of the stiletto-stabbed shoulder, infected monkey bites all over, newly severed penis foreskin - and way more smack than I've ever snorted up and stayed alive – all of it convinces me that passing out is probably the best thing all round right now.

Over the next indeterminable hours, I experienced a series of vague recollections and dreams, nice and opiate-related or fitful and out of sheer exhaustion.

My eyes opened at least once in response to approaching footsteps down a grassy creek bank and a voice I recognized saying my name. I remembered looking up into a madly grinning, silver-mustachioed, twinkling-eyed face staring down at me and, for a tic, thinking this chap wants *to eat my face*.

But it was only police tracker and fellow Crocodile Cultist Jacob Kunmubilpilguru.

"That's a big crocodile you have there, Veggie," he might have said. "How's that brother's daughter of yours?" I might have asked - in *lingo*, mind – I'm a tribal guy.

...And I remember my head banging into the side of a helicopter on a beach and coming to in mid-flight, noticing Ann fussing over the butt-shot Chirp on a stretcher next to mine, still moaning in agony like a boy with a belly-ache.

And I have some recall of beckoning the paramedic on board close to me and, when close enough, whispering with appreciable conviction and as politely as I could, "You better get the Schedule 1

Drugs out *STAT*, the I.V. morphine. I'm about to start puking, and I'm afraid I might cause a bit of a fuss."

I woke to darkness in a private Darwin hospital bed several hours later, my right arm in a sling, right foot bandaged, left ankle in a cast, and all hooked up to tubes and dehydration paraphernalia with some low-level, beggar's painkillers in my biochemistry. I cast around, and there it was …like amazing grace, Mrs. Korda's green leather Prada overnight tote bag hanging by its blade-absorbing, double-thick strap off a chair in a dark corner. It was unzipped and my opened wallet sat atop my white-dusted jeans with driver's license photo showing. The Journal wasn't inside …but a one-kilo slab of pressed Armani Dragon brand heroin rested in the bottom of the all-purpose quality bag, floating on a soft bed of powder-dry, snort-ready scag.

I managed to stash the kilo behind the toilet cistern in my bathroom and shake out the powdered heroin into a handy bedpan, all the while fretting about the Journal and whether the police were reading entries concerning the whereabouts of illegal drugs. I supposed rescuers found my wallet in the Prada and rescued my belongings along with my body before anyone tweaked to the heroin.

When Pam arrives with the first birds the next morning, I come out of junkie-reverie expecting the police to be along directly behind her.

"Husband, you live …*still*," she says, all smiles and happy, rushing to my bedside and commencing inventory.

I start mumbling nonsense about participating in an Aboriginal blood-letting initiation ceremony, but she just shushes me, saying her sweetest, most caring, "You went to work a few days ago, and now you're all ...cut and broken in hospital. The tip of your willy is severed, and your breath is like a dead bird. It's druggie breath, Jack. Your pants were in some woman's overnight bag ...but don't worry *now* ...I'm sure there is an innocent explanation ...sleep, my brave warrior ...I'm here beside you."

As she brushes my ear with her lips, I'm hoping the police get here soon. "I'll protect you ...as always," says the wife with a knife with a name. And whispered soft and close in her native Shoshone, it sets my jelly spine aquiver ...*scare the Devil himself!*

Postscript

The Darwin Rehabilitation Centre is brand-new ...out near the Fanny Bay Race Track. The group therapy session on Thursday afternoons is held outdoors under shade cloth, so most of the recovering drunks, petrol-sniffers, junkies, cokeheads, meth addicts, and assorted other wasted riffraff can chain-smoke.

I sit next to *Steve*, a local rock station DJ with a strong affection for crystal methedrine and a Thursday regular. He's a small, thin man; a young speed freak with a curious obsessive-compulsive disorder when it comes to tobacco smoke - an amphetamine-addicted health nut - go figure, eh?

I always make sure I'm seated next to him and directly upwind when I light up, my second-hand smoke blowing in his face. He gets all twitchy, fake-coughing his useless complaints, and I try to estimate how long it'll take him to move. It's the only pathetic diversion from listening to our tiresome, *suspect* group leader, *Baz*.

Baz is a middle-aged, pot-bellied, thin-limbed, puffy-faced, shaven-headed man in a white business shirt and blue stubby shorts - a not-so-reformed drunk for my money. He's addressing the Thursday group.

"In today's session," says Baz, "we're going to talk about ...and explore ...*hate* ...what makes us so angry we can't contain it ...*blind rage* hatred ...*hate* that you can't pull back from. I know we all have it. Now, I'd like everyone to turn to the person on your right, introduce yourselves if you don't know them …and begin by listing the things that *really* make you see red …Jack, I see no one's sitting near you, so you're with me."

"You start," I say.

"OK …well, what I really *hate* is superficiality…and people thinking they're better than me, *irregardless* of …"

I'm here as part of a plea bargain with my wife. I convinced her to let me wean myself off the healthy little smack-jones that's inveigled itself into my biochemistry over recent weeks - rather than going cold turkey. She allowed me to retain about a quarter of a bed-pan's worth, gave me three months to get clean, and watched as I flushed the balance down the hospital toilet.

She never found out about the full kilo behind the cistern. I agreed to attend these excruciating rehab sessions once a week for the duration of my *recovery*. I've been completely clean for a week. I'm a bit ill-tempered at the moment.

I stayed in Darwin Hospital for ten days following the East Crocodile Island rescue. The rabies test was positive; the vaccine had to be imported from Jakarta, but it worked. The monkey bites were infected with an additional unidentified bacterium that cleared up with antibodies. My shoulder wound healed, as did the bullet hole in my foot. I contained myself with the secret smack, just tooting parsimoniously to add a certain *je n'sais quoi* to the hospital-grade crap - like any aging primitive would who could.

The federal police visited twice regarding missing heroin, a large pink-diamond ring, and the deaths of five people. They recovered the Journal and quizzed me for hours about this entry and that.

It turned out they'd had an eye on ole' Yousef for some time, originally as a people smuggler and more recently as he branched out his business. A search of the swamp where he disappeared never found his body, and everyone was pretty sure he ended up as the shit of another crocodile. They took the Prada away for testing, but that was the last I heard. I never saw it again.

They would have found traces but not much, and it wasn't *my* bag, and I don't know how it got to my hospital room (my pants notwithstanding). My statement to the coppers allowed that if the Journal recorded that the bag held a kilo slab and half again in powder, it probably did, but who knows what happened - maybe one of the rescue personnel knows something, maybe one of those Aborigines nicked it, or a bloody crocodile ate it.

And crashed plane rescue footage was all over the TV news for two or three days. The police returned the Journal after public prosecutors from a variety of jurisdictions concluded that no charges against me could reasonably be proved in a court of law because of *ambiguous culpability*. The coppers *knew*, though, but in the end, were reasonably happy with keeping two hundred and eighteen kilos *off the streets*, and their interest in Dr. Levague waned.

But this wasn't before the Journal was copied and sent to the

Coroner's Office, Feral Animal Control, NT Conservation Commission, RSPCA (Snakes and Reptile Division), Commonwealth Quarantine Service, border protection authorities - everyone and his goddamn mother's brother …and a certain colleague, Prof. Athol Pine, a stickler for ethics and an anthropologist of minor regard with some previous experience in Arnhem Land.

Apparently, the Territorial Office of Public Prosecution was concerned that the Journal might contain culturally secret, sacred data that might be *taboo*. Pine apparently 'cleared' the East Crocodile Island entries as 'safe' for restricted circulation and then evidently 'sold' the story to some two-bit publishing house. I reluctantly agreed to his money offer; the damage to my privacy was done …and his wife's kind of hot.

Since then, I've received calls from the Dutch Historical Association demanding that I return a seventeenth-century Dutch guilder. I gave it to Pam, and she's secreted it away in her traditional Shoshone medicine bag with other special small old things. To get it back, they'll have to negotiate with Mrs. Skinning.

I've received an endless stream of threats from certain religious organizations, and surprisingly, the Atheist Association of Australia seems to think they have a copyright over the name *ATHEISTMAN*. Well, they can kiss my godless ass and talk to my hungry Pentecostalist lawyer.

Incredibly, the Darwin Shakespearian Society charged me with plagiarizing a few words of the Bard, but I'm just a typewriting monkey who got lucky over a long time. When I see something in writing, I'll see someone in court. Until then, *bite me!*

Jacob Kunmubilpilguru and a few clansmen stayed on at East Crocodile Island after the dramatic rescue. It seems he somehow knew the plane went down - where and when it happened - knew that Chirp had swiped the Mother's Brother Sister's Son stone and knew to follow the Armani's tire tracks from GUMO Airport west to the mouth of the Woolen River - and *knew* to tow a dinghy. He'd have never made it in that old red sedan of his ...good-old Mattius Korda and the man's warm responsiveness to extortion.

You may well ask how Jacob *knew* all this. Answer: The stone *called* ...ask a stupid question ...In fact, he'd heard on the community's emergency radio frequency that the Lorina was hit by lightning and that it was trying to return to GUMO but might have to make an emergency landing at a remote airstrip along the coast somewhere. A missing plane and fresh, unauthorized vehicle tracks heading west from the airport were intriguing enough to tweak interest and lead his expert tracker's nose right to us. Incidentally, Chirp was sentenced to a traditional leg-spearing for unauthorized use of the stone, but his shot butt was a mitigating circumstance, and the penalty was rescinded on appeal. The *TWO MEN* stone was eventually repatriated to Minjininga.

My croc and a few of the slower babies were eaten by the clan over a day or two - all in breach of traditional totemic prohibitions, mind - but what the hell, rules are made ...What was left would have made a stylish set of luggage to shame a Prada, but the carcass just rotted in the swamp until it was consumed by the snapping baby cuties that Jacob didn't cook.

Jacob formally complained to RCC about *'unauthorized use of Aboriginal land for transporting dangerous substances',* and it was never clear in my mind whether he really knew or cared about the difference between heroin powder and yellowcake powder; it was all just 'dangerous,' very expensive *powder*, white or yellow.

RCC was so embarrassed for giving Yousef a job and having their GUMO facilities used to smuggle contraband that they provided a research grant to properly record the East Crocodile Island cave drawings (now UNESCO Listed *Levague EA01*), and when I could stand Pam's post-hospital custodial scrutiny at home no longer, I took off for a fortnight's work at my daily rate with a kilo of smack still fresh as a daisy in yellow clothed, dragon-stamped slab. But after a week's *research*, mostly spent planting a crop of *Gorilla Glue No. 4* along the creek and recreating in the little water-spring pool near the cave, I found the lights in *Casino de Scag* getting too bright, my nerves and my junkie resolve frazzling, and Old Lefty, One-Eye Bob, me, Paddy and the Dutchman ran out of conversation.

It was a close call, really - my life was shining lower in the West, and I was hearing a lot of the Beatles - so I stashed the bulk of the kilo of smack in the Dutchman's ribcage and sealed up Levague EA01 for later …much later. I went back home early and surrendered unto Her Majesty.

Was there preternatural prescience in the cave drawings? Tell me what you reckon – *jacqueslevague@gmail.com*. I have a bridge you might like to buy.

RCC also gave Jacob funds to develop the potential of the old leper colony into a kind of macabre tourist attraction. But the ghosts had to be banished properly, and a bunch of old fellas from Minjininga (me included) conducted the prescribed rituals and dances. Appropriately, I thought, Chirp Kunmubilpilguru is now in charge of the tourist project, assisted by Ann (now *just* Ann – plain and simple, and with no *e*) Quigley. I'm told the tour they have in mind covers the period from the leper days up to the *East Crocodile Island Tragedy* and features actual locations where victims met their grizzly ends - just like in the book.

I've also had some dealings with Prof. Athol Pine, a pompous frump of a man if ever there was one. I'm a little stressed out now, and I intend to deal with Athol the Asshole in due course. But I'm not the type to make a formal complaint to the Anthropological Federation Ethics Committee - I'm more of a set-your-car-on-fire kind of guy.

… Baz's discourse on things he hates has become an indecipherable, moaning, groaning muffle. He's on the ground, trying desperately to roll about, but my knee has his throat pinned down tight. His two hands are trying to pry off mine, which are clamped down hard on his mouth and pressing his nose flat against his face so he can't breathe …

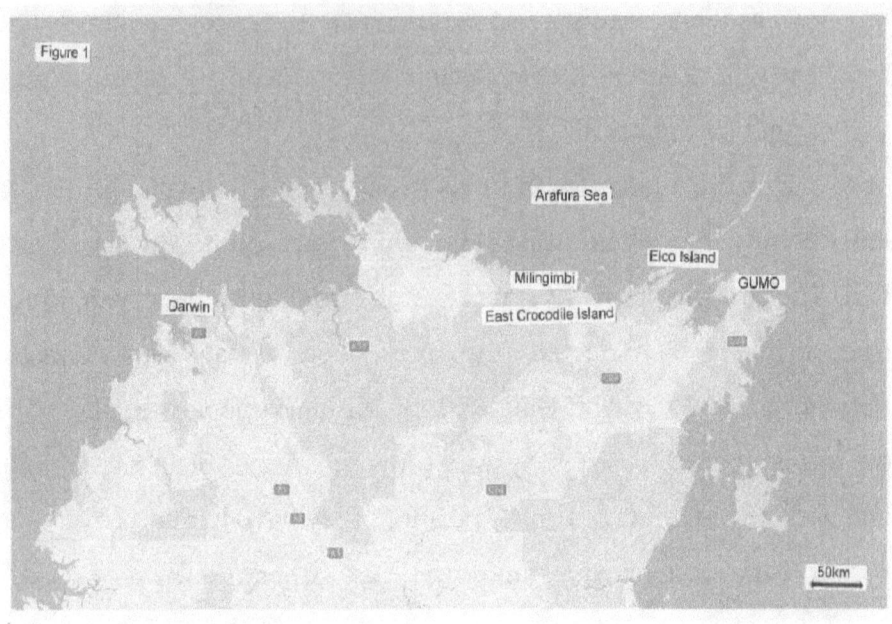

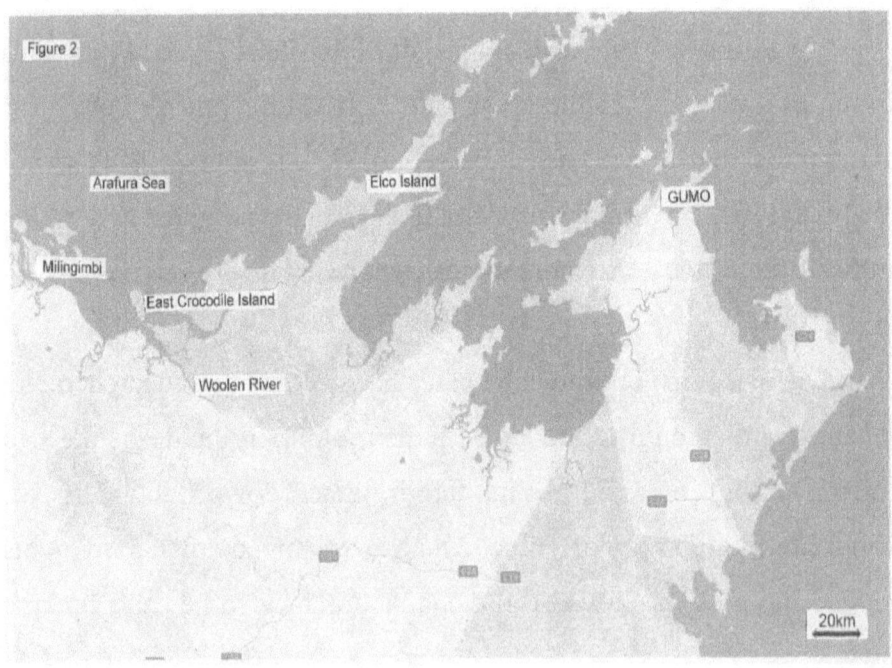

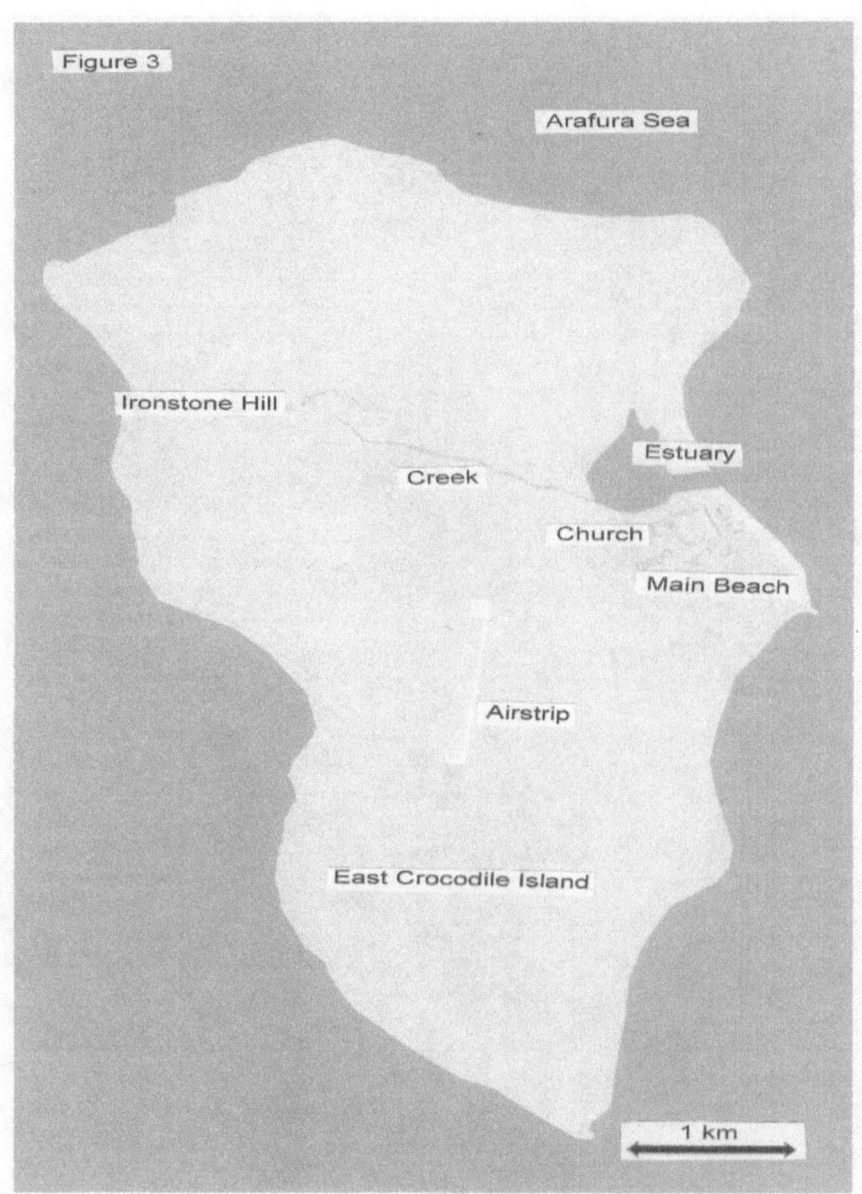

Figure 3

Arafura Sea

Ironstone Hill

Estuary

Creek

Church

Main Beach

Airstrip

East Crocodile Island

1 km

375

www.ingramcontent.com/pod-product-compliance
Lightning Source LLC
Chambersburg PA
CBHW051525250626
47156CB00001B/229